MIKE MAIHACK

CLEOPATRA
IN SPACE

BOOK TWO
THE THIEF AND THE SWORD

AN IMPRINT OF
■SCHOLASTIC

Library of Congress Control Number: 2014939603

ISBN 978-0-545-52844-3 (hardcover)
ISBN 978-0-545-52845-0 (paperback)

10 9 8 7 6 5 4 3   19 20 21

Printed in China   62
First edition, May 2015
Color flatting by Dan Conner and Kate Carleton
Edited by Cassandra Pelham
Book design by Phil Falco
Creative Director: David Saylor

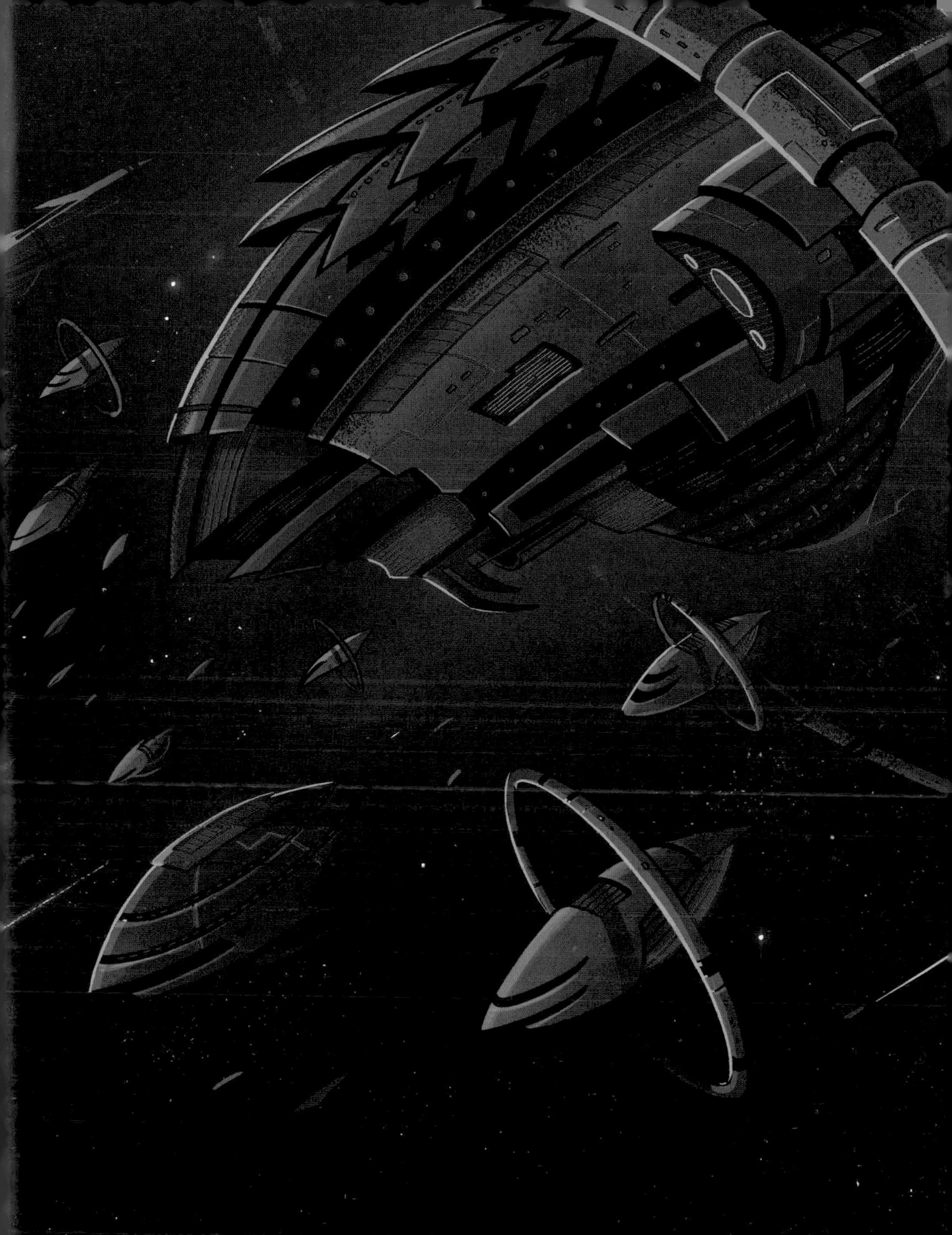

CHAPTER ONE

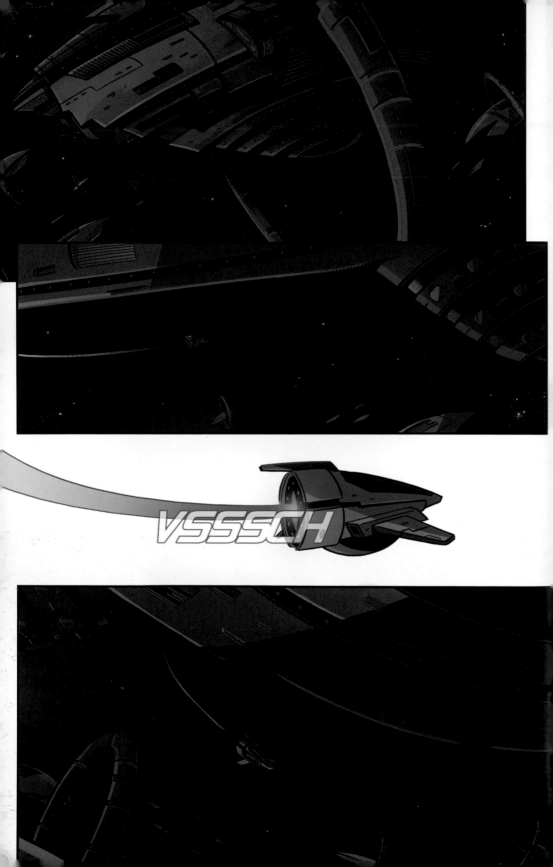

VSSSCH

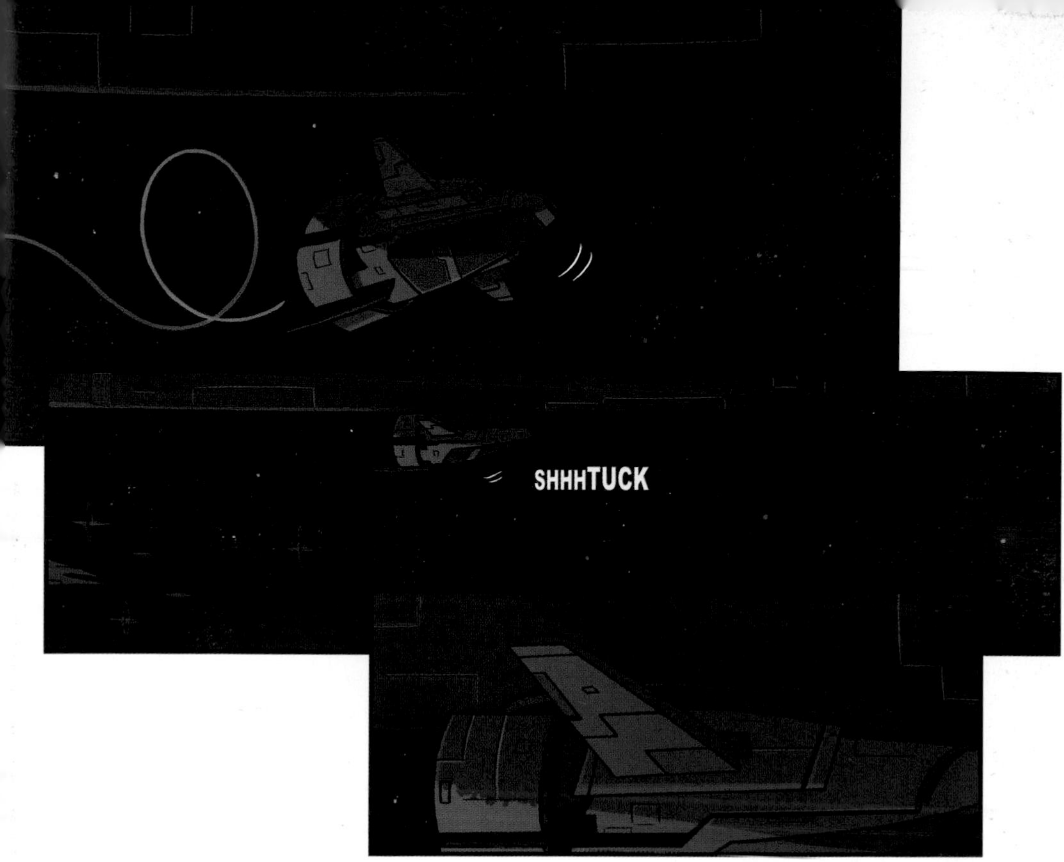
SHHHTUCK

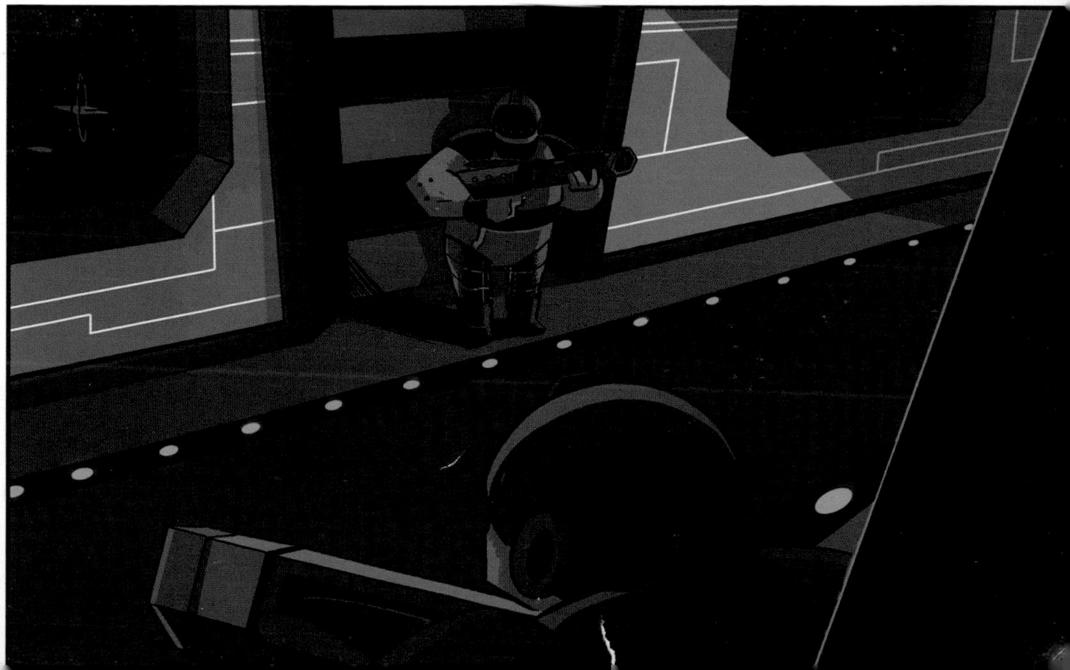

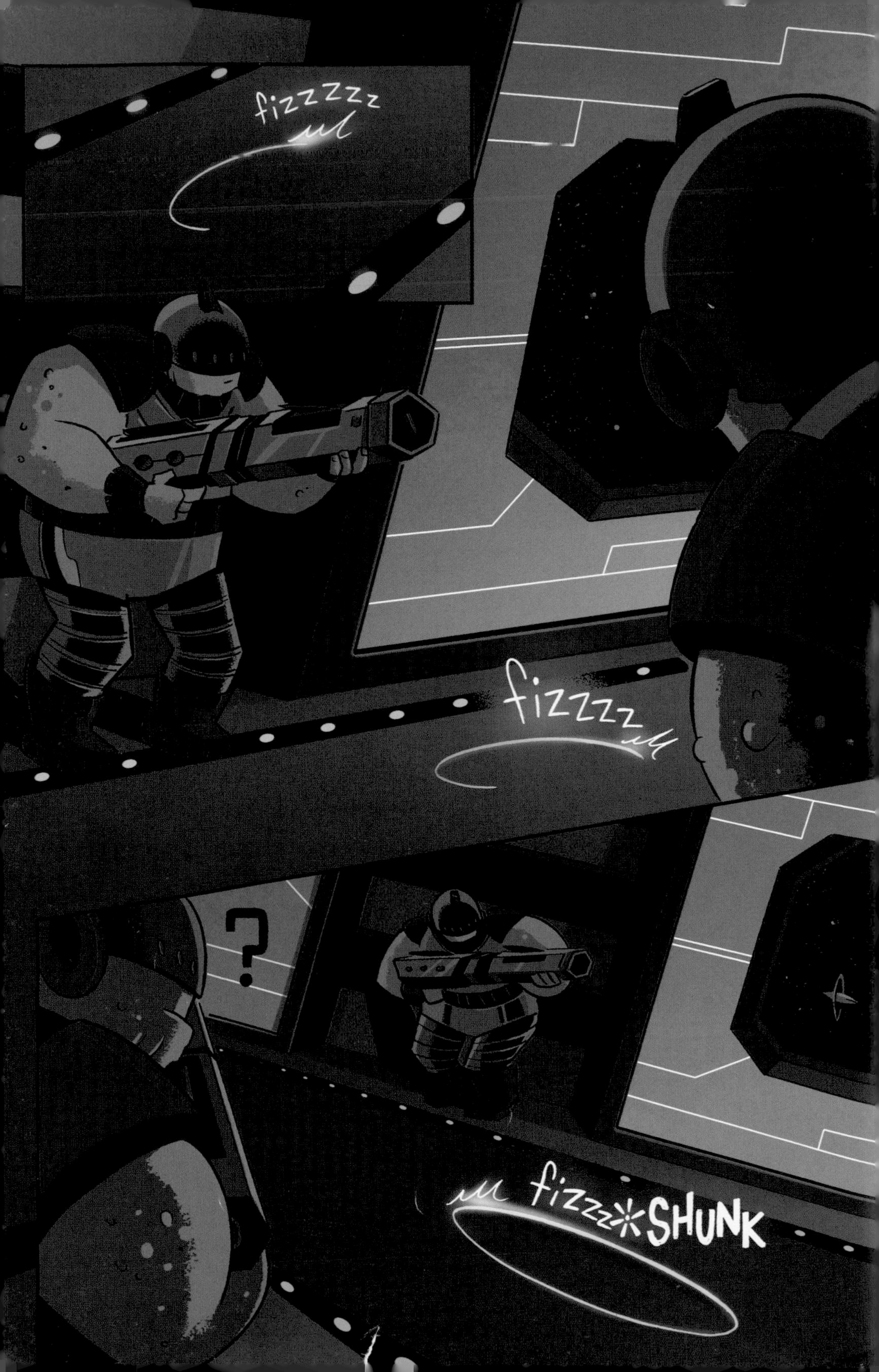
fizzzzz
fizzzzz
?
fizzz*SHUNK

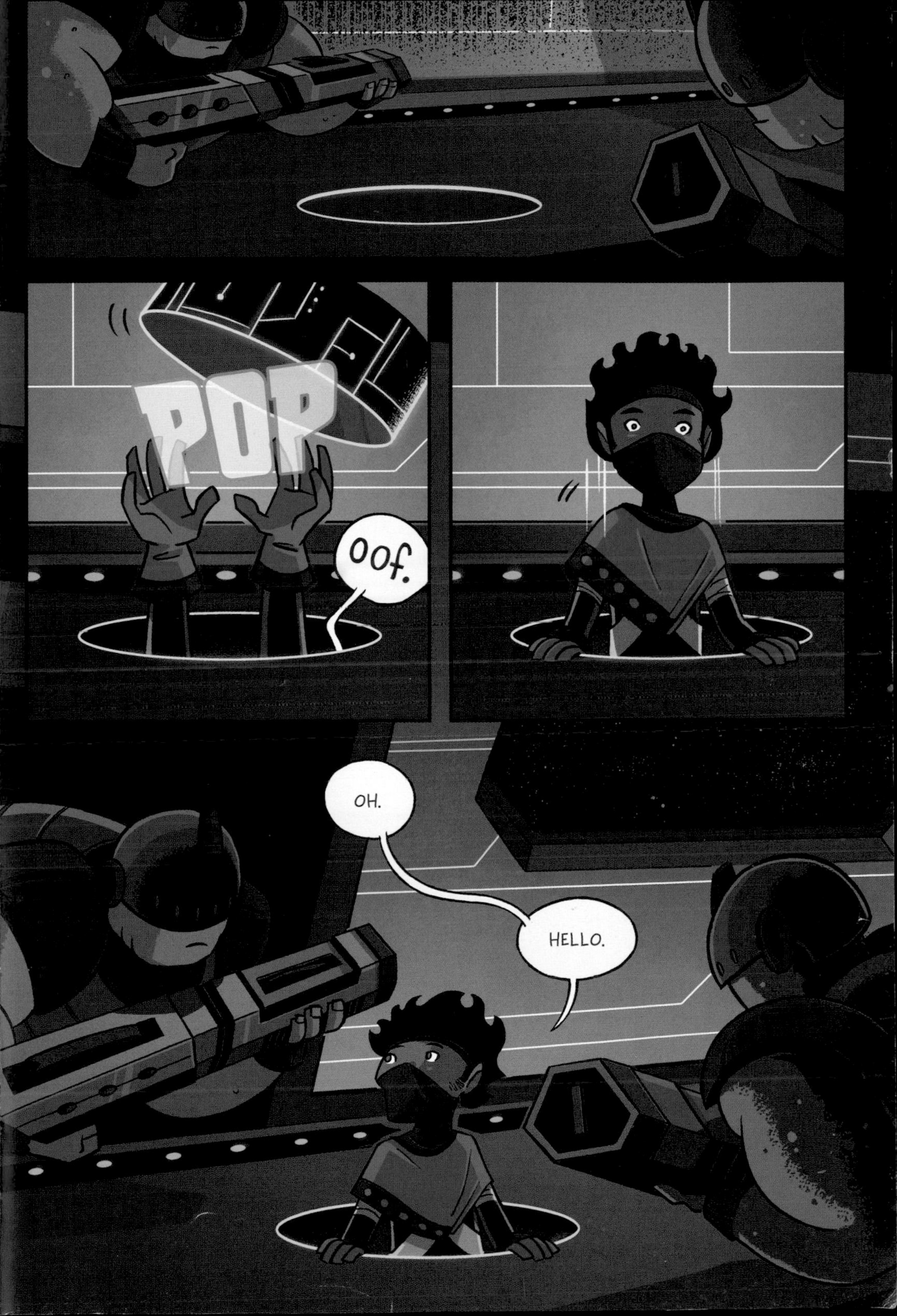
POP
oof.
OH.
HELLO.

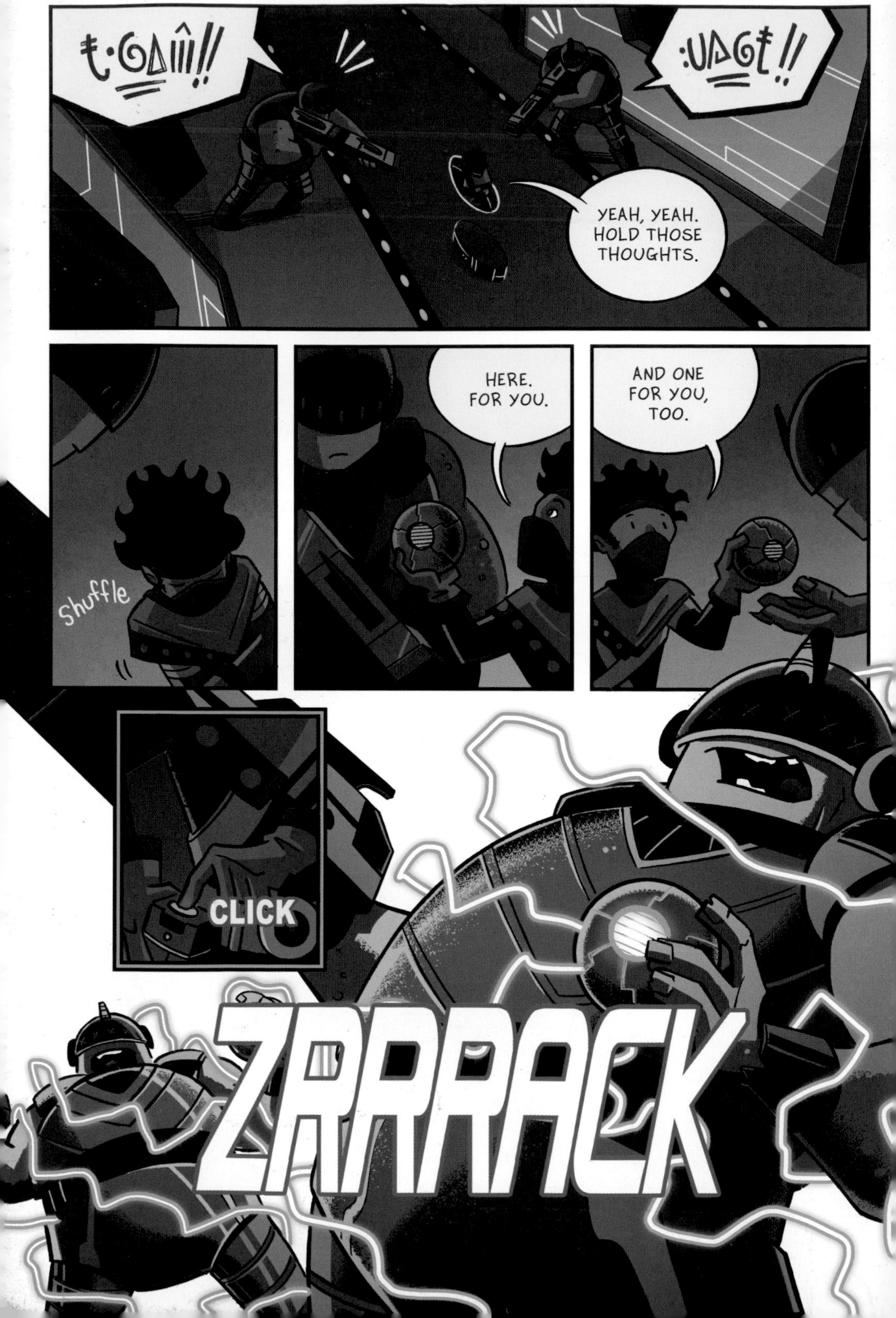
YEAH, YEAH. HOLD THOSE THOUGHTS.
shuffle
HERE. FOR YOU.
AND ONE FOR YOU, TOO.
CLICK
ZRRRACK

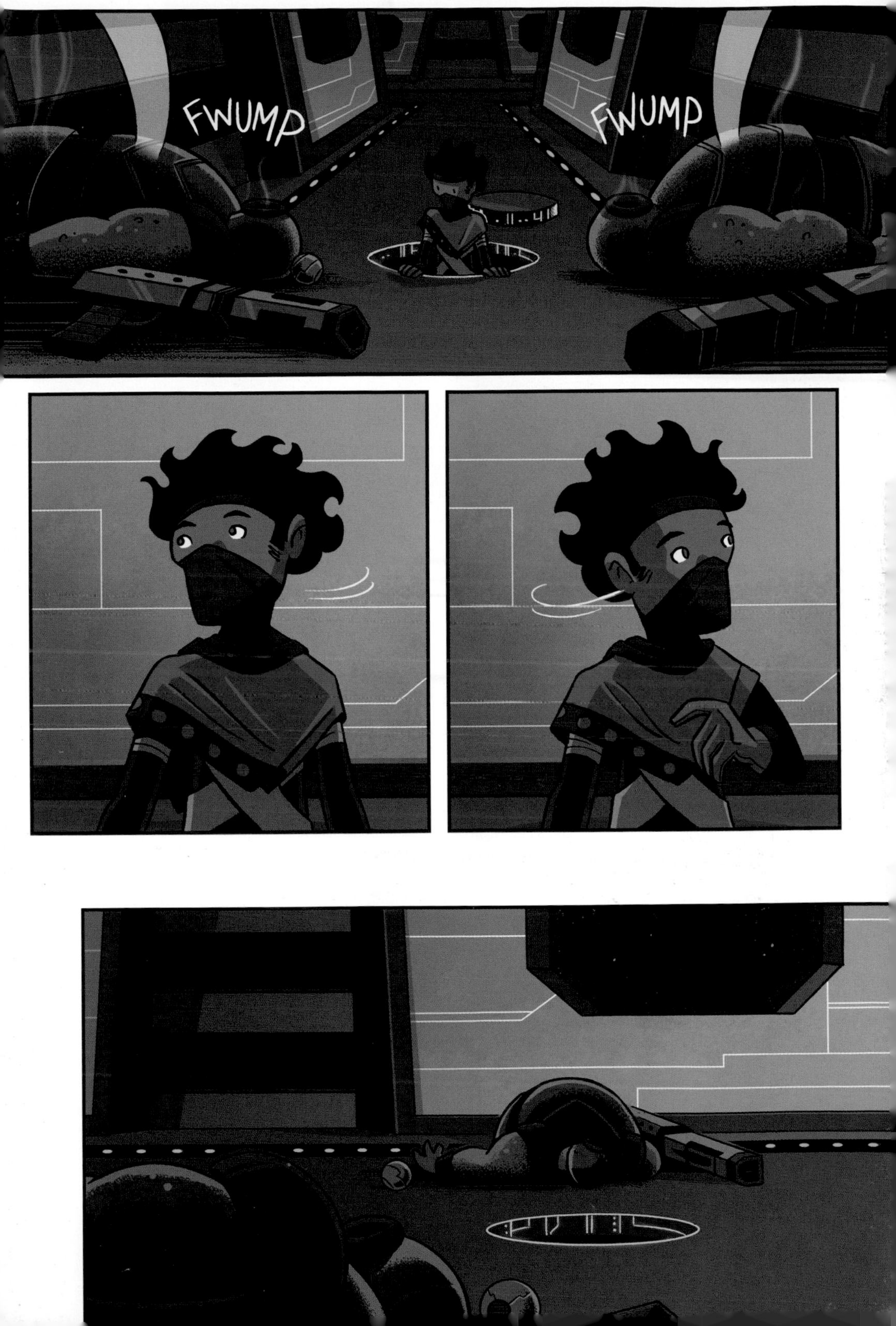
FWUMP
FWUMP

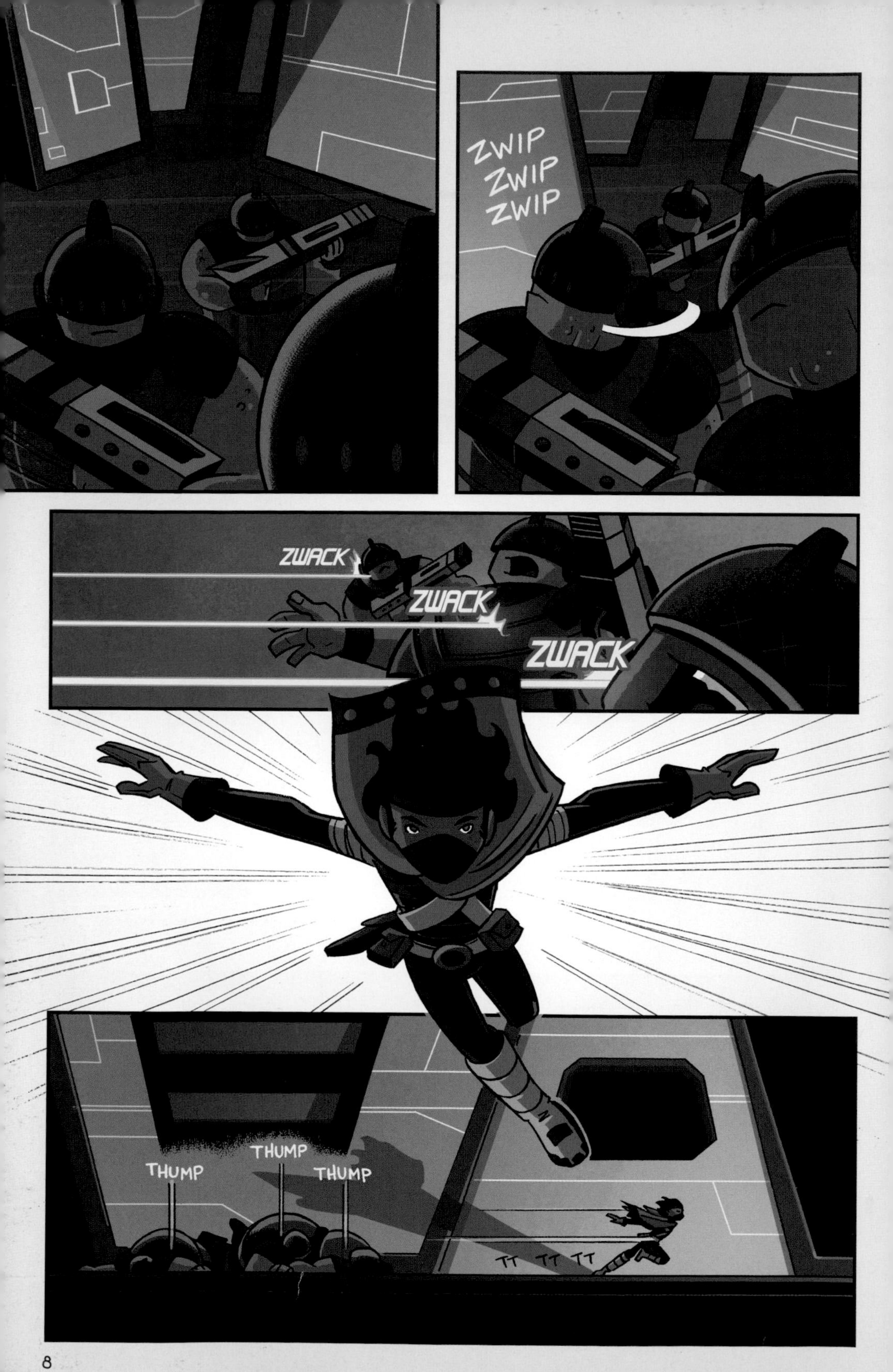
ZWIP
ZWIP
ZWIP
ZWACK
ZWACK
ZWACK
THUMP
THUMP
THUMP
TT TT TT

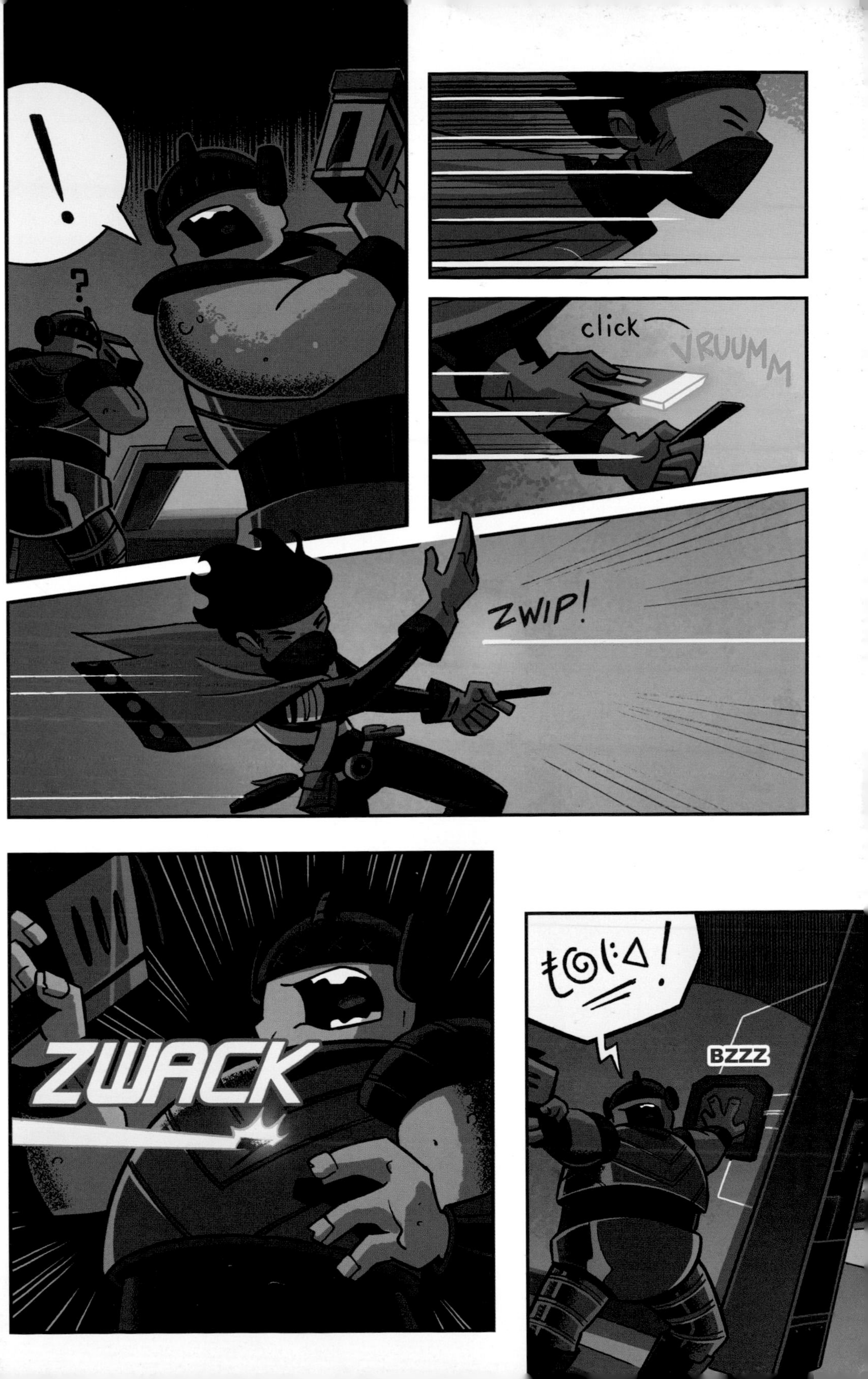
!
?
click
VRUUMM
ZWIP!
ZWACK
BZZZ

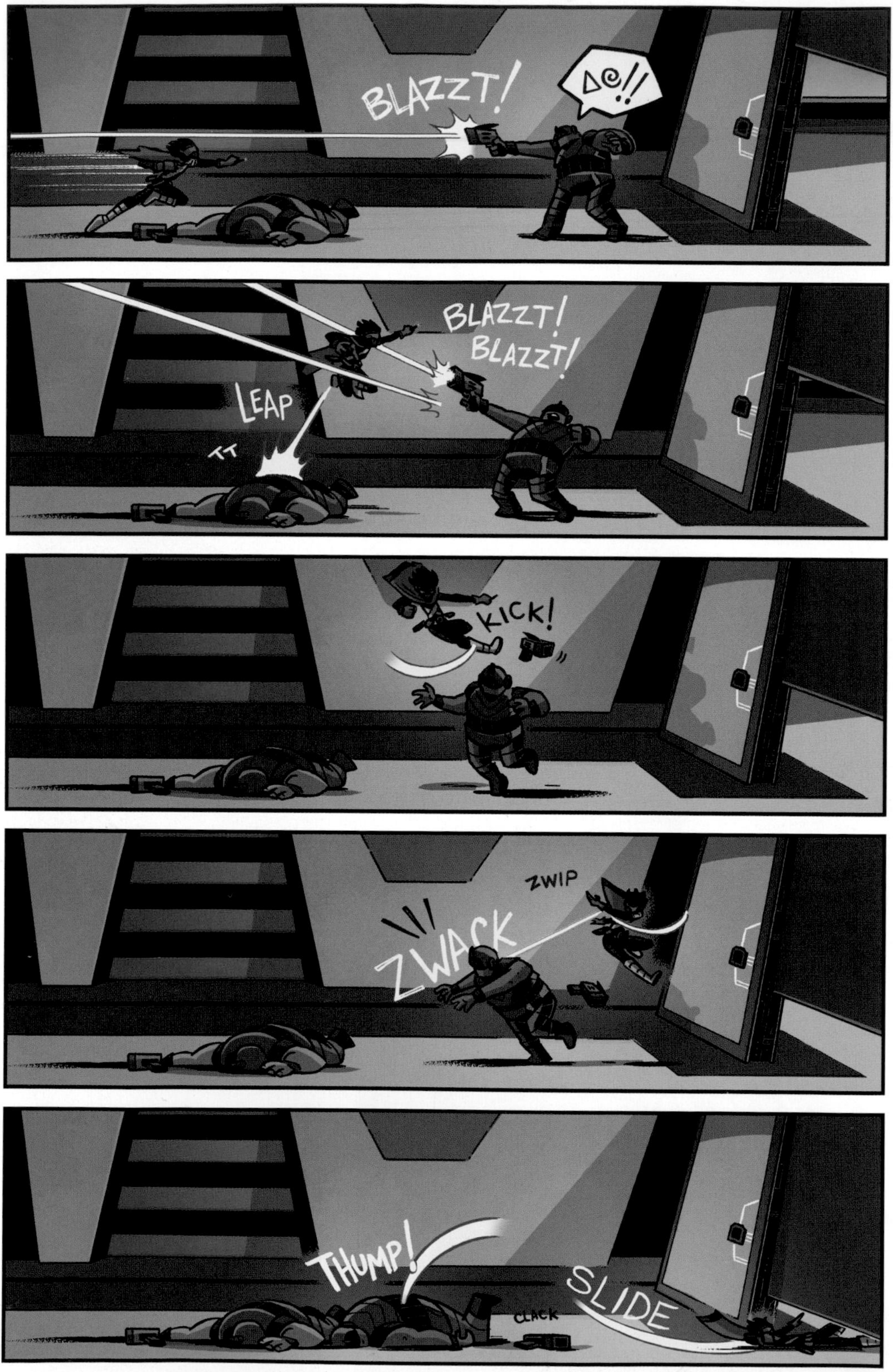
BLAZZT!
BLAZZT!
BLAZZT!
LEAP
KICK!
ZWIP
ZWACK
THUMP!
CLACK
SLIDE

SLAM!

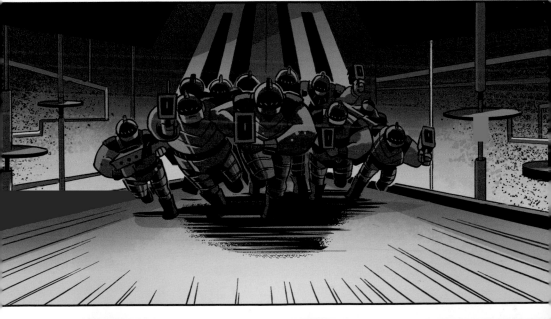

toss

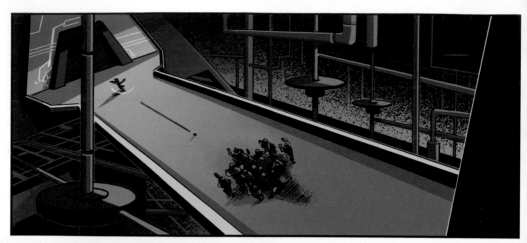

BLEEP

ZRRACK!

ZWIP
ZWIP ZWIP ZWIP
ZWIP

ZWACK

ZWACK

ZWACK ZWACK

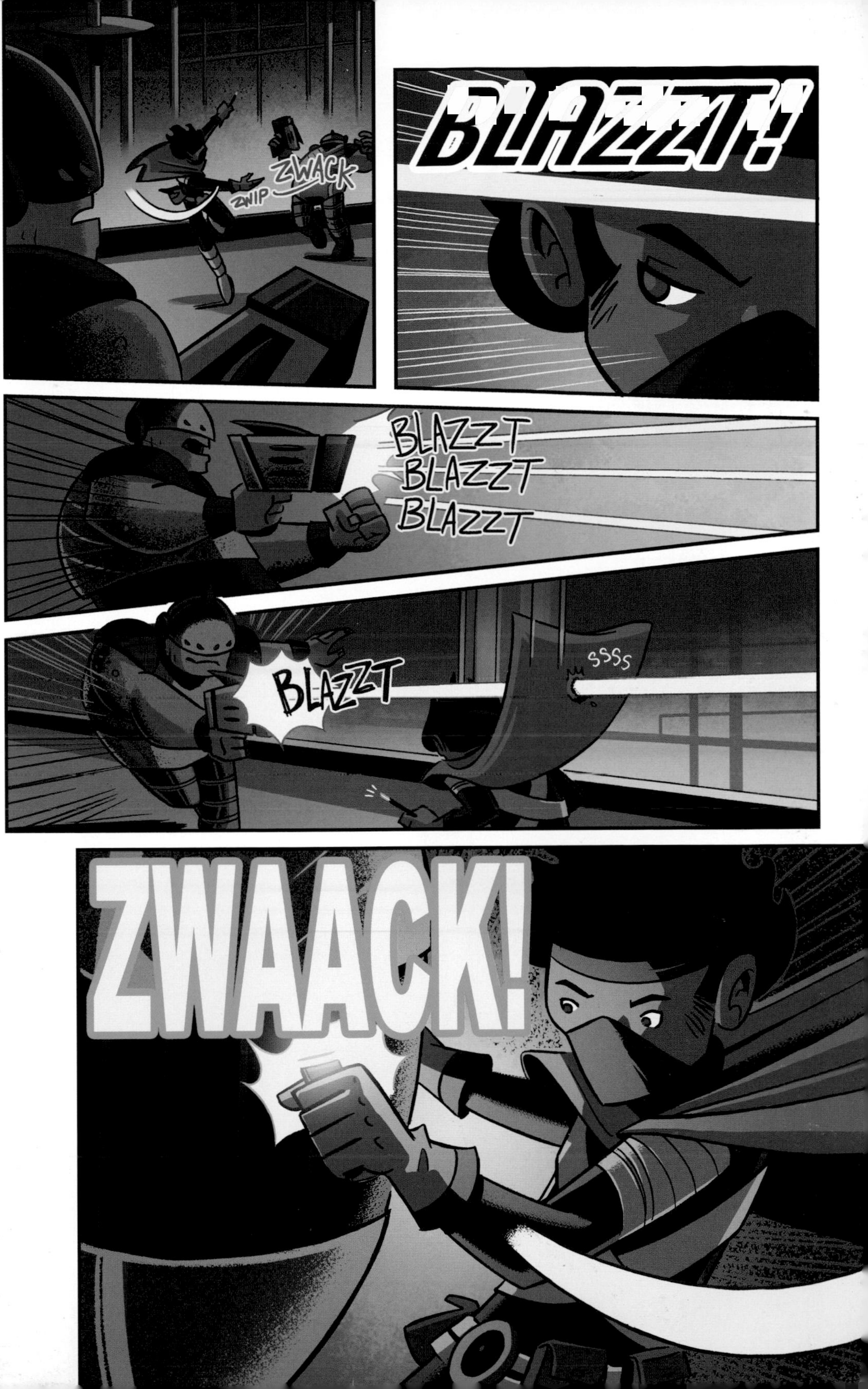
ZWIP
ZWACK
BLAZZT!
BLAZZT
BLAZZT
BLAZZT
BLAZZT
SSSS
ZWAACK!

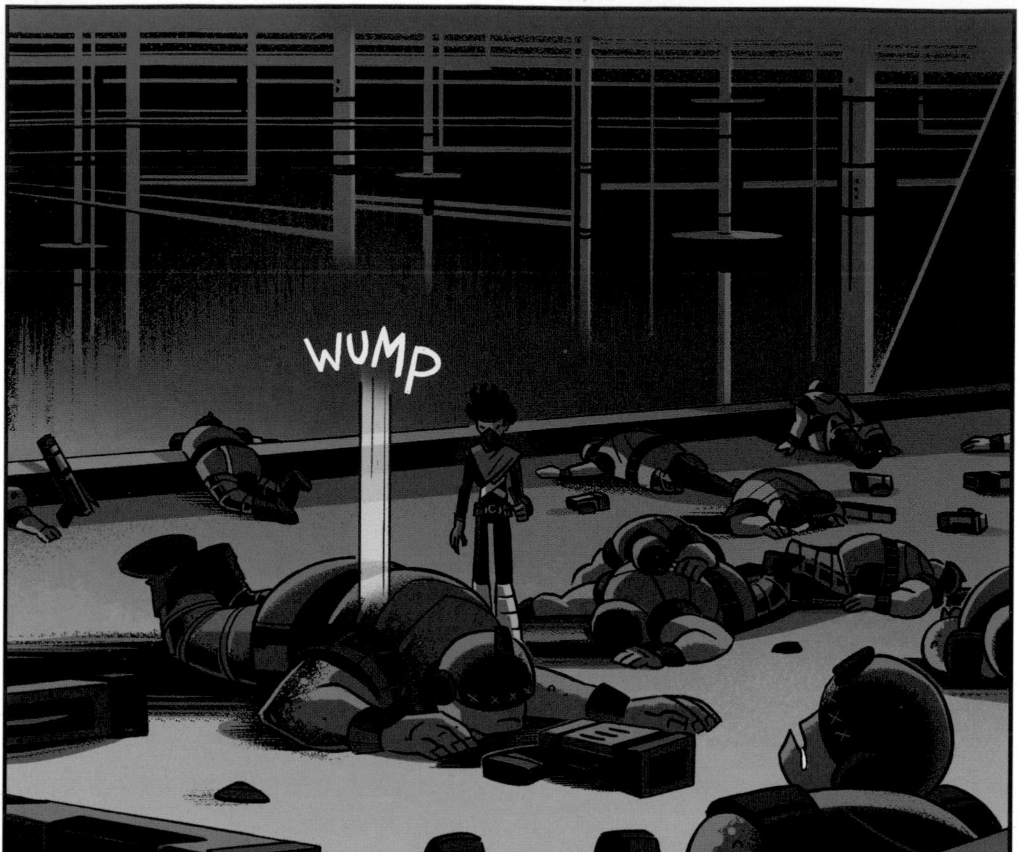
WUMP
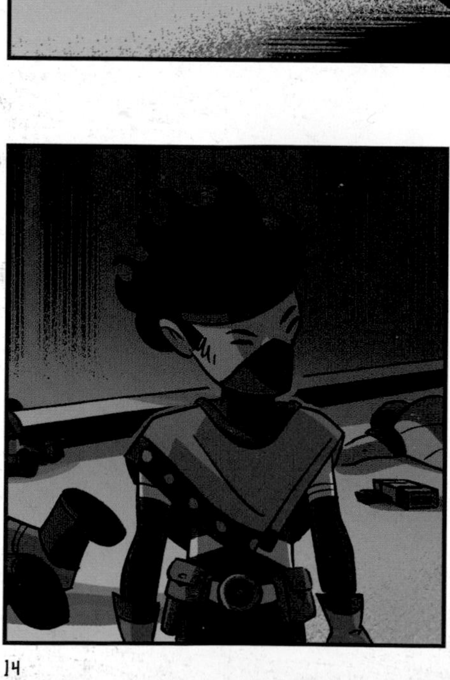
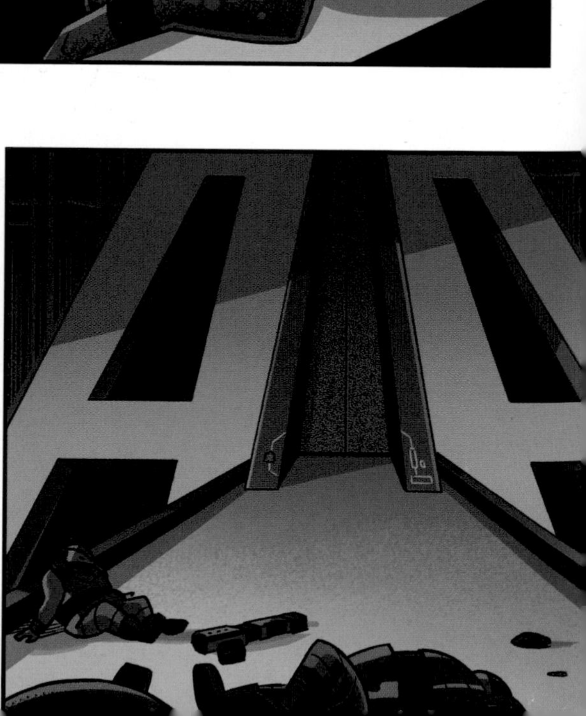

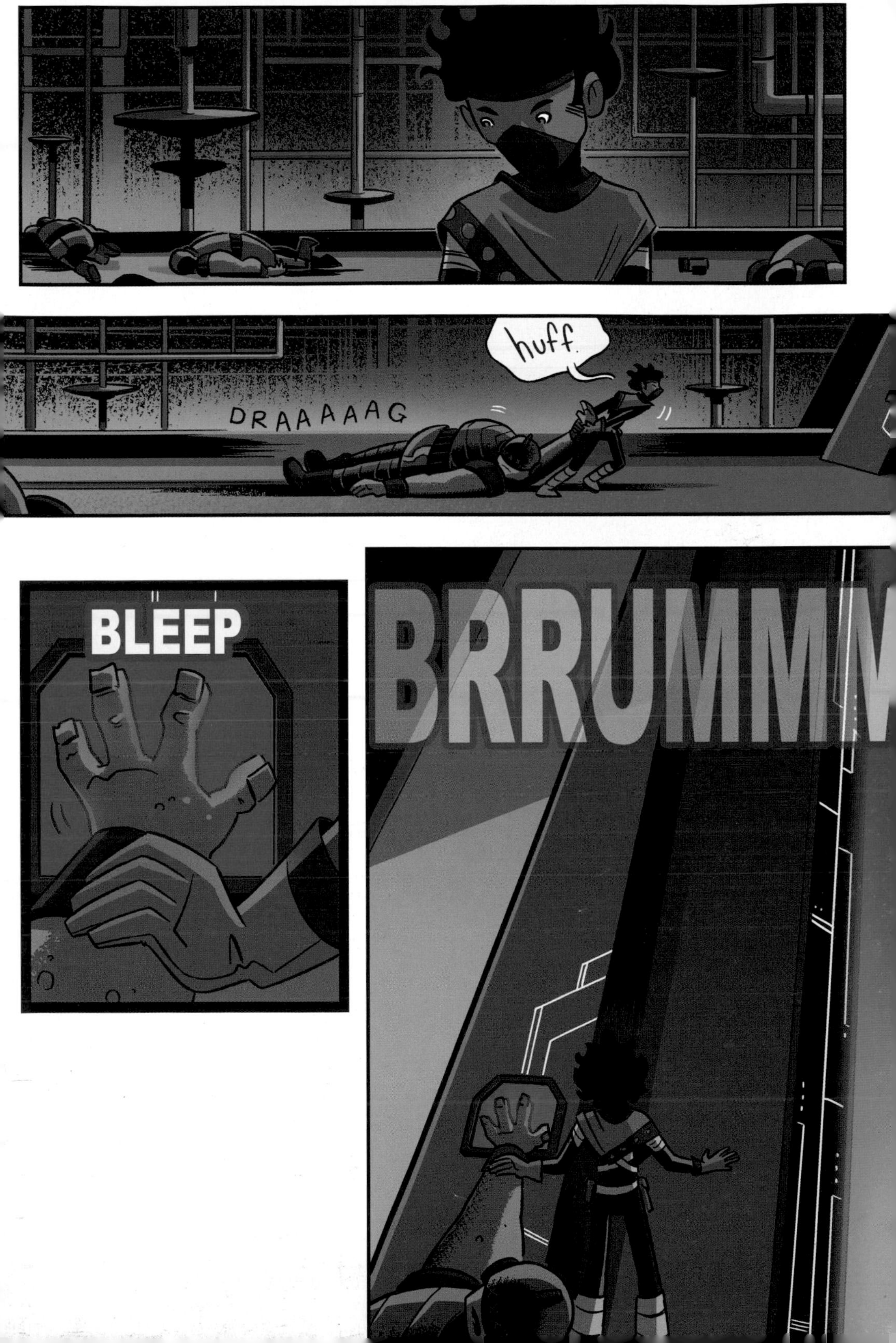
huff.
DRAAAAAG
BLEEP
BRRUMMM

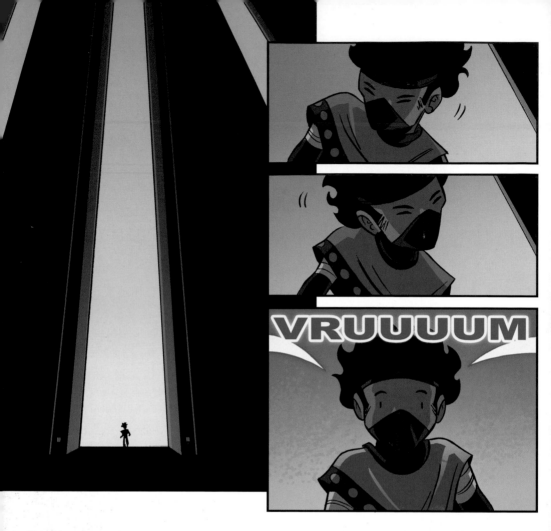

VRUUUUM

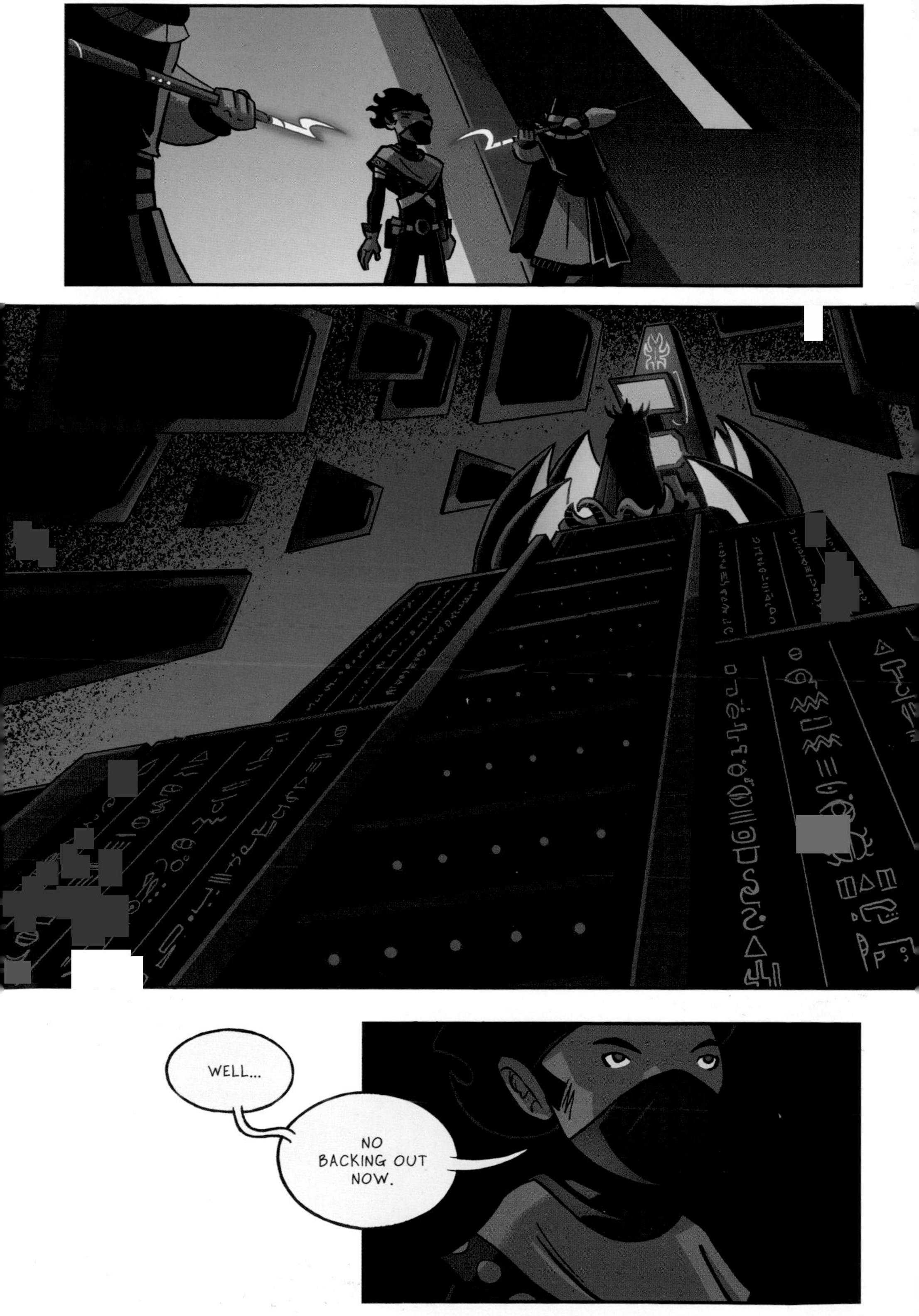
WELL...
NO BACKING OUT NOW.

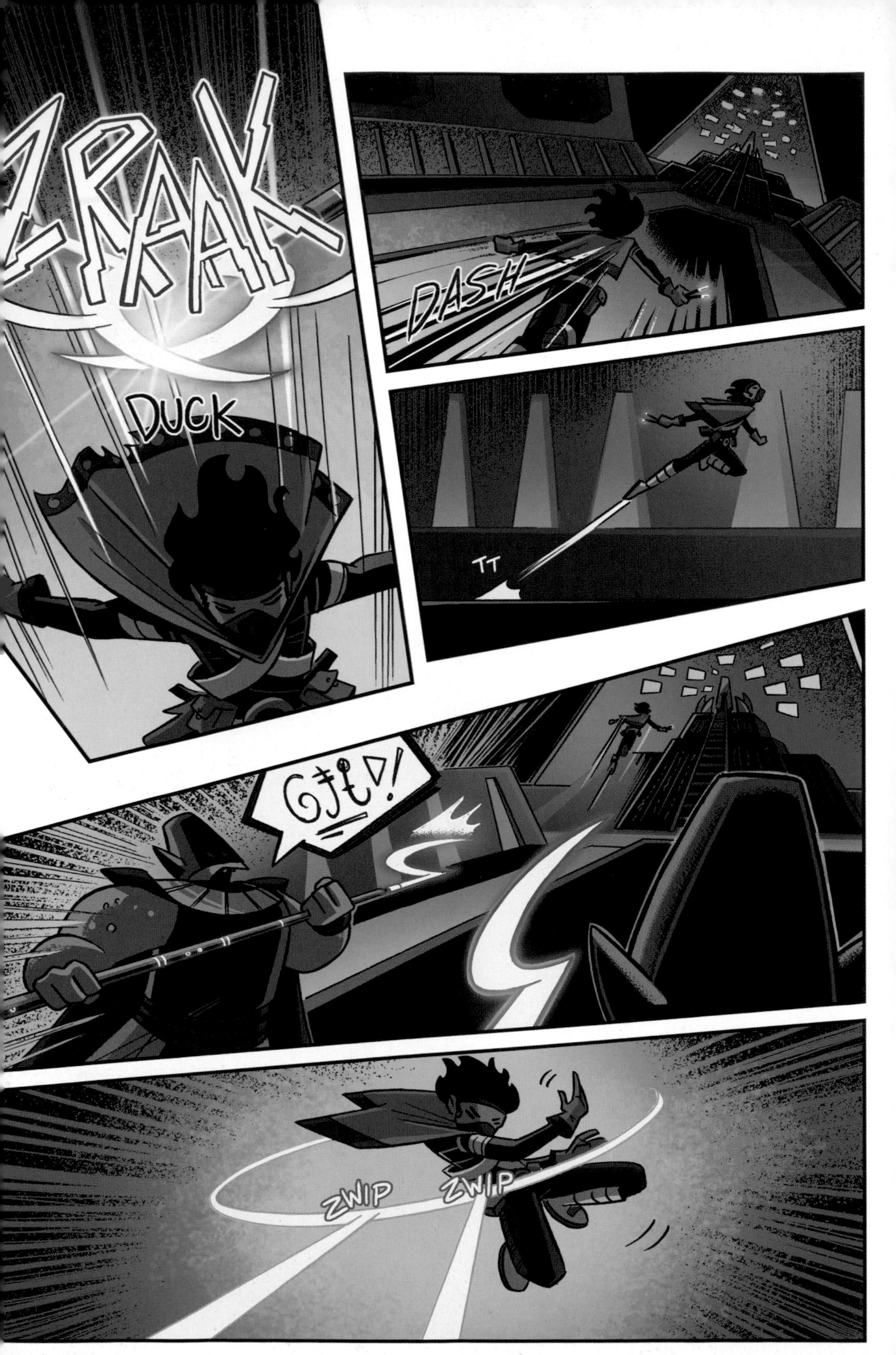
ZRAAK
DUCK
DASH
TT
ZWIP
ZWIP

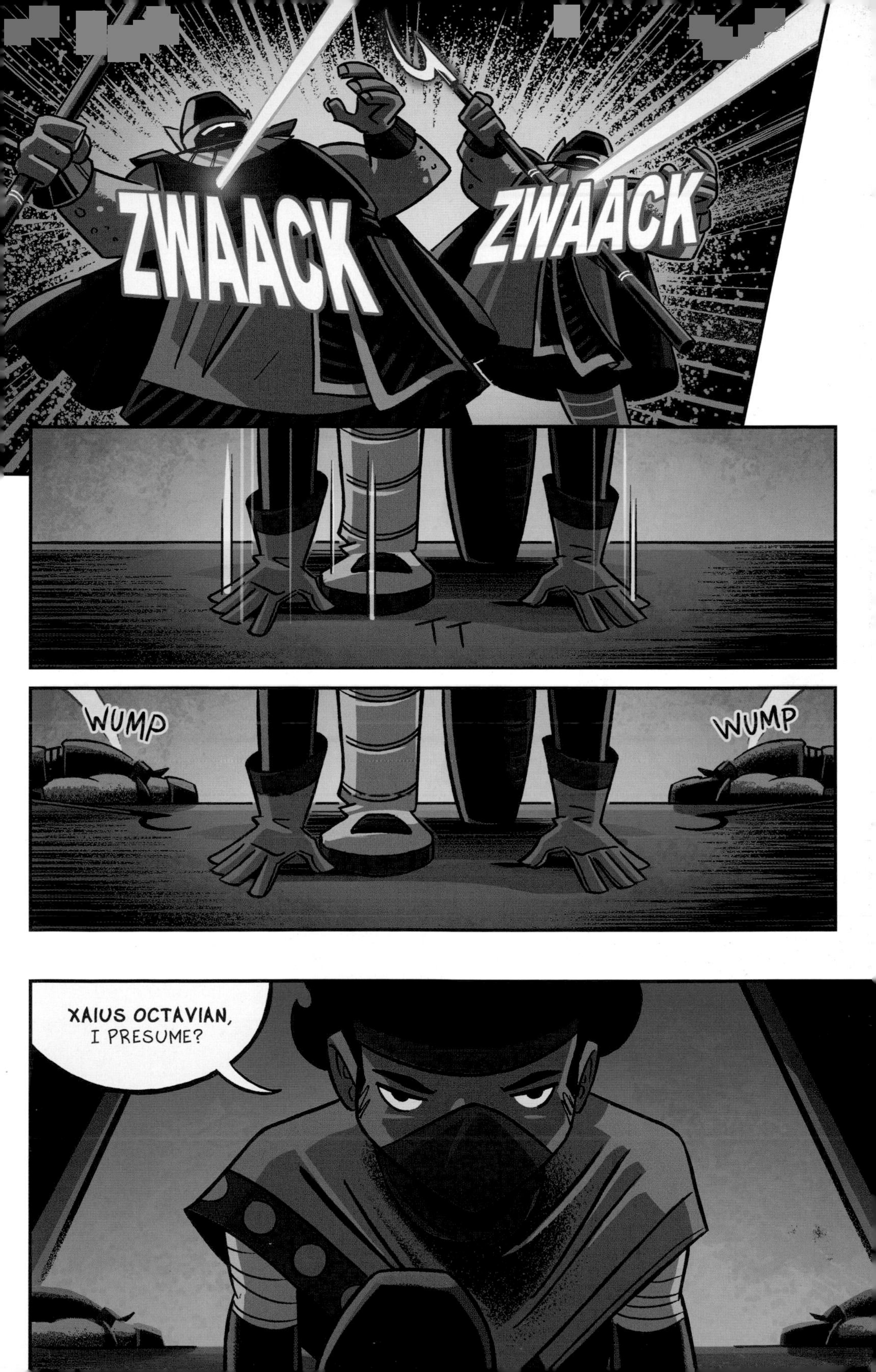
ZWAACK
ZWAACK
TT
WUMP
WUMP
XAIUS OCTAVIAN, I PRESUME?

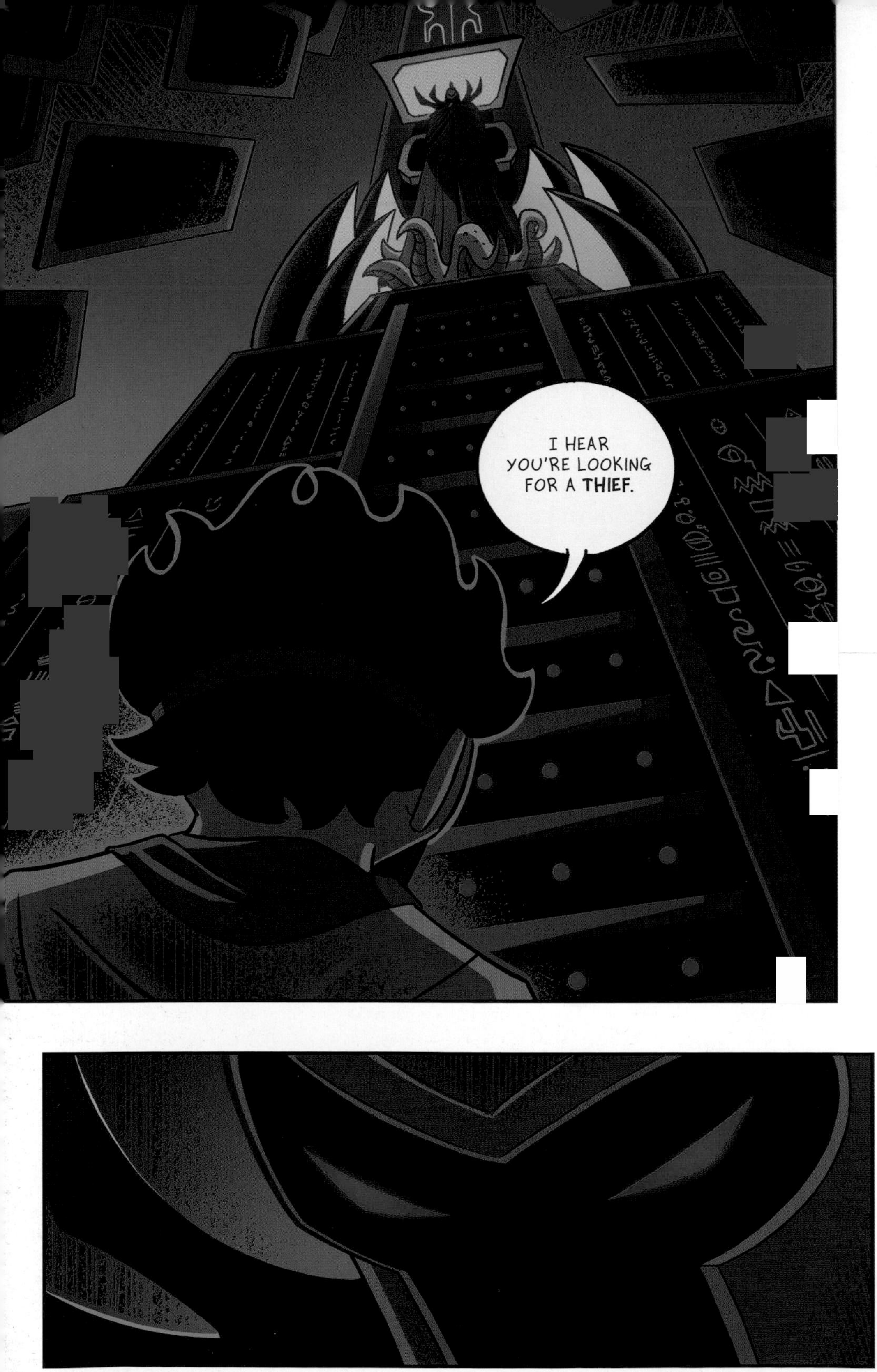
I HEAR YOU'RE LOOKING FOR A **THIEF**.

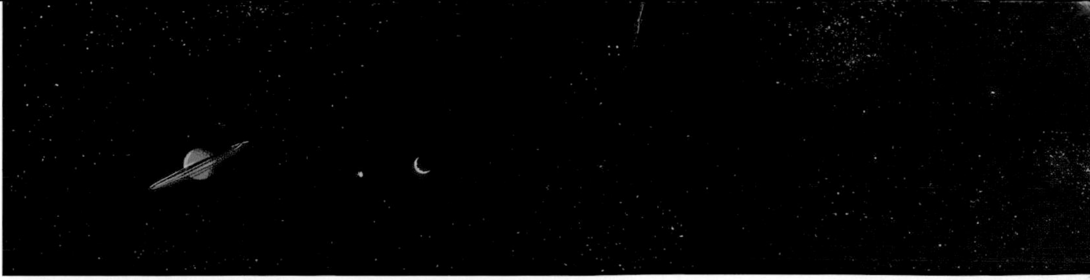

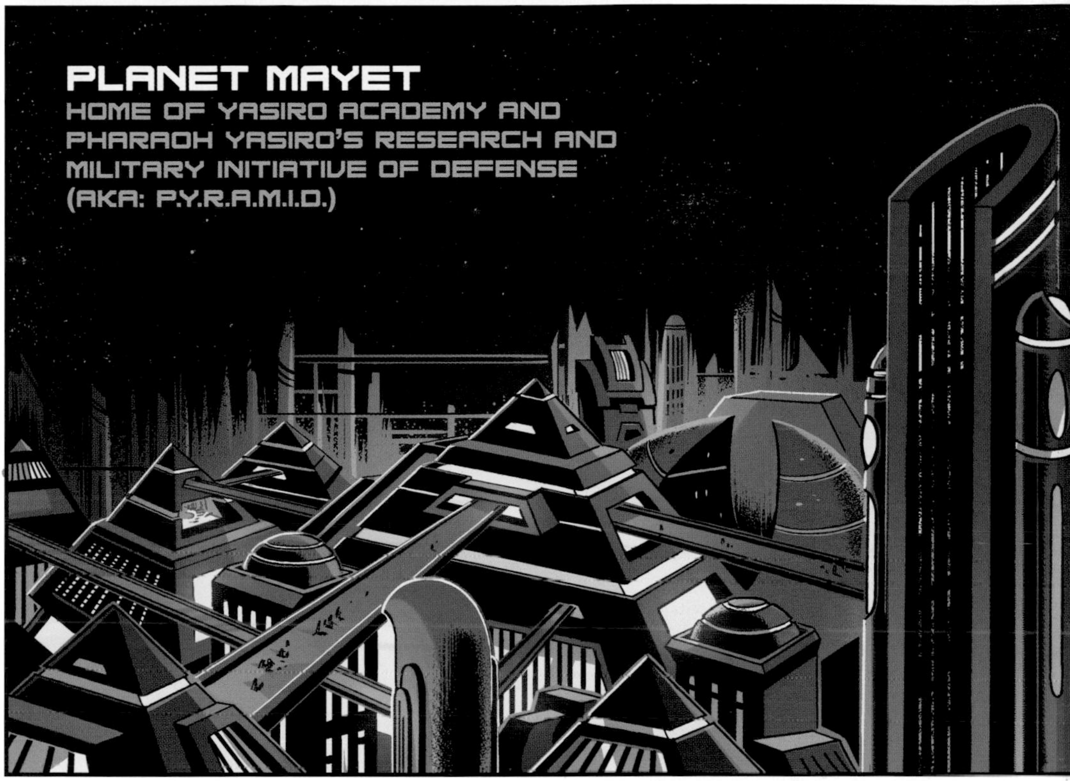
PLANET MAYET
HOME OF YASIRO ACADEMY AND PHARAOH YASIRO'S RESEARCH AND MILITARY INITIATIVE OF DEFENSE (AKA: P.Y.R.A.M.I.D.)

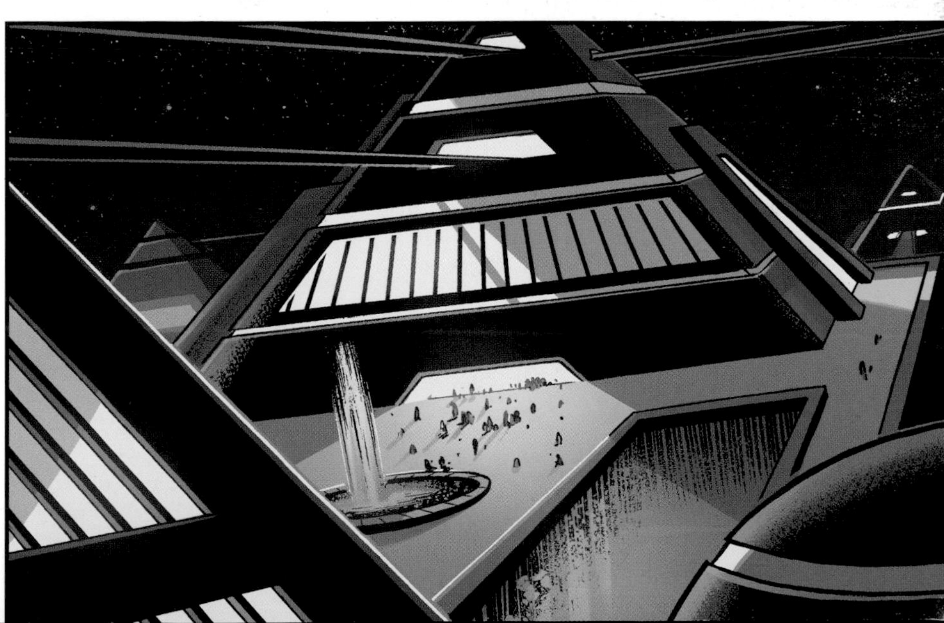

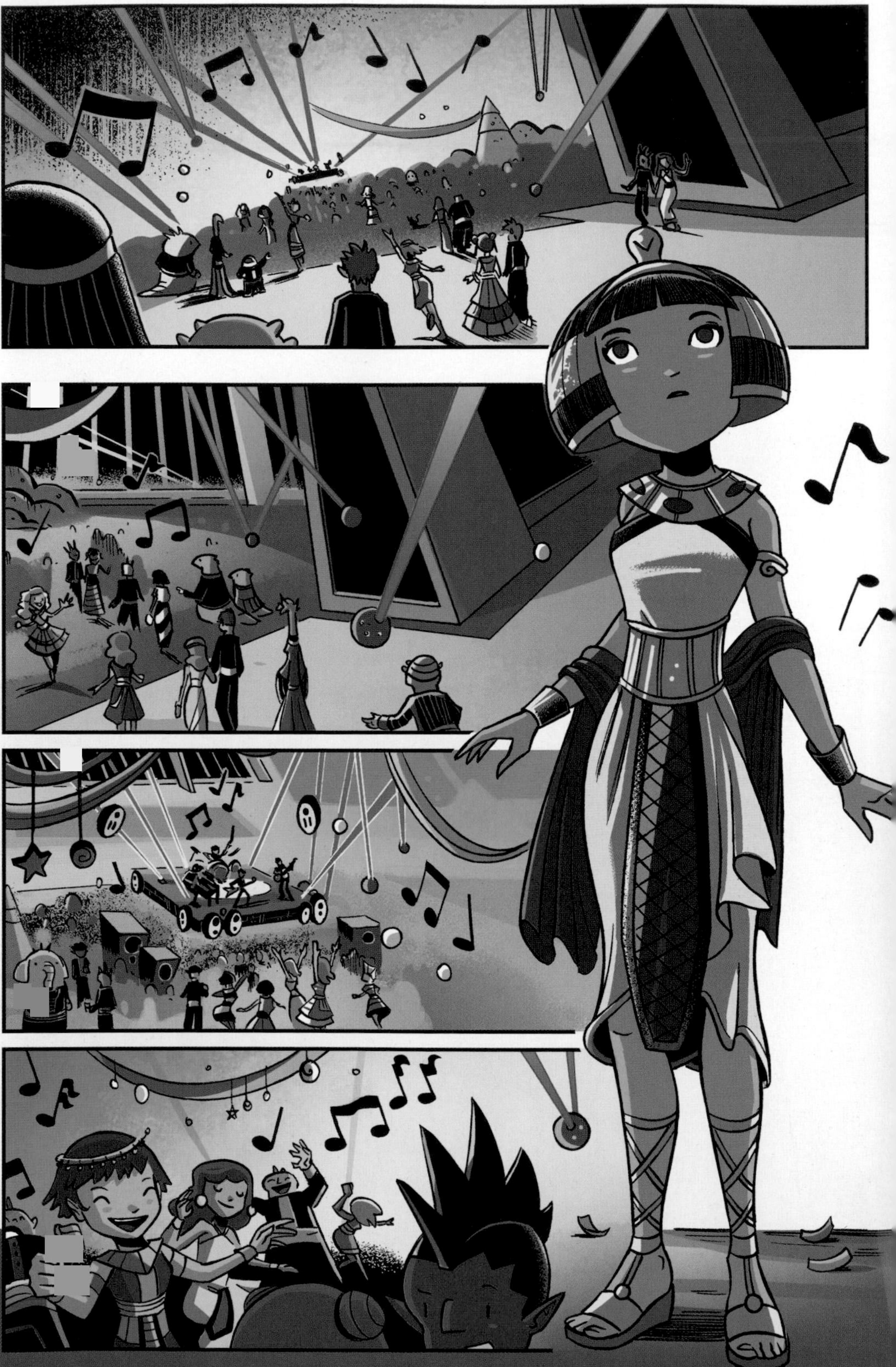

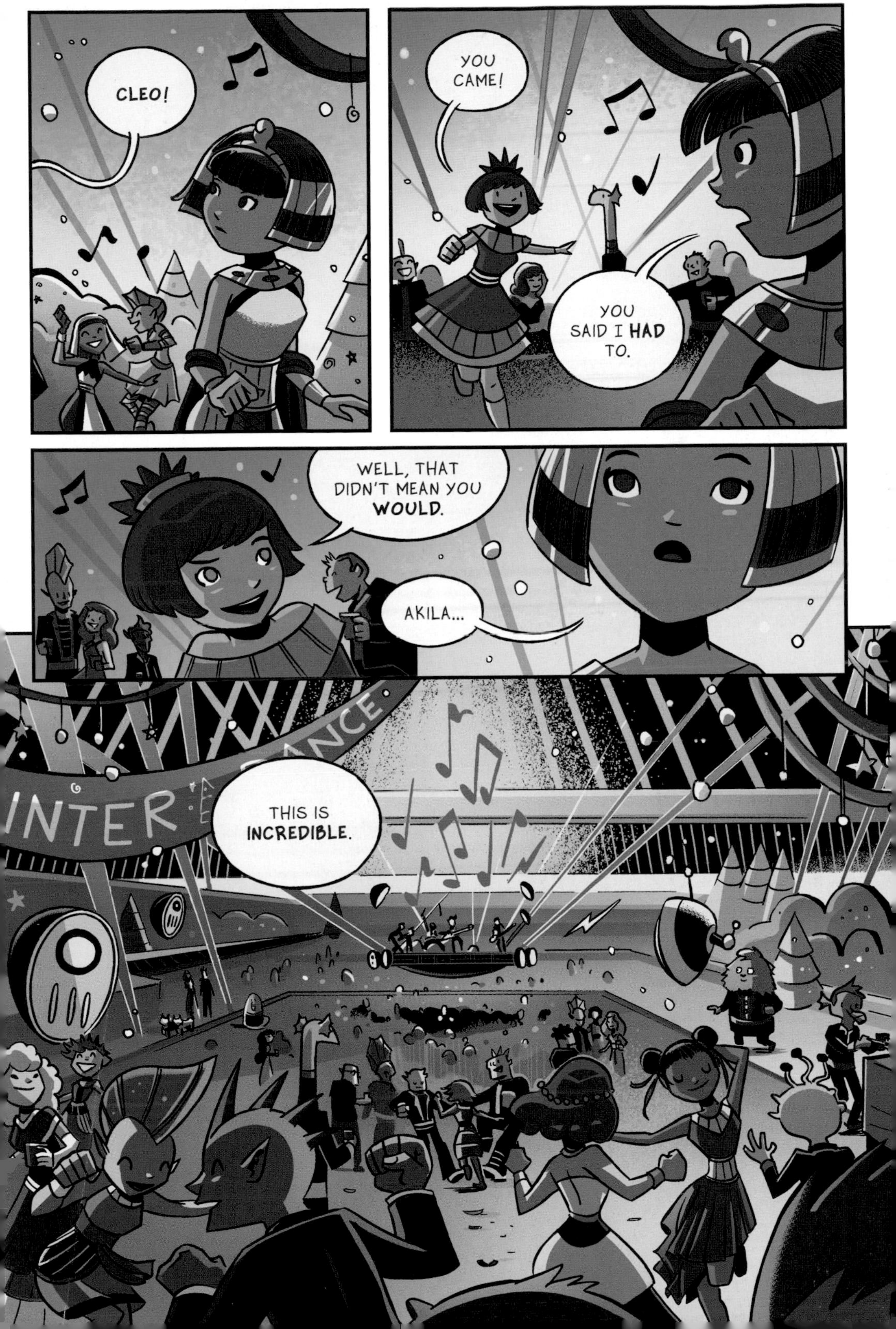
CLEO!
YOU CAME!
YOU SAID I HAD TO.
WELL, THAT DIDN'T MEAN YOU WOULD.
AKILA...
INTER
THIS IS INCREDIBLE.

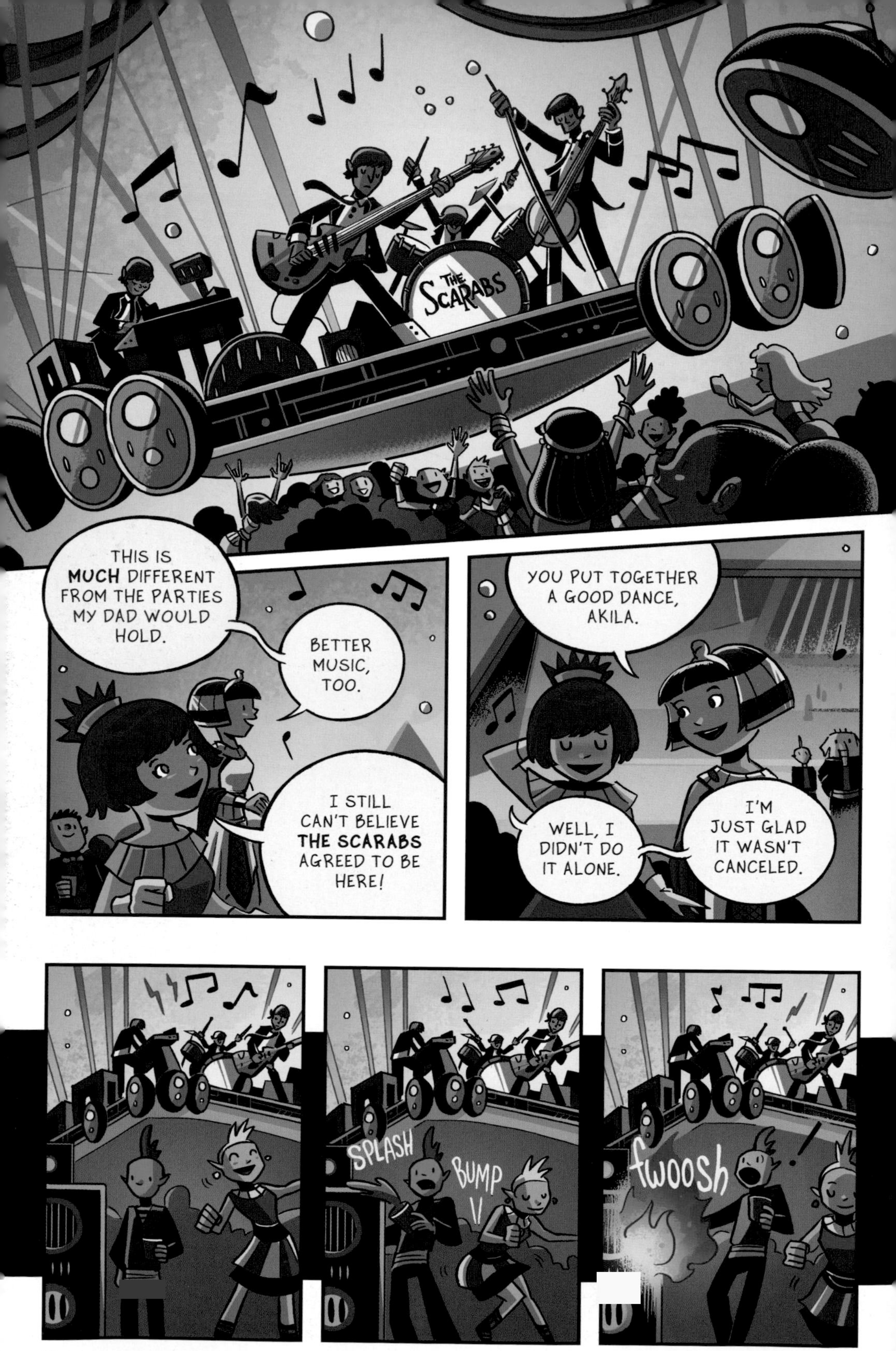
THE SCARABS
THIS IS MUCH DIFFERENT FROM THE PARTIES MY DAD WOULD HOLD.
BETTER MUSIC, TOO.
I STILL CAN'T BELIEVE THE SCARABS AGREED TO BE HERE!
YOU PUT TOGETHER A GOOD DANCE, AKILA.
WELL, I DIDN'T DO IT ALONE.
I'M JUST GLAD IT WASN'T CANCELED.
SPLASH
BUMP
fwoosh
!

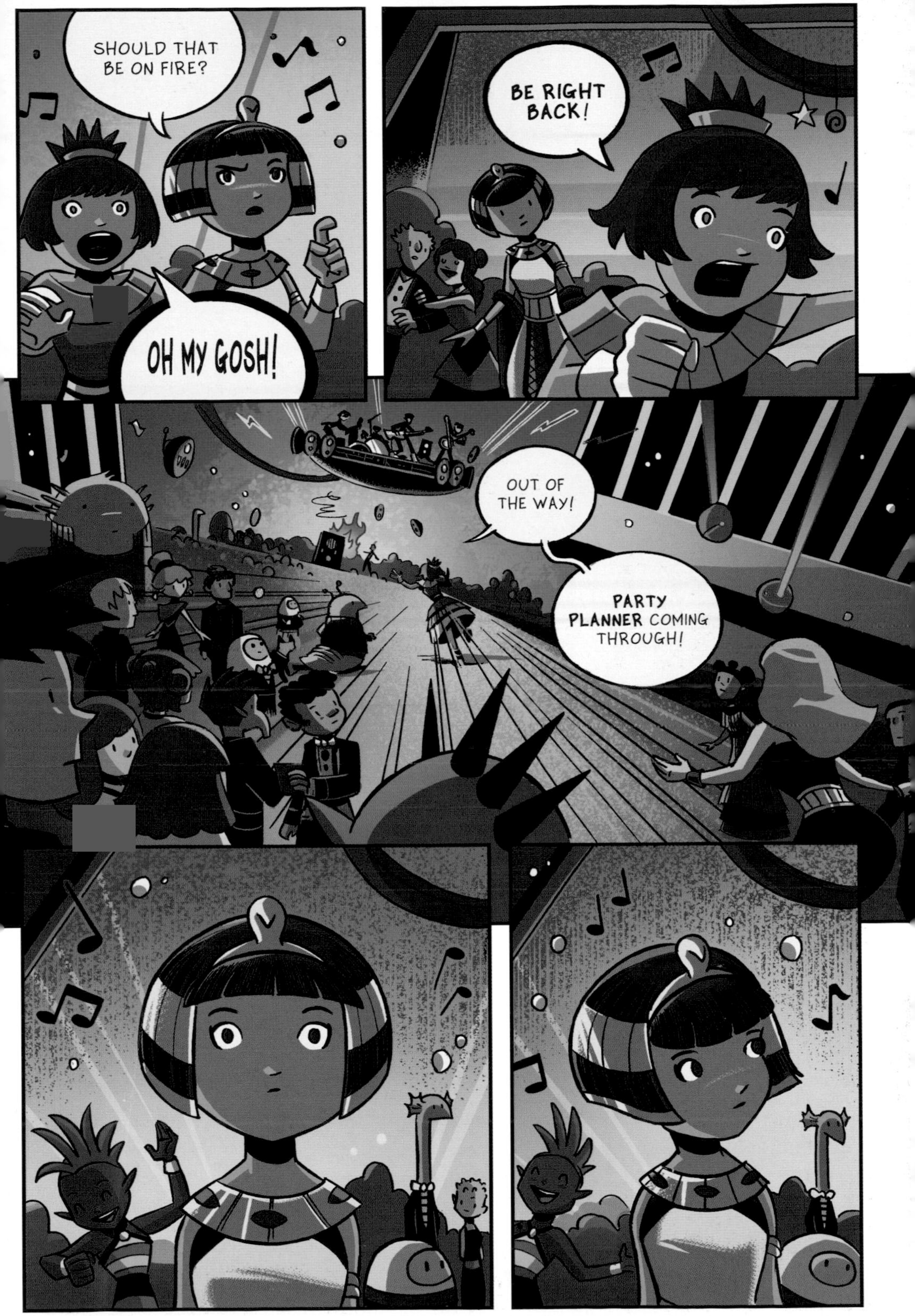
SHOULD THAT BE ON FIRE?
OH MY GOSH!
BE RIGHT BACK!
OUT OF THE WAY!
PARTY PLANNER COMING THROUGH!

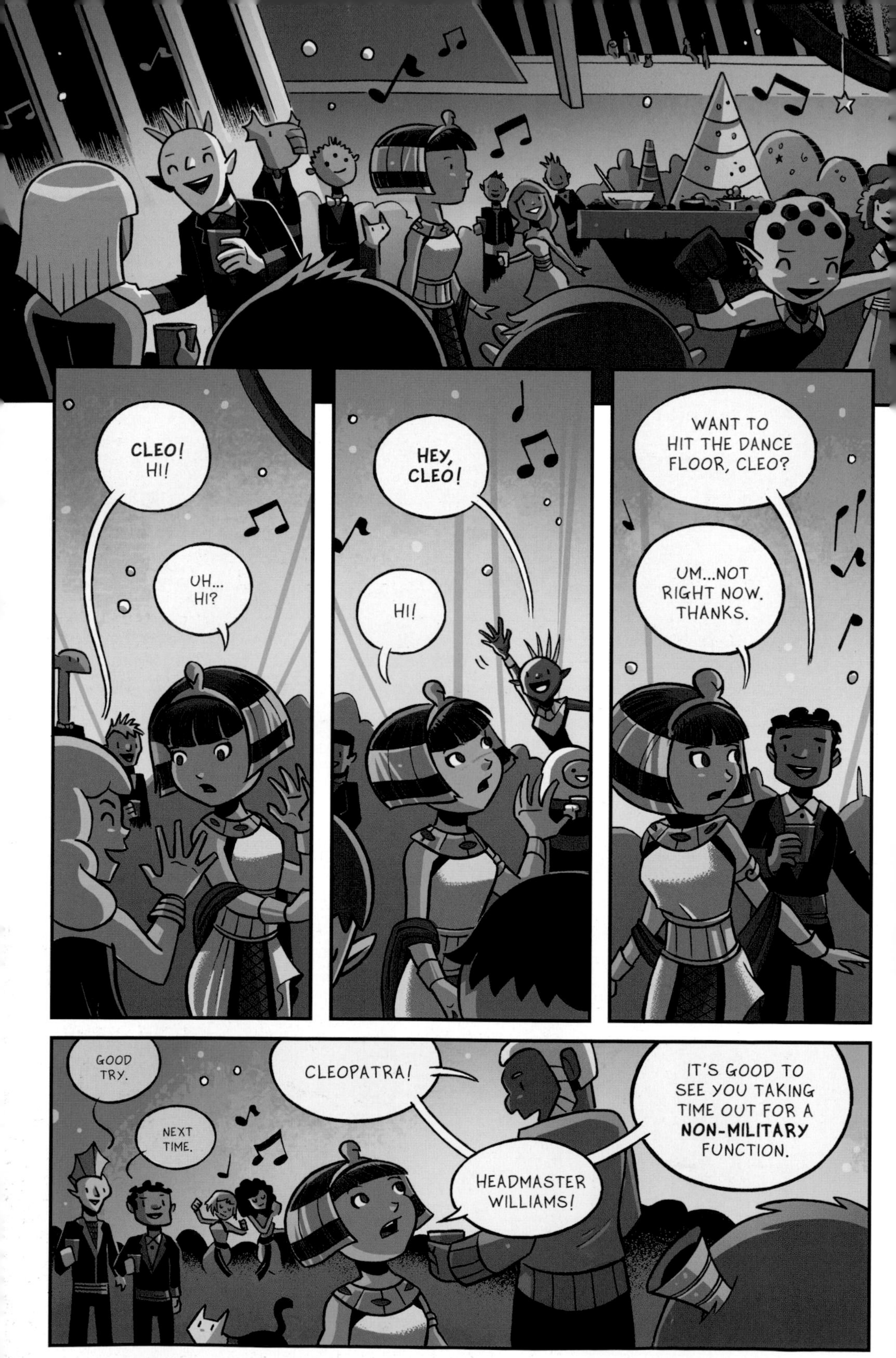
CLEO! HI!
UH... HI?
HEY, CLEO!
HI!
WANT TO HIT THE DANCE FLOOR, CLEO?
UM...NOT RIGHT NOW. THANKS.
GOOD TRY.
NEXT TIME.
CLEOPATRA!
HEADMASTER WILLIAMS!
IT'S GOOD TO SEE YOU TAKING TIME OUT FOR A **NON-MILITARY** FUNCTION.

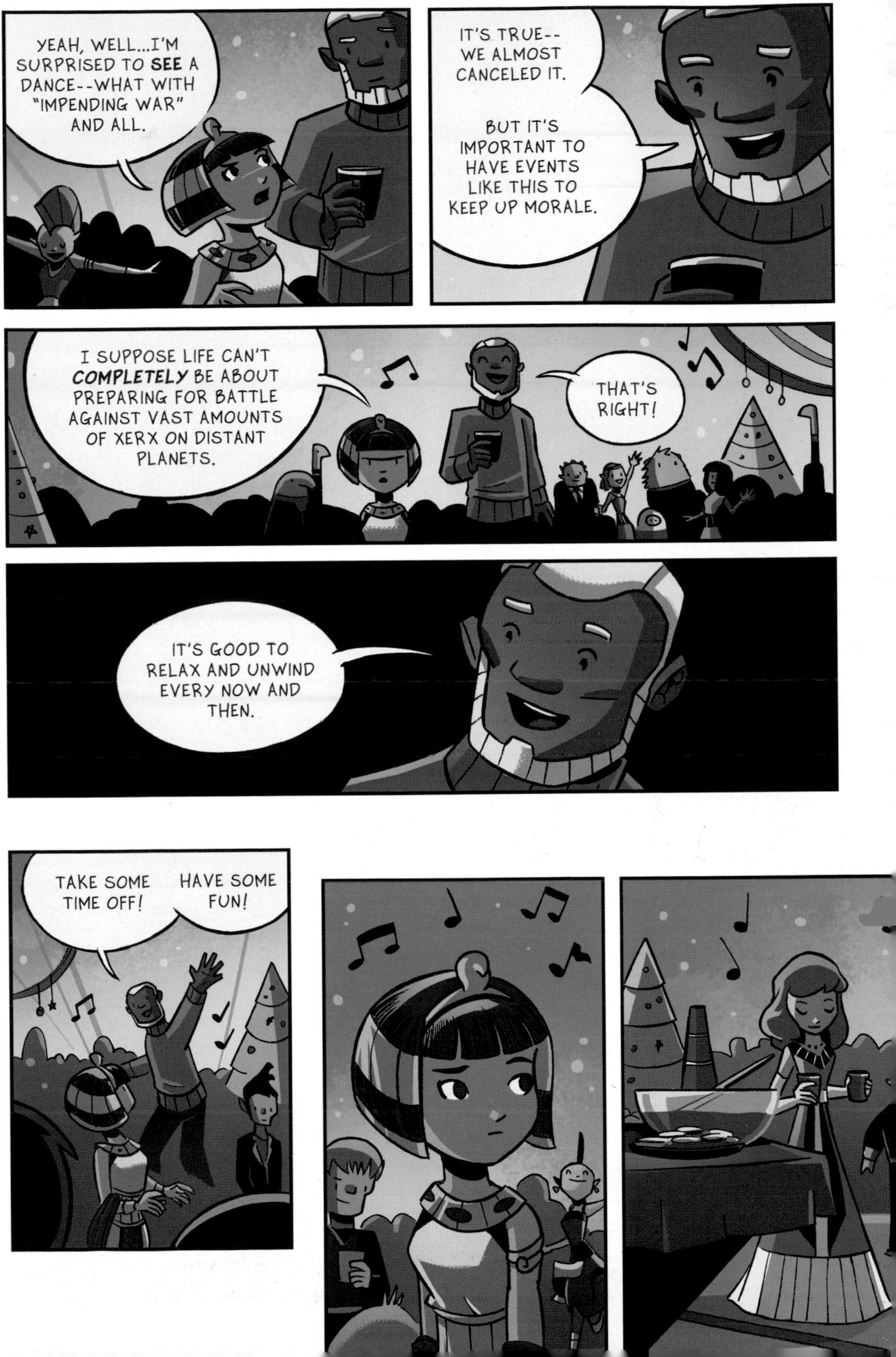
YEAH, WELL...I'M SURPRISED TO **SEE** A DANCE--WHAT WITH "IMPENDING WAR" AND ALL.
IT'S TRUE-- WE ALMOST CANCELED IT.
BUT IT'S IMPORTANT TO HAVE EVENTS LIKE THIS TO KEEP UP MORALE.
I SUPPOSE LIFE CAN'T ***COMPLETELY*** BE ABOUT PREPARING FOR BATTLE AGAINST VAST AMOUNTS OF XERX ON DISTANT PLANETS.
THAT'S RIGHT!
IT'S GOOD TO RELAX AND UNWIND EVERY NOW AND THEN.
TAKE SOME TIME OFF!
HAVE SOME FUN!

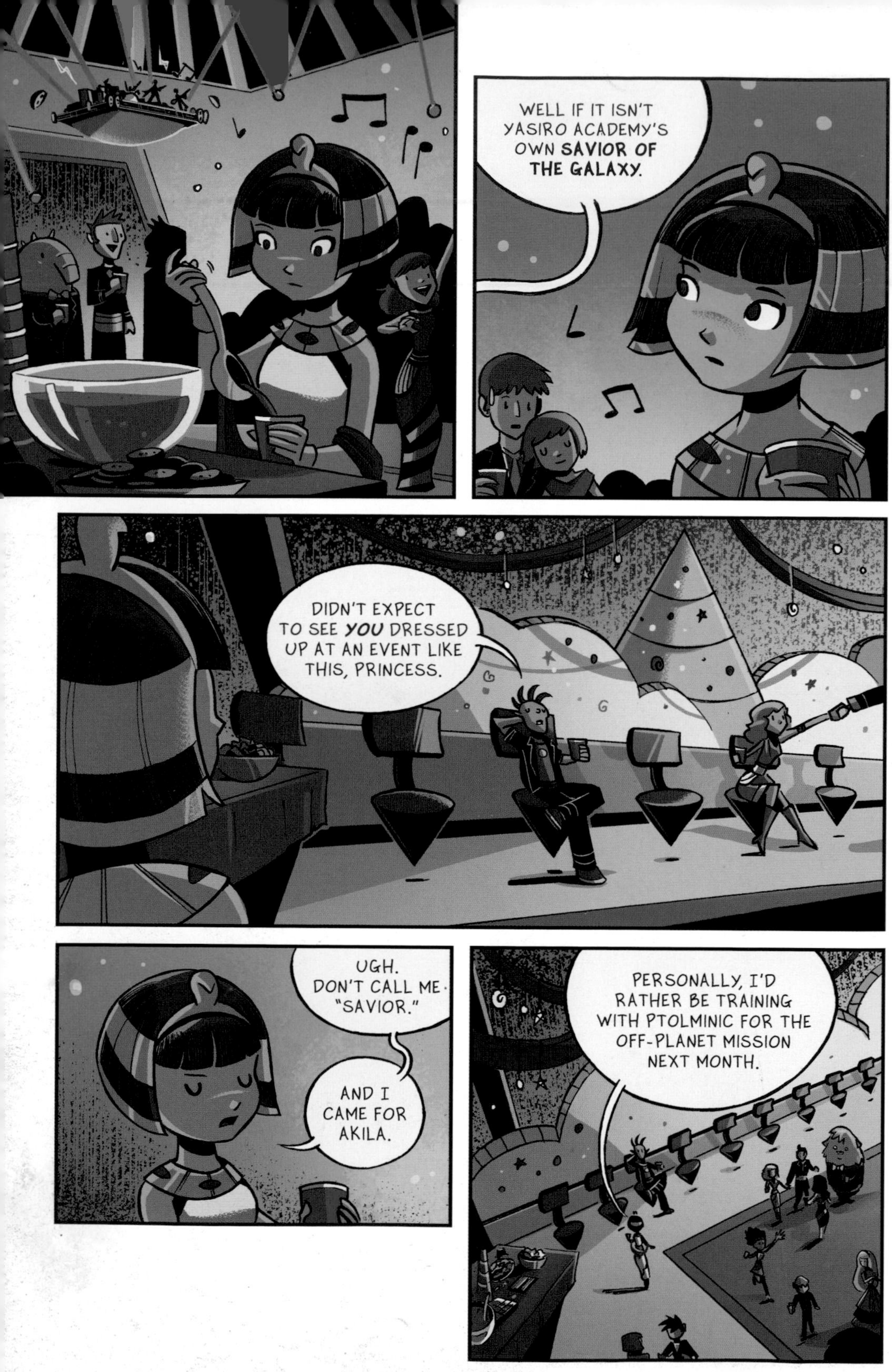
WELL IF IT ISN'T YASIRO ACADEMY'S OWN **SAVIOR OF THE GALAXY.**
DIDN'T EXPECT TO SEE ***YOU*** DRESSED UP AT AN EVENT LIKE THIS, PRINCESS.
UGH. DON'T CALL ME "SAVIOR."
AND I CAME FOR AKILA.
PERSONALLY, I'D RATHER BE TRAINING WITH PTOLMINIC FOR THE OFF-PLANET MISSION NEXT MONTH.

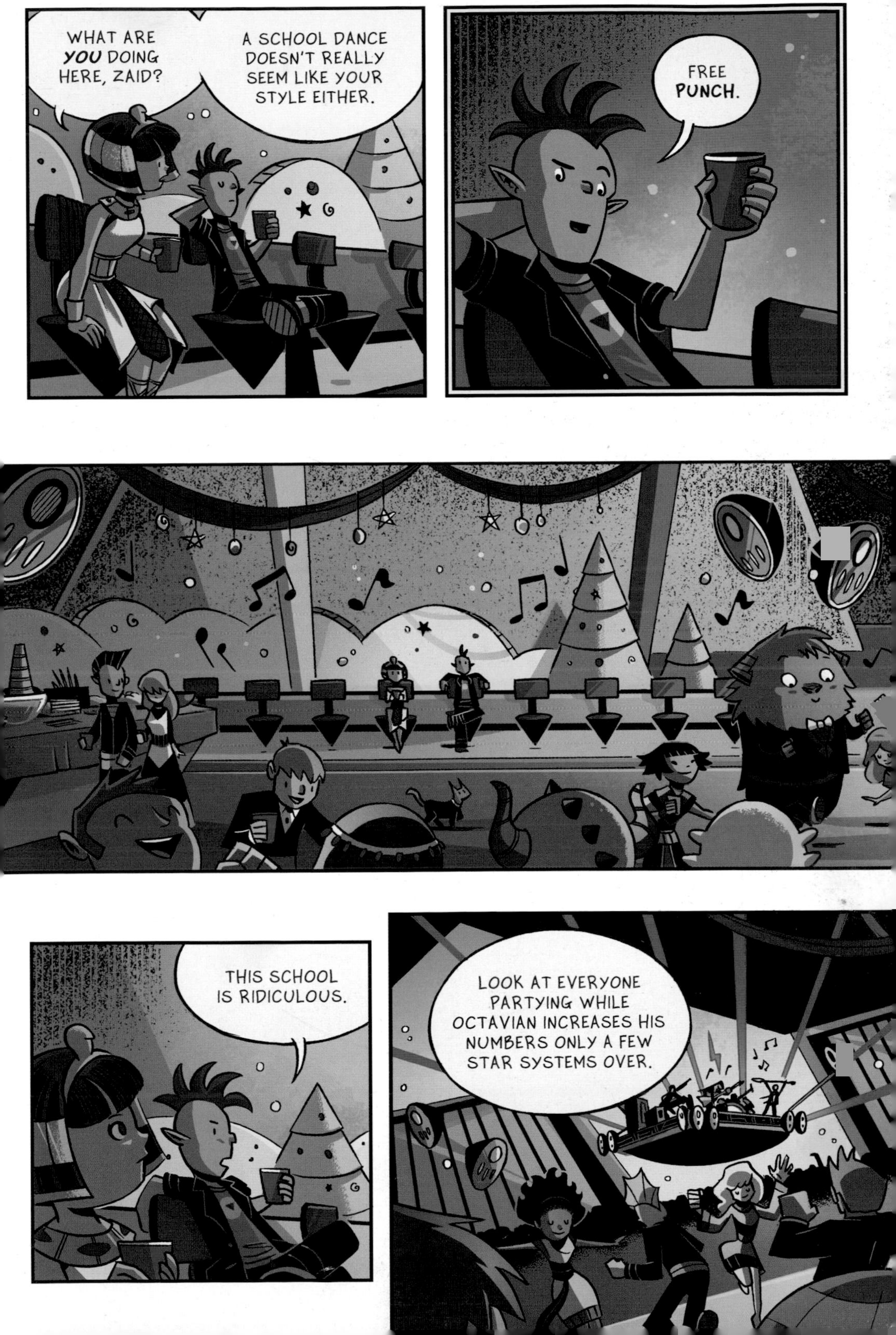
WHAT ARE *YOU* DOING HERE, ZAID?
A SCHOOL DANCE DOESN'T REALLY SEEM LIKE YOUR STYLE EITHER.
FREE **PUNCH.**
THIS SCHOOL IS RIDICULOUS.
LOOK AT EVERYONE PARTYING WHILE OCTAVIAN INCREASES HIS NUMBERS ONLY A FEW STAR SYSTEMS OVER.

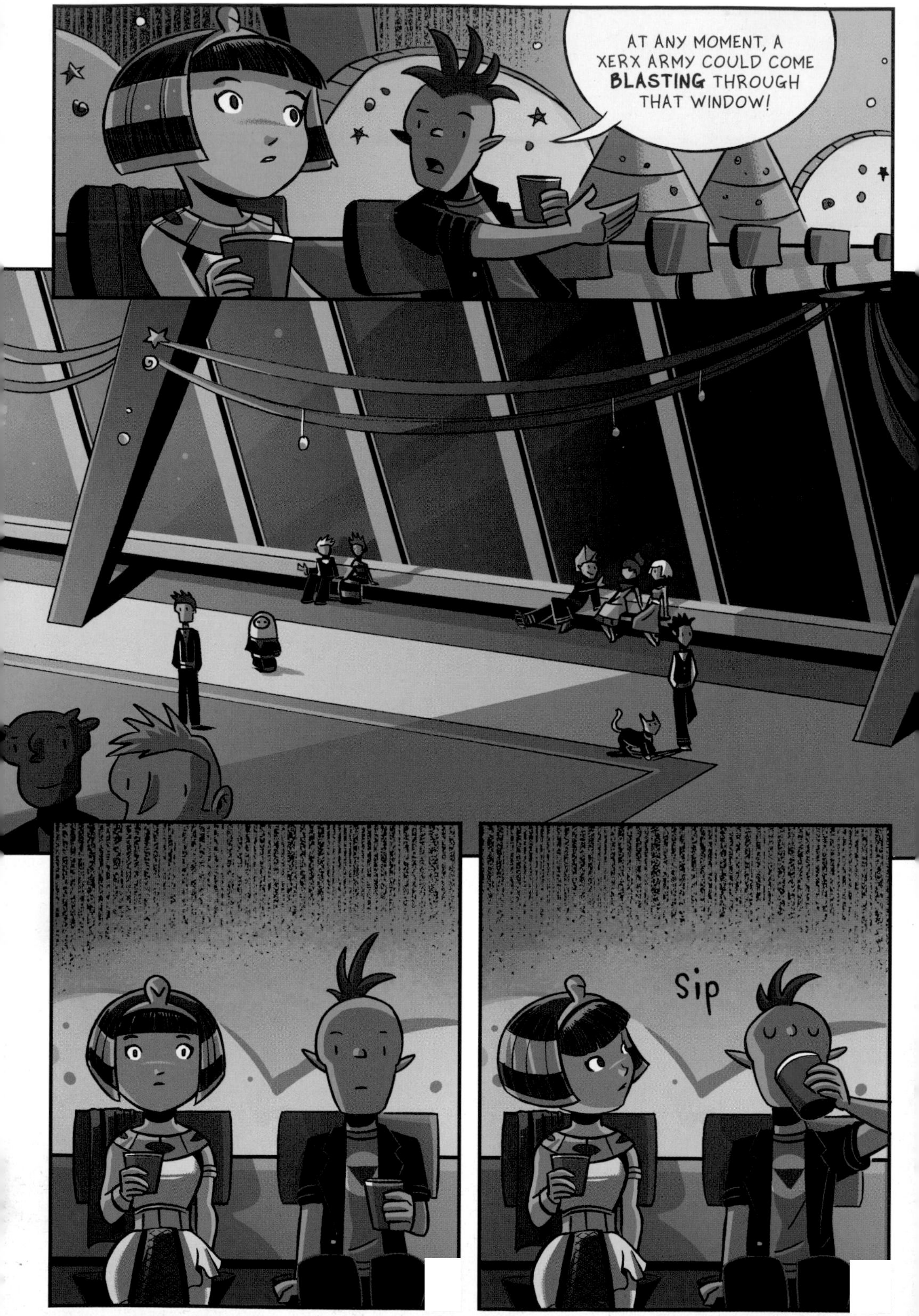
AT ANY MOMENT, A XERX ARMY COULD COME **BLASTING** THROUGH THAT WINDOW!
Sip

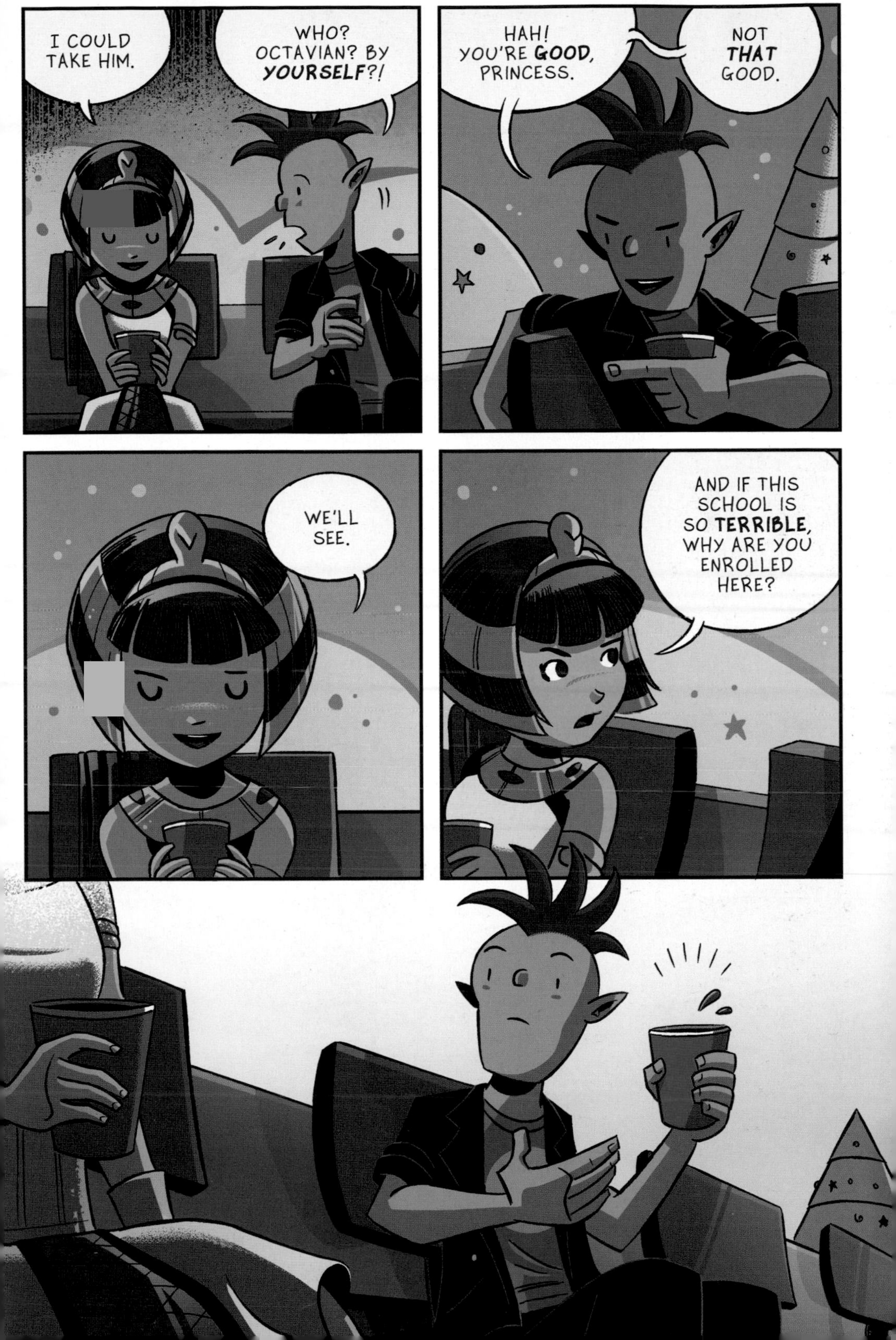
I COULD TAKE HIM.
WHO? OCTAVIAN? BY YOURSELF?!
HAH! YOU'RE GOOD, PRINCESS.
NOT THAT GOOD.
WE'LL SEE.
AND IF THIS SCHOOL IS SO TERRIBLE, WHY ARE YOU ENROLLED HERE?

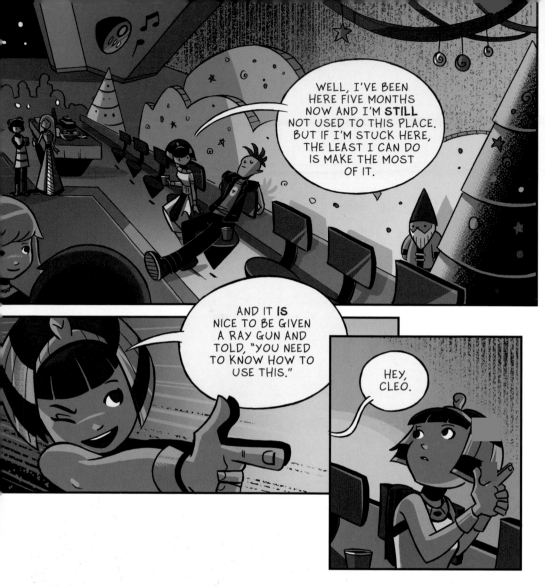

WELL, I'VE BEEN HERE FIVE MONTHS NOW AND I'M **STILL** NOT USED TO THIS PLACE. BUT IF I'M STUCK HERE, THE LEAST I CAN DO IS MAKE THE MOST OF IT.

AND IT **IS** NICE TO BE GIVEN A RAY GUN AND TOLD, "YOU NEED TO KNOW HOW TO USE THIS."

HEY, CLEO.

OH HEY, BRIAN.

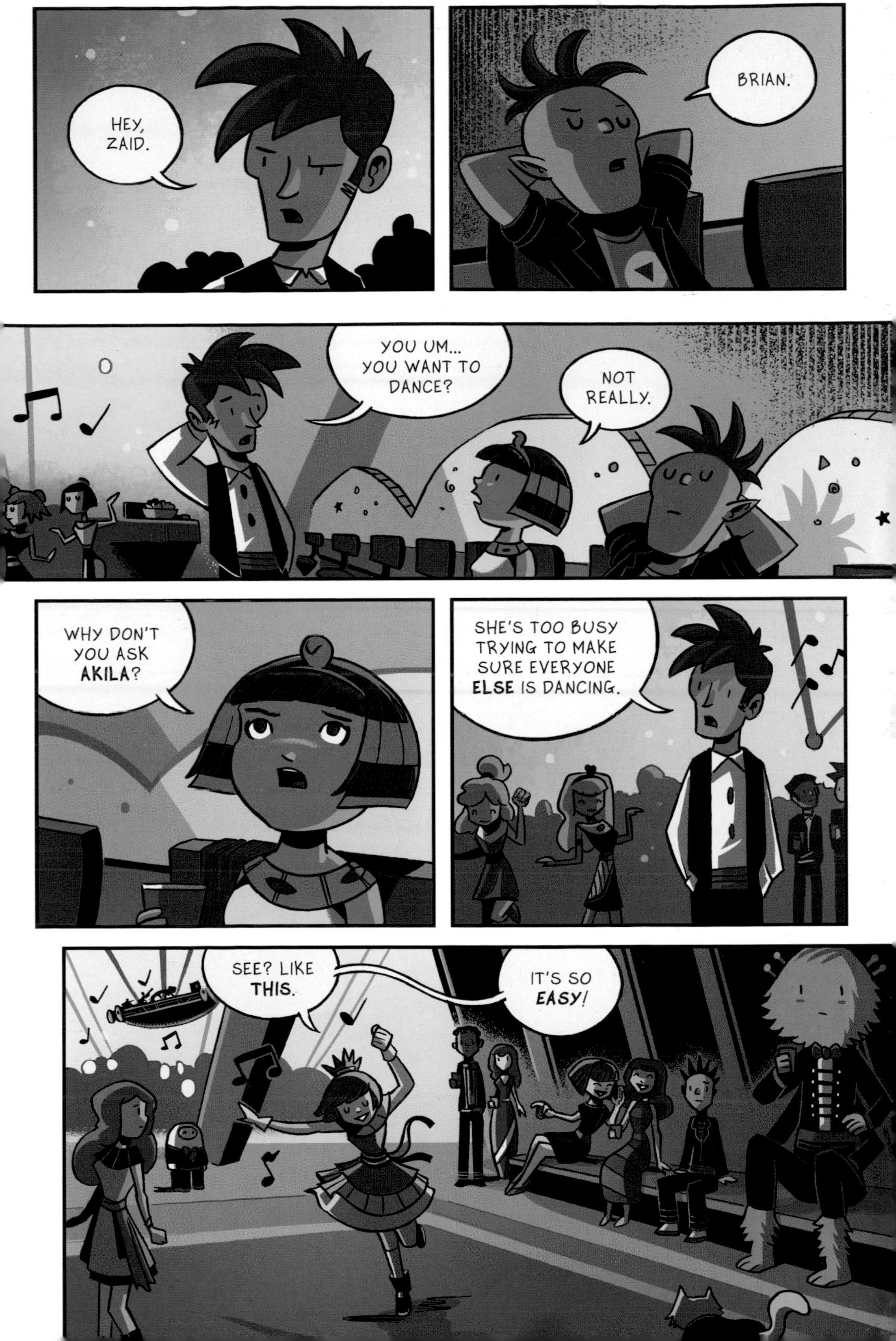
HEY, ZAID.
BRIAN.
YOU UM... YOU WANT TO DANCE?
NOT REALLY.
WHY DON'T YOU ASK AKILA?
SHE'S TOO BUSY TRYING TO MAKE SURE EVERYONE ELSE IS DANCING.
SEE? LIKE THIS.
IT'S SO EASY!

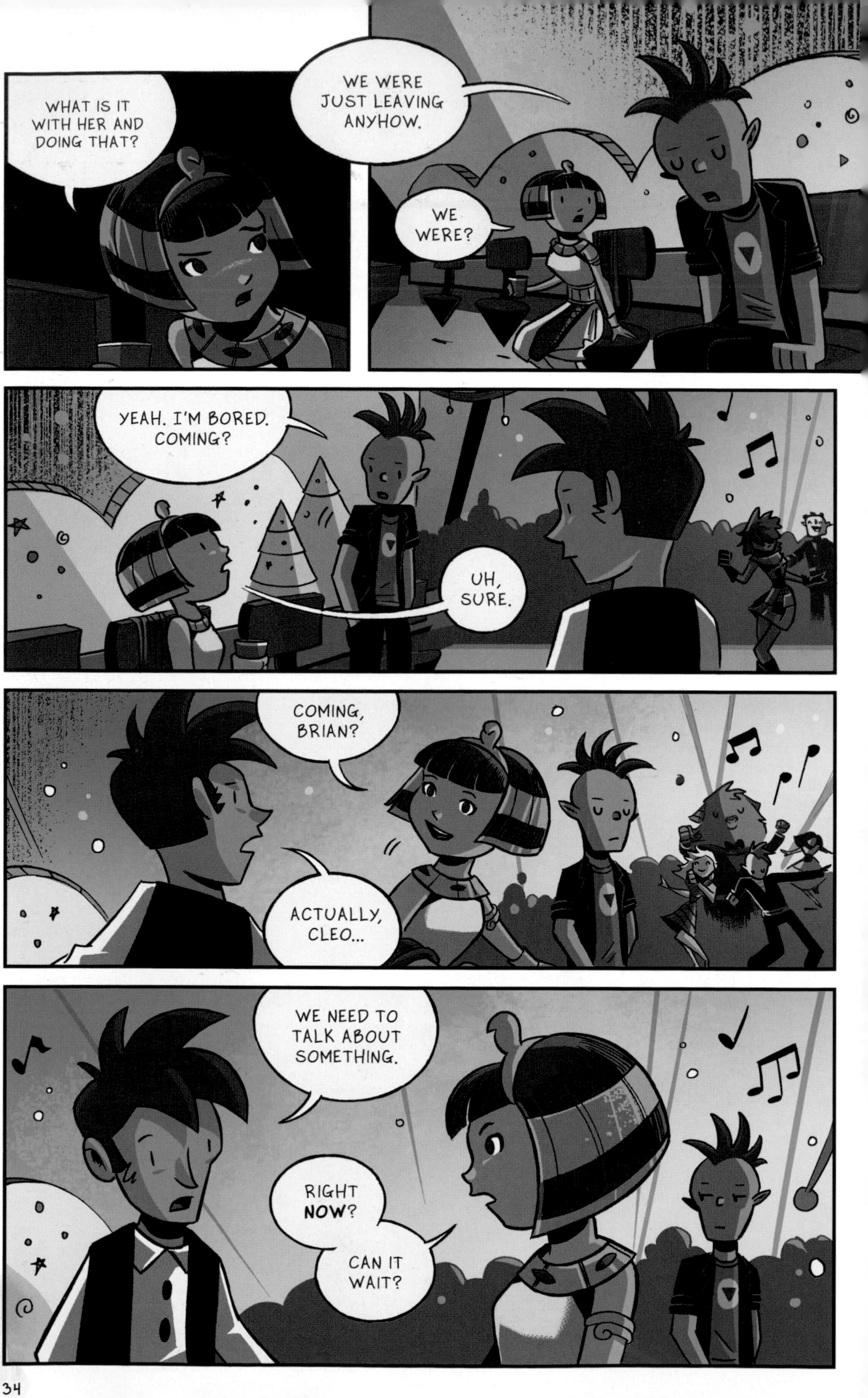
WHAT IS IT WITH HER AND DOING THAT?
WE WERE JUST LEAVING ANYHOW.
WE WERE?
YEAH. I'M BORED. COMING?
UH, SURE.
COMING, BRIAN?
ACTUALLY, CLEO...
WE NEED TO TALK ABOUT SOMETHING.
RIGHT **NOW**?
CAN IT WAIT?

YEAH, I SUPPOSE.

OKAY, SEE YA!

TRY TO GET A DANCE IN WITH AKILA WHY DON'T YOU!

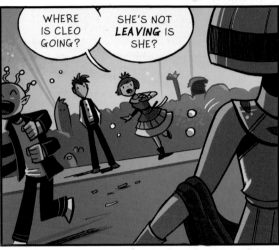

WHERE IS CLEO GOING?

SHE'S NOT *LEAVING* IS SHE?

I DON'T THINK DANCES ARE HER THING.

THAT'S **CRAZY** TALK!

DANCES ARE **FUN**.

EVERYBODY LOVES FUN.

SHYONI AND STEVE DON'T LOOK LIKE THEY LOVE FUN.

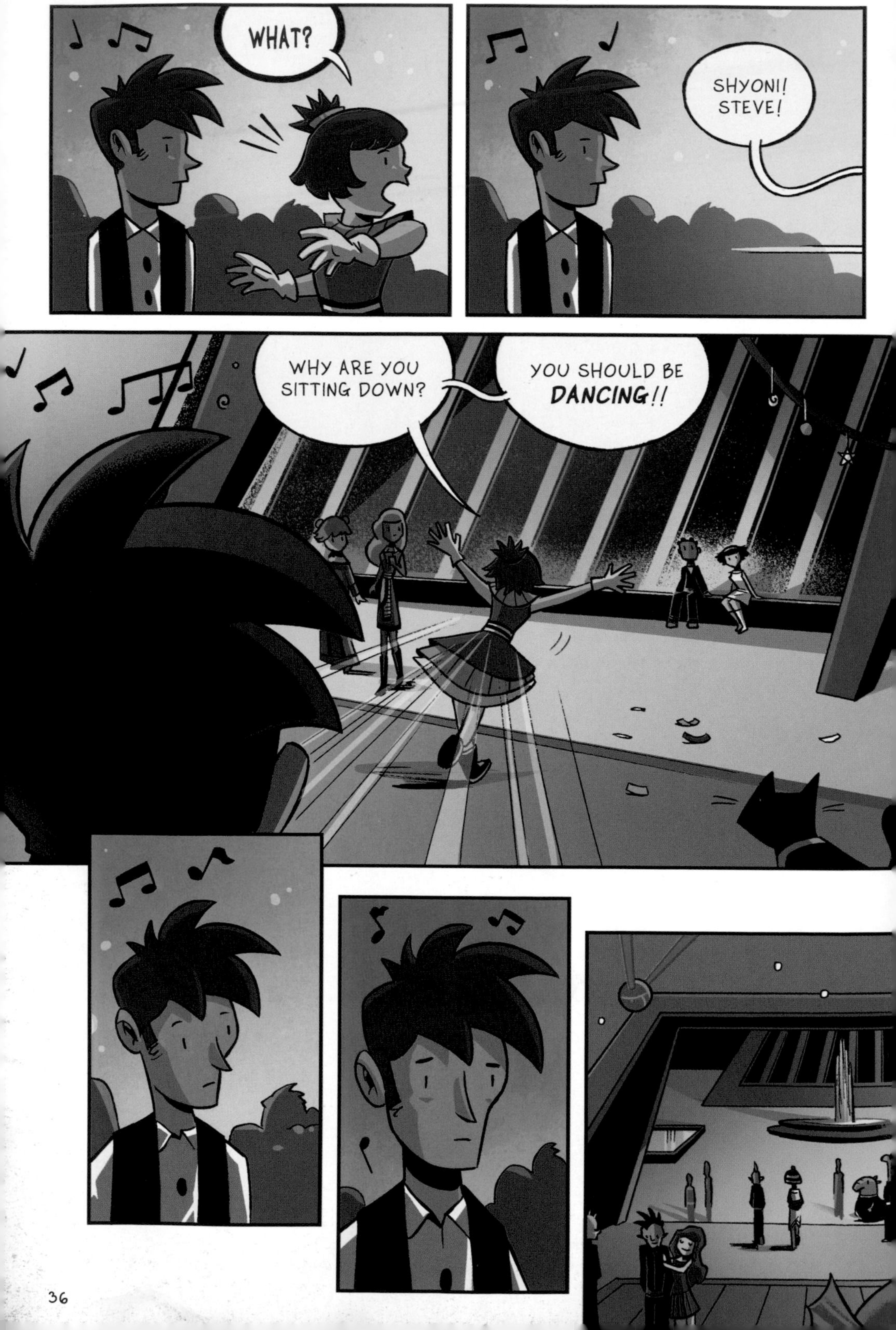
WHAT?
SHYONI! STEVE!
WHY ARE YOU SITTING DOWN?
YOU SHOULD BE DANCING!!

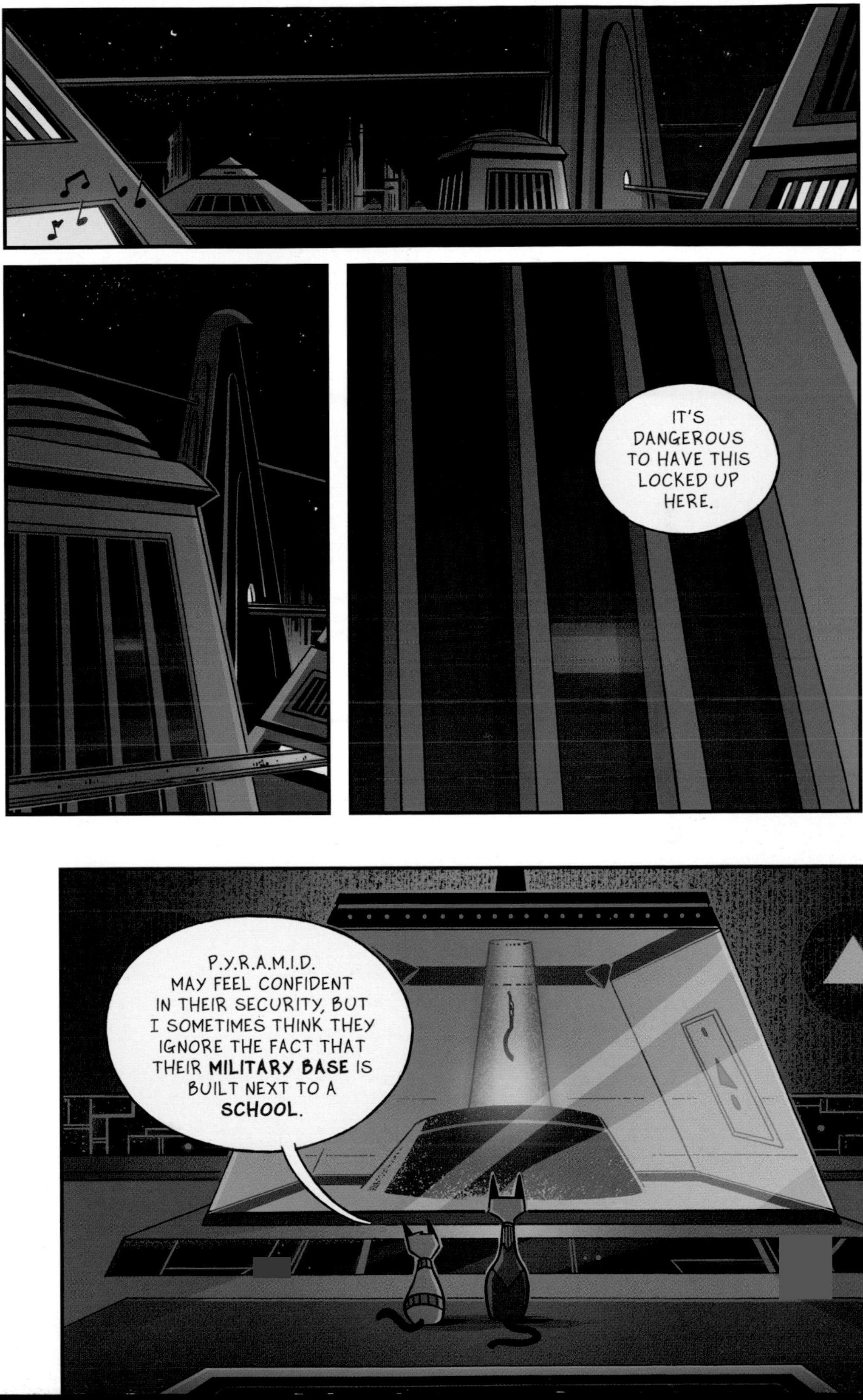
IT'S DANGEROUS TO HAVE THIS LOCKED UP HERE.
P.Y.R.A.M.I.D. MAY FEEL CONFIDENT IN THEIR SECURITY, BUT I SOMETIMES THINK THEY IGNORE THE FACT THAT THEIR **MILITARY BASE** IS BUILT NEXT TO A **SCHOOL**.

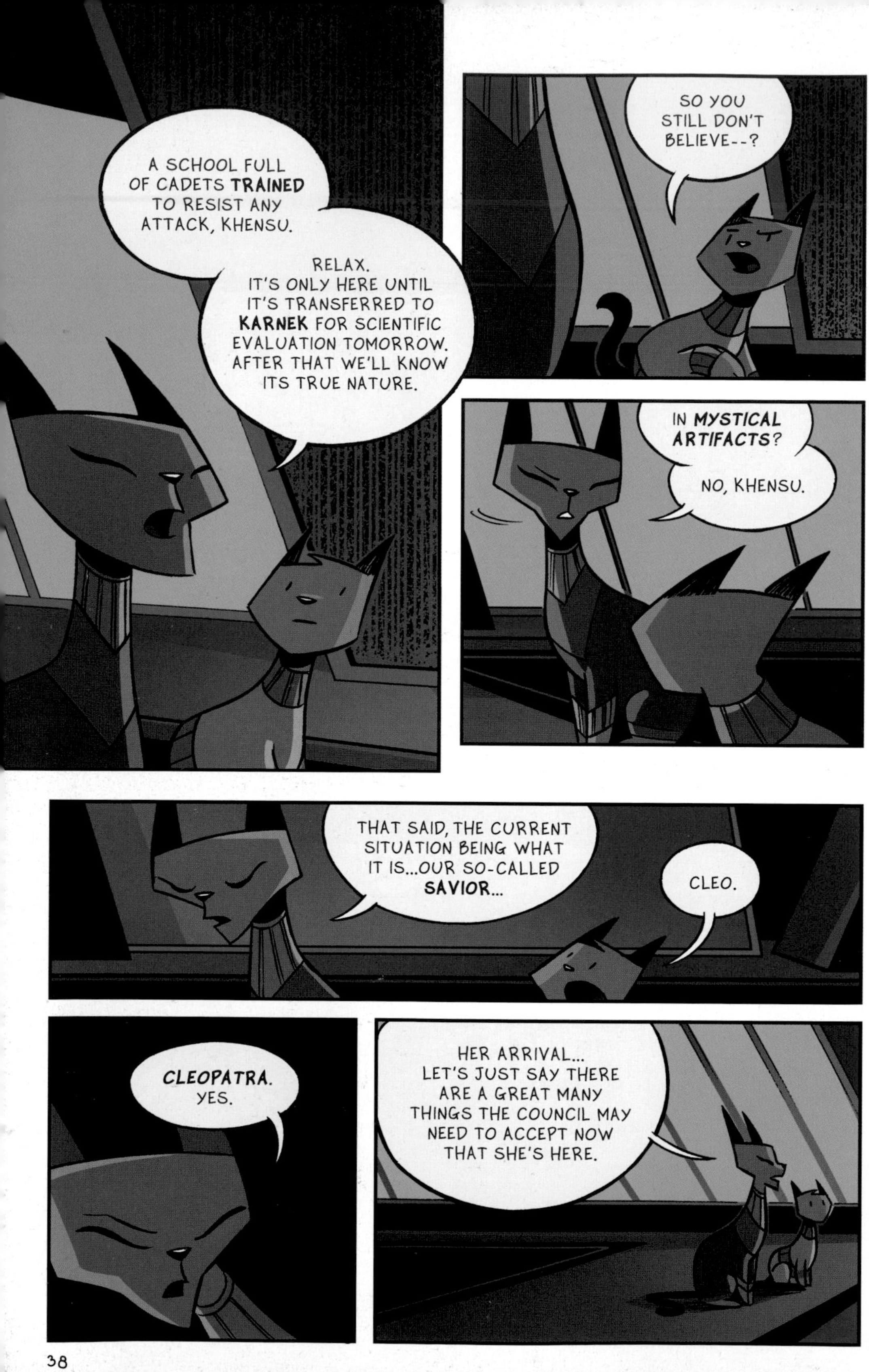
A SCHOOL FULL OF CADETS **TRAINED** TO RESIST ANY ATTACK, KHENSU.
RELAX. IT'S ONLY HERE UNTIL IT'S TRANSFERRED TO **KARNEK** FOR SCIENTIFIC EVALUATION TOMORROW. AFTER THAT WE'LL KNOW ITS TRUE NATURE.
SO YOU STILL DON'T BELIEVE--?
IN **MYSTICAL ARTIFACTS**?
NO, KHENSU.
THAT SAID, THE CURRENT SITUATION BEING WHAT IT IS...OUR SO-CALLED **SAVIOR**...
CLEO.
CLEOPATRA. YES.
HER ARRIVAL... LET'S JUST SAY THERE ARE A GREAT MANY THINGS THE COUNCIL MAY NEED TO ACCEPT NOW THAT SHE'S HERE.

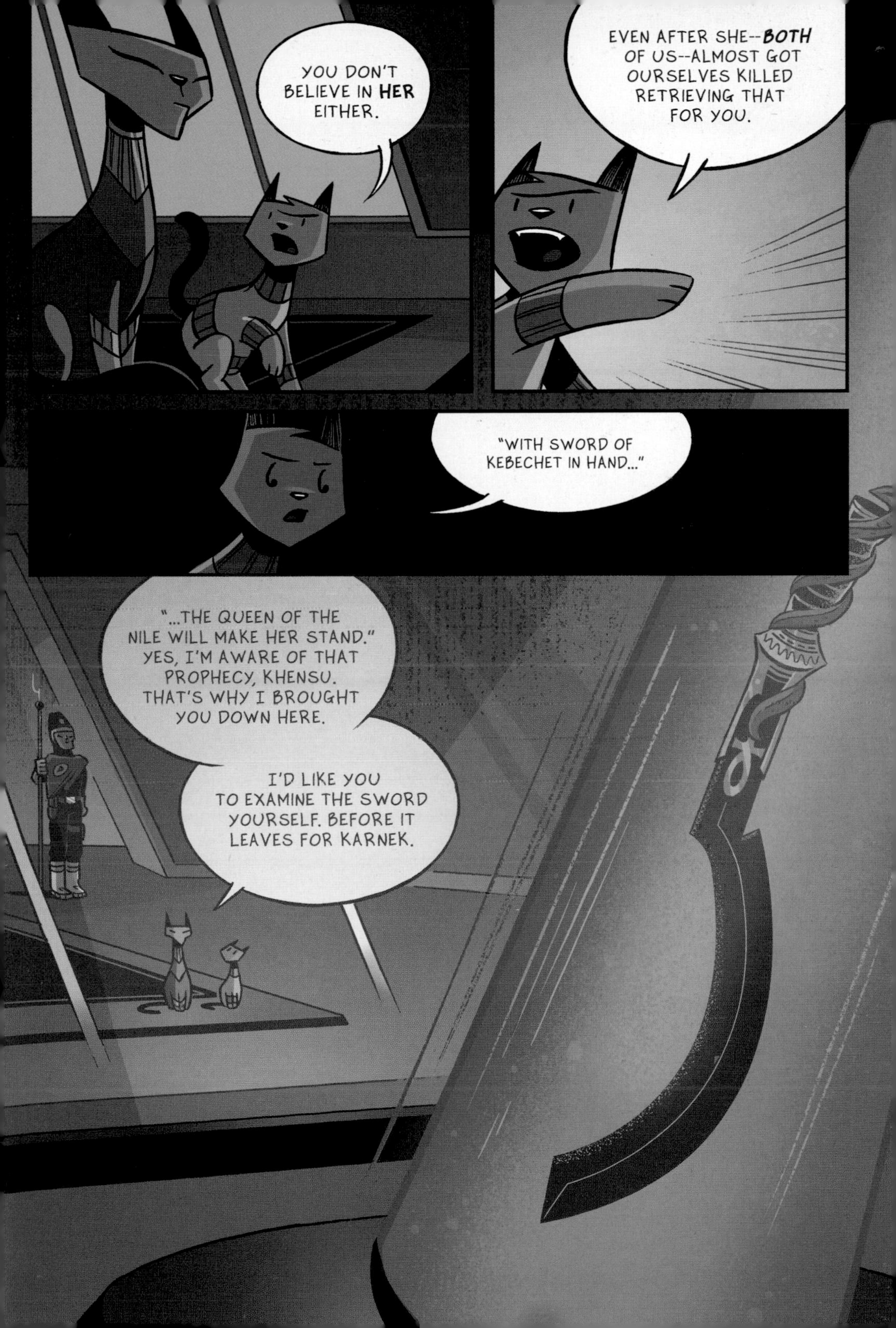
YOU DON'T BELIEVE IN **HER** EITHER.
EVEN AFTER SHE--**BOTH** OF US--ALMOST GOT OURSELVES KILLED RETRIEVING THAT FOR YOU.
"WITH SWORD OF KEBECHET IN HAND..."
"...THE QUEEN OF THE NILE WILL MAKE HER STAND." YES, I'M AWARE OF THAT PROPHECY, KHENSU. THAT'S WHY I BROUGHT YOU DOWN HERE.
I'D LIKE YOU TO EXAMINE THE SWORD YOURSELF. BEFORE IT LEAVES FOR KARNEK.

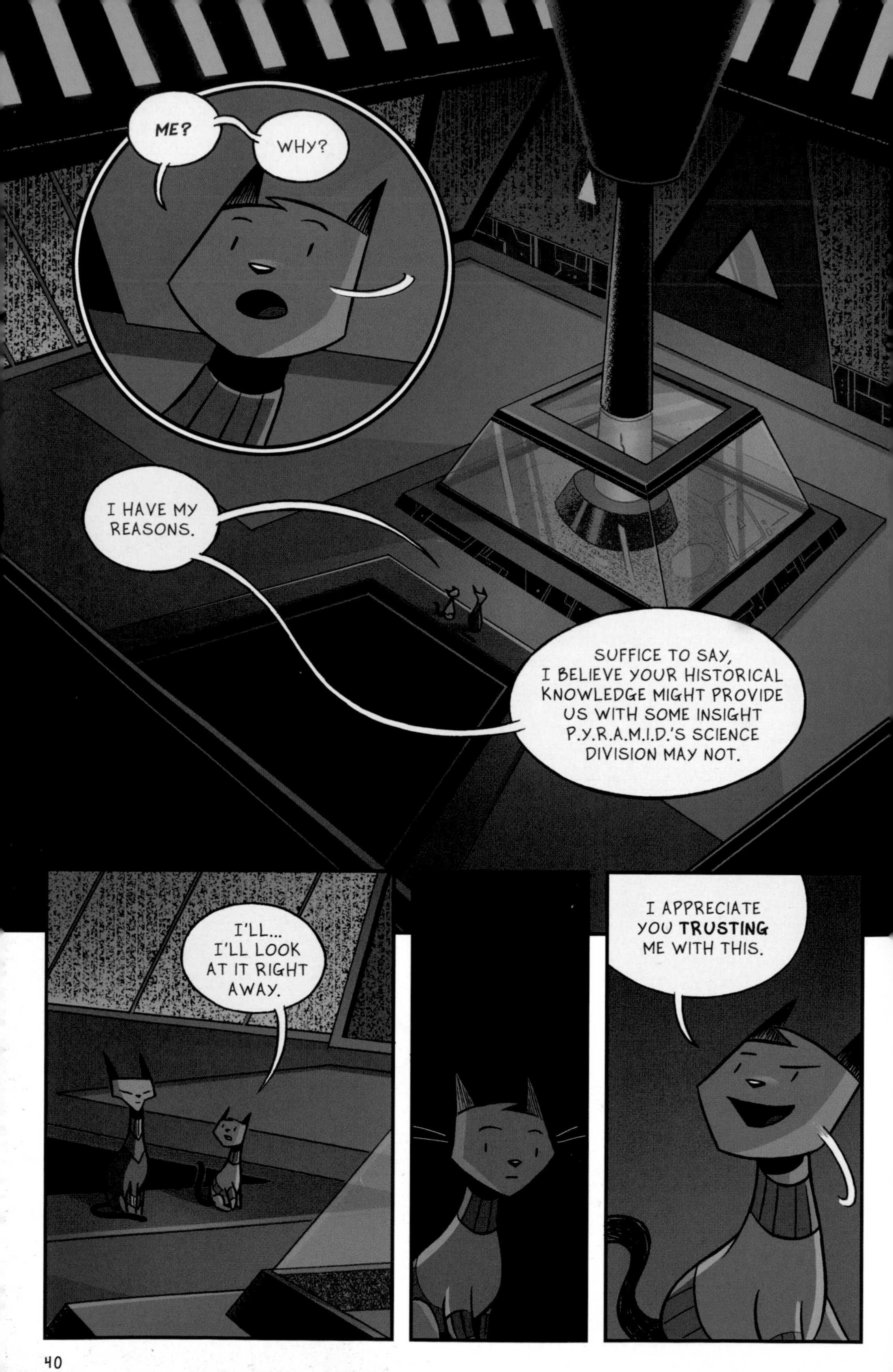
ME?
WHY?
I HAVE MY REASONS.
SUFFICE TO SAY, I BELIEVE YOUR HISTORICAL KNOWLEDGE MIGHT PROVIDE US WITH SOME INSIGHT P.Y.R.A.M.I.D.'S SCIENCE DIVISION MAY NOT.
I'LL... I'LL LOOK AT IT RIGHT AWAY.
I APPRECIATE YOU **TRUSTING** ME WITH THIS.

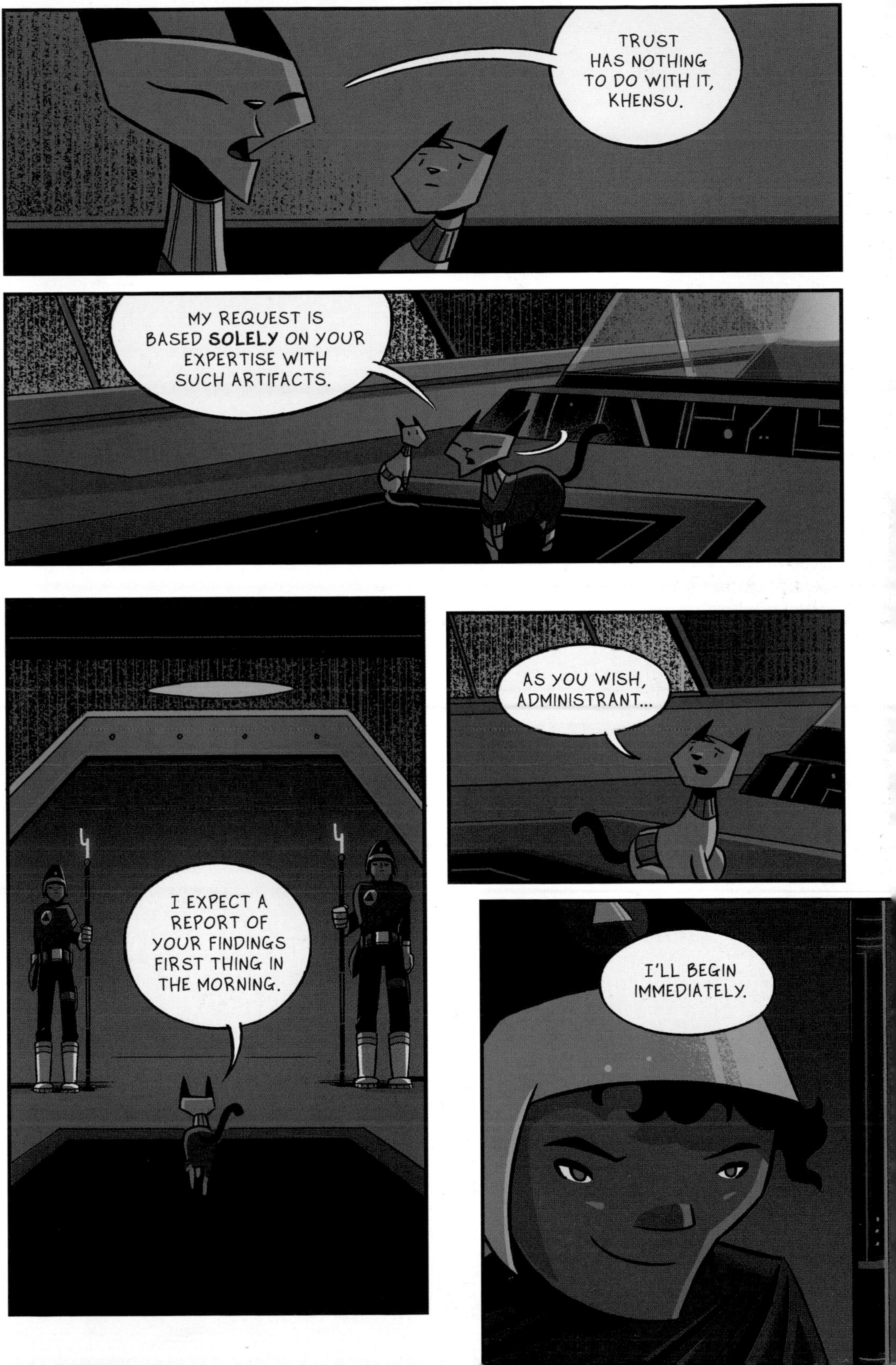
TRUST HAS NOTHING TO DO WITH IT, KHENSU.
MY REQUEST IS BASED **SOLELY** ON YOUR EXPERTISE WITH SUCH ARTIFACTS.
AS YOU WISH, ADMINISTRANT...
I EXPECT A REPORT OF YOUR FINDINGS FIRST THING IN THE MORNING.
I'LL BEGIN IMMEDIATELY.

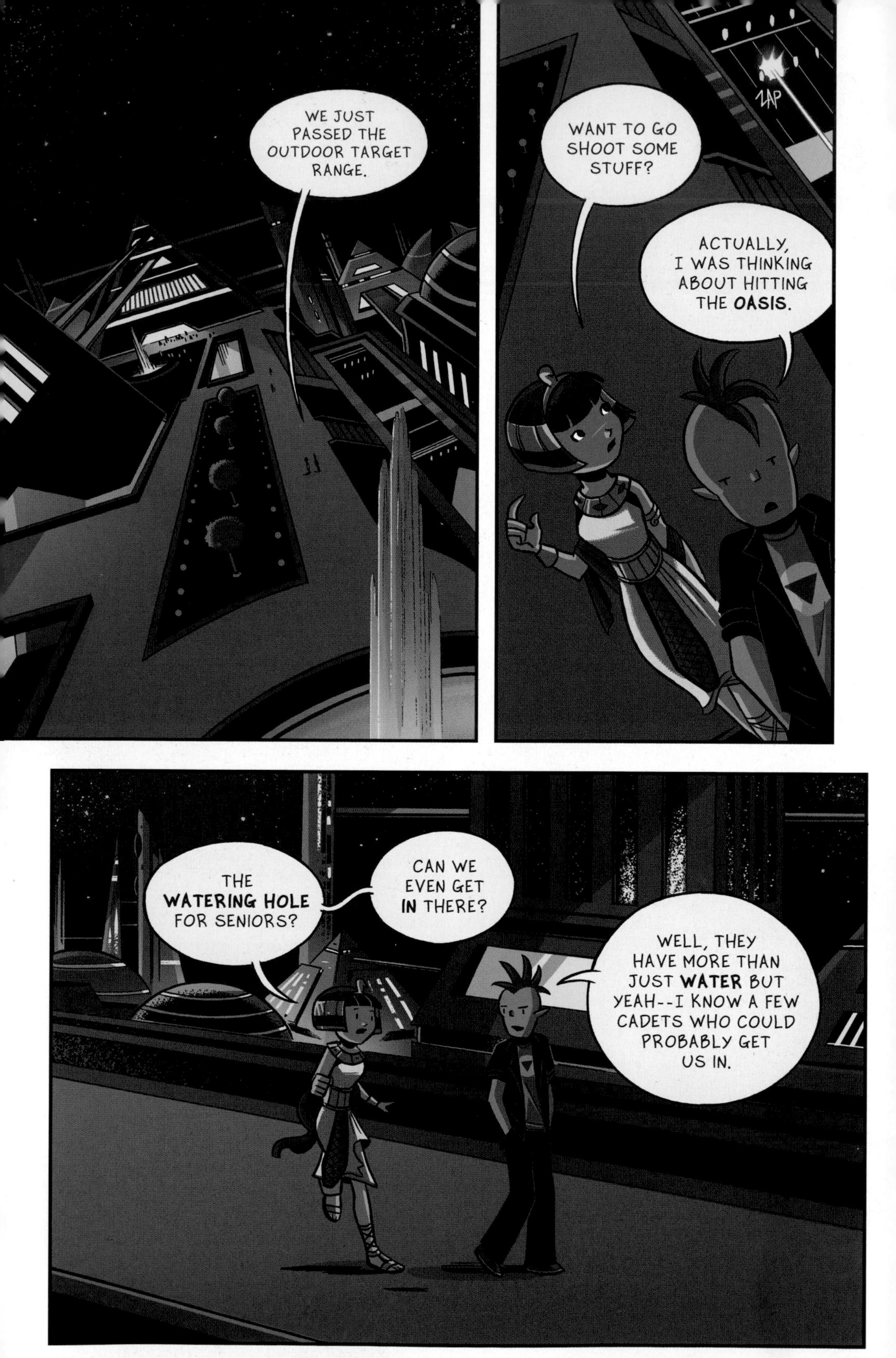
WE JUST PASSED THE OUTDOOR TARGET RANGE.
ZAP
WANT TO GO SHOOT SOME STUFF?
ACTUALLY, I WAS THINKING ABOUT HITTING THE **OASIS.**
THE **WATERING HOLE** FOR SENIORS?
CAN WE EVEN GET **IN** THERE?
WELL, THEY HAVE MORE THAN JUST **WATER** BUT YEAH--I KNOW A FEW CADETS WHO COULD PROBABLY GET US IN.

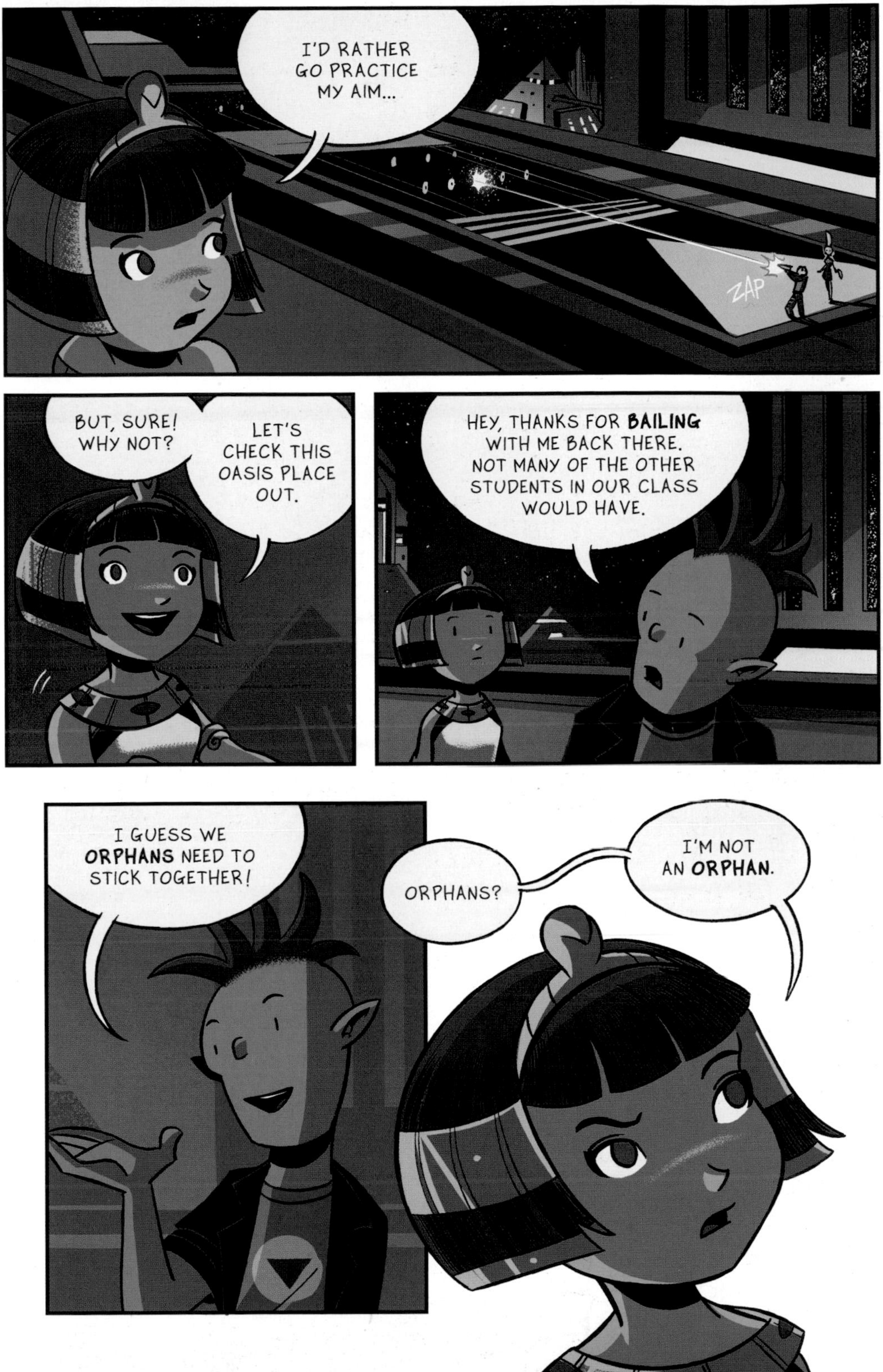

I'D RATHER GO PRACTICE MY AIM...
ZAP
BUT, SURE! WHY NOT?
LET'S CHECK THIS OASIS PLACE OUT.
HEY, THANKS FOR **BAILING** WITH ME BACK THERE. NOT MANY OF THE OTHER STUDENTS IN OUR CLASS WOULD HAVE.
I GUESS WE **ORPHANS** NEED TO STICK TOGETHER!
ORPHANS?
I'M NOT AN **ORPHAN**.

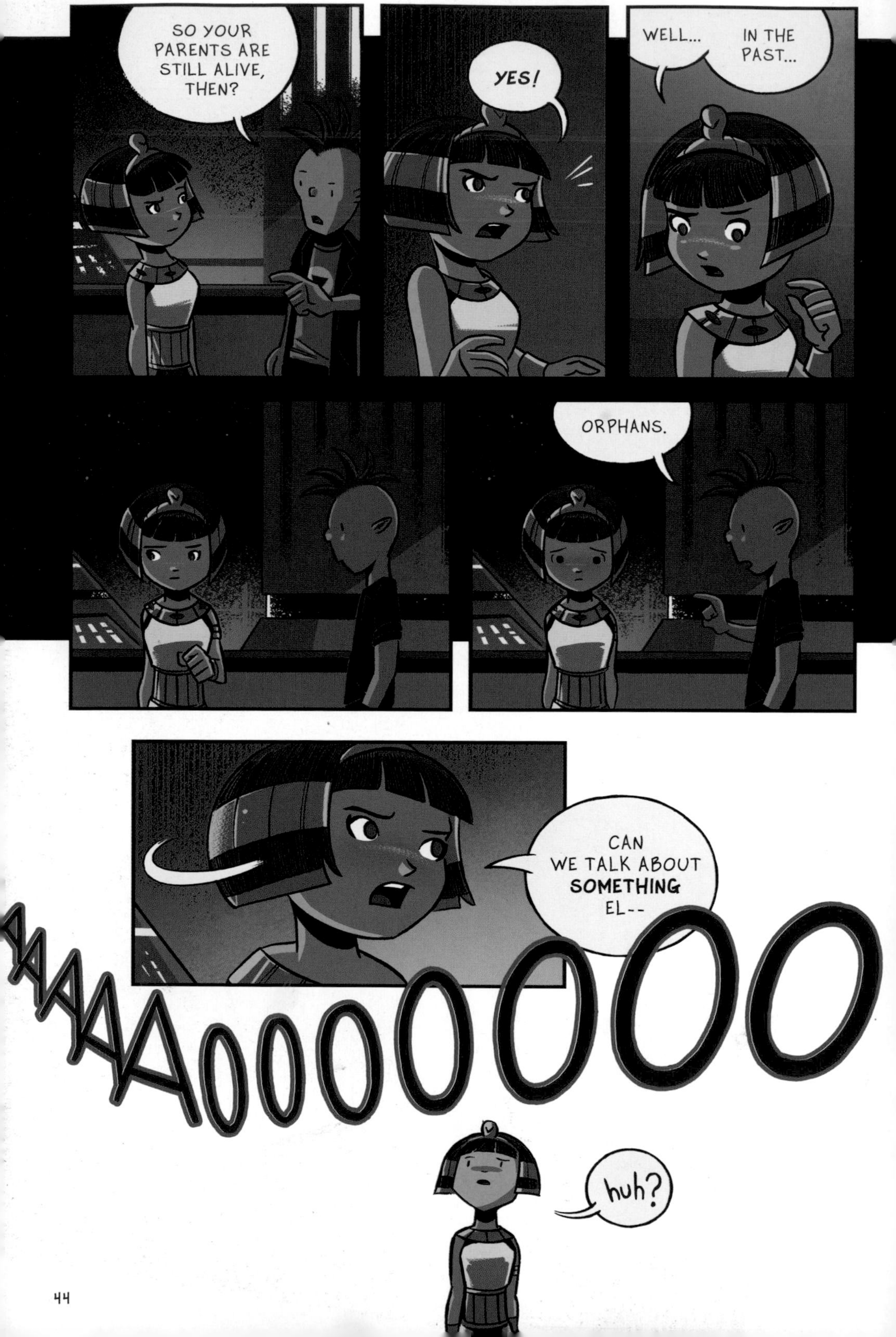

SO YOUR PARENTS ARE STILL ALIVE, THEN?
YES!
WELL...
IN THE PAST...
ORPHANS.
CAN WE TALK ABOUT SOMETHING EL--
AAAAAOOOOOOOOOO
huh?

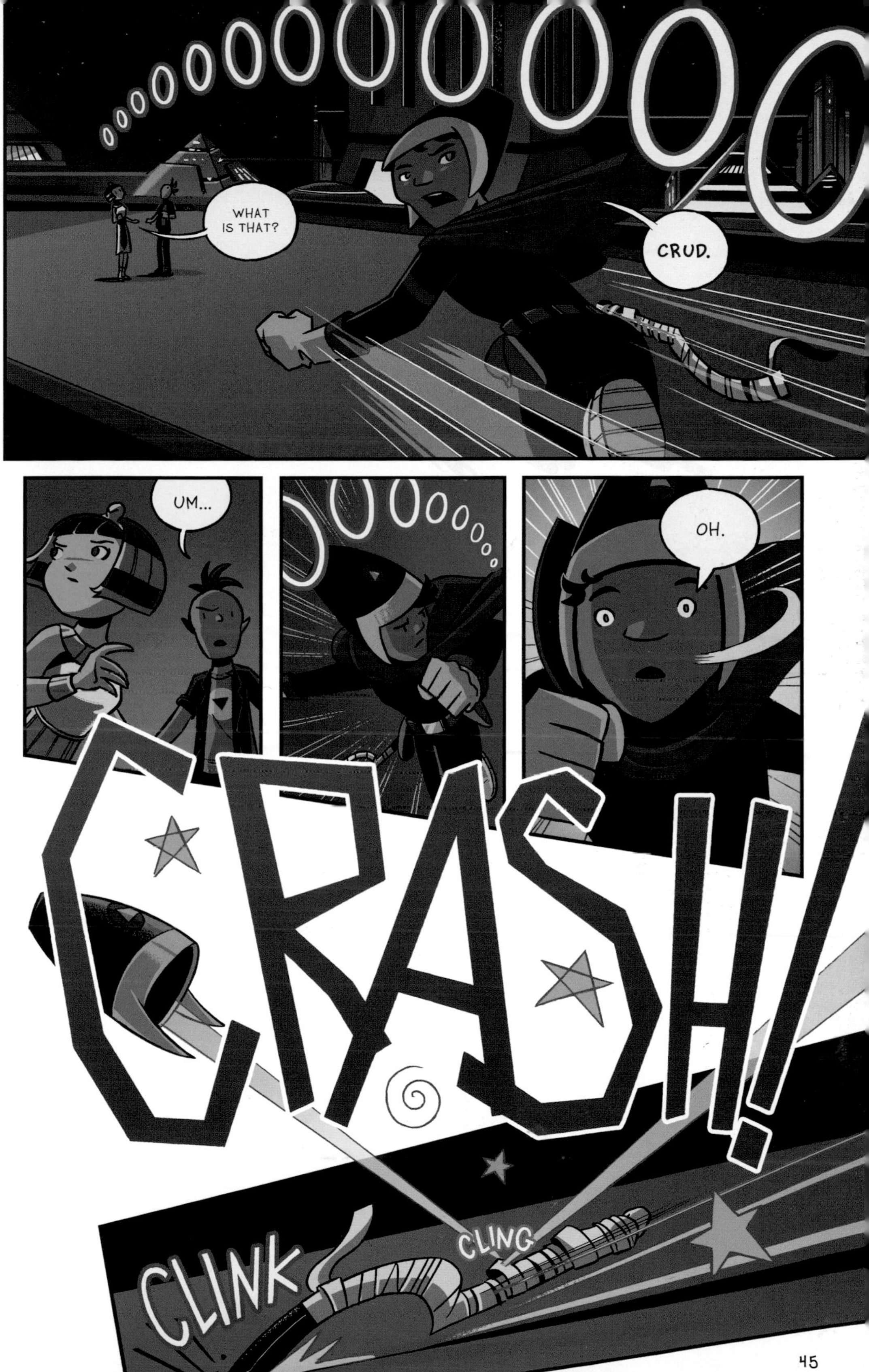
OOOOOOOOOOOO
WHAT IS THAT?
CRUD.
UM...
OOOOOOOO
OH.
CRASH!!
CLINK
CLING

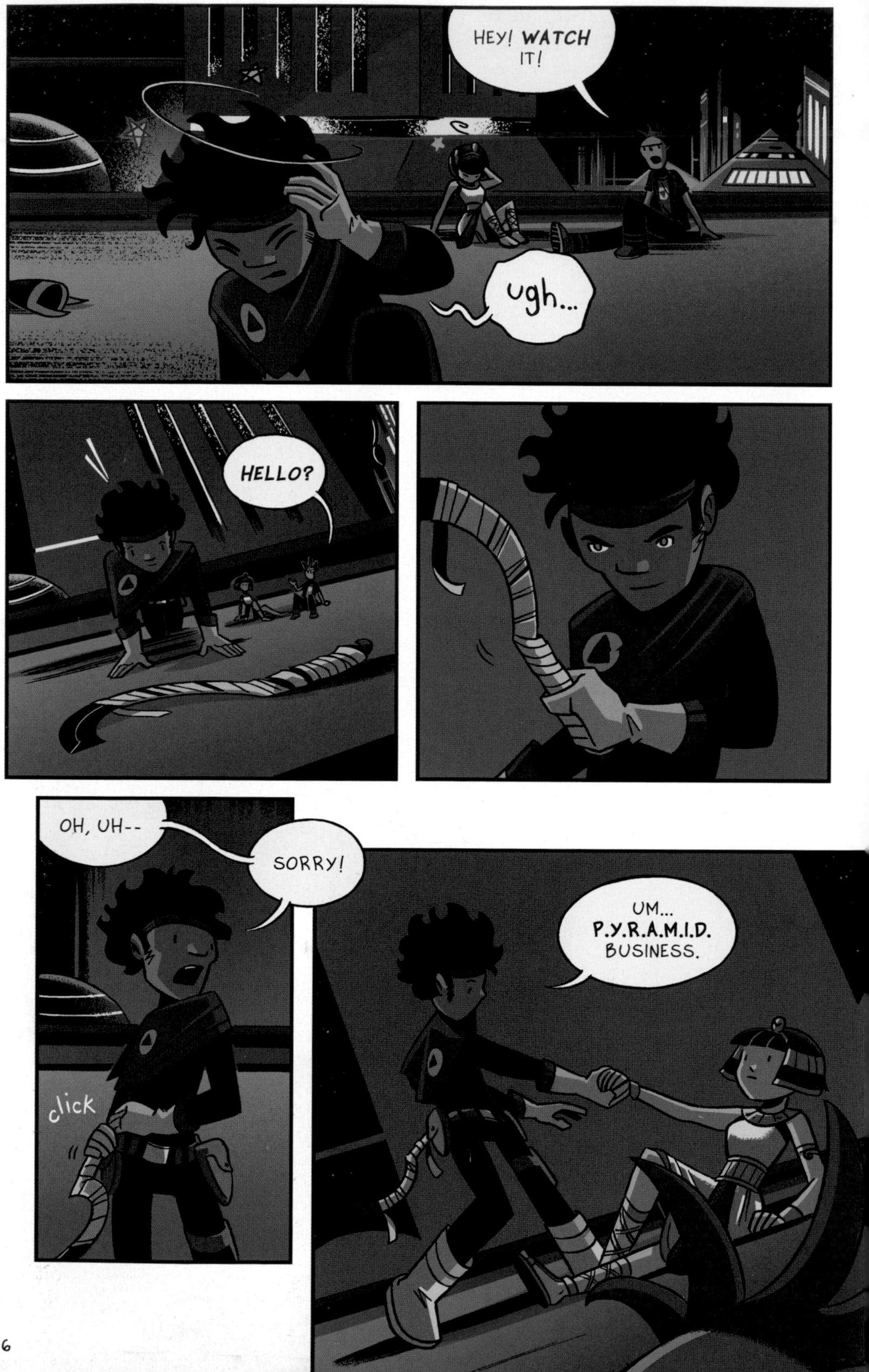
HEY! WATCH IT!
ugh...
HELLO?
OH, UH--
SORRY!
click
UM... P.Y.R.A.M.I.D. BUSINESS.

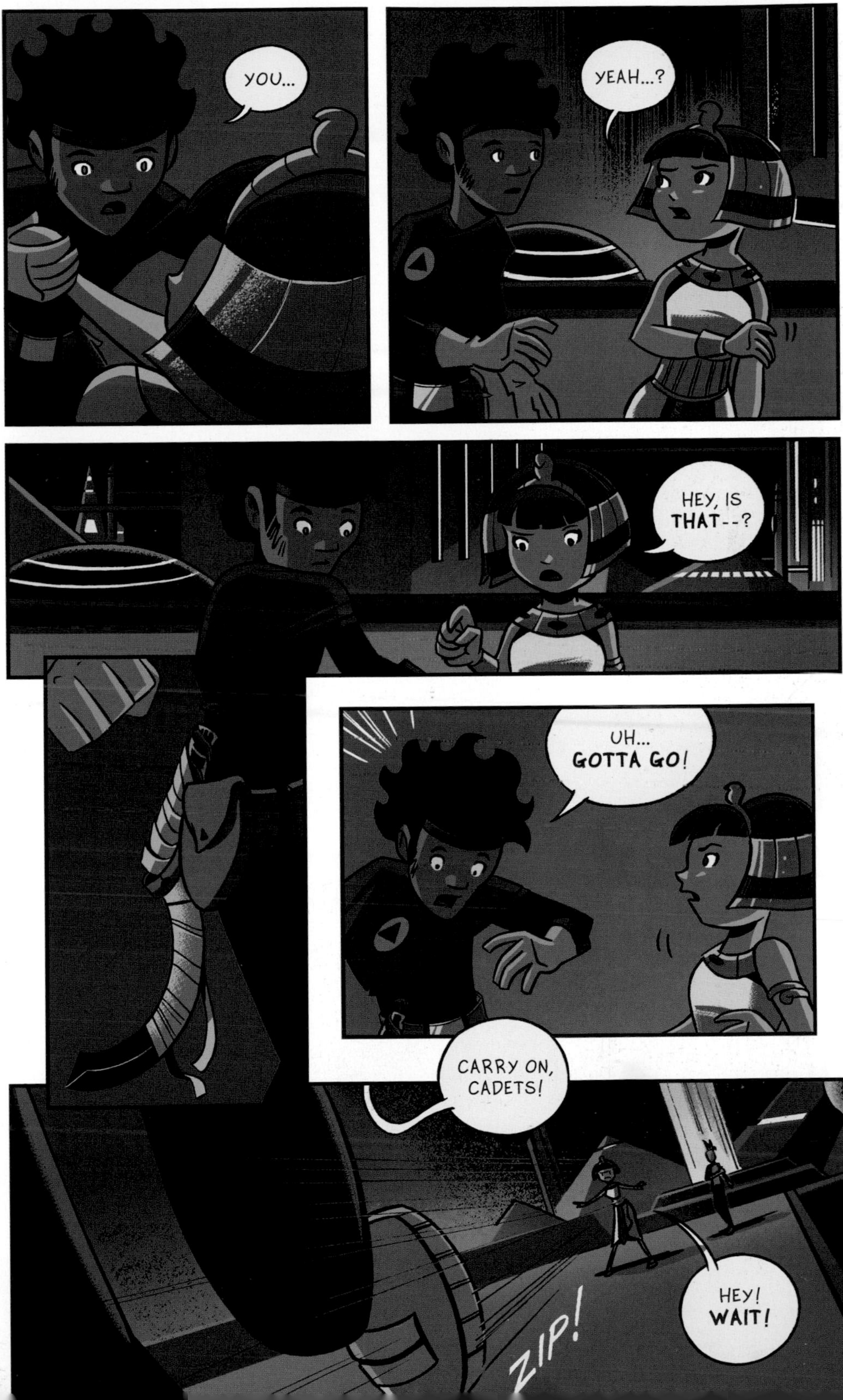
YOU...
YEAH...?
HEY, IS THAT--?
UH... GOTTA GO!
CARRY ON, CADETS!
HEY! WAIT!
ZIP!

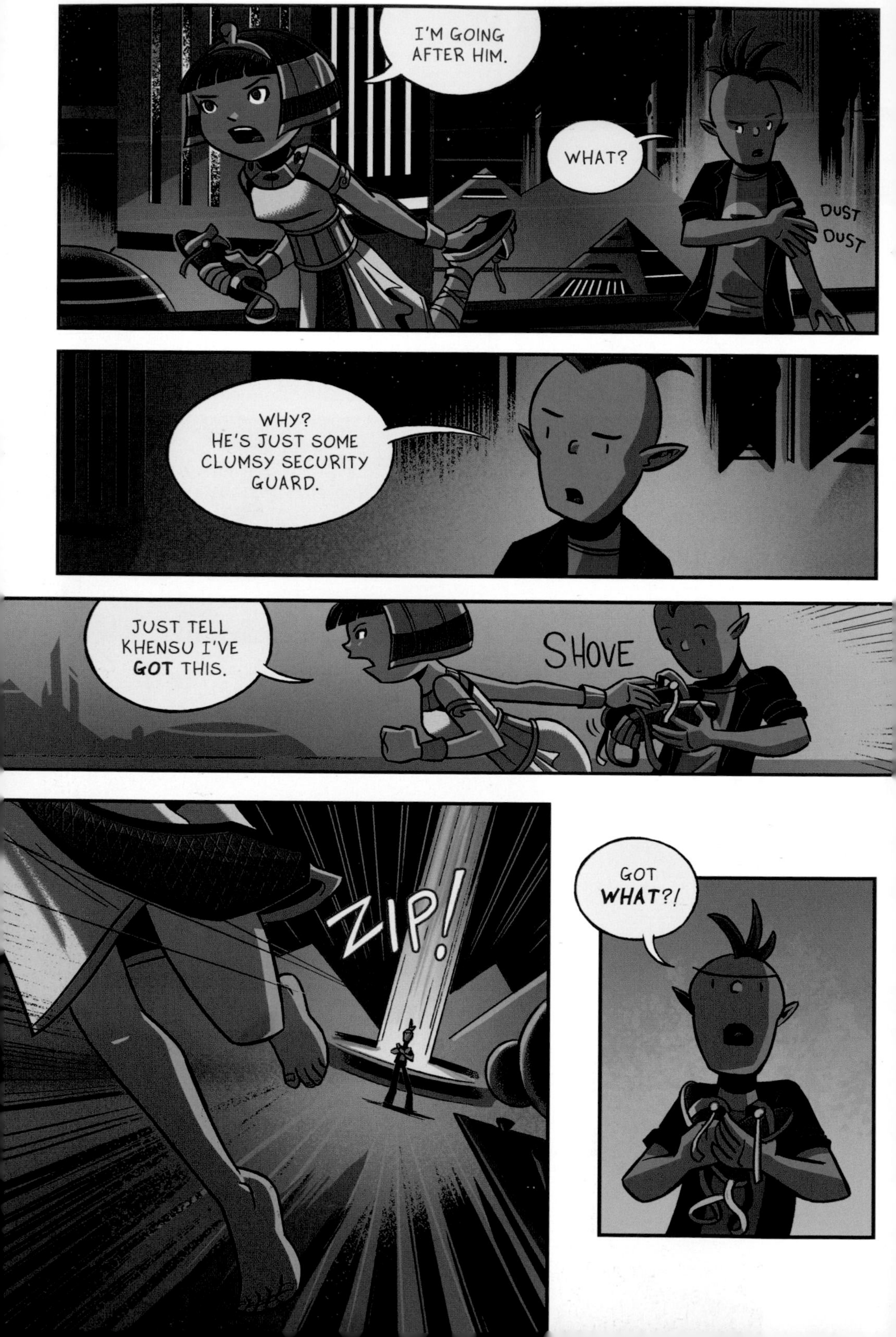
I'M GOING AFTER HIM.
WHAT?
DUST DUST
WHY? HE'S JUST SOME CLUMSY SECURITY GUARD.
JUST TELL KHENSU I'VE **GOT** THIS.
SHOVE
ZIP!
GOT **WHAT**?!

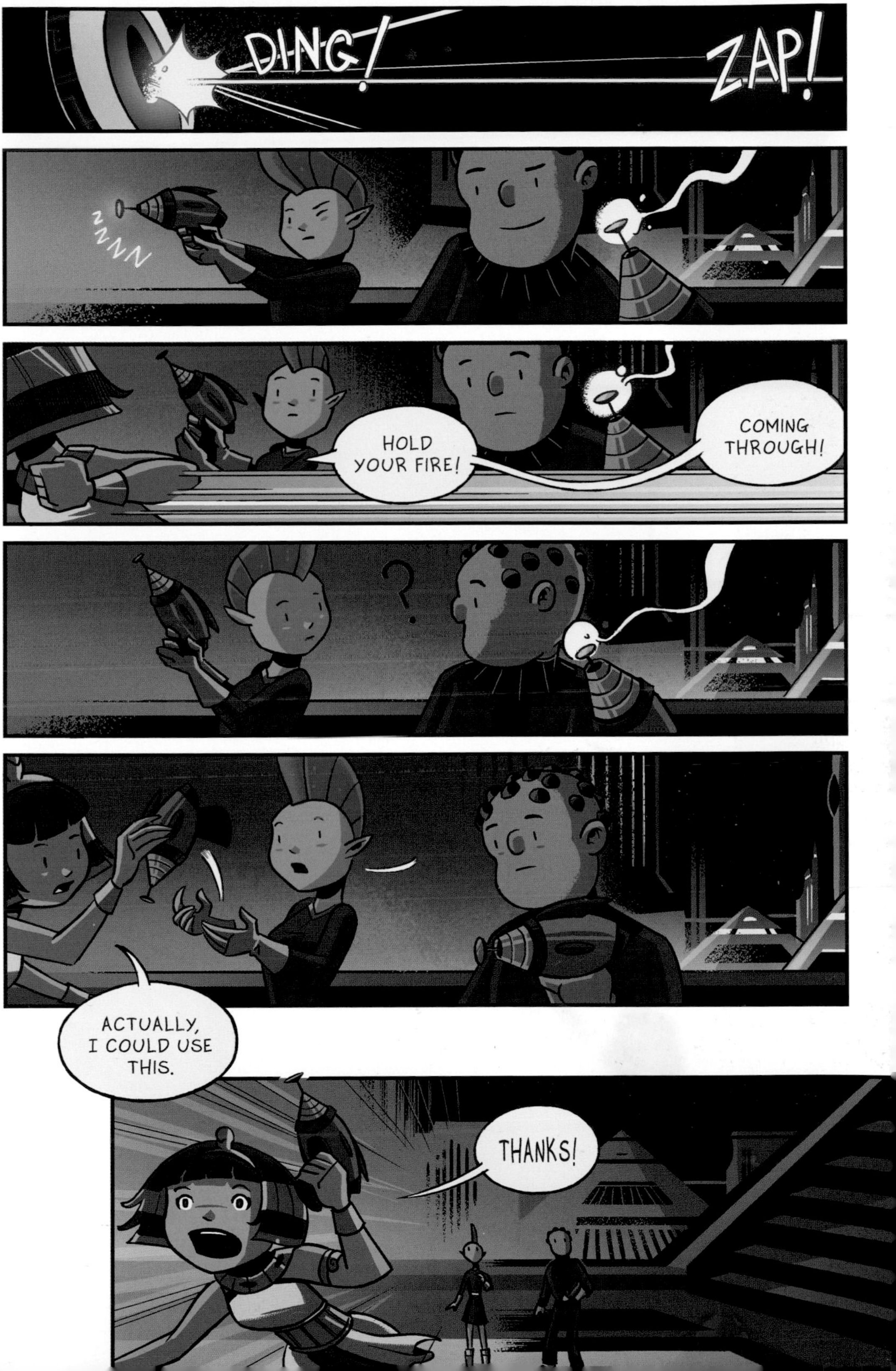
DING!
ZAP!
ZNNN
HOLD YOUR FIRE!
COMING THROUGH!
?
ACTUALLY, I COULD USE THIS.
THANKS!

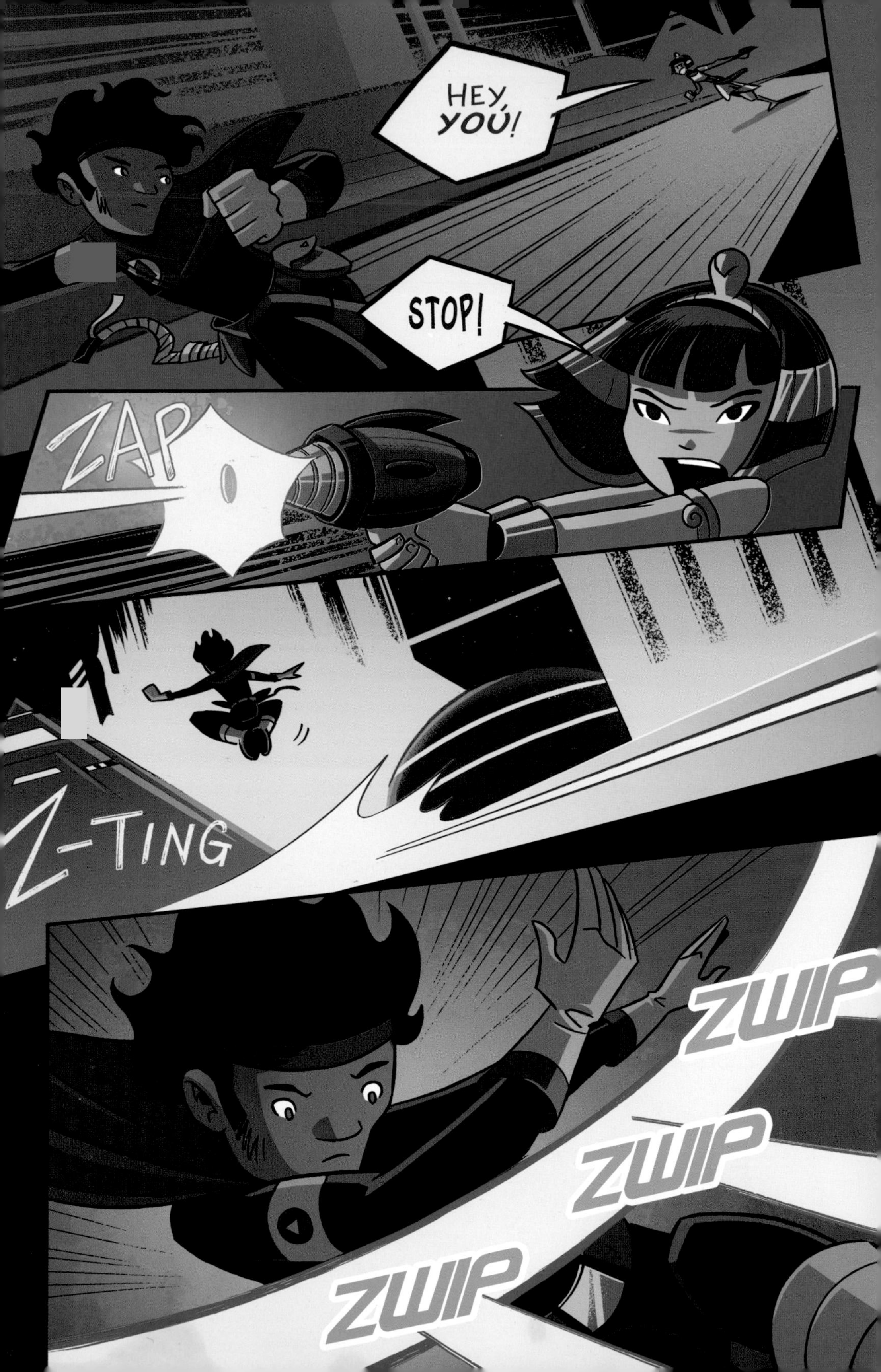
HEY, YOU!
STOP!
ZAP
Z-TING
ZWIP
ZWIP
ZWIP

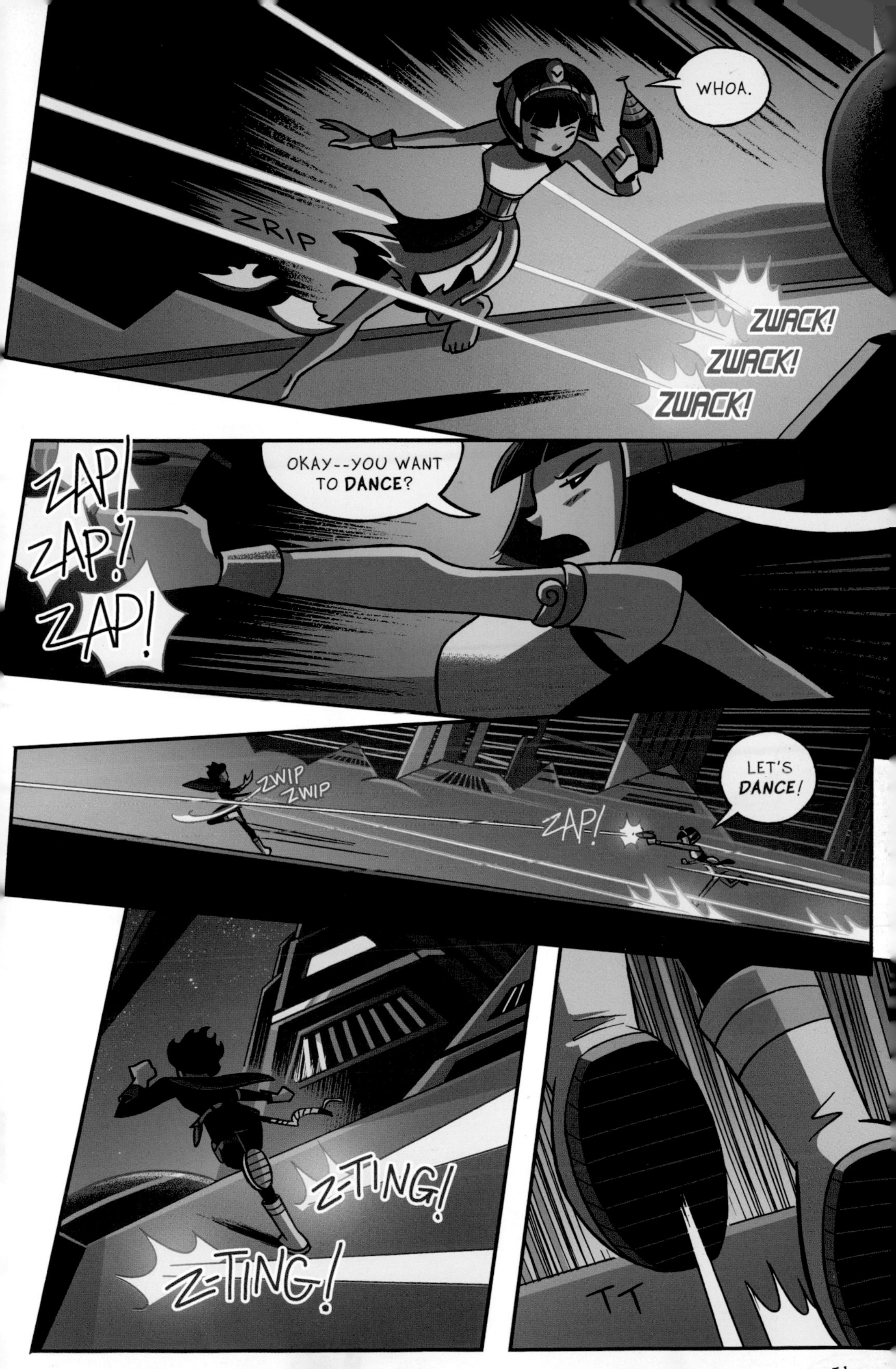
WHOA.
ZRIP
ZWACK!
ZWACK!
ZWACK!
ZAP!
ZAP!
ZAP!
OKAY--YOU WANT TO DANCE?
ZWIP
ZWIP
ZAP!
LET'S DANCE!
Z-TING!
Z-TING!
TT

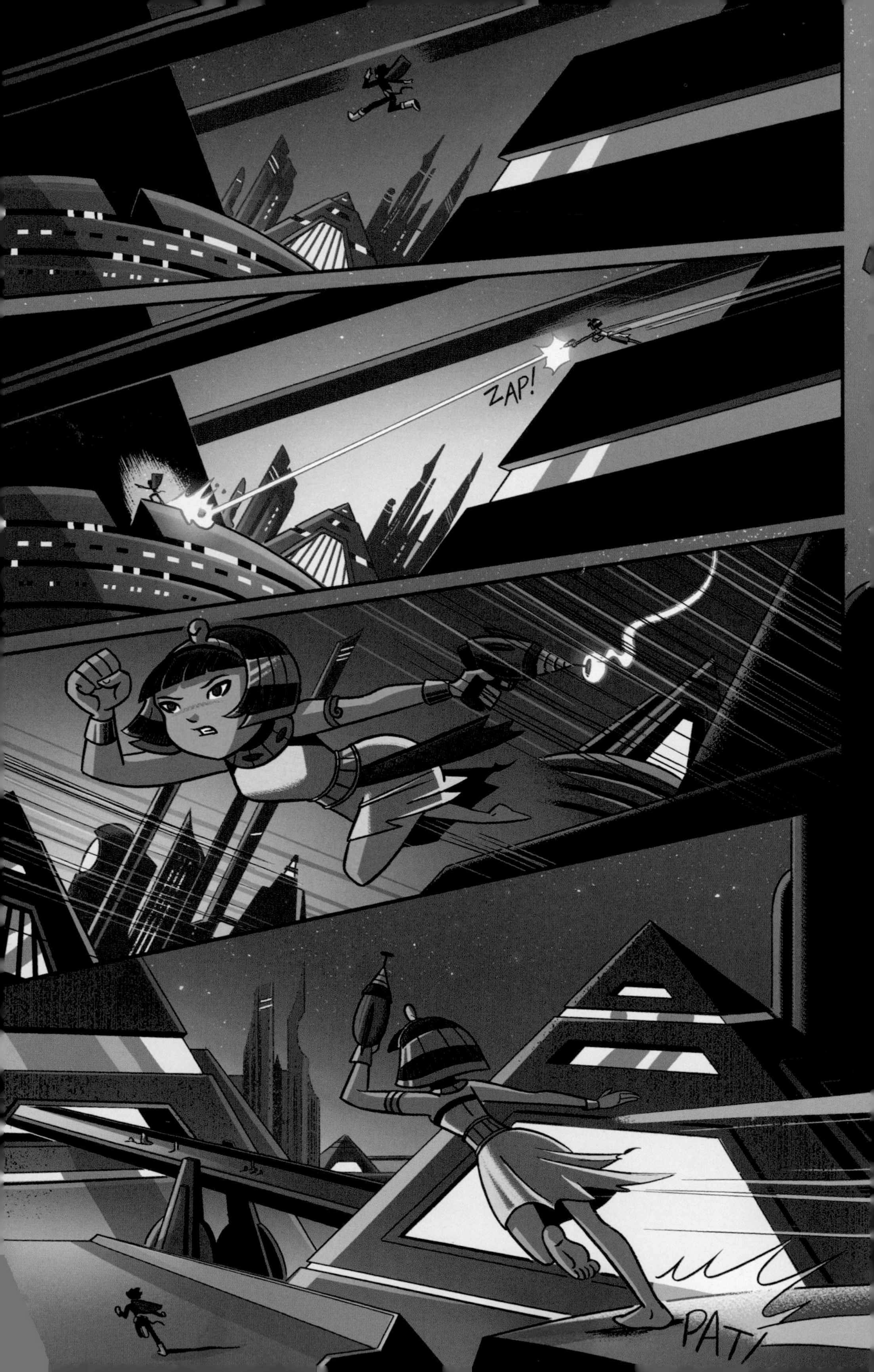
ZAP!
PAT!

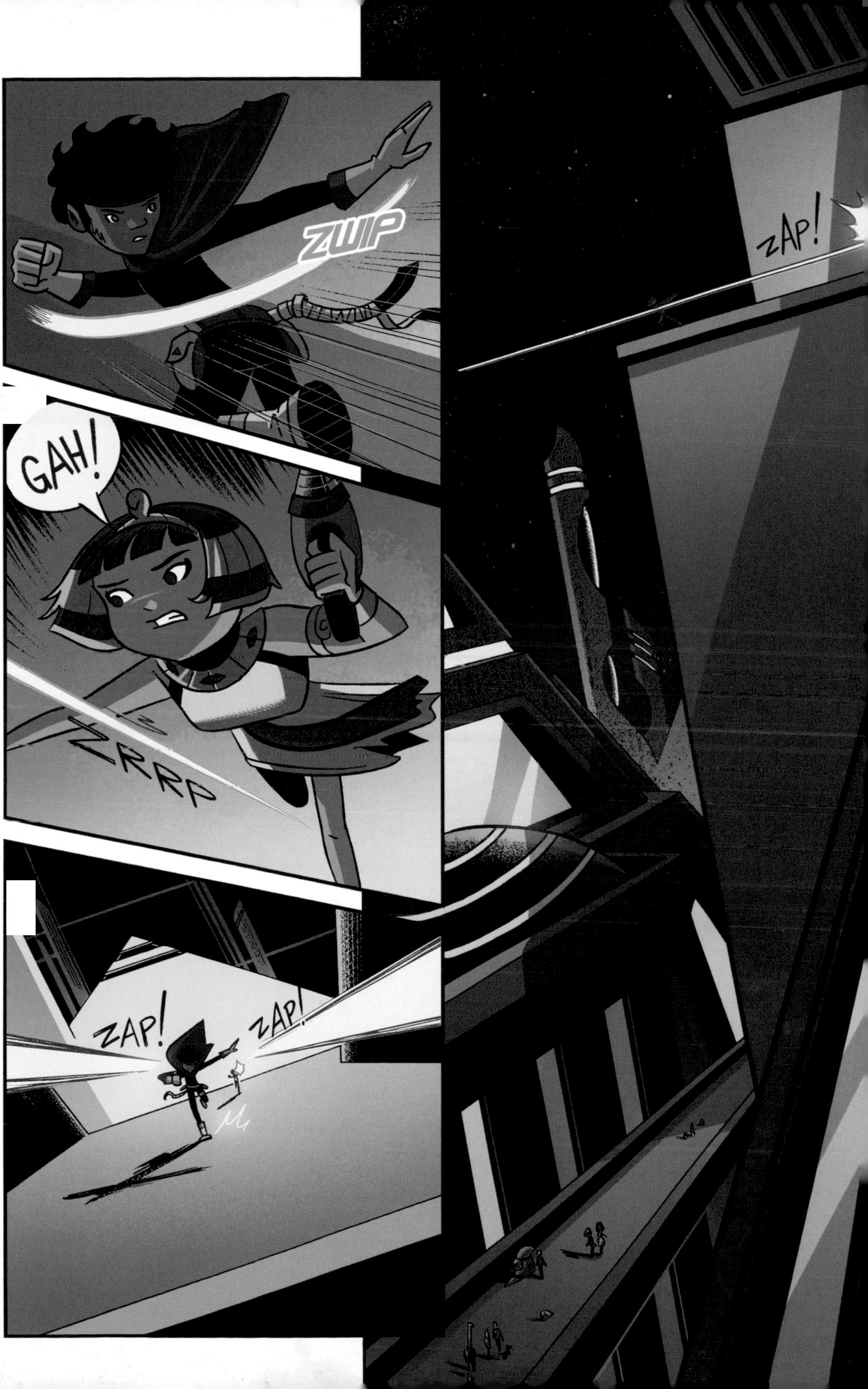
ZWIP
ZAP!
GAH!
ZRRRP
ZAP!
ZAP!

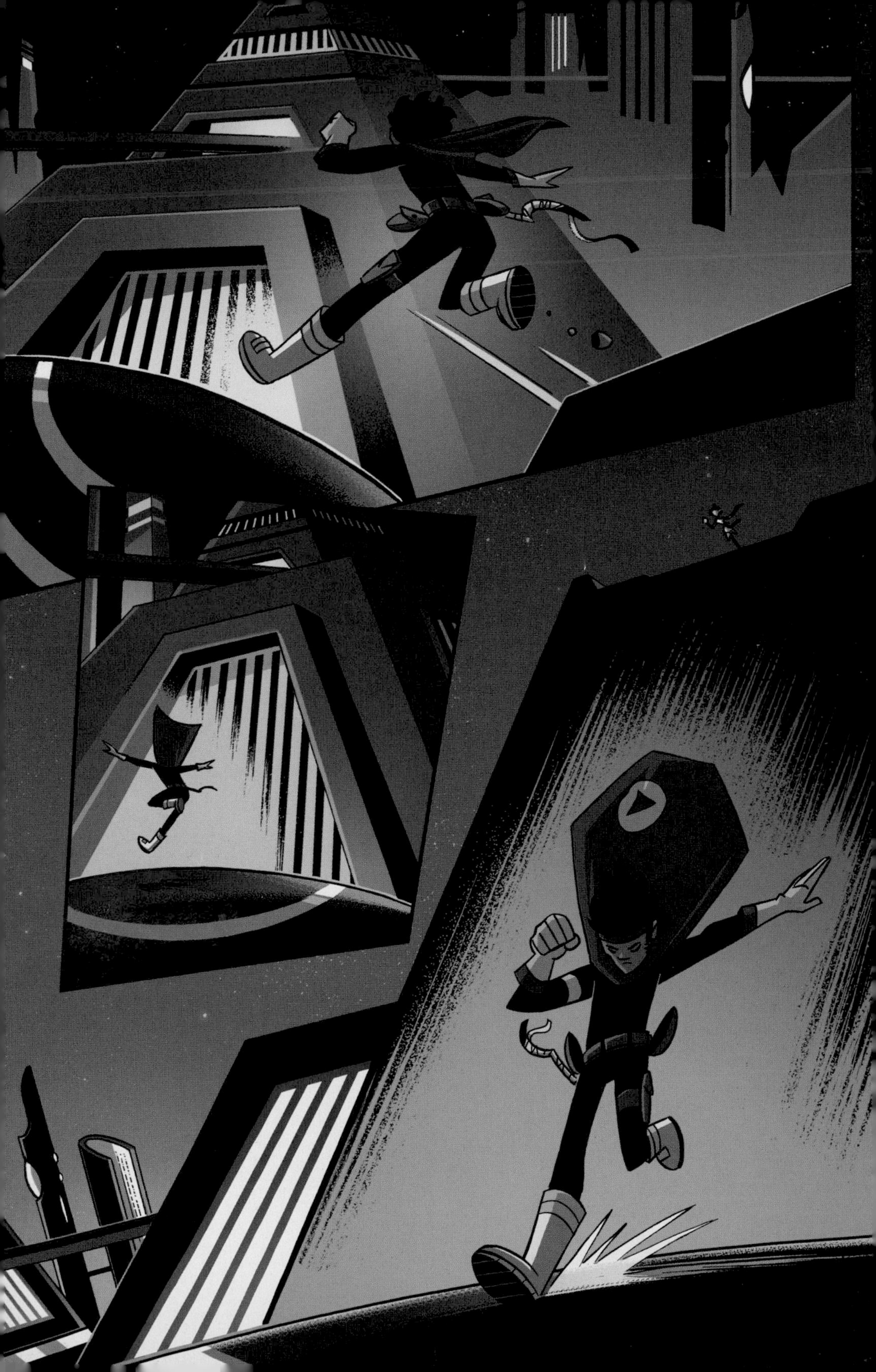

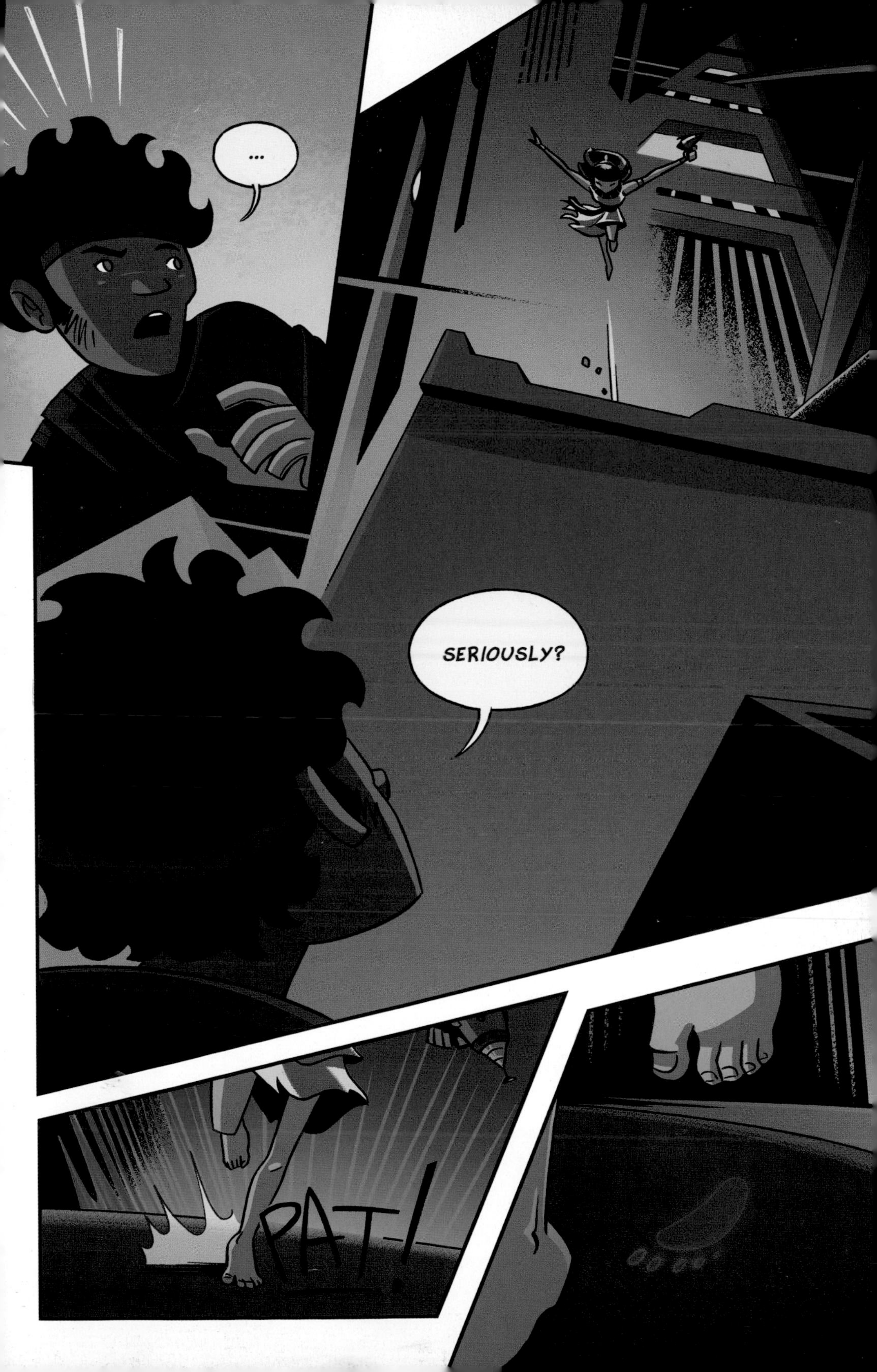
...
SERIOUSLY?
PAT!

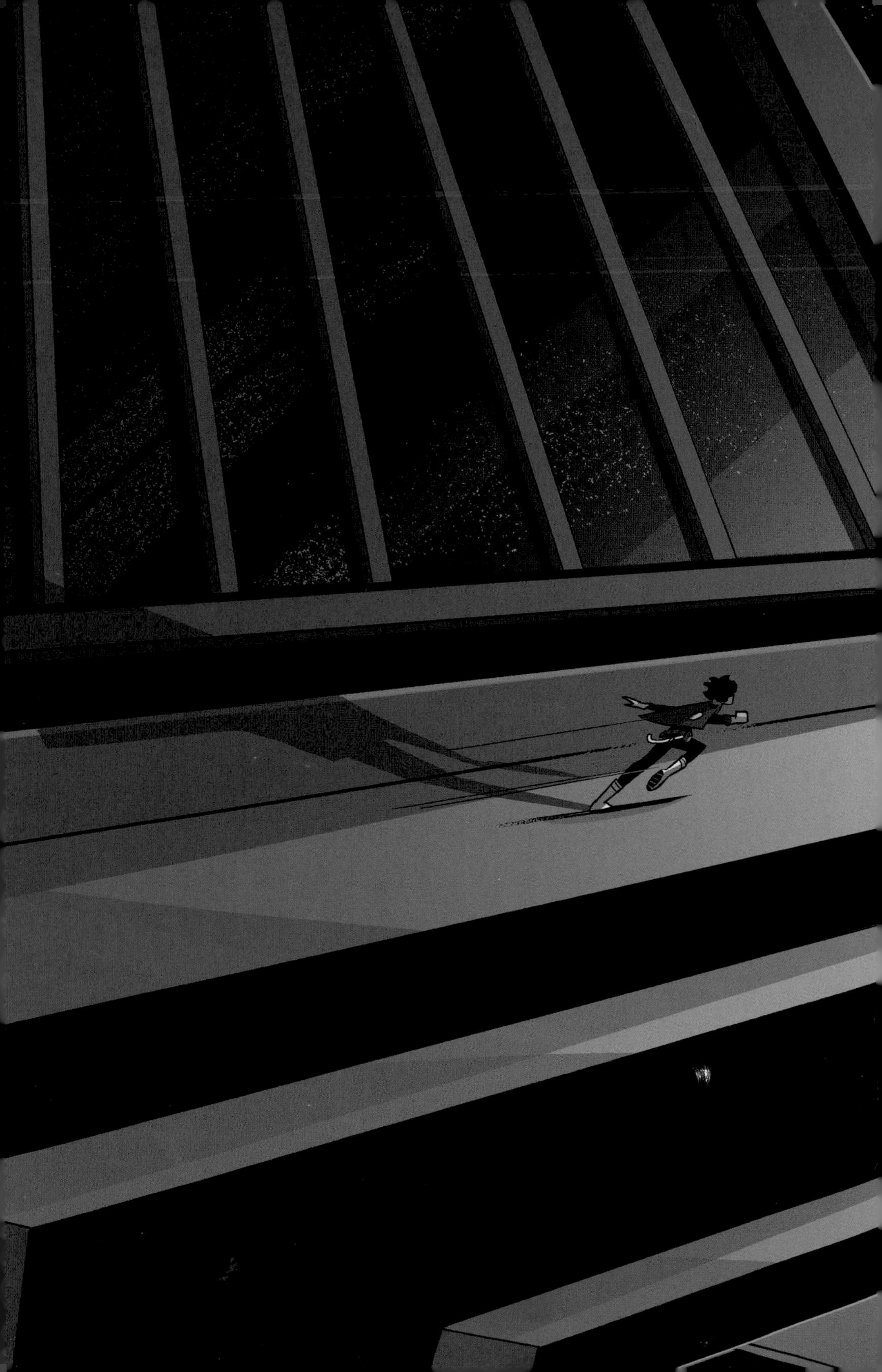

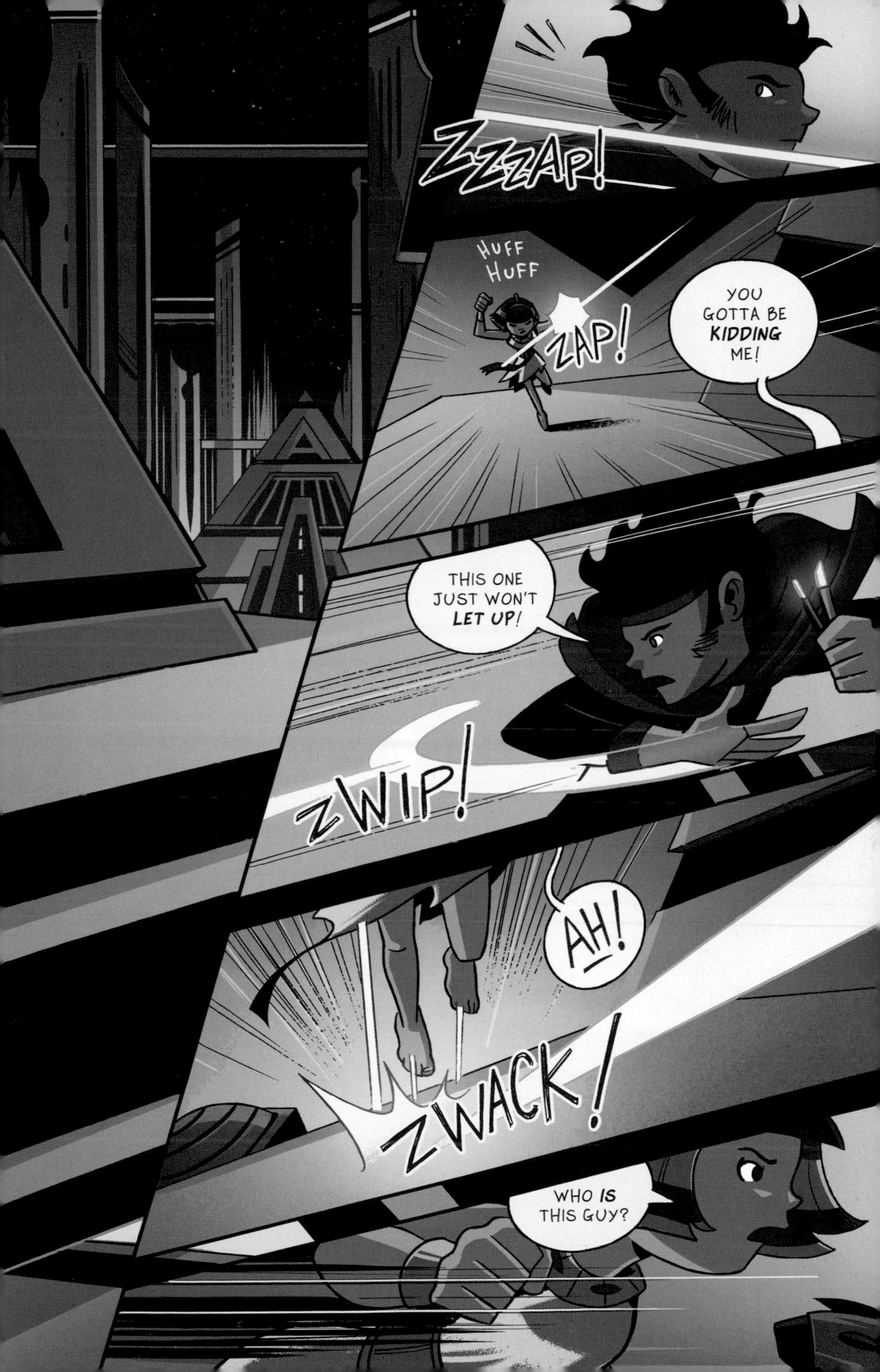
ZZZAP!
HUFF HUFF
ZAP!
YOU GOTTA BE KIDDING ME!
THIS ONE JUST WON'T LET UP!
ZWIP!
AH!
ZWACK!
WHO IS THIS GUY?

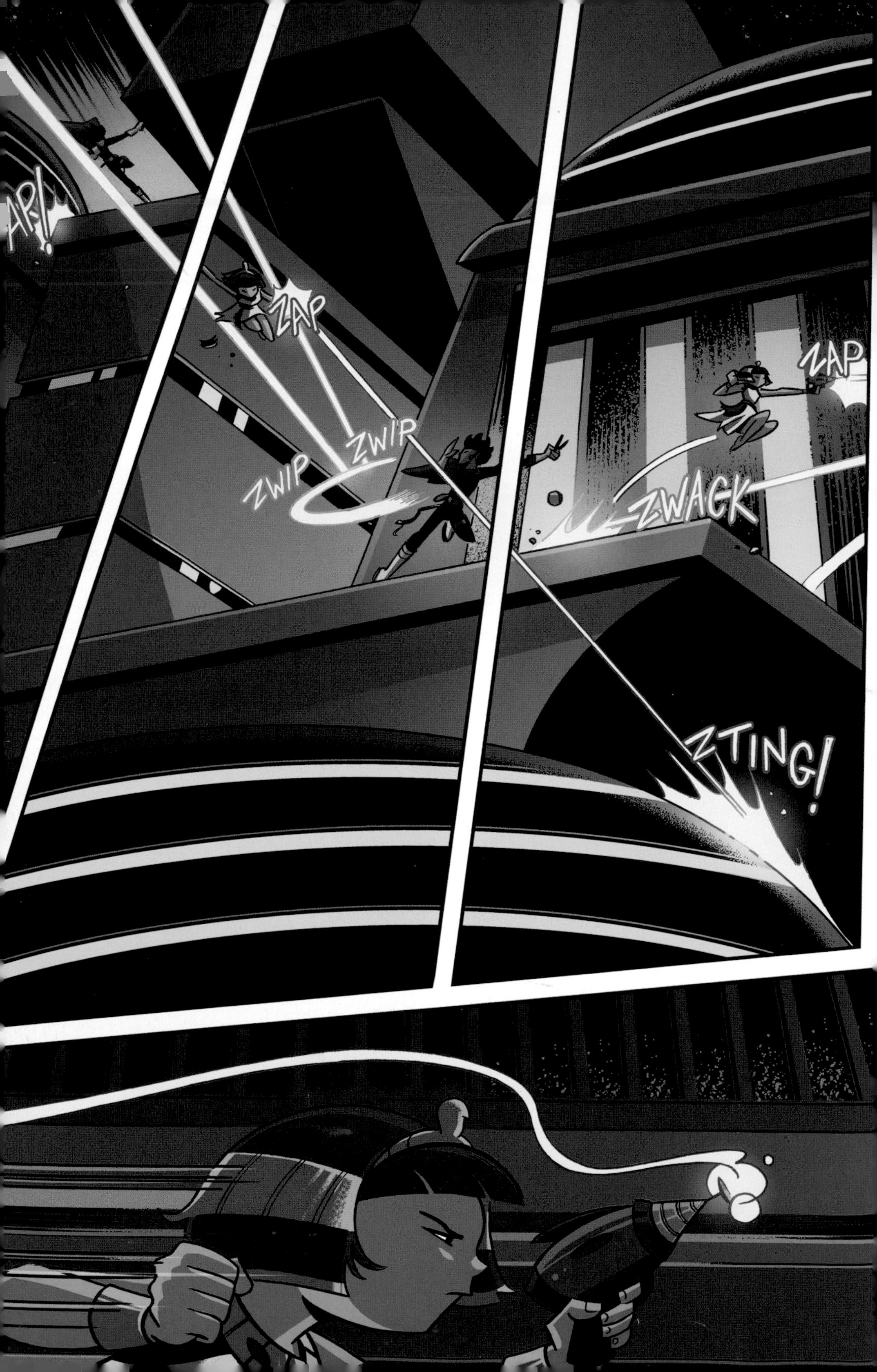
AP!
ZAP
ZWIP
ZWIP
ZAP
ZWACK
ZTING!

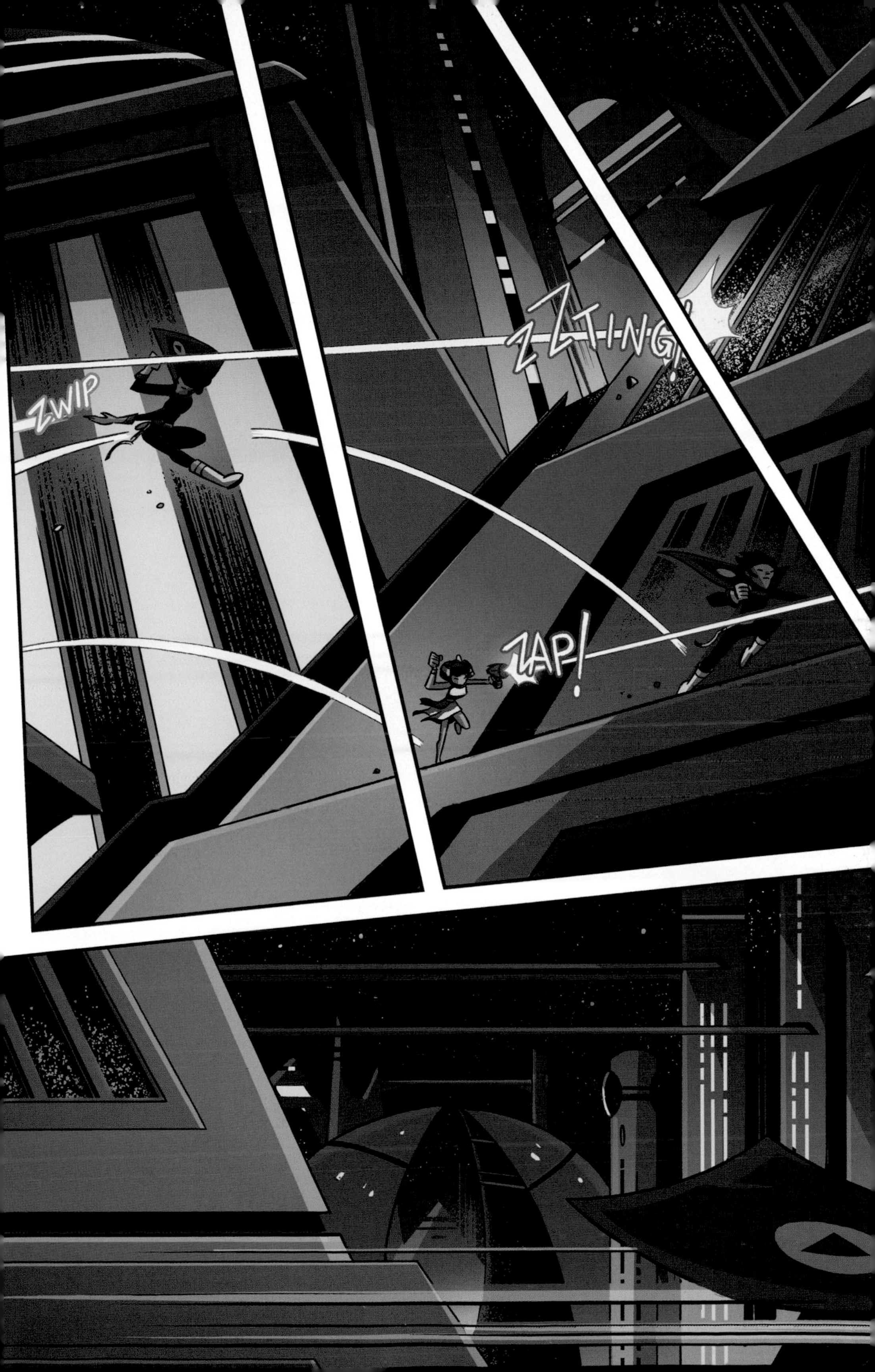
ZWIP
ZZTING!
ZAP!

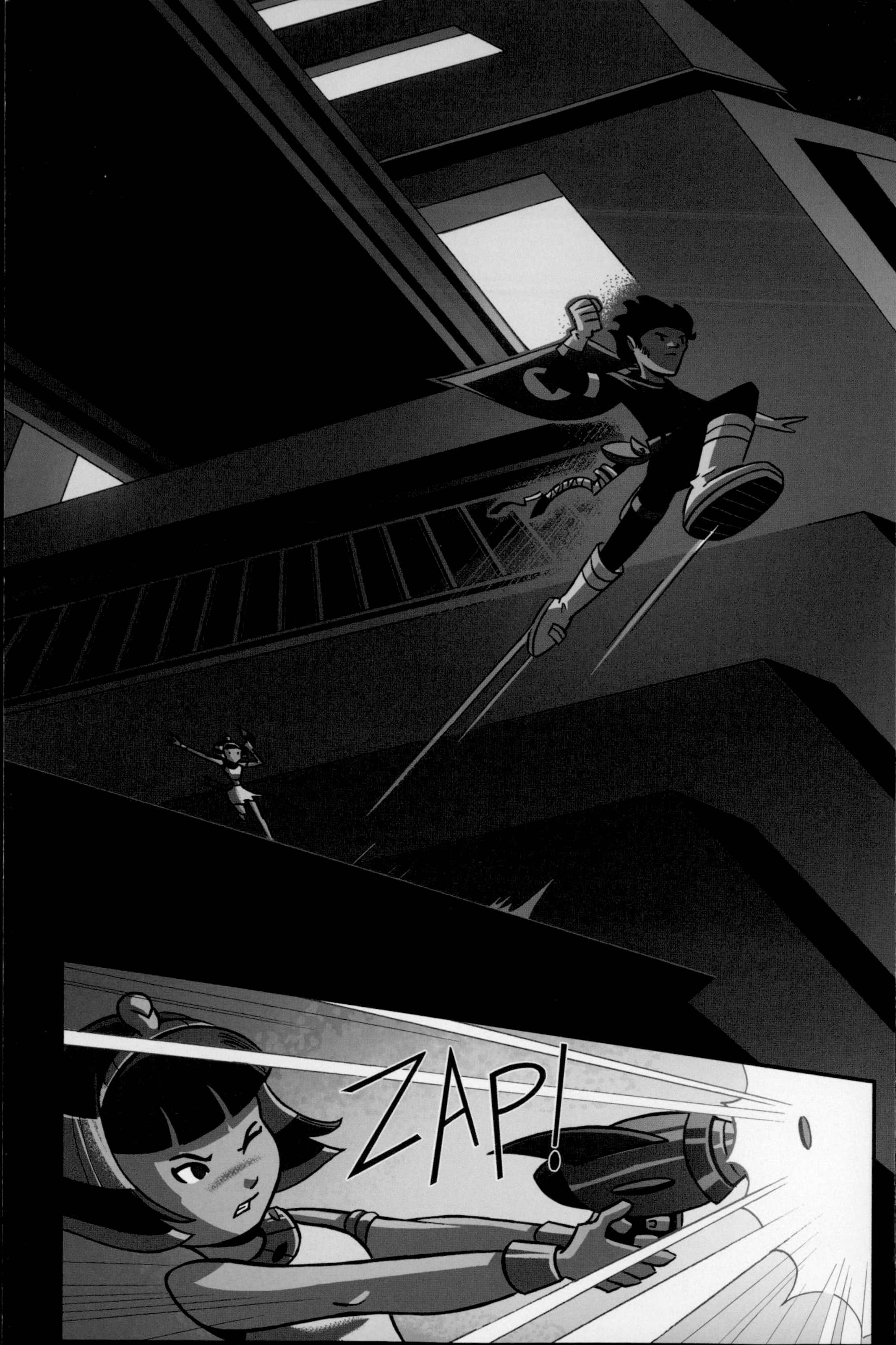
ZAP!

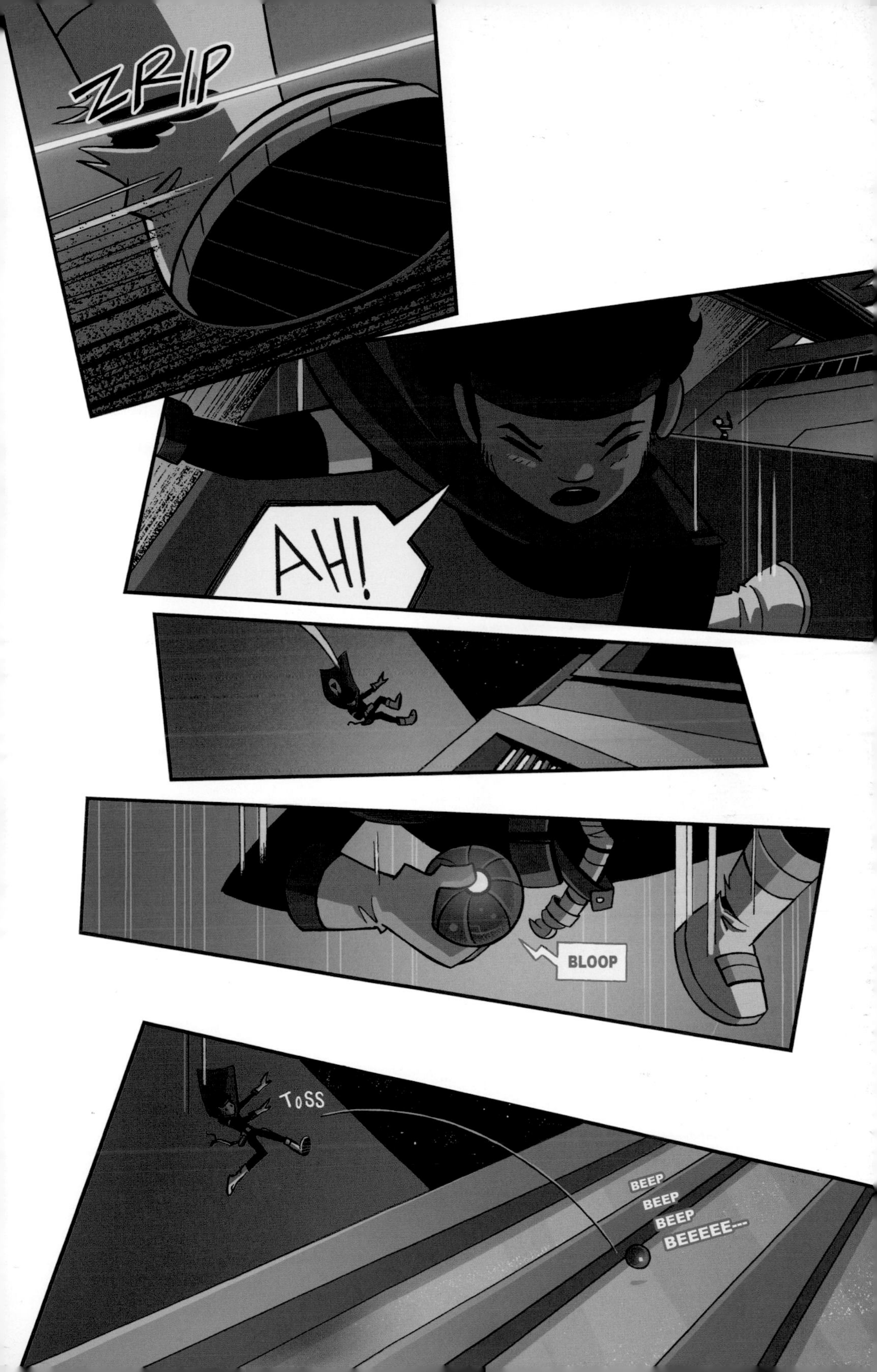
ZRIP
AH!
BLOOP
TOSS
BEEP
BEEP
BEEP
BEEEEE--

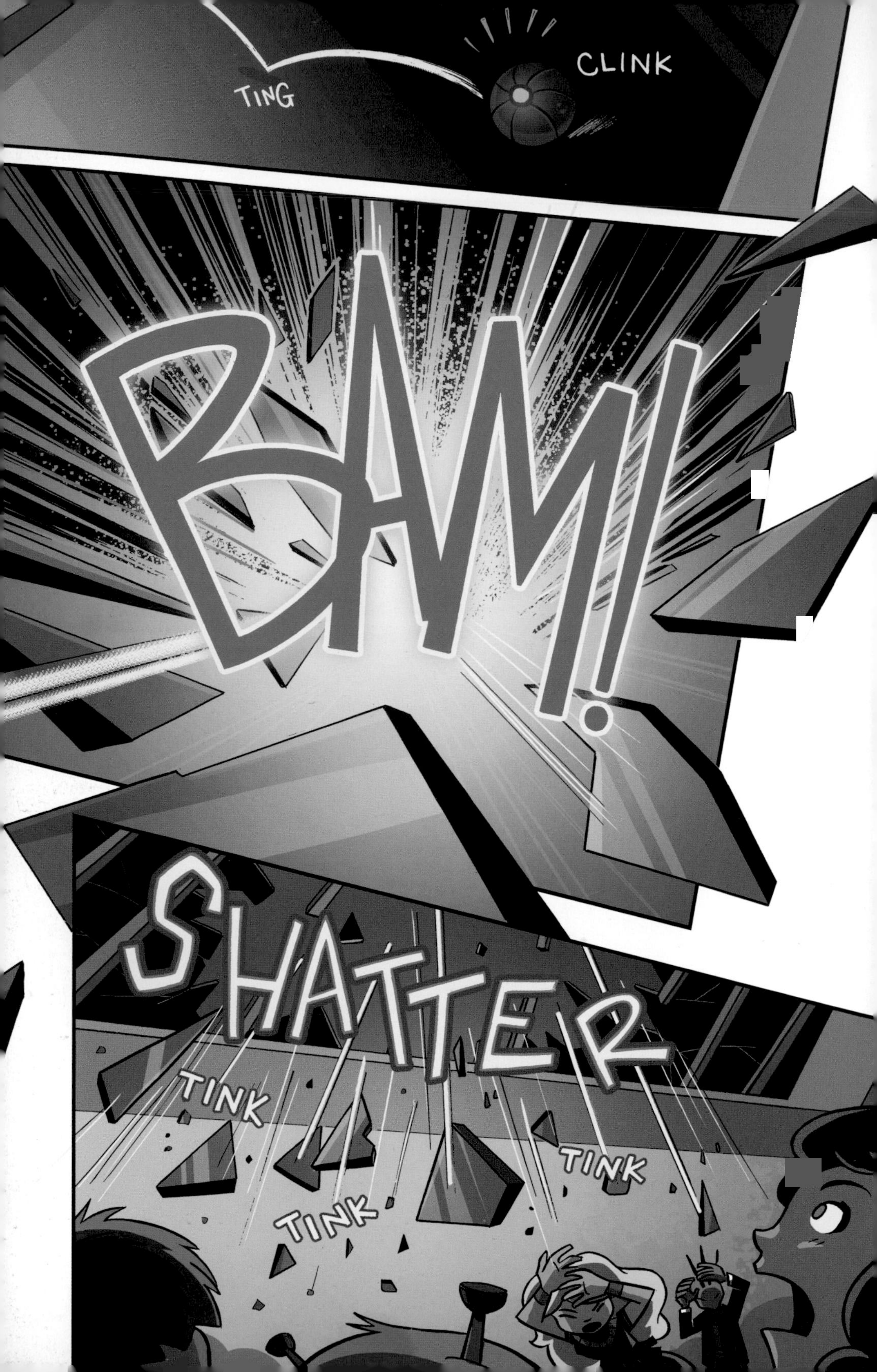
TING
CLINK
BAM!
SHATTER
TINK
TINK
TINK

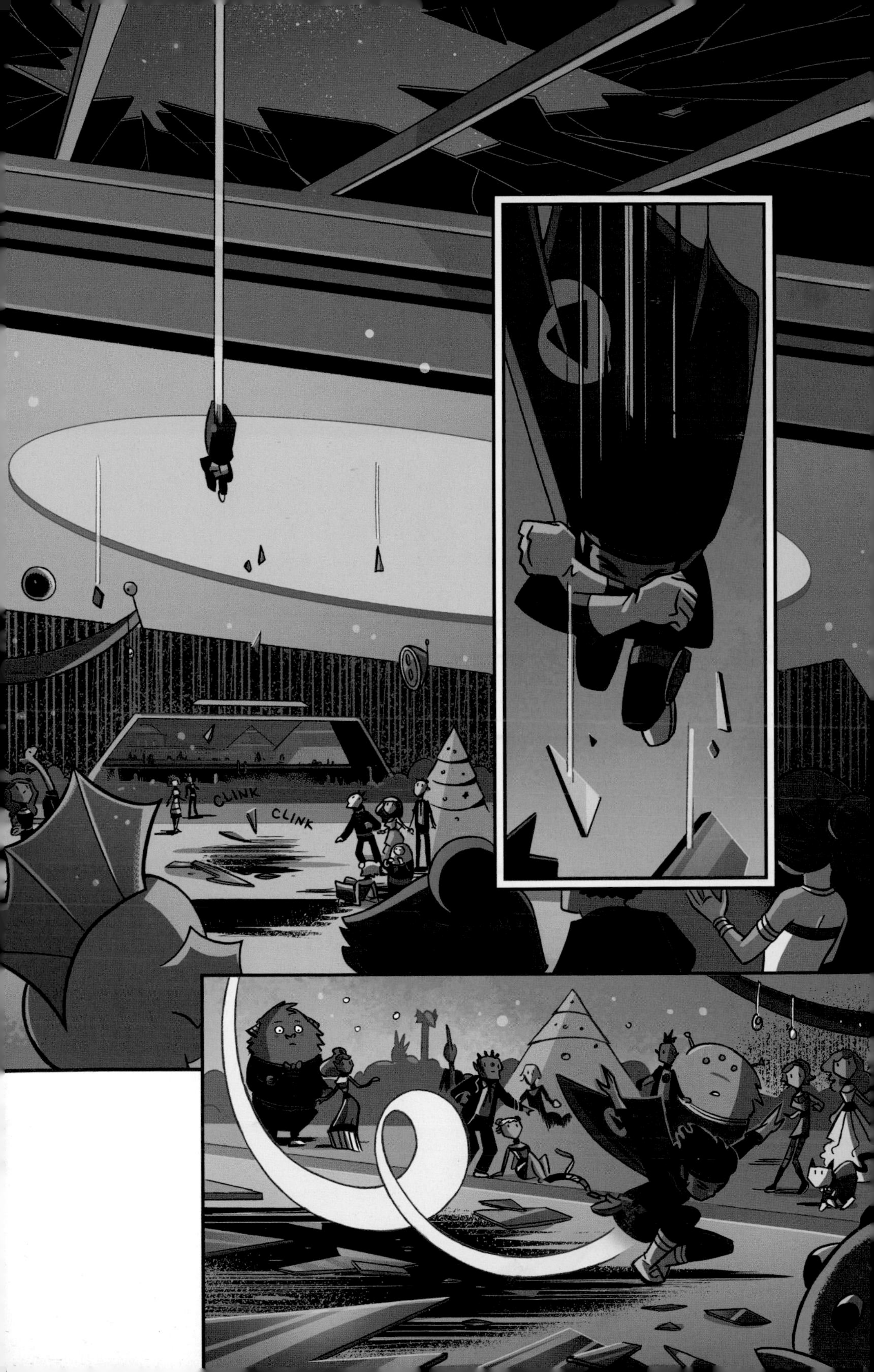
CLINK
CLINK

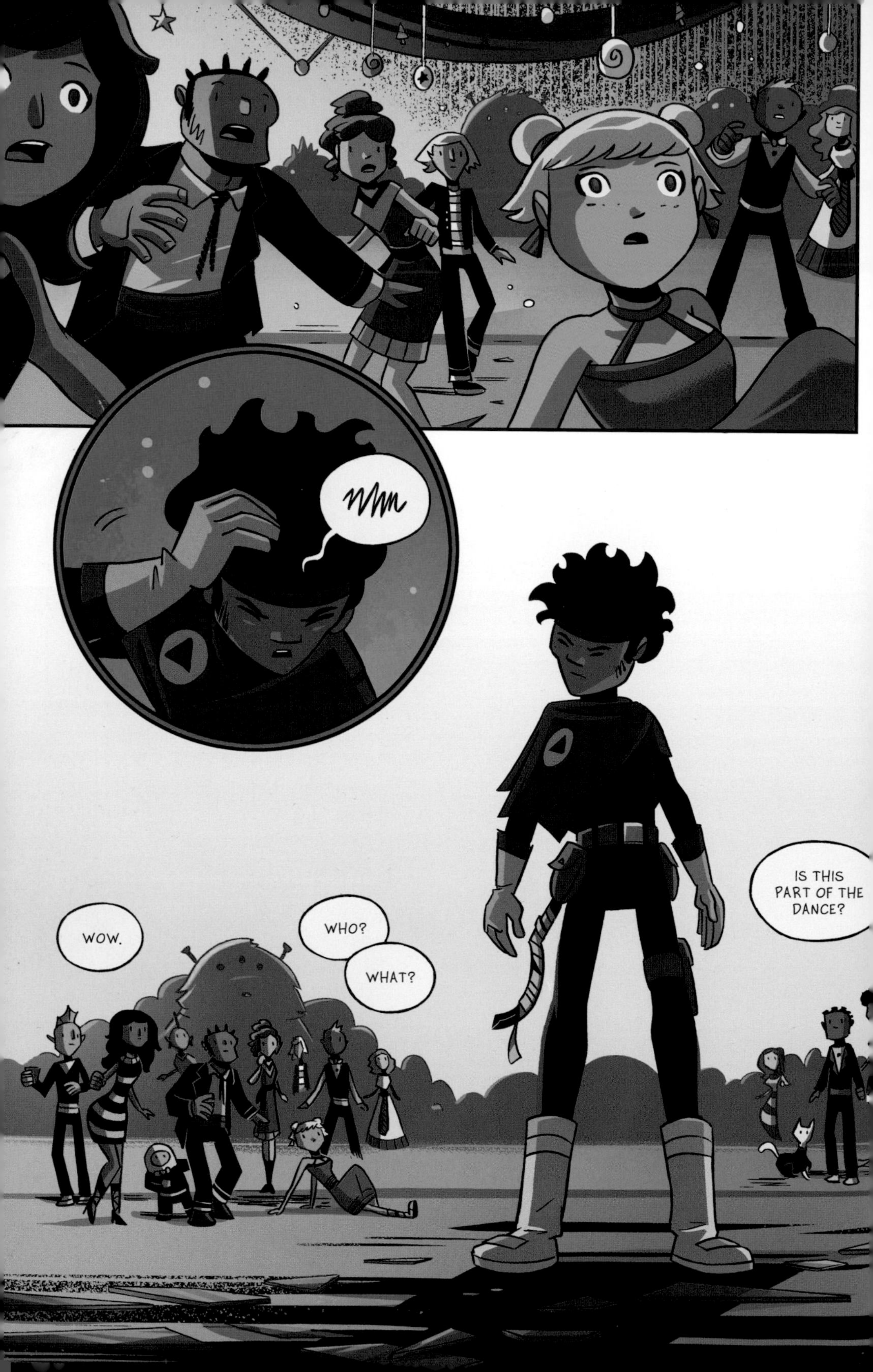
WOW.
WHO?
WHAT?
IS THIS PART OF THE DANCE?

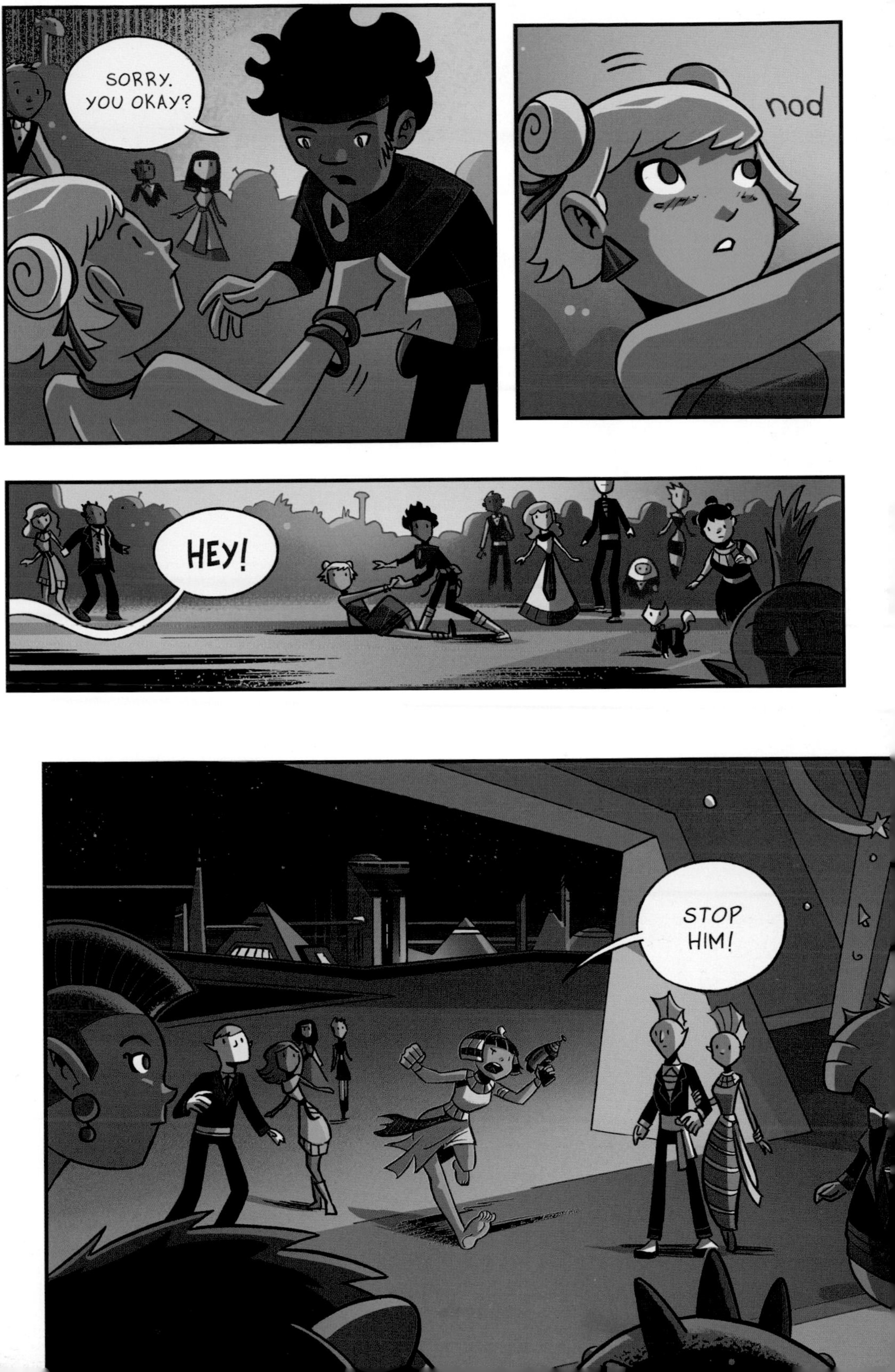
SORRY. YOU OKAY?
nod
HEY!
STOP HIM!

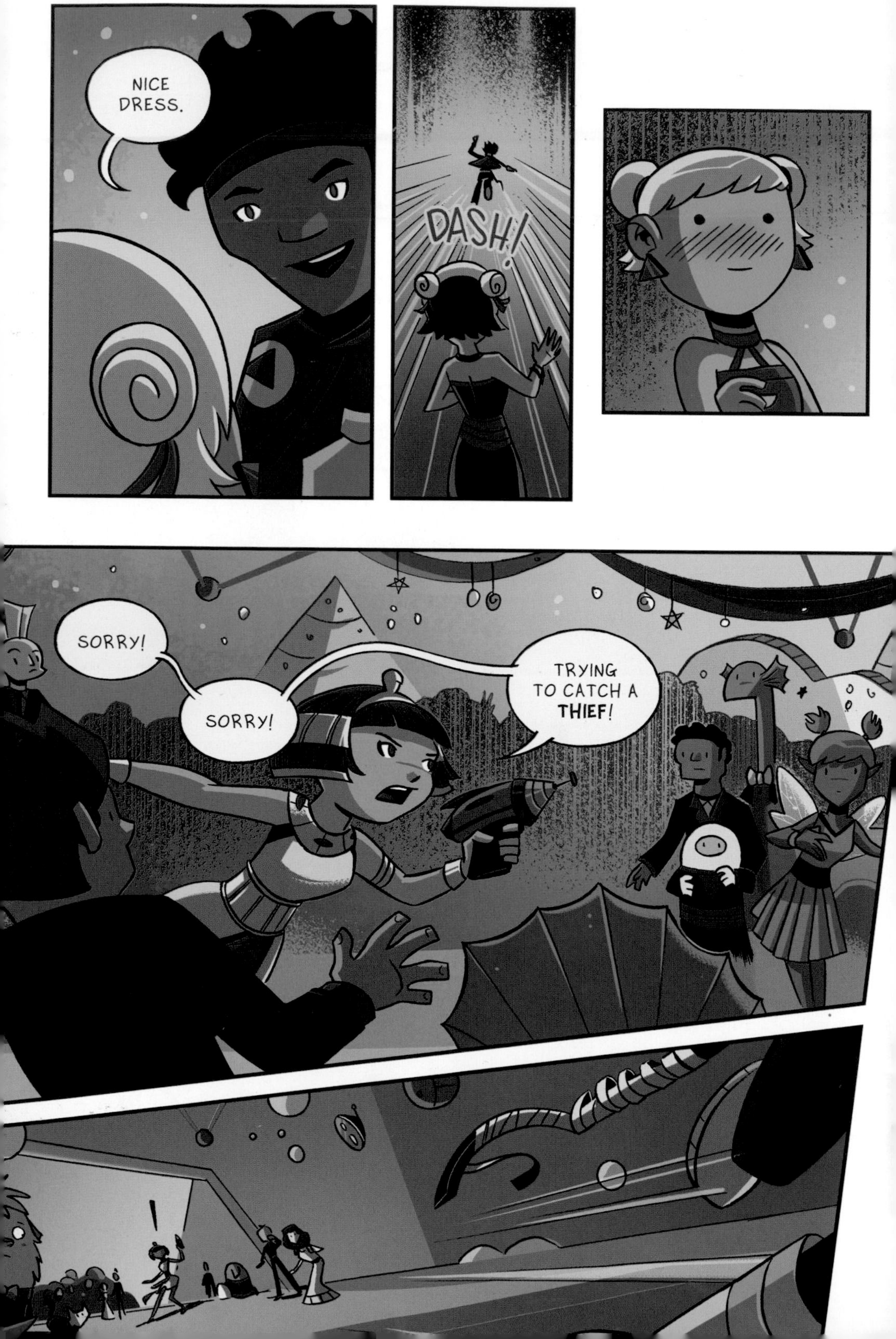
NICE DRESS.
DASH!
SORRY!
SORRY!
TRYING TO CATCH A **THIEF**!
!

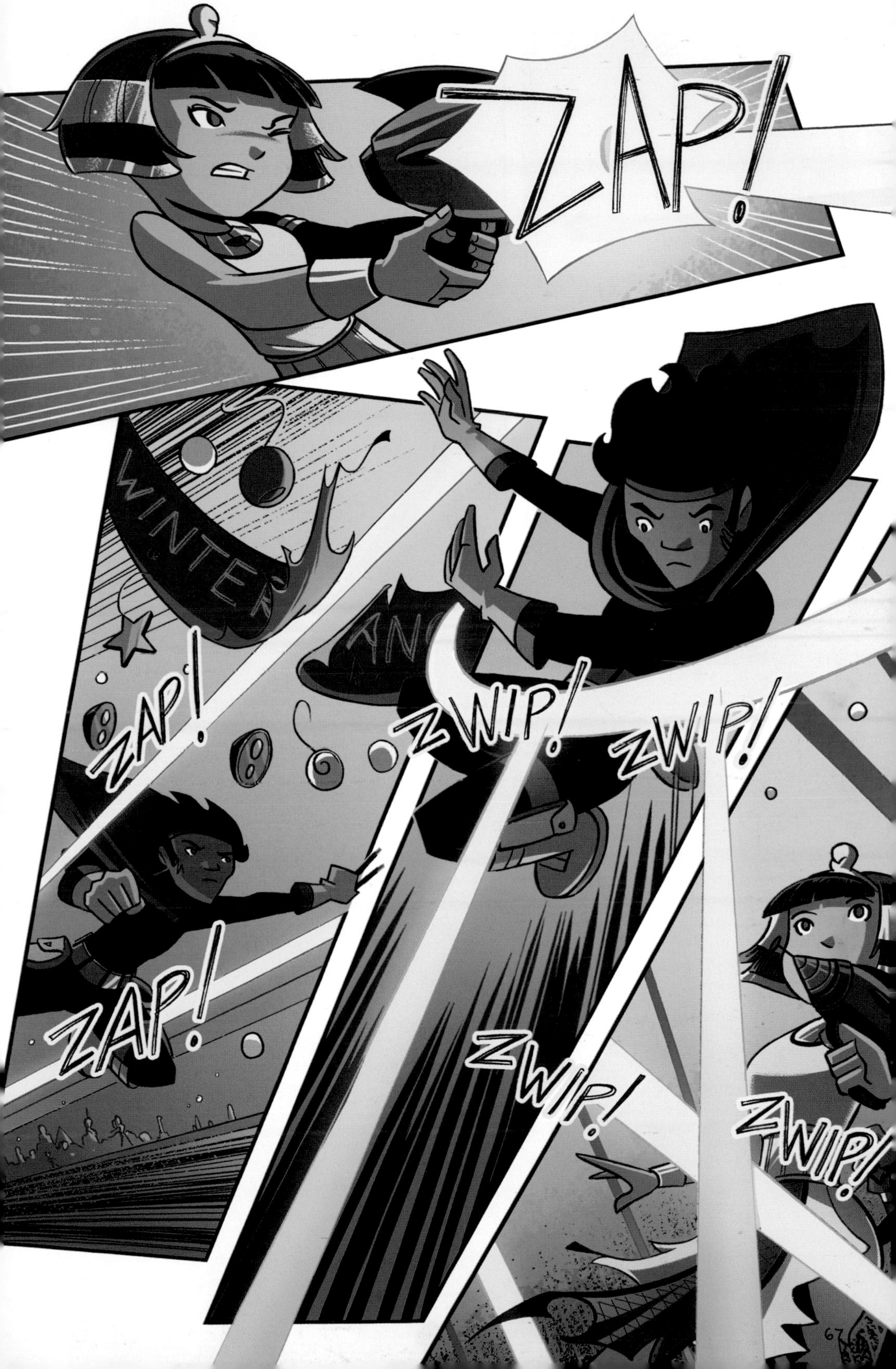
ZAP!
WINTER
ZAP!
ZWIP!
ZWIP!
ZAP!
ZWIP!
ZWIP!

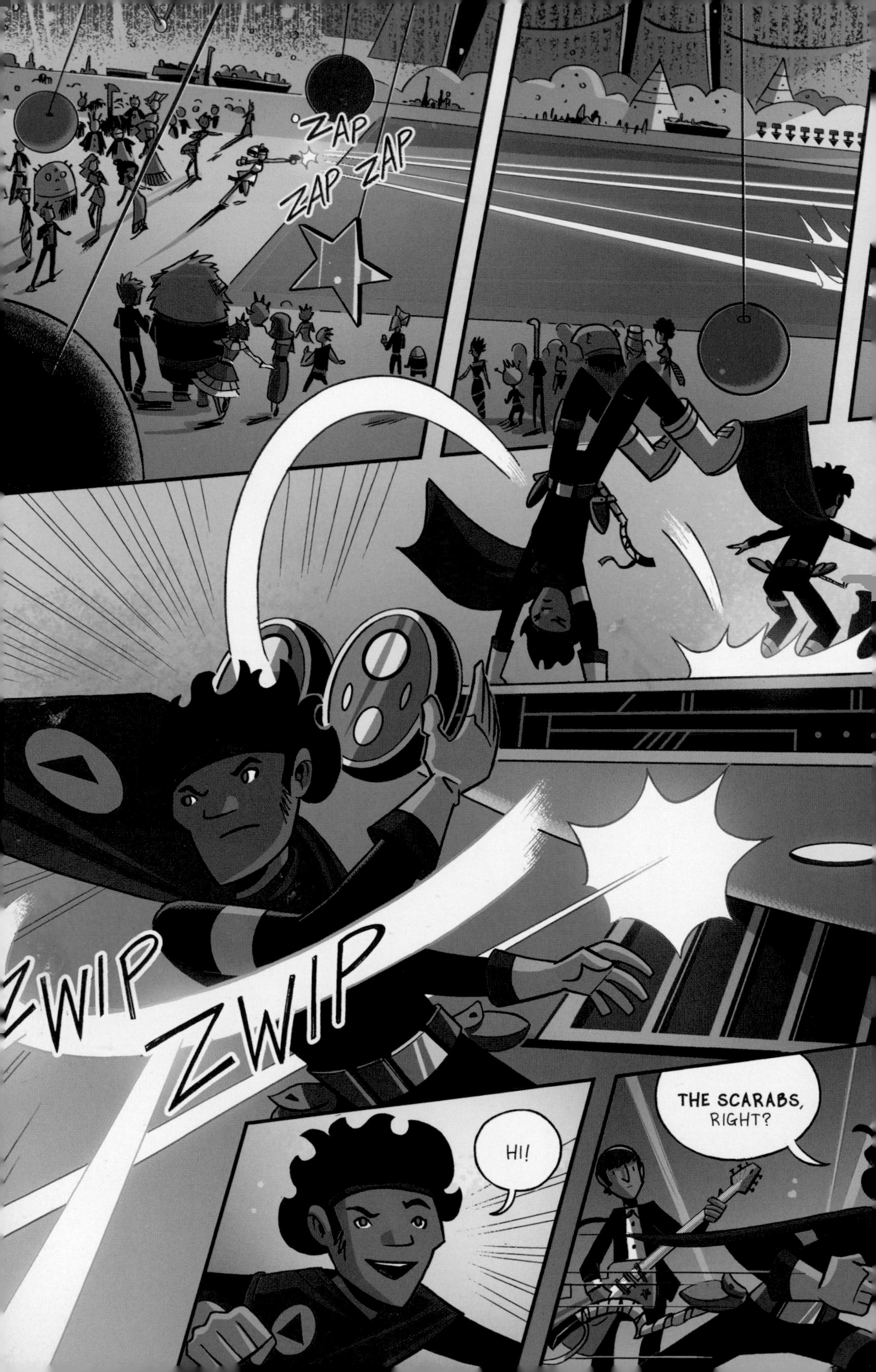

ZAP
ZAP ZAP
ZWIP ZWIP
HI!
THE SCARABS, RIGHT?

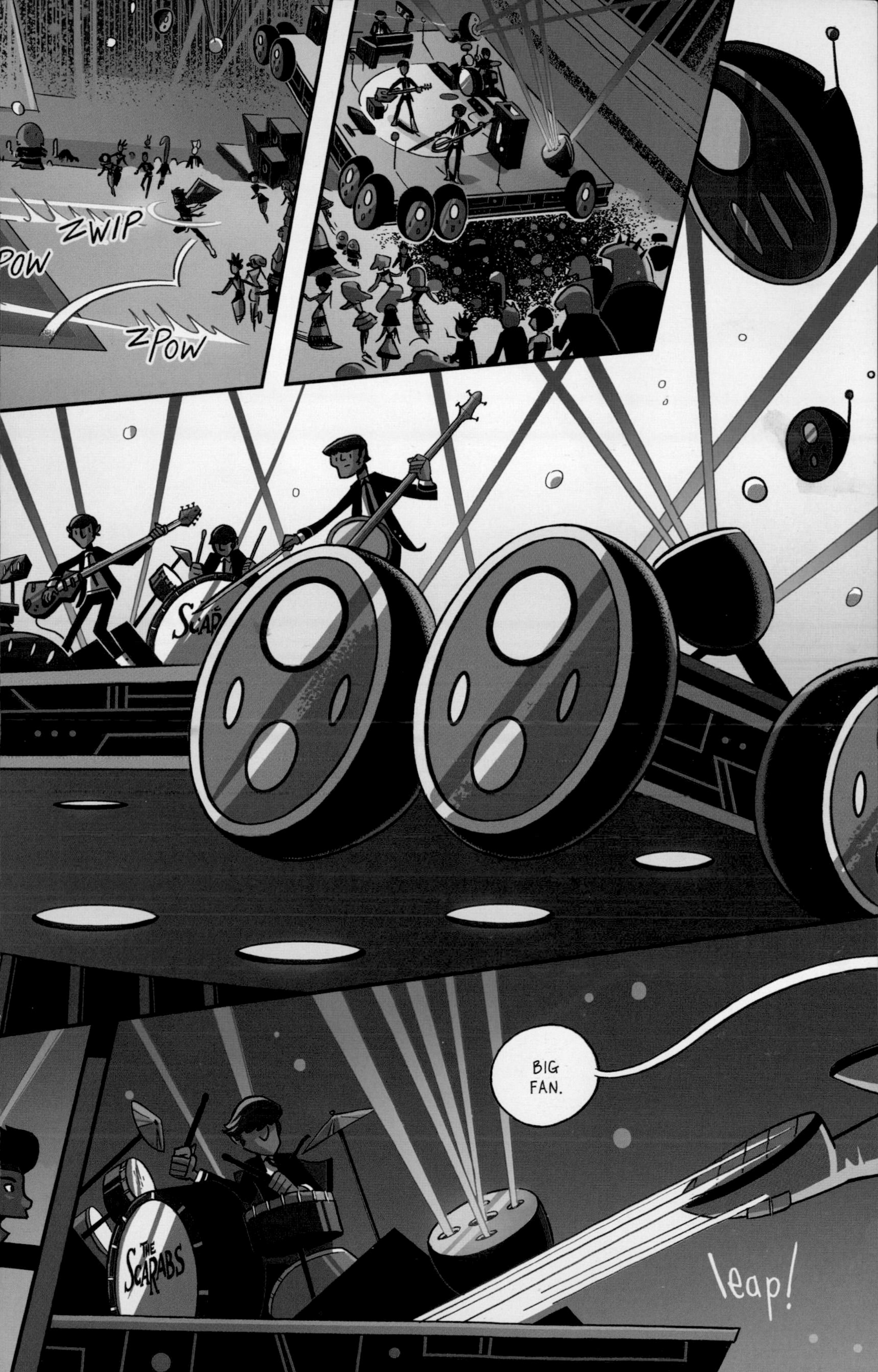
ZWIP
POW
ZPOW
THE SCARABS
BIG FAN.
leap!

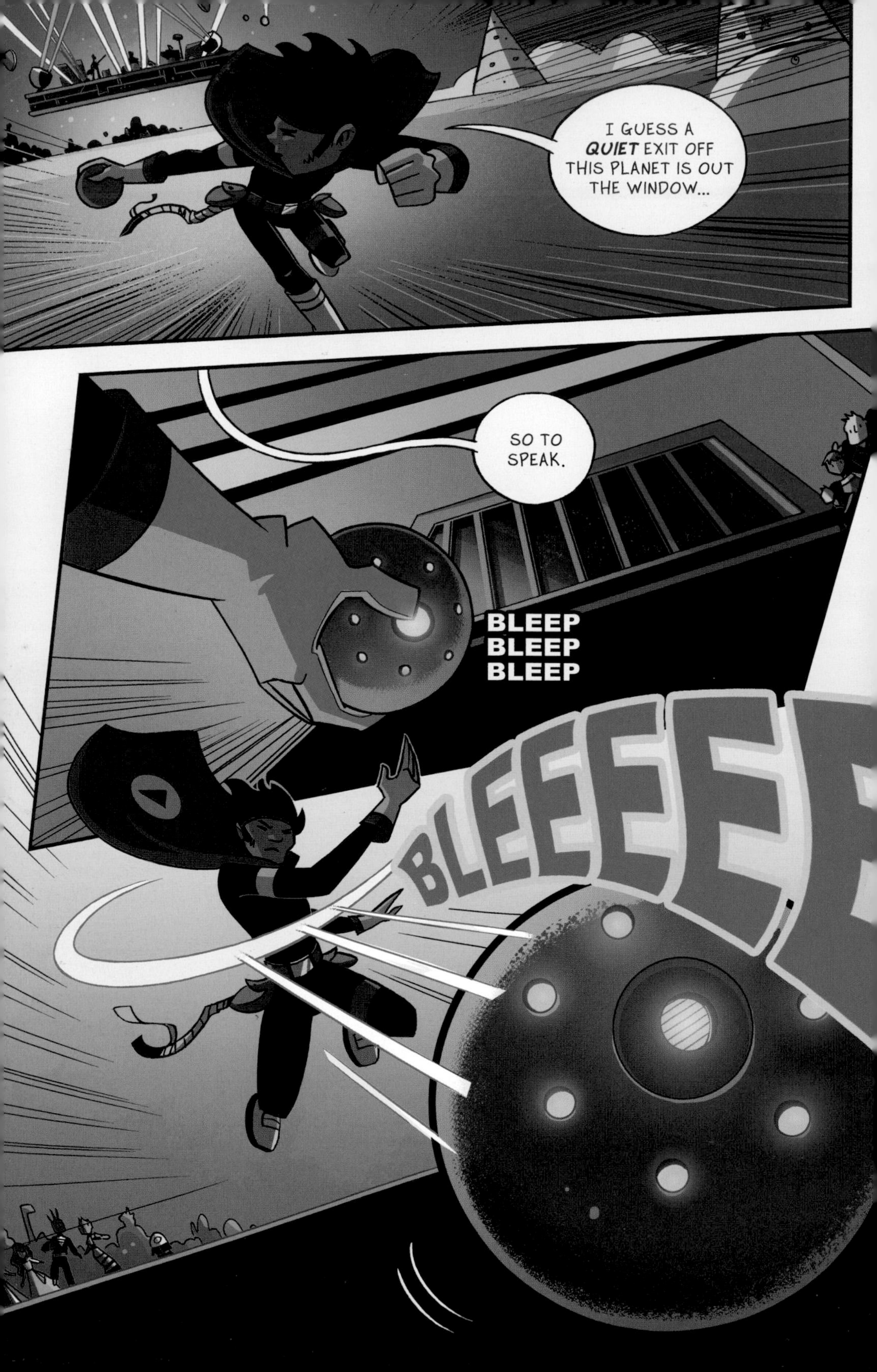
I GUESS A QUIET EXIT OFF THIS PLANET IS OUT THE WINDOW...
SO TO SPEAK.
BLEEP
BLEEP
BLEEP

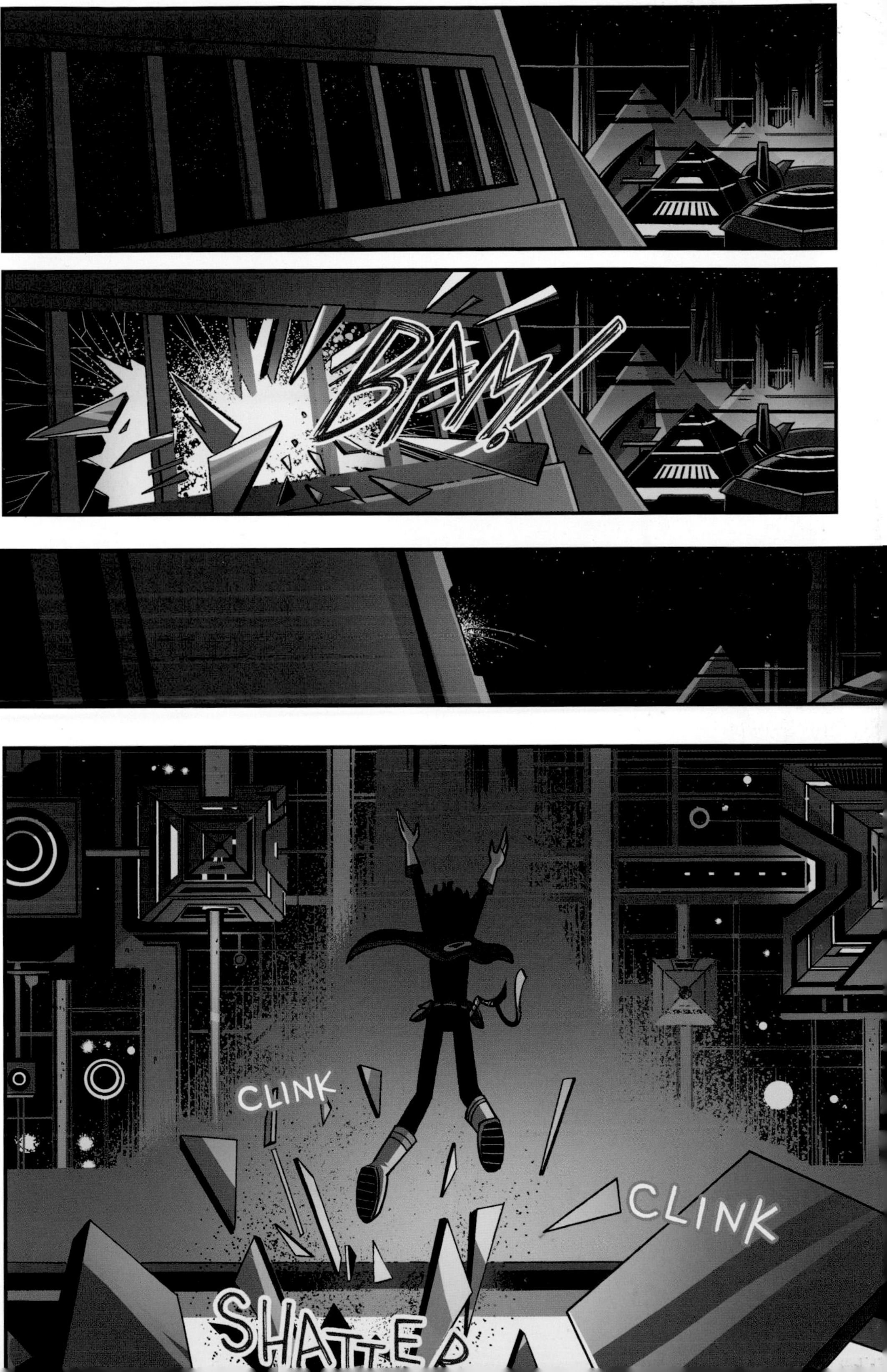
BAM!
CLINK
CLINK
SHATTE

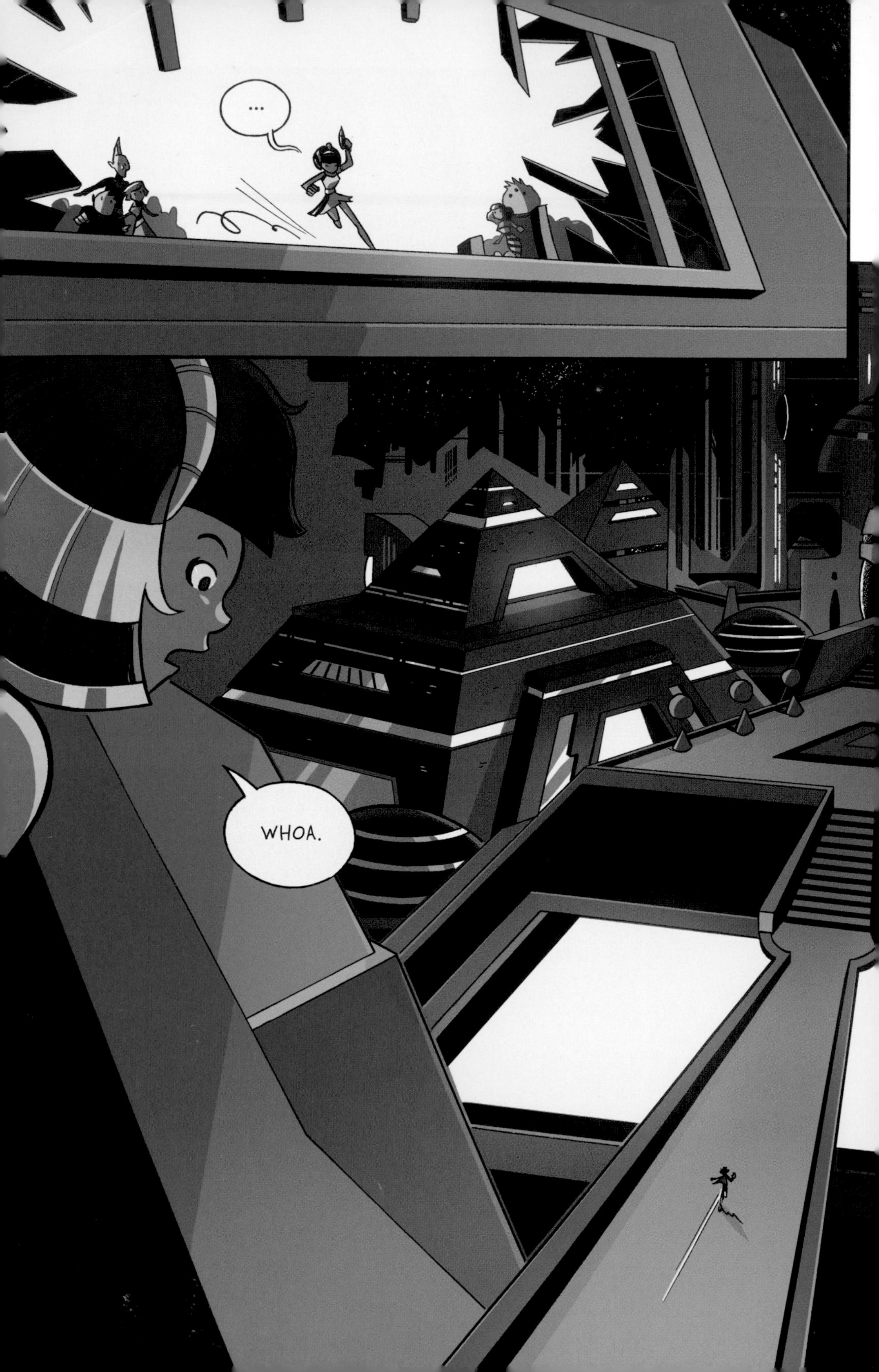
...
WHOA.

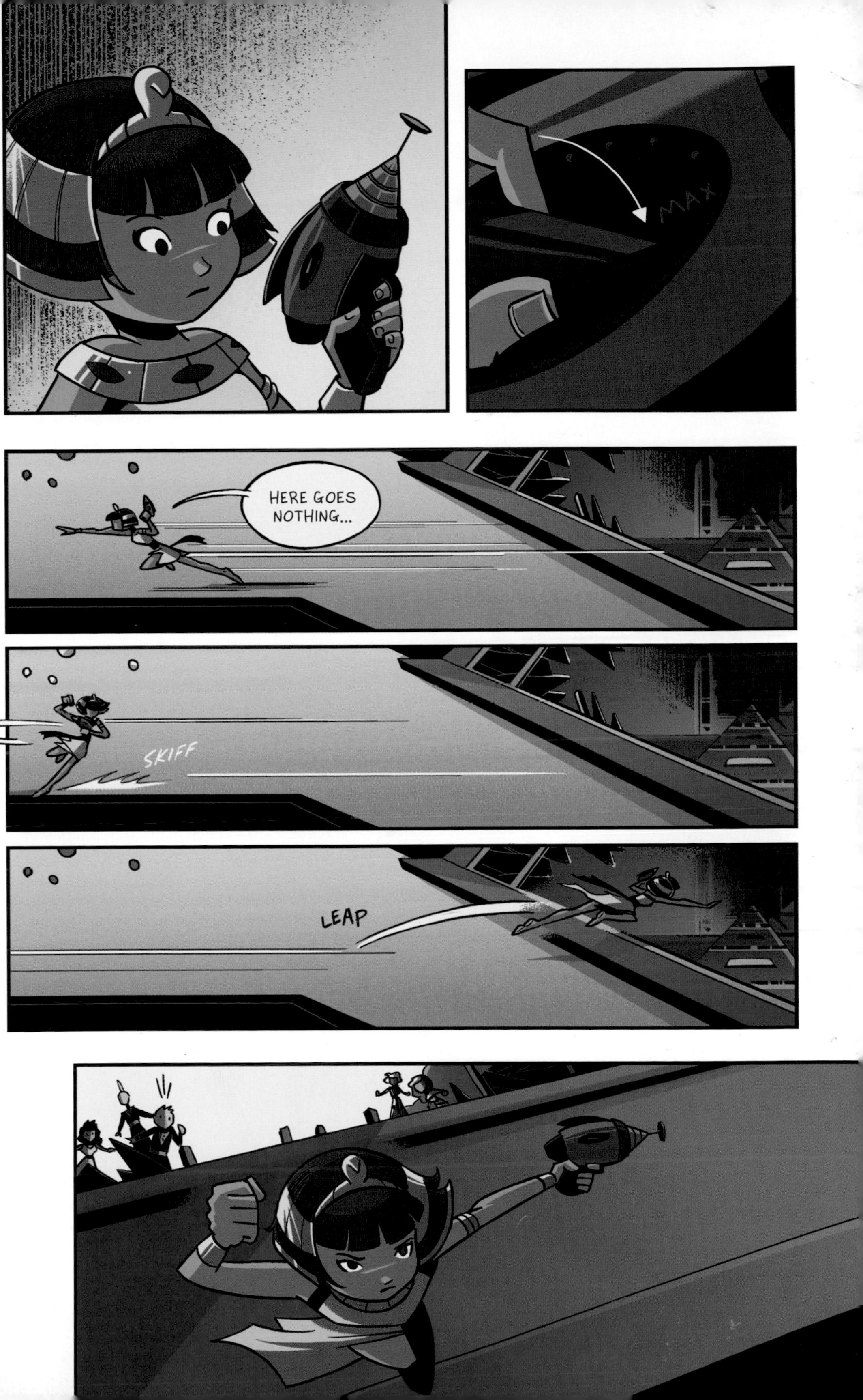
MAX
HERE GOES NOTHING...
SKIFF
LEAP

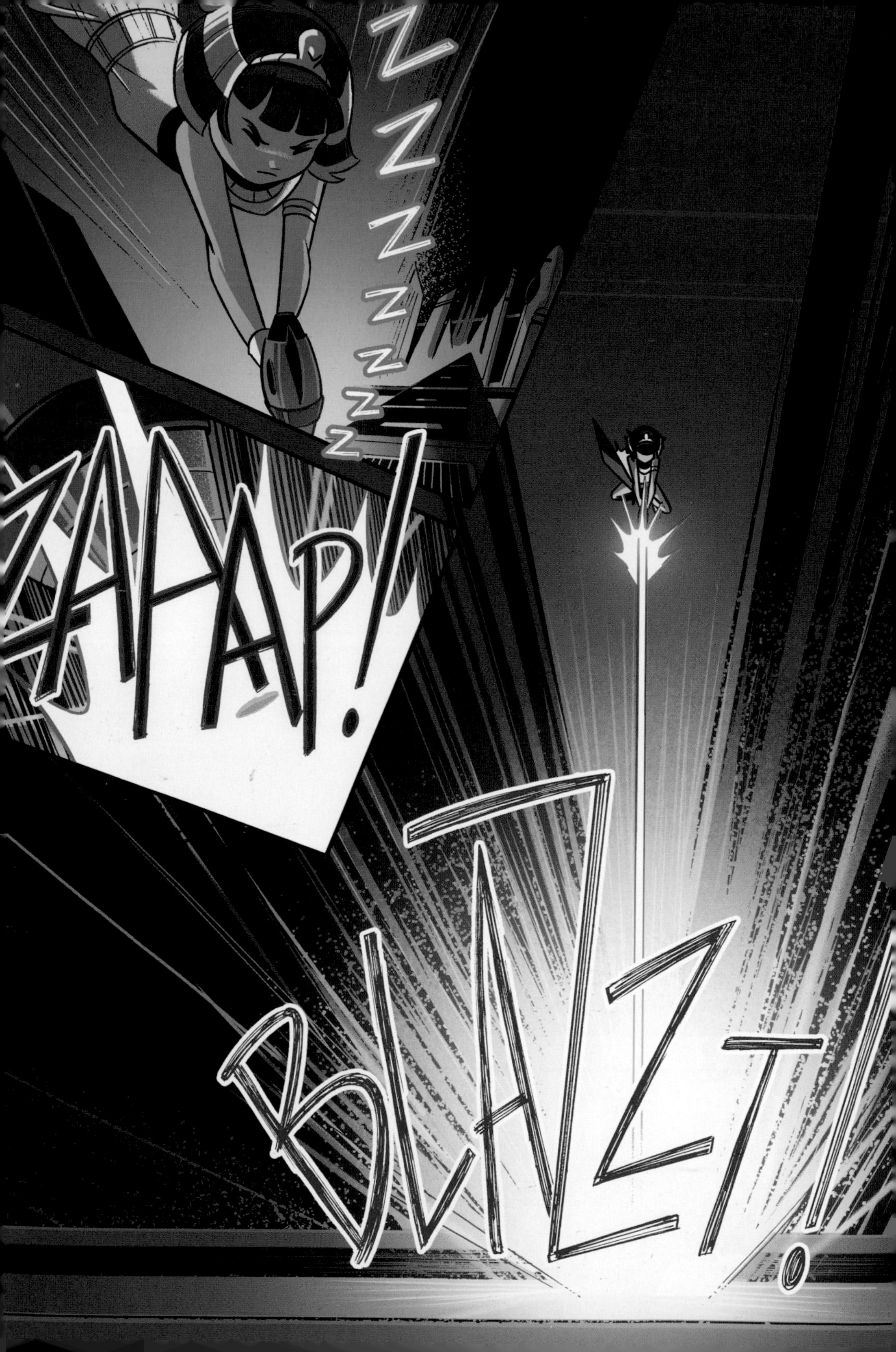
ZZZZZZZZZ
ZAPAP!
BLAZT!

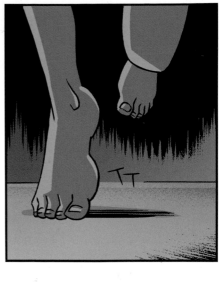

CADETS!

STAY AWAY FROM THE WINDOW!

WOW.

DID YOU **SEE** THAT?

I THINK I'M IN LOVE.

HUH.

WAIT TILL I TELL PTOLMINIC ABOUT **THAT!**

VRRRRR—

—RRRRUM

STEALTH SHIP?!

OF COURSE HE HAS A STEALTH SHIP.

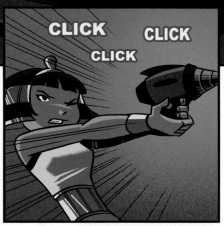

CLICK
CLICK
CLICK

GAH!

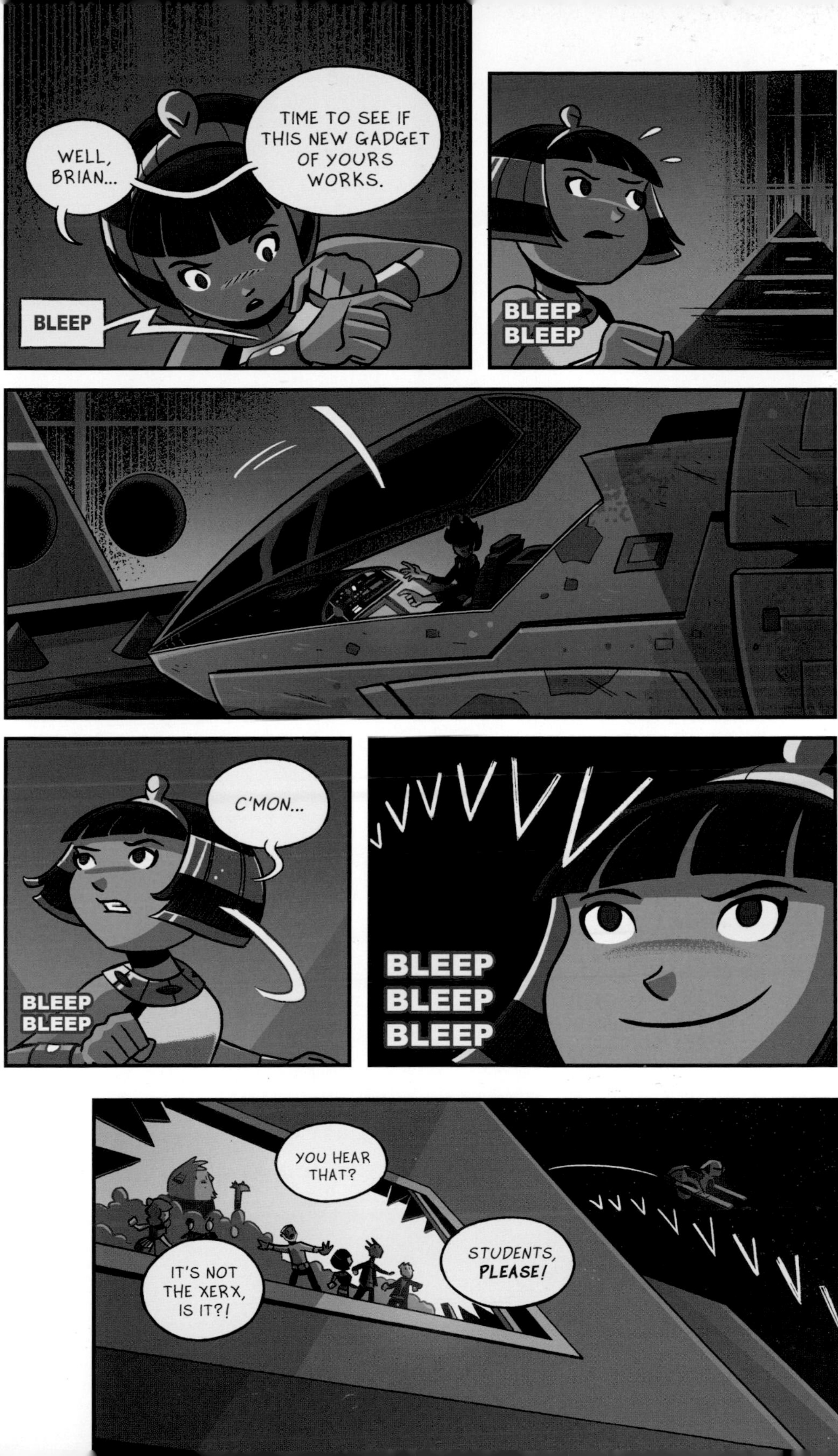

WELL, BRIAN...
TIME TO SEE IF THIS NEW GADGET OF YOURS WORKS.
BLEEP
BLEEP BLEEP
C'MON...
BLEEP BLEEP
BLEEP BLEEP BLEEP
YOU HEAR THAT?
IT'S NOT THE XERX, IS IT?!
STUDENTS, **PLEASE!**

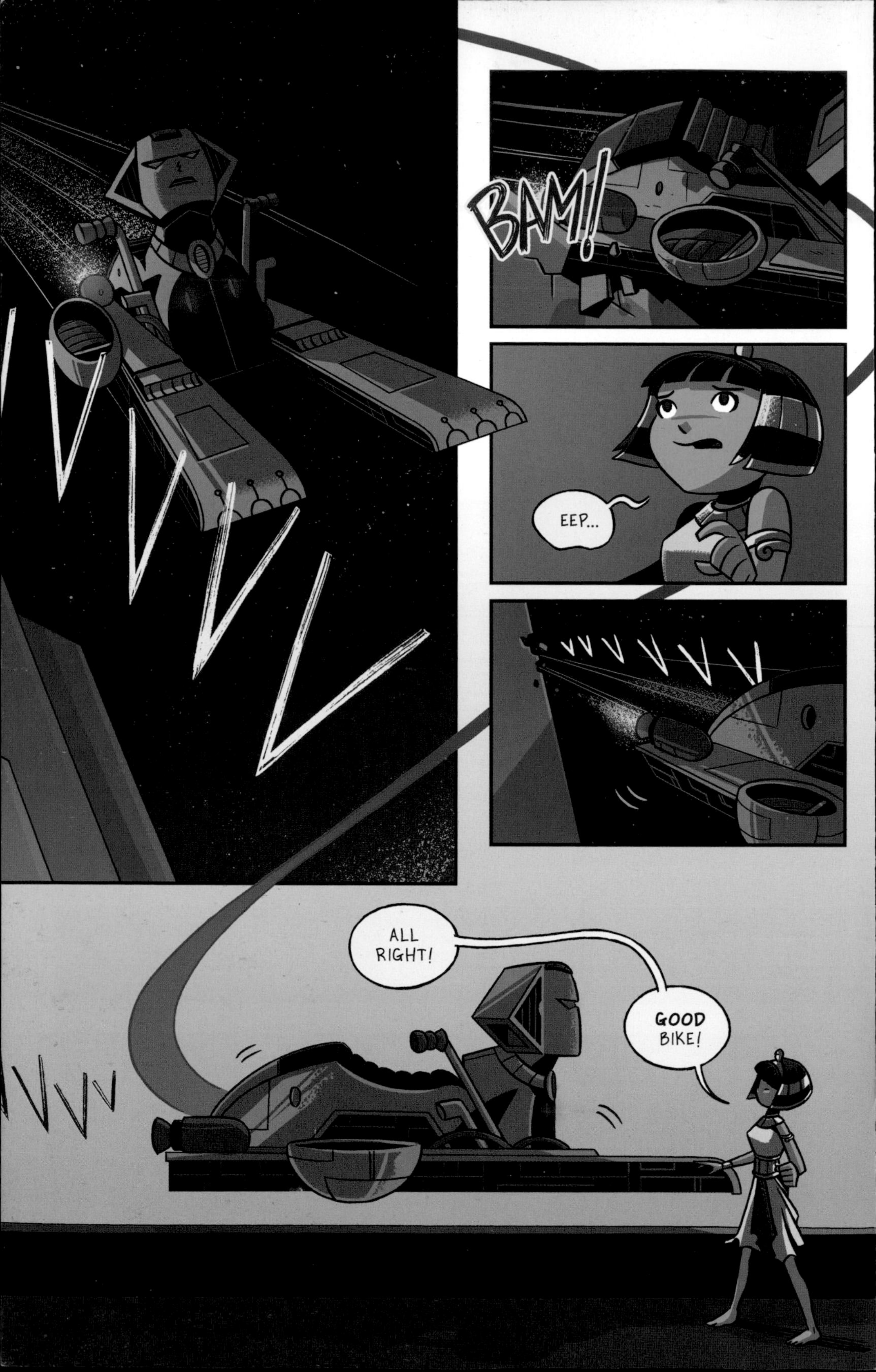
BAM!!
EEP...
ALL RIGHT!
GOOD BIKE!

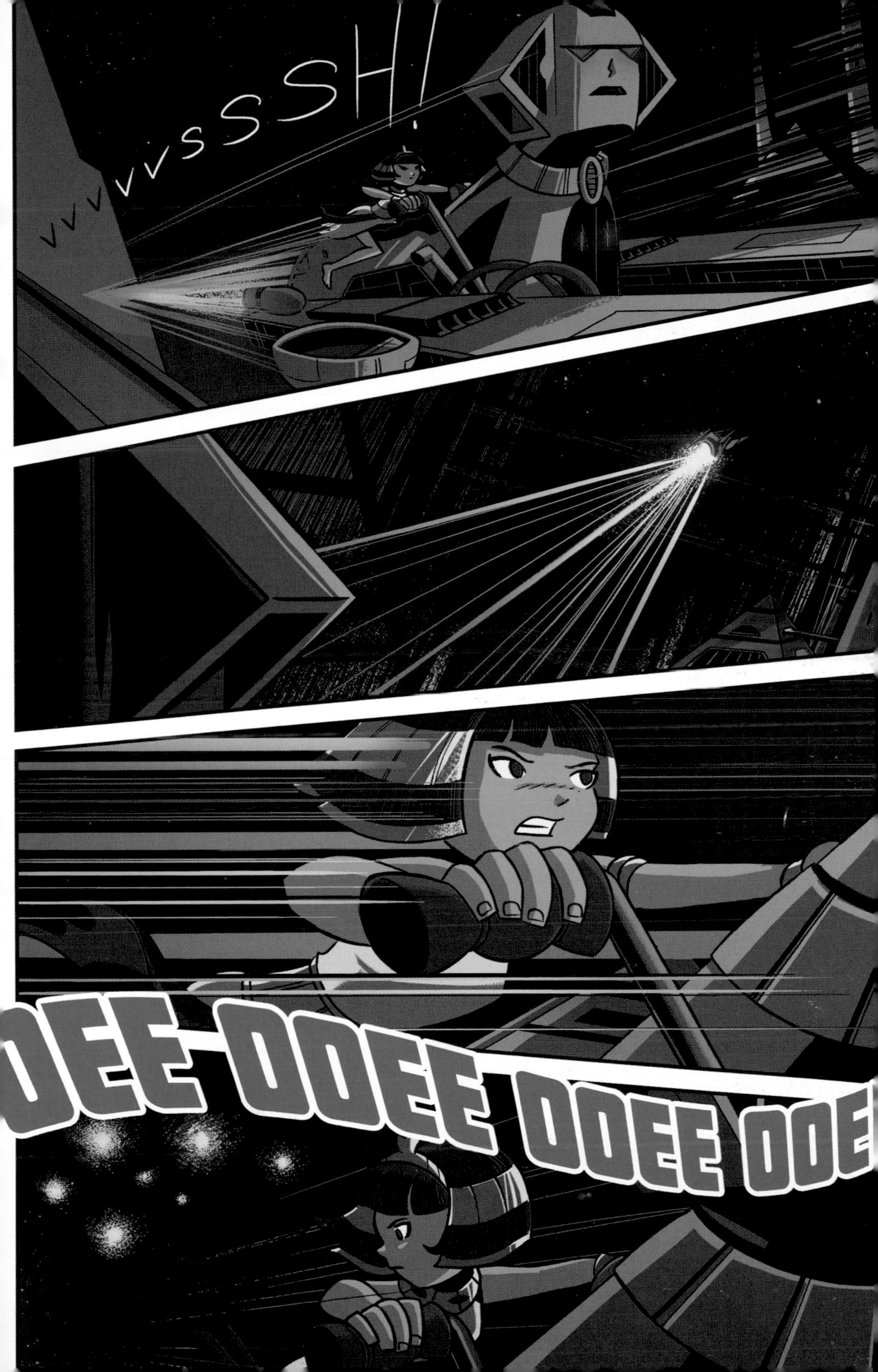
VVVVVVVSSSSH!
OOEE OOEE OOEE OOE

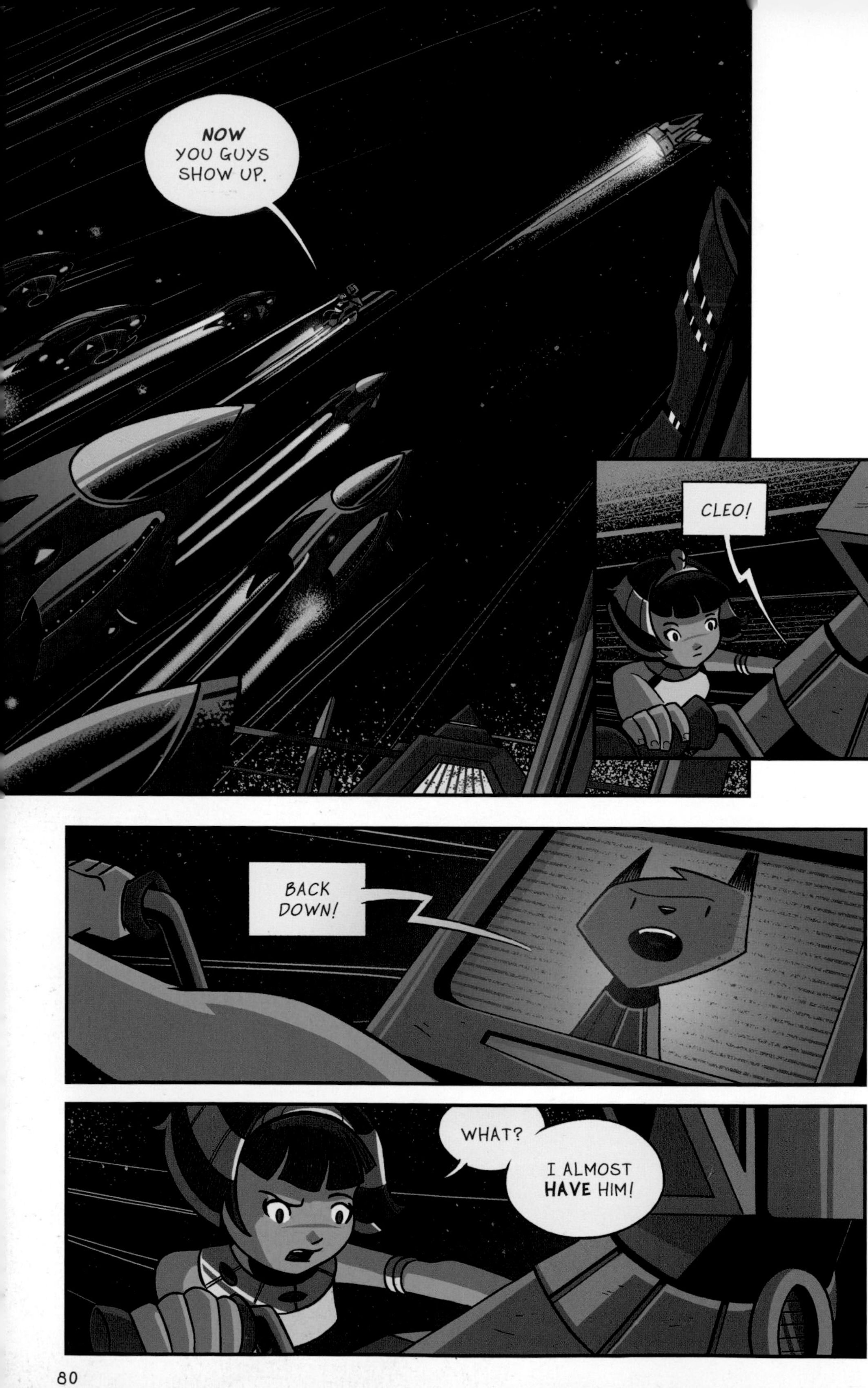
NOW YOU GUYS SHOW UP.
CLEO!
BACK DOWN!
WHAT?
I ALMOST HAVE HIM!

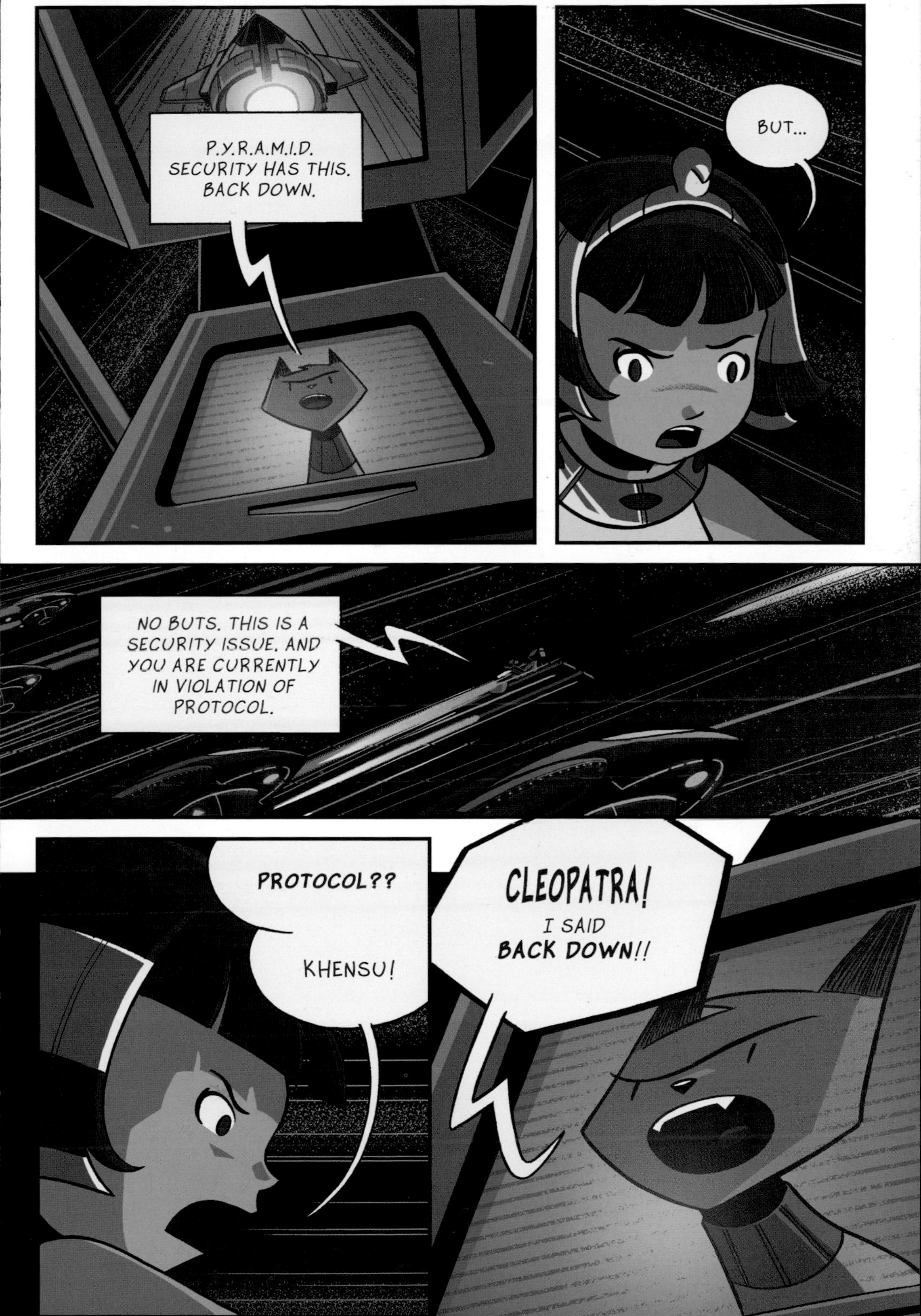
P.Y.R.A.M.I.D. SECURITY HAS THIS. BACK DOWN.
BUT...
NO BUTS. THIS IS A SECURITY ISSUE. AND YOU ARE CURRENTLY IN VIOLATION OF PROTOCOL.
PROTOCOL??
KHENSU!
CLEOPATRA! I SAID BACK DOWN!!

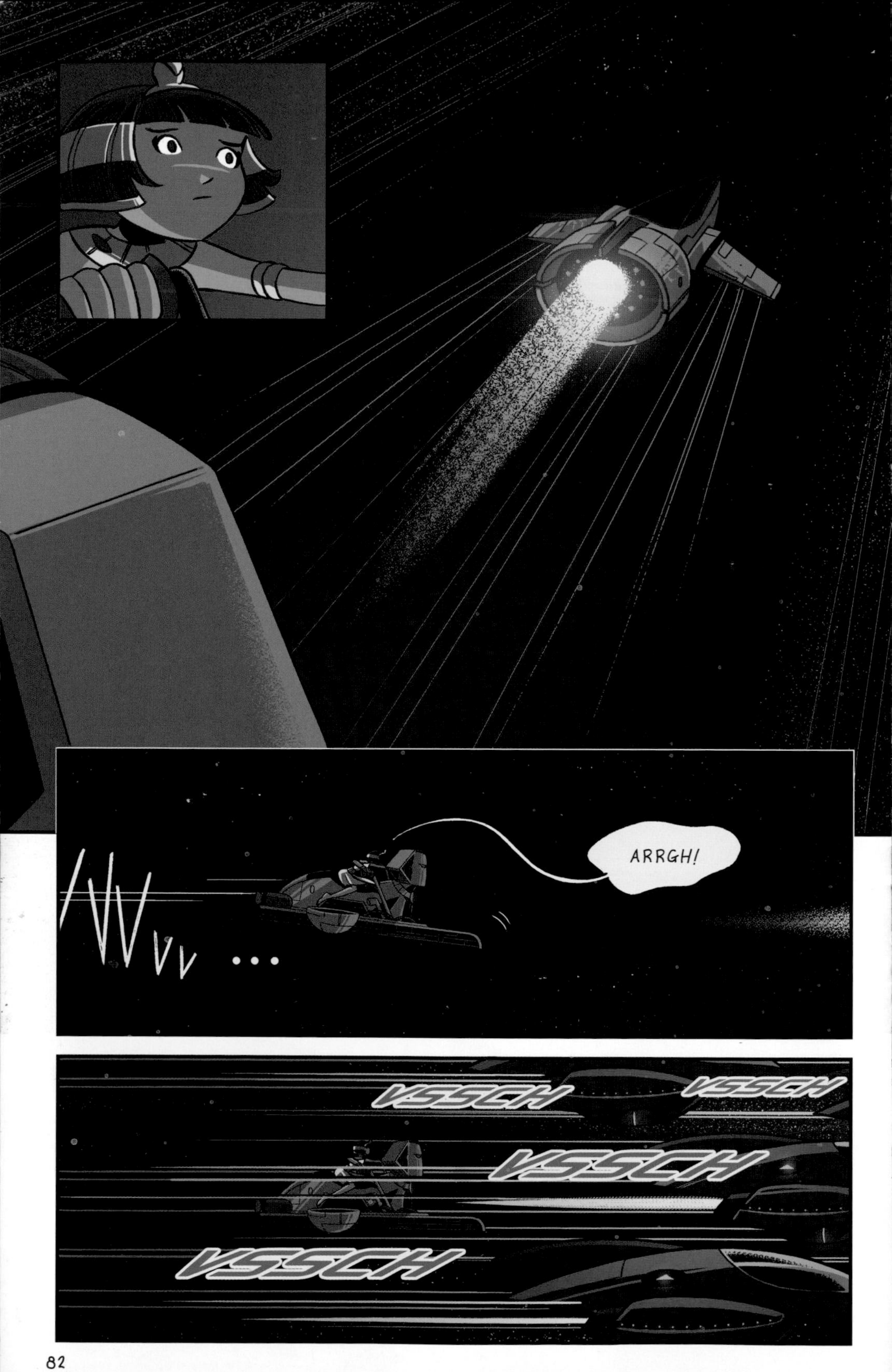
VVVvv ...
ARRGH!
VSSCH
VSSCH
VSSCH
VSSCH

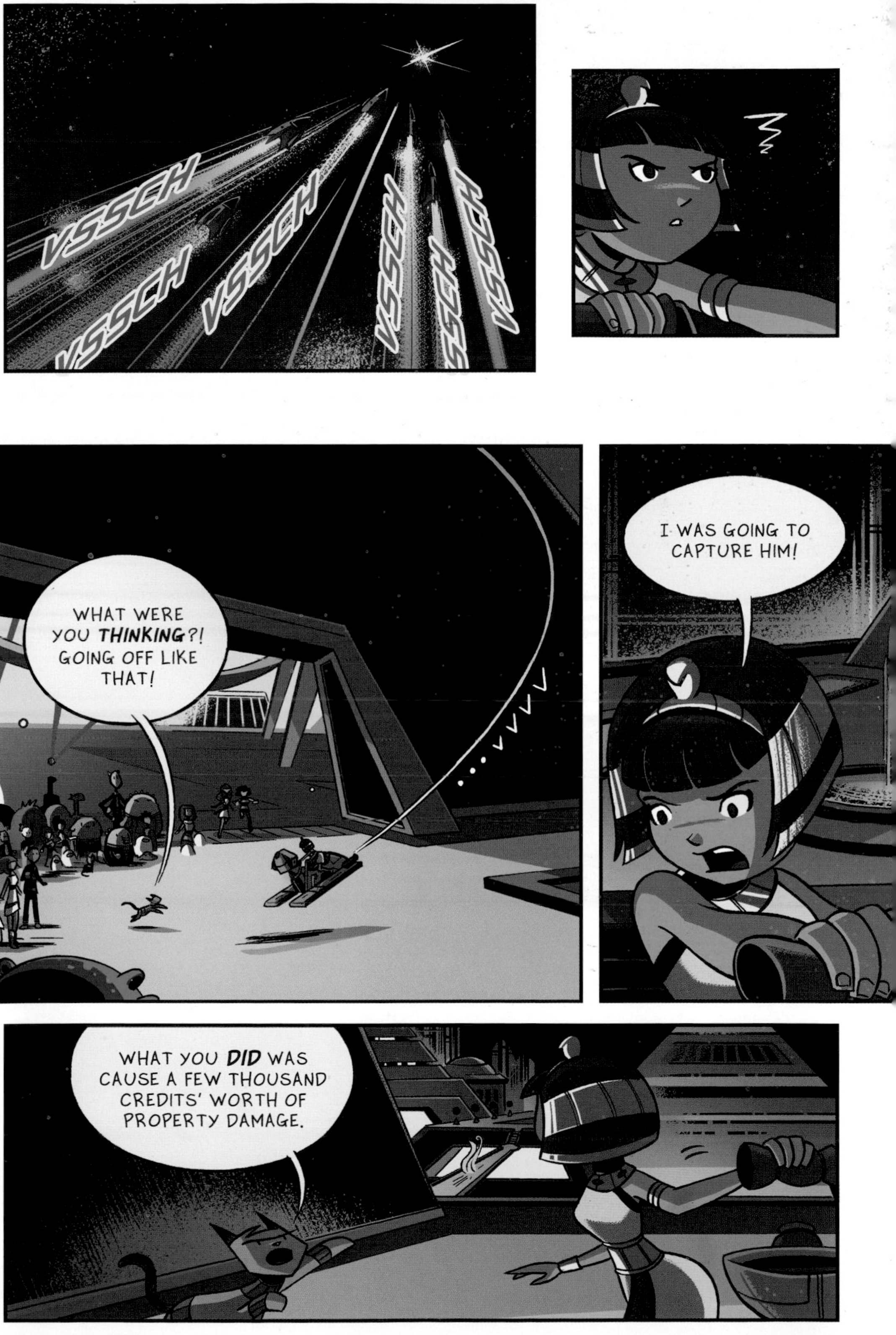
VSSCH
VSSCH
VSSCH
VSSCH
VSSCH
VSSCH
WHAT WERE YOU THINKING?! GOING OFF LIKE THAT!
I WAS GOING TO CAPTURE HIM!
WHAT YOU DID WAS CAUSE A FEW THOUSAND CREDITS' WORTH OF PROPERTY DAMAGE.

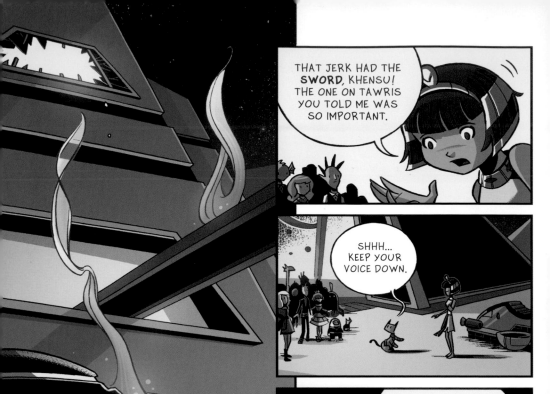

THAT JERK HAD THE **SWORD**, KHENSU! THE ONE ON TAWRIS YOU TOLD ME WAS SO IMPORTANT.

SHHH... KEEP YOUR VOICE DOWN.

THERE ARE CERTAIN THINGS YOU DON'T KNOW ABOUT, CLEO.

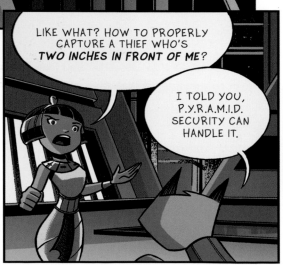

LIKE WHAT? HOW TO PROPERLY CAPTURE A THIEF WHO'S **TWO INCHES IN FRONT OF ME?**

I TOLD YOU, P.Y.R.A.M.I.D. SECURITY CAN HANDLE IT.

I COULD HAVE HANDLED IT!

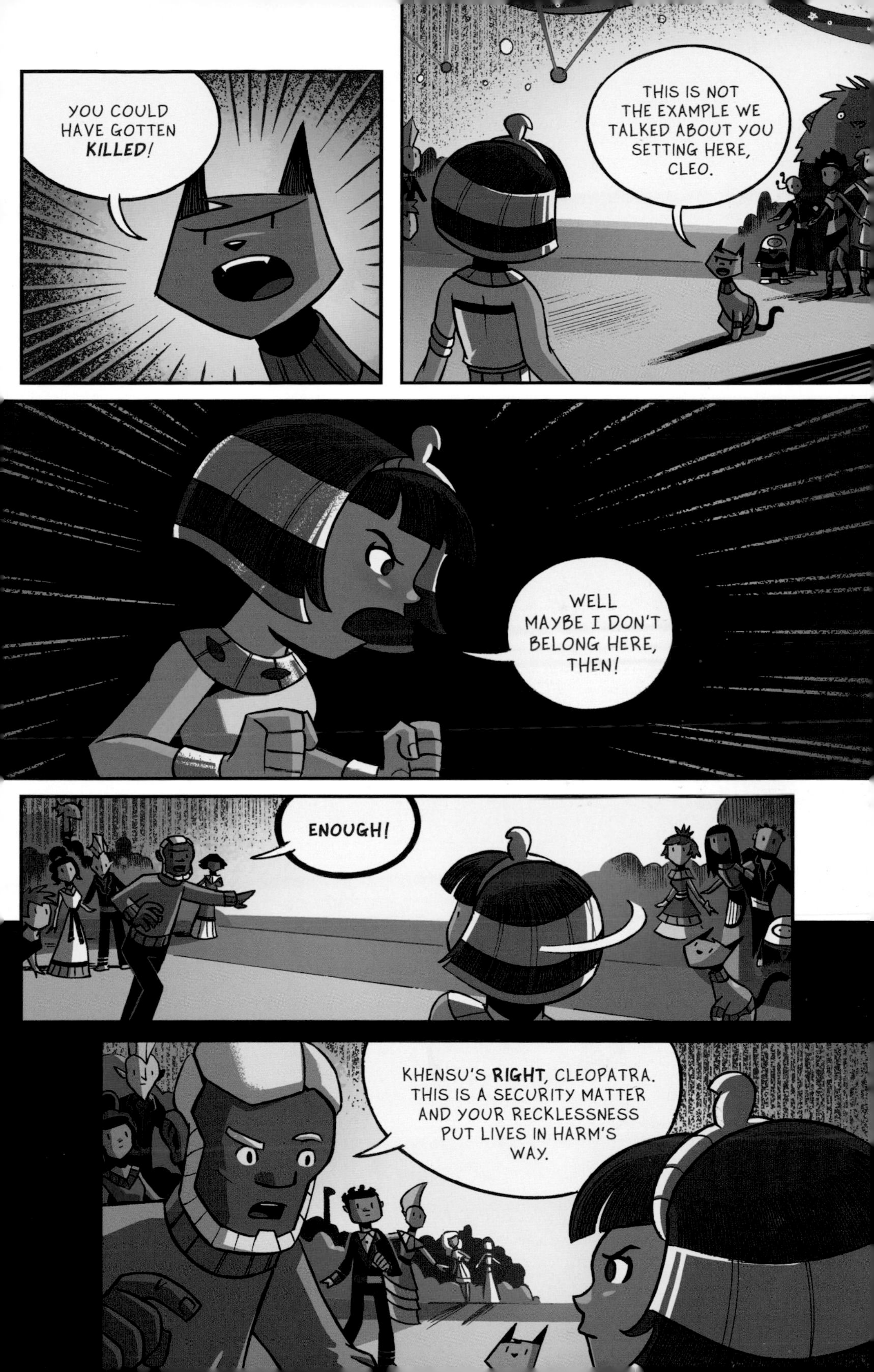
YOU COULD HAVE GOTTEN **KILLED**!
THIS IS NOT THE EXAMPLE WE TALKED ABOUT YOU SETTING HERE, CLEO.
WELL MAYBE I DON'T BELONG HERE, THEN!
ENOUGH!
KHENSU'S **RIGHT**, CLEOPATRA. THIS IS A SECURITY MATTER AND YOUR RECKLESSNESS PUT LIVES IN HARM'S WAY.

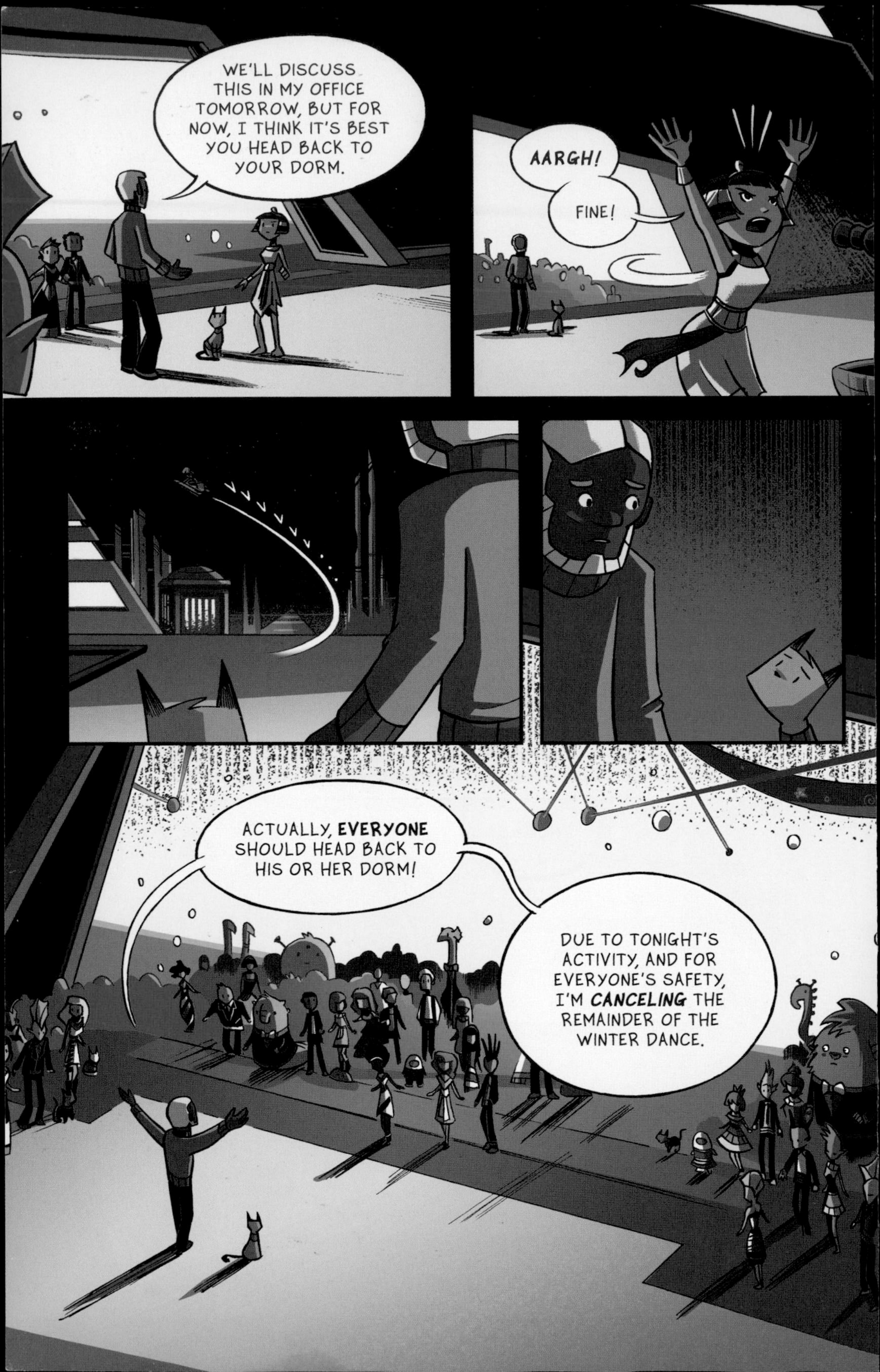
WE'LL DISCUSS THIS IN MY OFFICE TOMORROW, BUT FOR NOW, I THINK IT'S BEST YOU HEAD BACK TO YOUR DORM.
AARGH!
FINE!
ACTUALLY, EVERYONE SHOULD HEAD BACK TO HIS OR HER DORM!
DUE TO TONIGHT'S ACTIVITY, AND FOR EVERYONE'S SAFETY, I'M CANCELING THE REMAINDER OF THE WINTER DANCE.

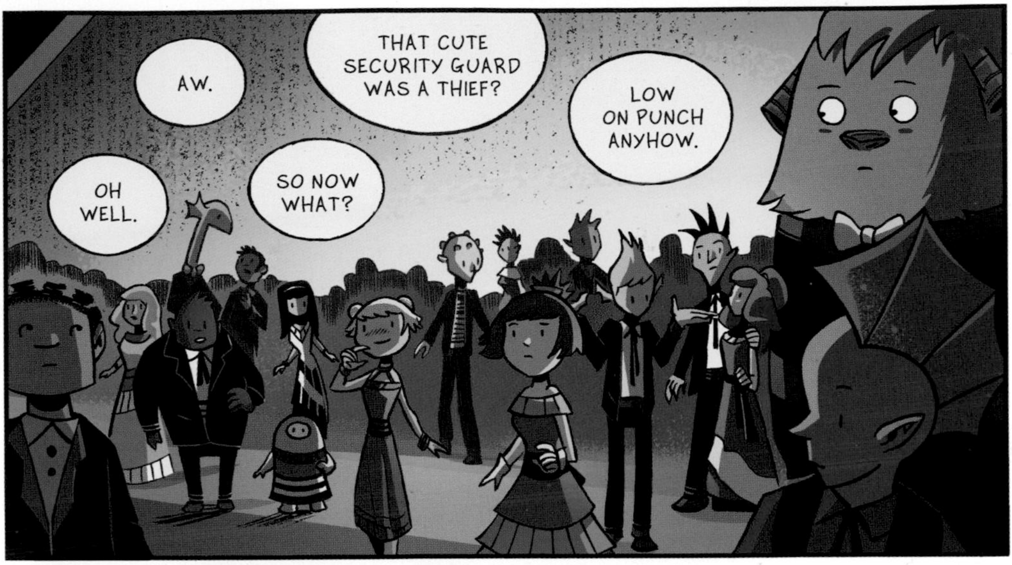
OH WELL.
AW.
SO NOW WHAT?
THAT CUTE SECURITY GUARD WAS A THIEF?
LOW ON PUNCH ANYHOW.

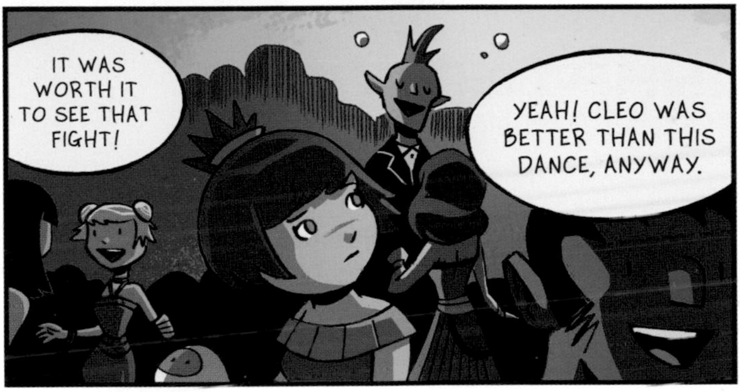
IT WAS WORTH IT TO SEE THAT FIGHT!
YEAH! CLEO WAS BETTER THAN THIS DANCE, ANYWAY.

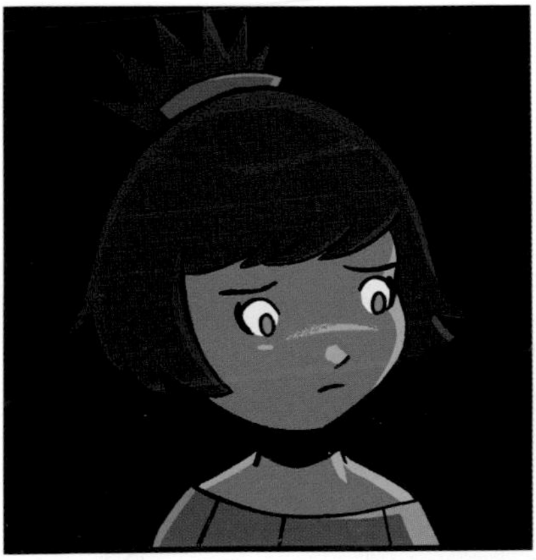

CHAPTER TWO

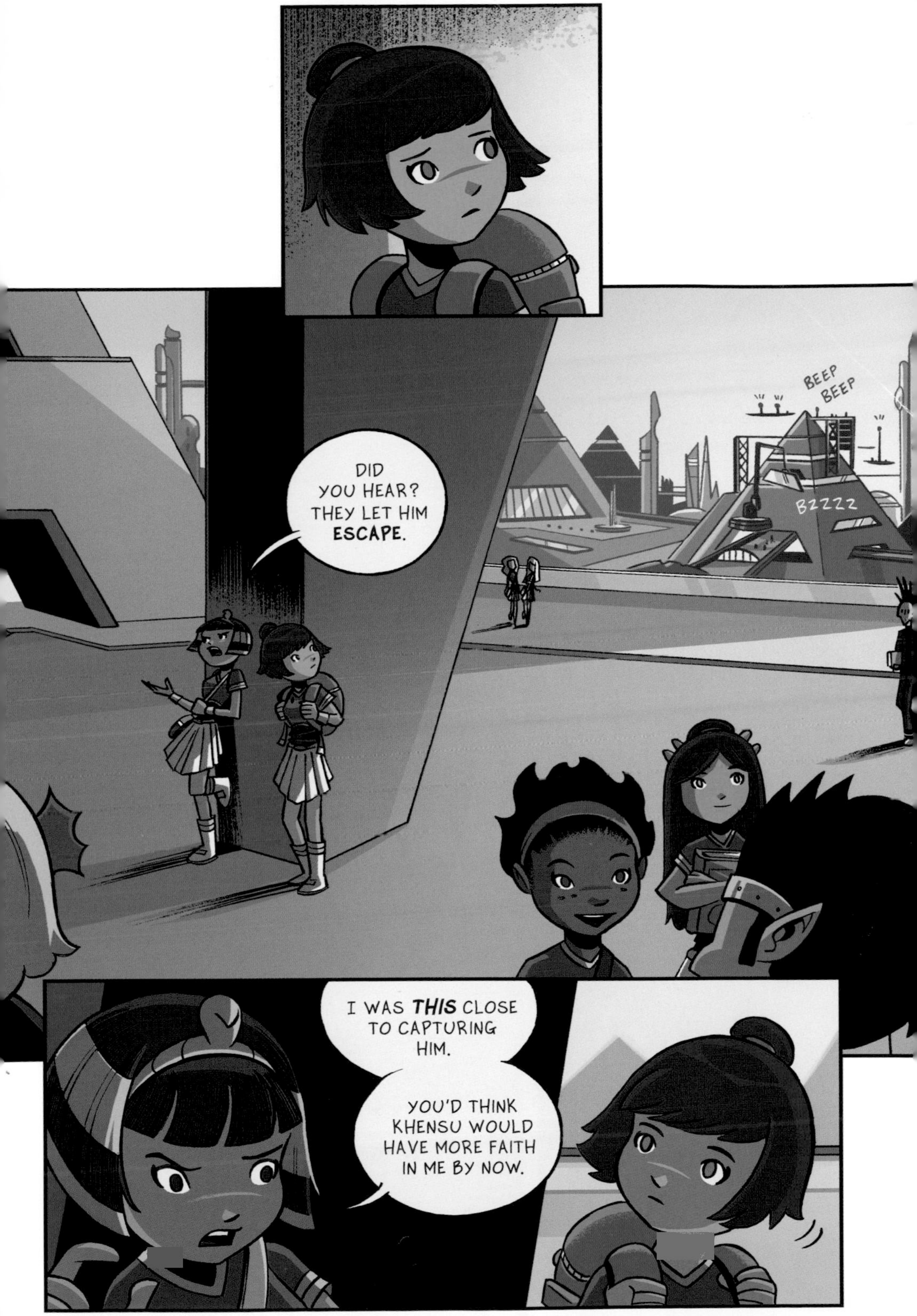
DID YOU HEAR? THEY LET HIM **ESCAPE.**
BEEP BEEP
BZZZZ
I WAS **THIS** CLOSE TO CAPTURING HIM.
YOU'D THINK KHENSU WOULD HAVE MORE FAITH IN ME BY NOW.

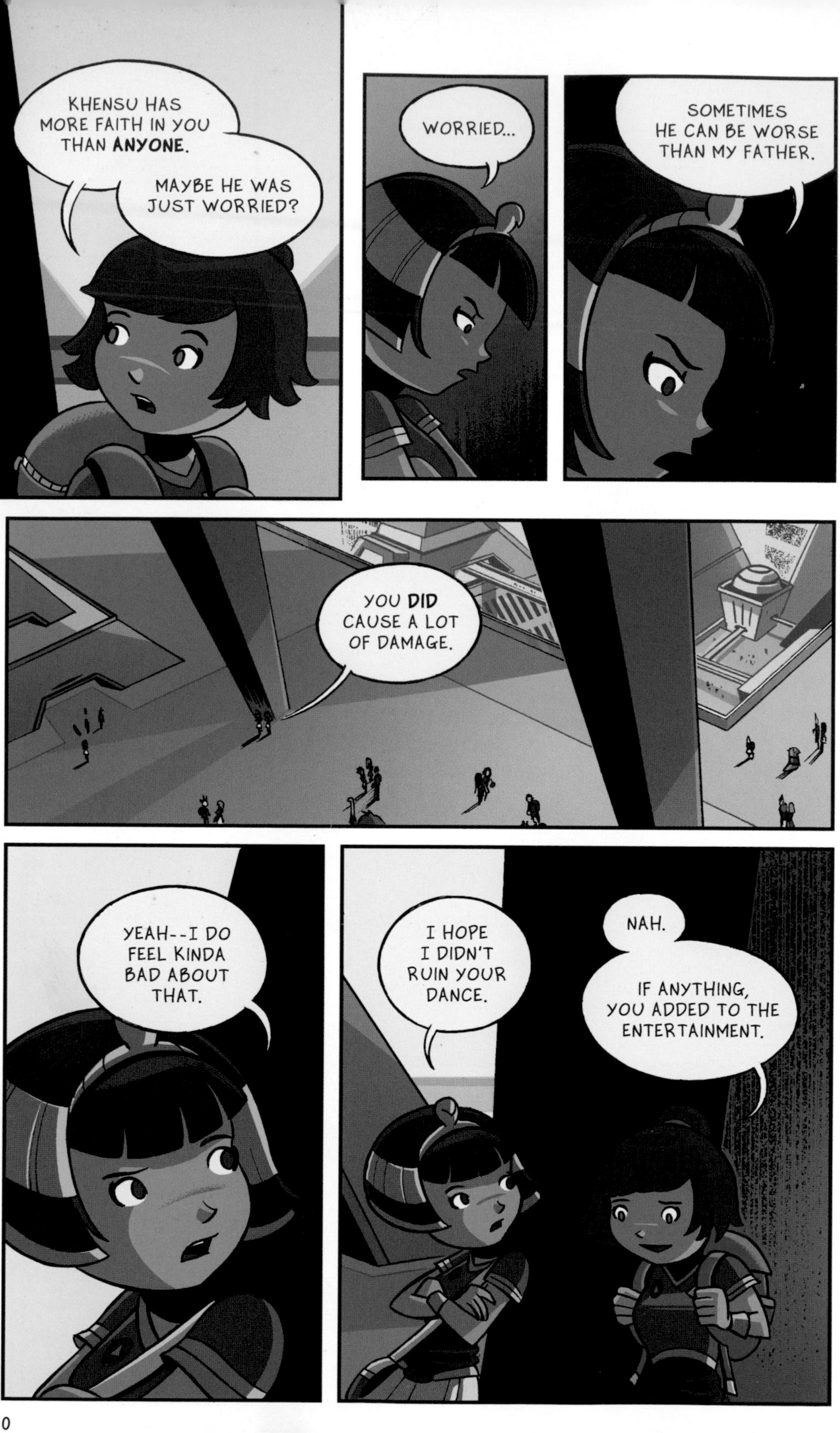
KHENSU HAS MORE FAITH IN YOU THAN **ANYONE**.
MAYBE HE WAS JUST WORRIED?
WORRIED...
SOMETIMES HE CAN BE WORSE THAN MY FATHER.
YOU **DID** CAUSE A LOT OF DAMAGE.
YEAH--I DO FEEL KINDA BAD ABOUT THAT.
I HOPE I DIDN'T RUIN YOUR DANCE.
NAH.
IF ANYTHING, YOU ADDED TO THE ENTERTAINMENT.

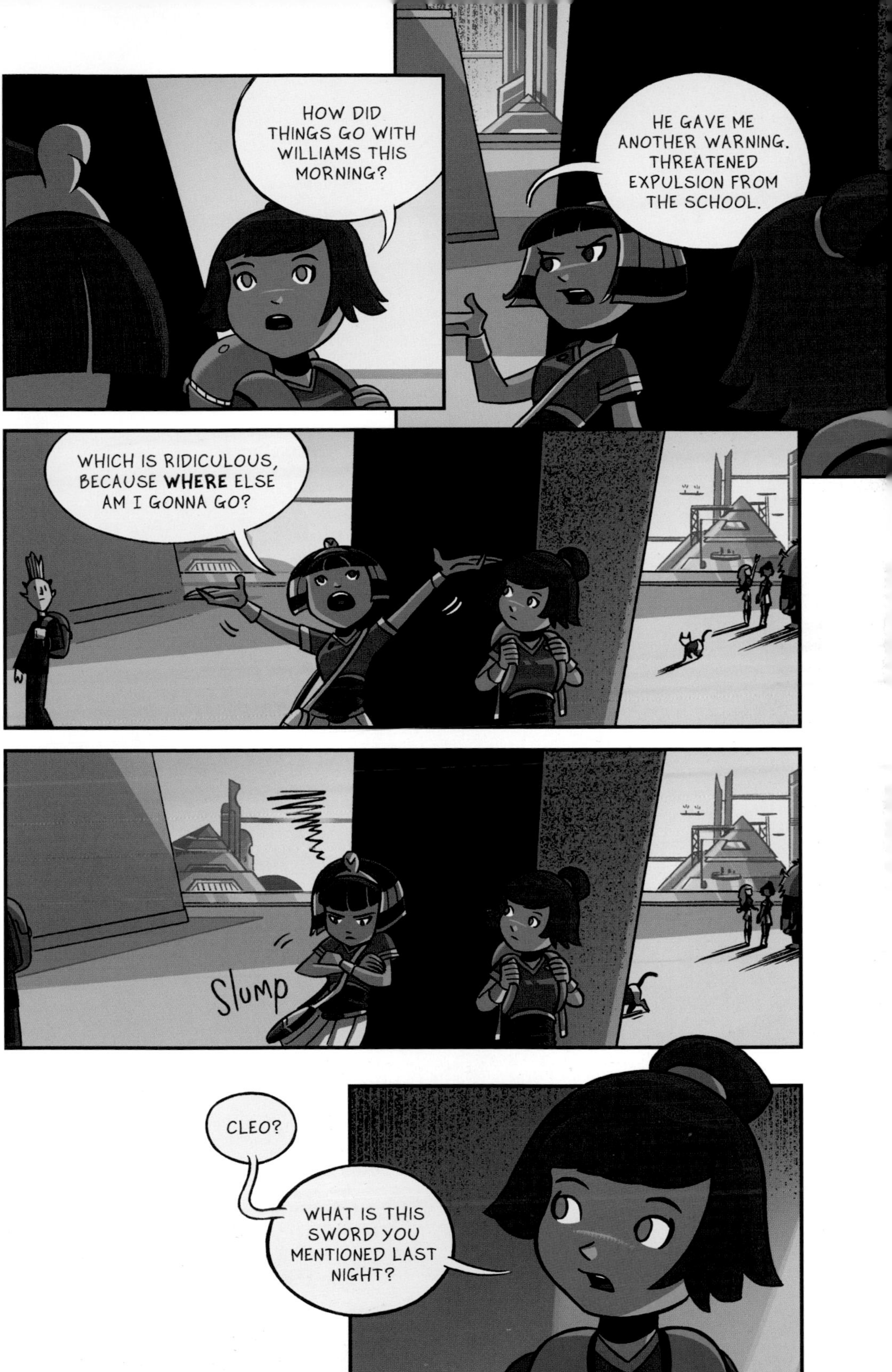
HOW DID THINGS GO WITH WILLIAMS THIS MORNING?
HE GAVE ME ANOTHER WARNING. THREATENED EXPULSION FROM THE SCHOOL.
WHICH IS RIDICULOUS, BECAUSE **WHERE** ELSE AM I GONNA GO?
Slump
CLEO?
WHAT IS THIS SWORD YOU MENTIONED LAST NIGHT?

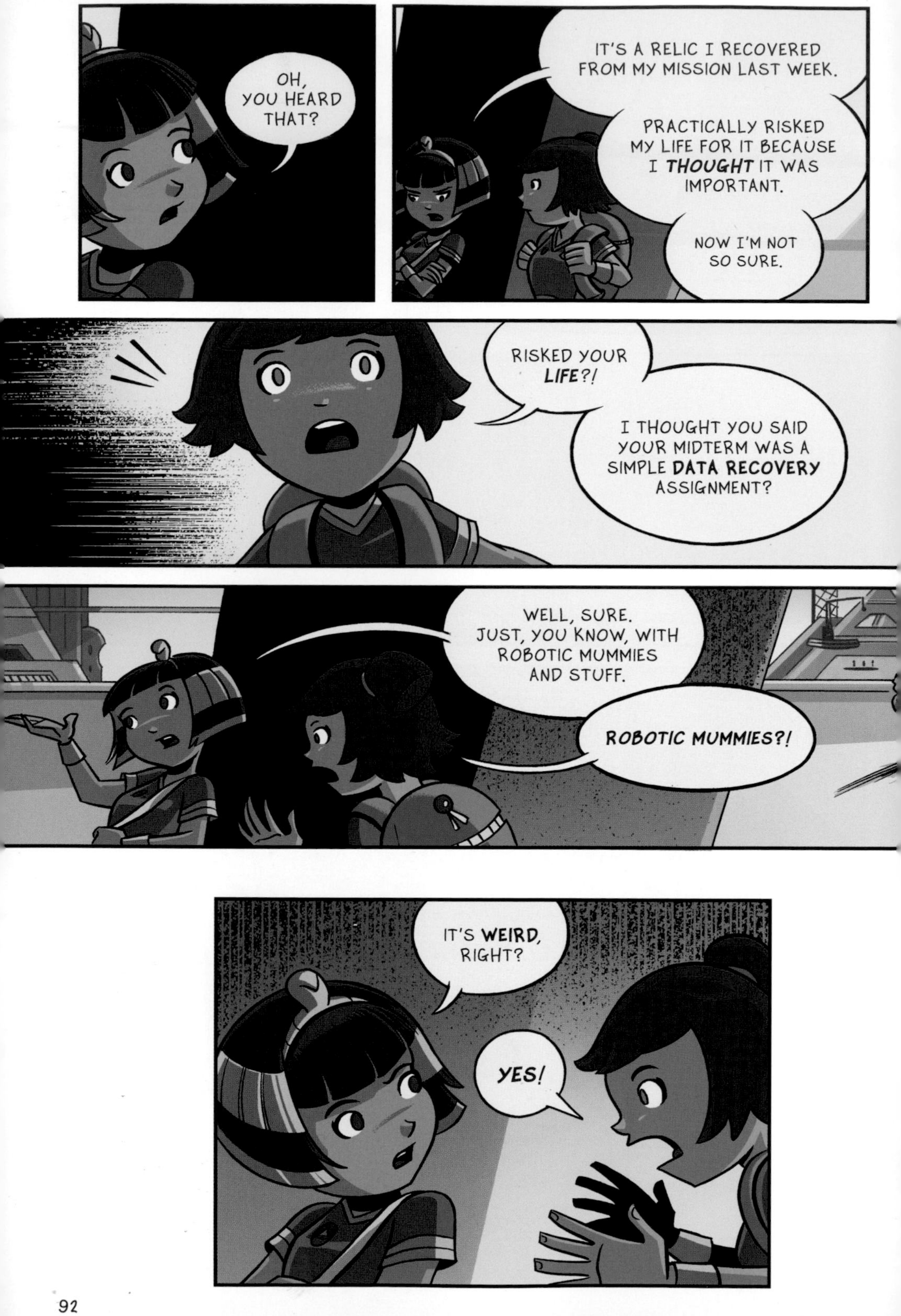
OH, YOU HEARD THAT?
IT'S A RELIC I RECOVERED FROM MY MISSION LAST WEEK.
PRACTICALLY RISKED MY LIFE FOR IT BECAUSE I **THOUGHT** IT WAS IMPORTANT.
NOW I'M NOT SO SURE.
RISKED YOUR **LIFE**?!
I THOUGHT YOU SAID YOUR MIDTERM WAS A SIMPLE **DATA RECOVERY** ASSIGNMENT?
WELL, SURE. JUST, YOU KNOW, WITH ROBOTIC MUMMIES AND STUFF.
ROBOTIC MUMMIES?!
IT'S **WEIRD**, RIGHT?
YES!

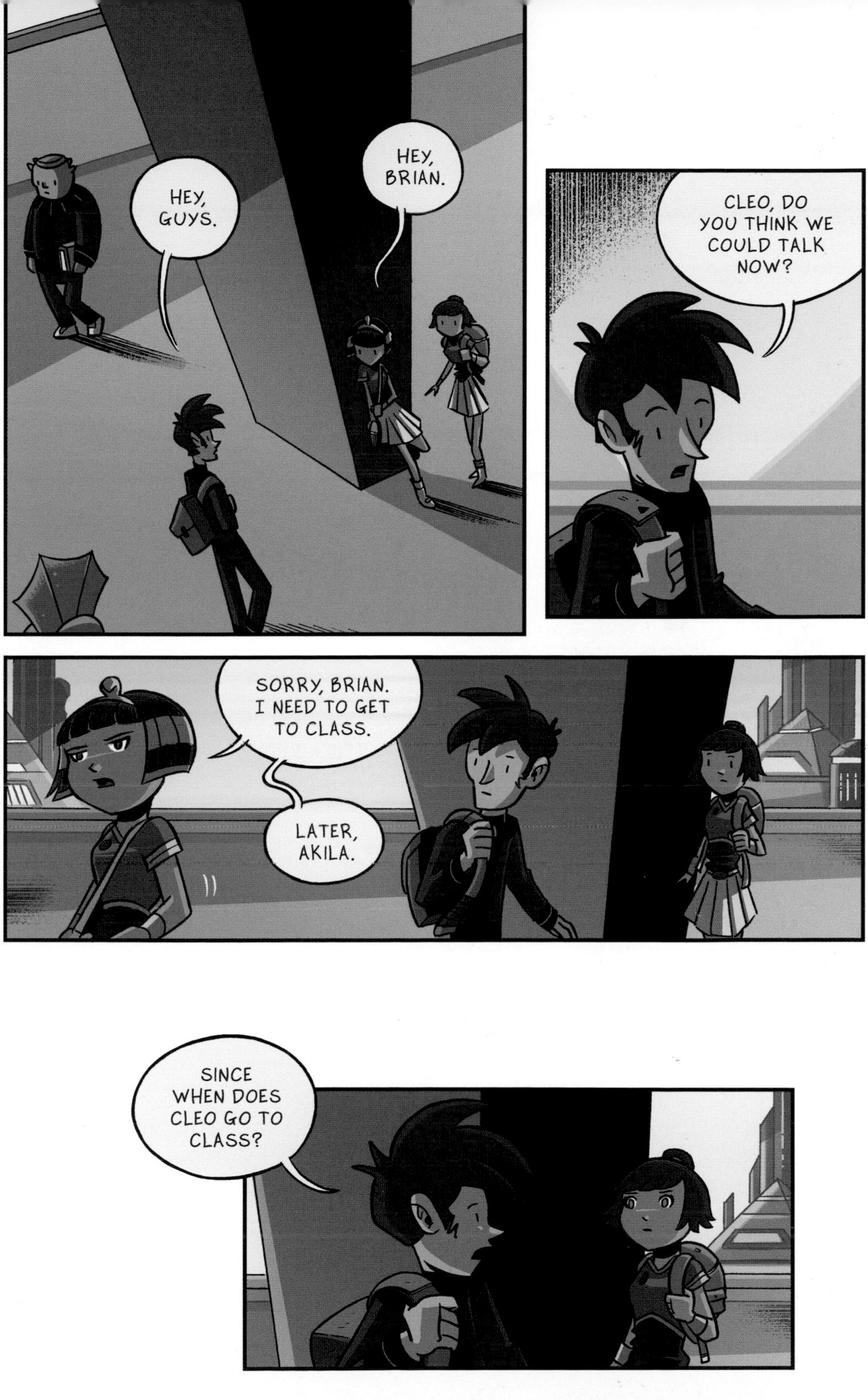
HEY, GUYS.
HEY, BRIAN.
CLEO, DO YOU THINK WE COULD TALK NOW?
SORRY, BRIAN. I NEED TO GET TO CLASS.
LATER, AKILA.
SINCE WHEN DOES CLEO GO TO CLASS?

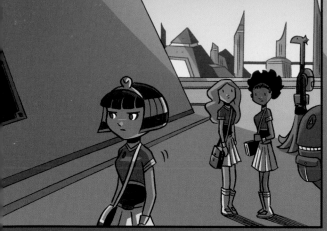

CLEOPATRA HAS ARRIVED!

REMEMBER THE WORDS OF THE SCROLL
(PHARAOH YASIRO TRANSLATION)

A HERO WILL ARRIVE FROM EARTH.
DAUGHTER OF AULETES, DESCENDANT OF SOTER.
WHEN THE MOON OF DUAT HAS TOUCHED ITS PEAK
ON THE EVE OF THE GOLDEN LION.

SHE WILL WEAR THE CROWN OF THE IBIS.
SHE WILL JOIN IN YOUR FIGHT.
SHE WILL CONTAIN LOST KNOWLEDGE.
SHE WILL OFFER HOPE FROM YOUR BLIGHT.
THE SERPENT WILL FALL BY HER SWORD.
THE APE WILL COWER BY HER MIGHT.
THE SPIDER WILL GROW DEAF BY HER WORD.
THE JACKAL WILL COLLAPSE BY HER SIGHT.

SHE WILL COMMAND THE ARMIES OF FIRE.
SHE WILL COMMAND THE NIGHT.
SHE WILL EXTINGUISH AN EMPIRE.
SHE WILL PUT AN END TO THEIR PLIGHT.
FEAR HAS BEEN BANISHED.
BLACKNESS BURNS WHITE.
SING PRAISES TO THE QUEEN OF THE NILE!
FOR SHE HAS TURNED DARKNESS TO LIGHT.

CLEO!

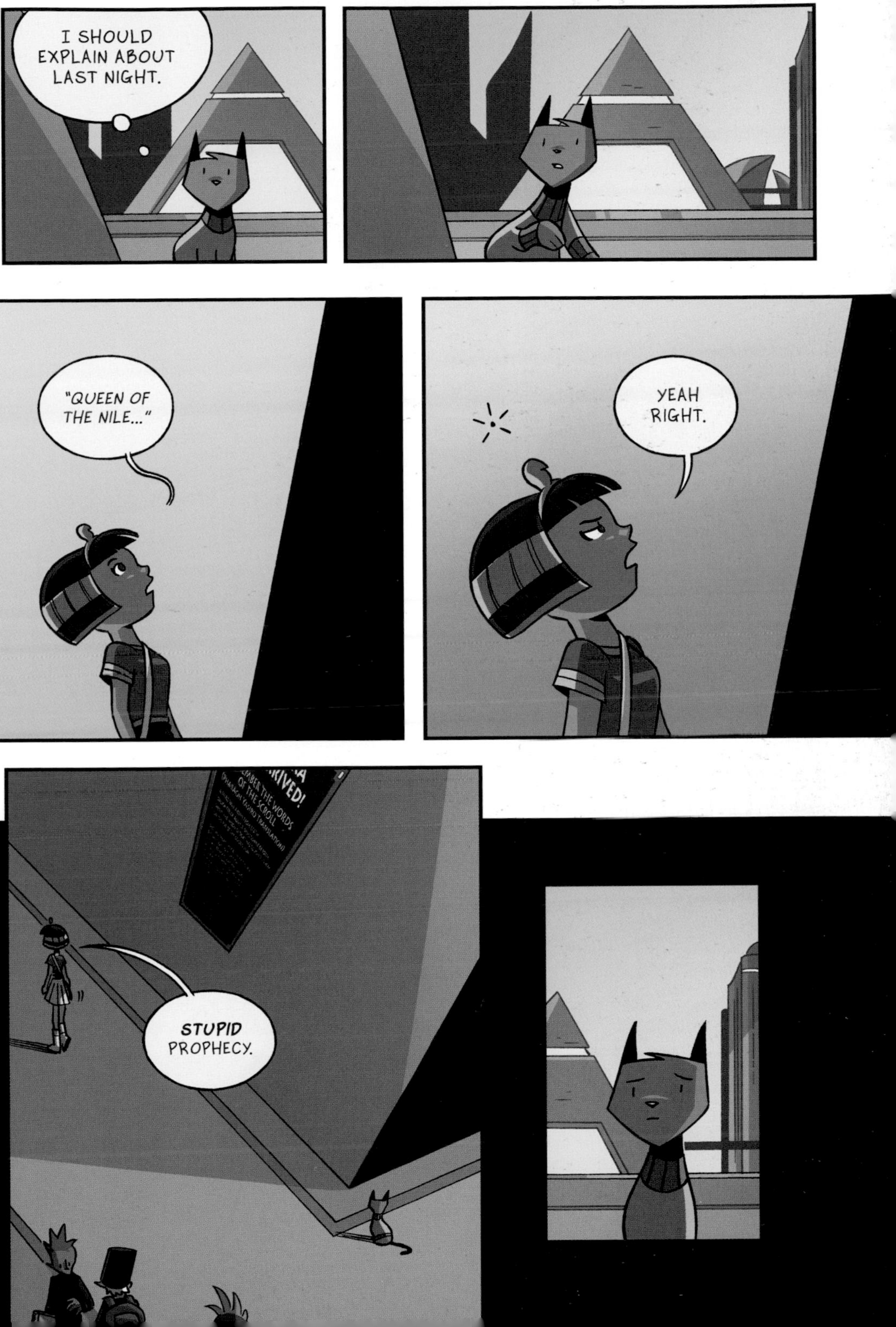
I SHOULD EXPLAIN ABOUT LAST NIGHT.
"QUEEN OF THE NILE..."
YEAH RIGHT.
STUPID PROPHECY.

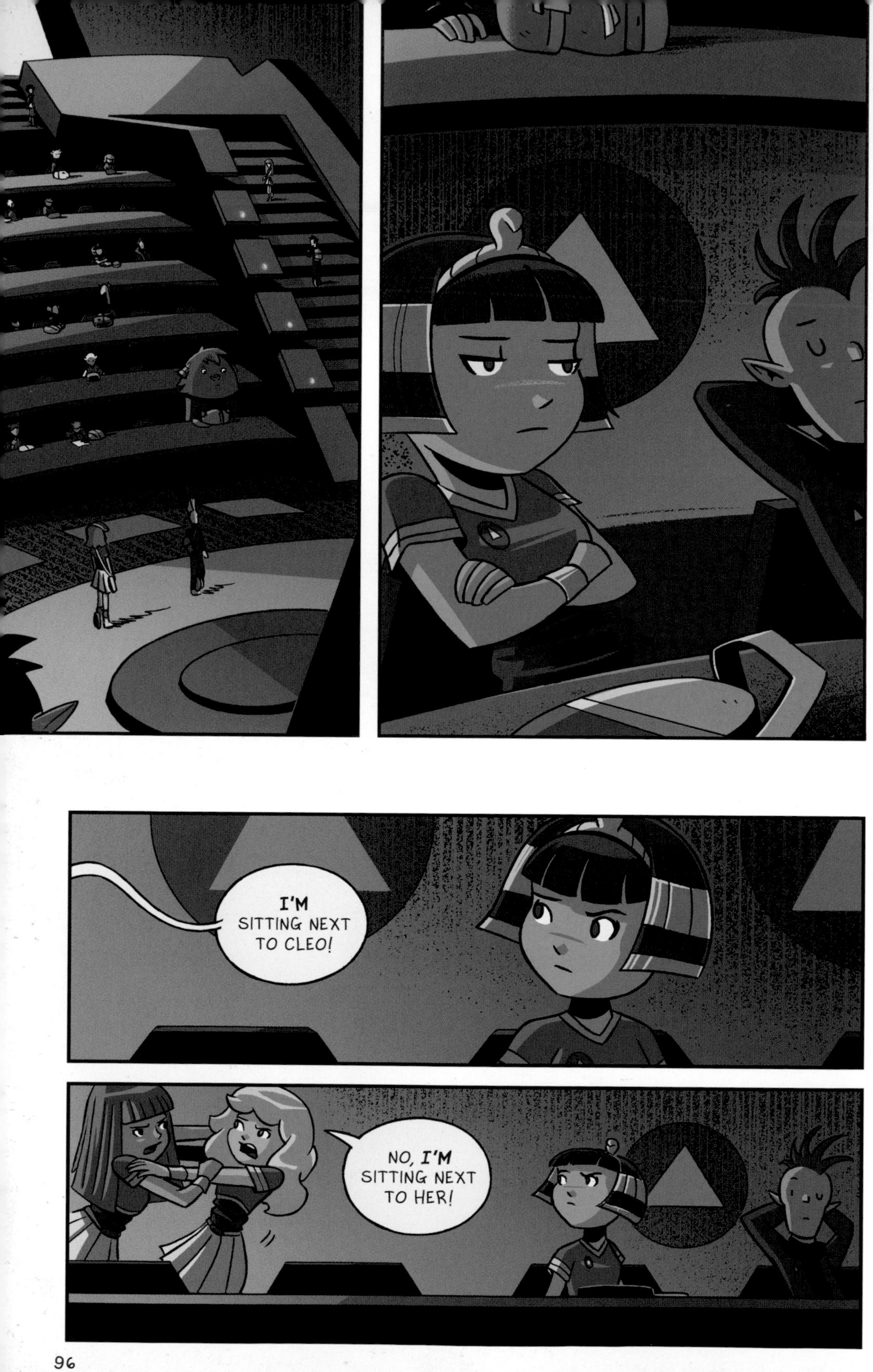
I'M SITTING NEXT TO CLEO!
NO, I'M SITTING NEXT TO HER!

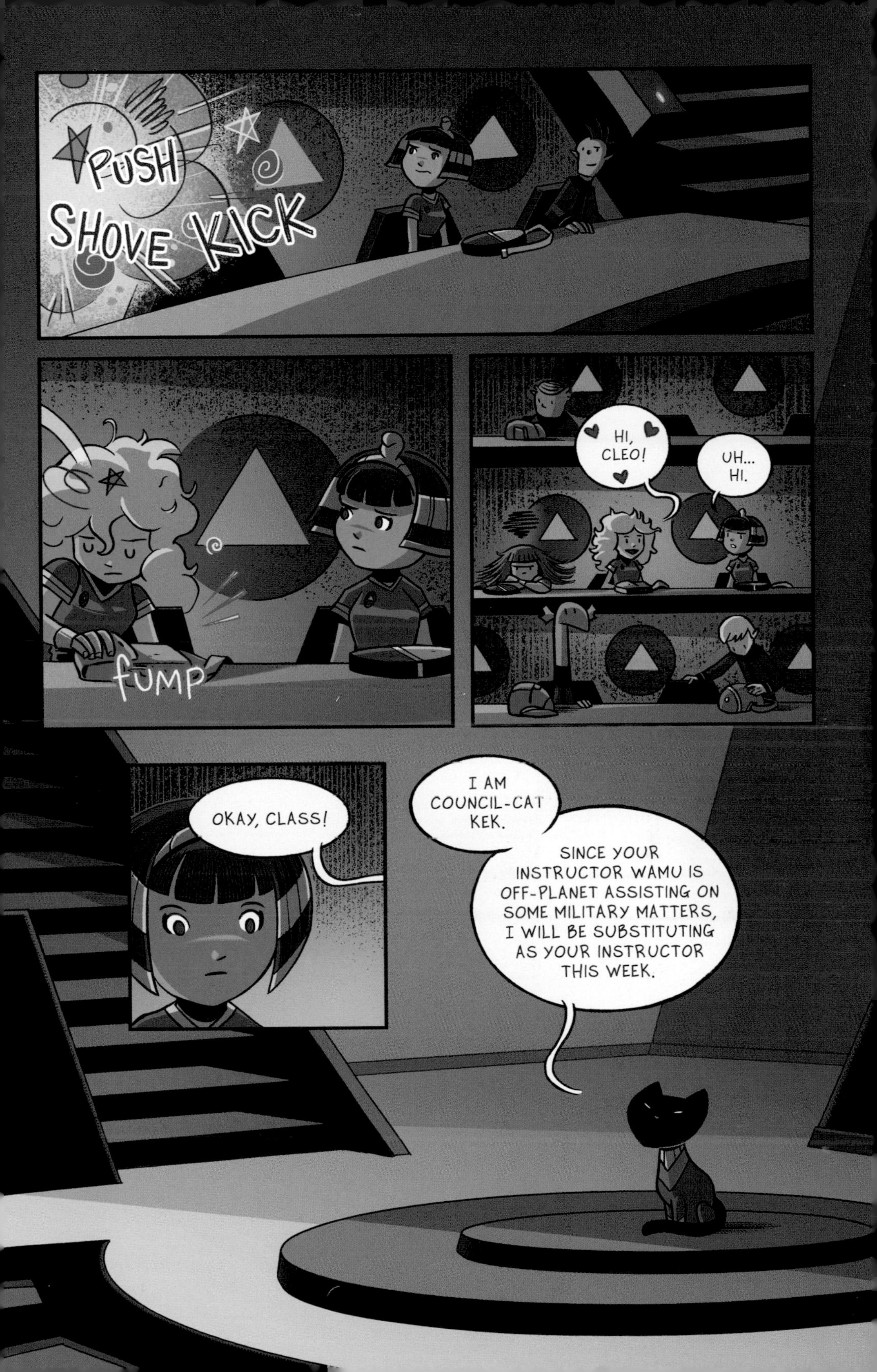
PUSH
SHOVE
KICK
fUMP
HI, CLEO!
UH... HI.
OKAY, CLASS!
I AM COUNCIL-CAT KEK.
SINCE YOUR INSTRUCTOR WAMU IS OFF-PLANET ASSISTING ON SOME MILITARY MATTERS, I WILL BE SUBSTITUTING AS YOUR INSTRUCTOR THIS WEEK.

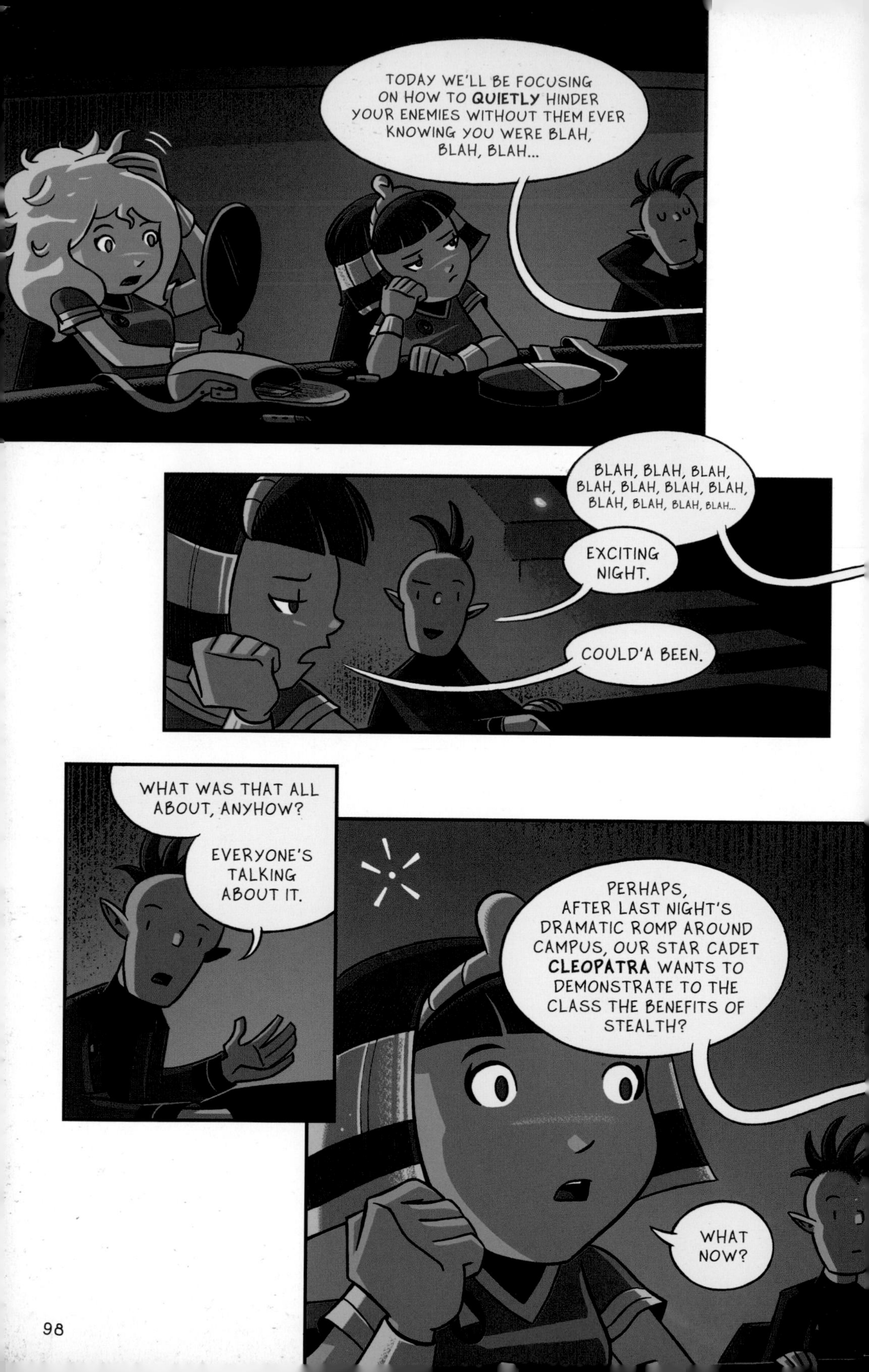
TODAY WE'LL BE FOCUSING ON HOW TO **QUIETLY** HINDER YOUR ENEMIES WITHOUT THEM EVER KNOWING YOU WERE BLAH, BLAH, BLAH...
BLAH, BLAH, BLAH, BLAH, BLAH, BLAH, BLAH, BLAH, BLAH, BLAH, BLAH...
EXCITING NIGHT.
COULD'A BEEN.
WHAT WAS THAT ALL ABOUT, ANYHOW?
EVERYONE'S TALKING ABOUT IT.
PERHAPS, AFTER LAST NIGHT'S DRAMATIC ROMP AROUND CAMPUS, OUR STAR CADET **CLEOPATRA** WANTS TO DEMONSTRATE TO THE CLASS THE BENEFITS OF STEALTH?
WHAT NOW?

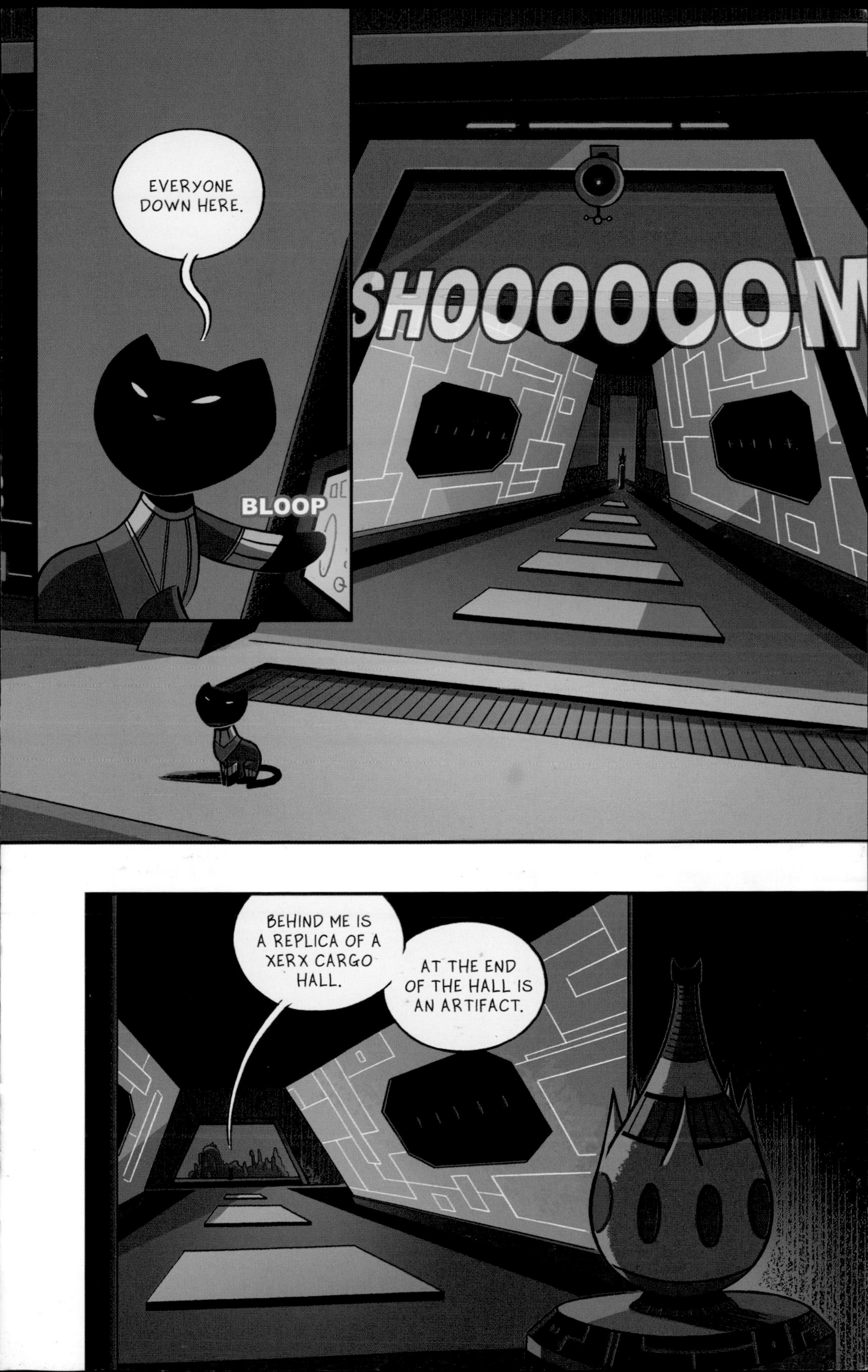
EVERYONE DOWN HERE.
BLOOP
SHOOOOOOOM
BEHIND ME IS A REPLICA OF A XERX CARGO HALL.
AT THE END OF THE HALL IS AN ARTIFACT.

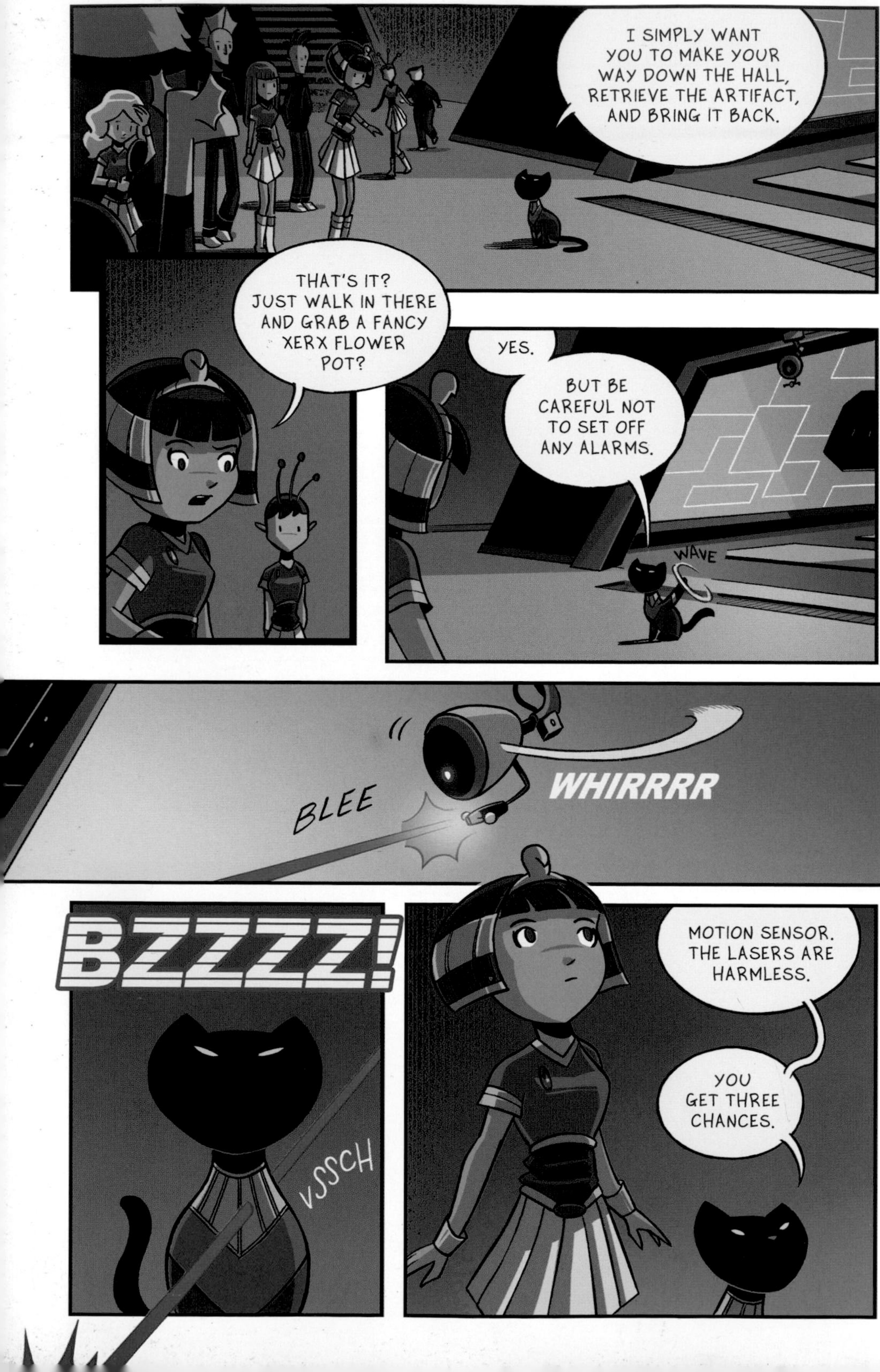

I SIMPLY WANT YOU TO MAKE YOUR WAY DOWN THE HALL, RETRIEVE THE ARTIFACT, AND BRING IT BACK.
THAT'S IT? JUST WALK IN THERE AND GRAB A FANCY XERX FLOWER POT?
YES.
BUT BE CAREFUL NOT TO SET OFF ANY ALARMS.
WAVE
WHIRRRR
BLEE
BZZZZ!
VSSCH
MOTION SENSOR. THE LASERS ARE HARMLESS.
YOU GET THREE CHANCES.

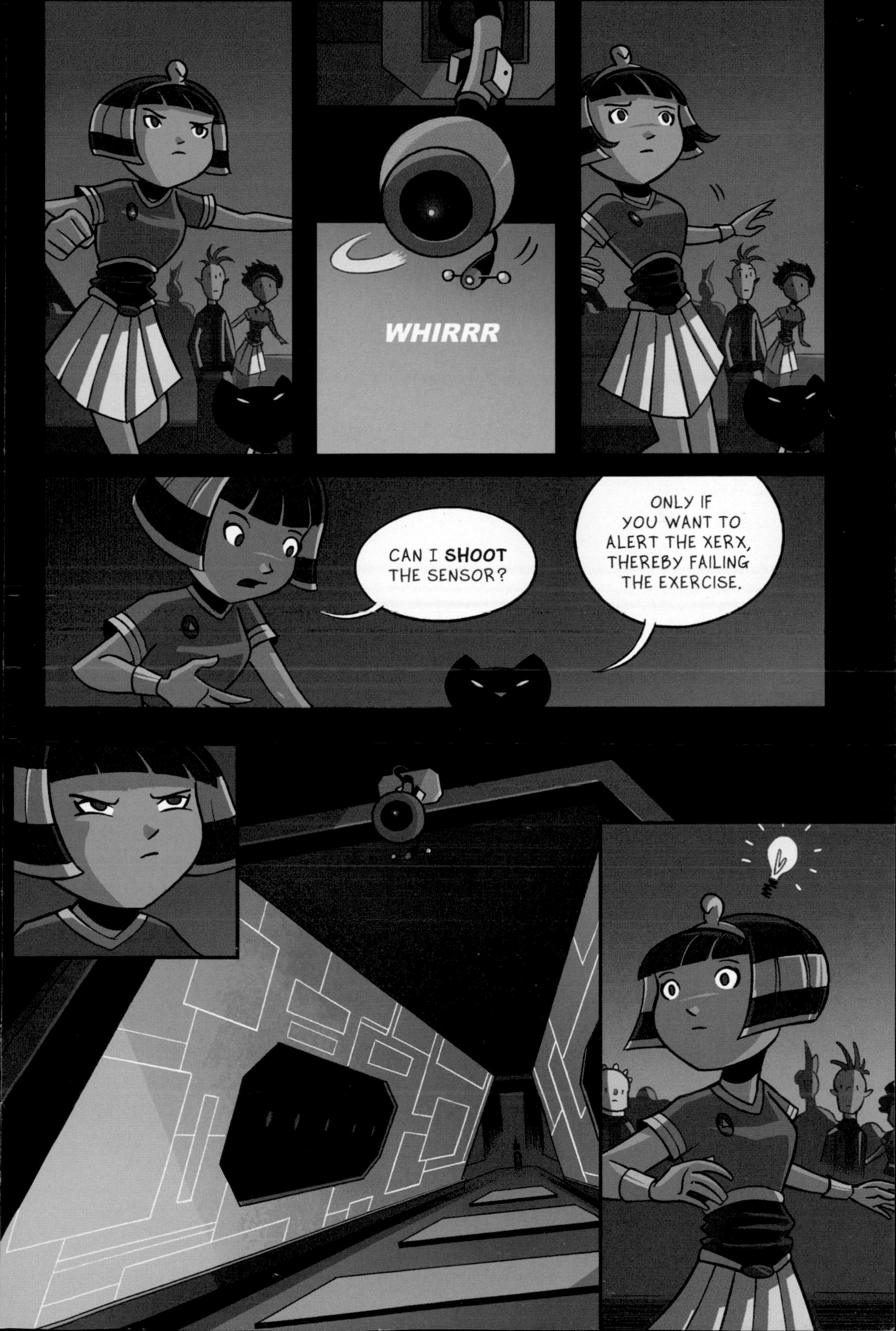
WHIRRR
CAN I SHOOT THE SENSOR?
ONLY IF YOU WANT TO ALERT THE XERX, THEREBY FAILING THE EXERCISE.

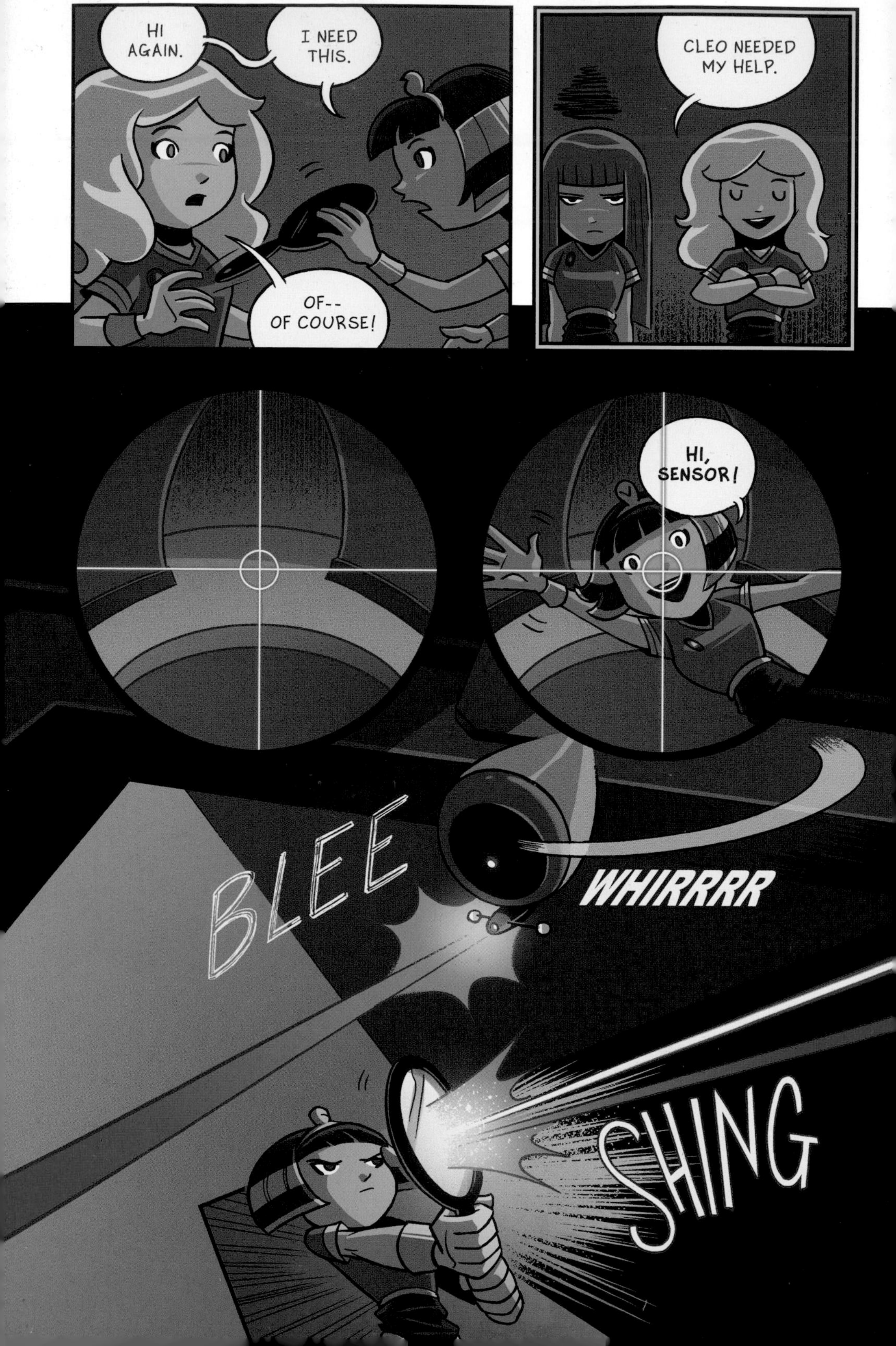
HI AGAIN.
I NEED THIS.
OF-- OF COURSE!
CLEO NEEDED MY HELP.
HI, SENSOR!
BLEE
WHIRRRR
SHING

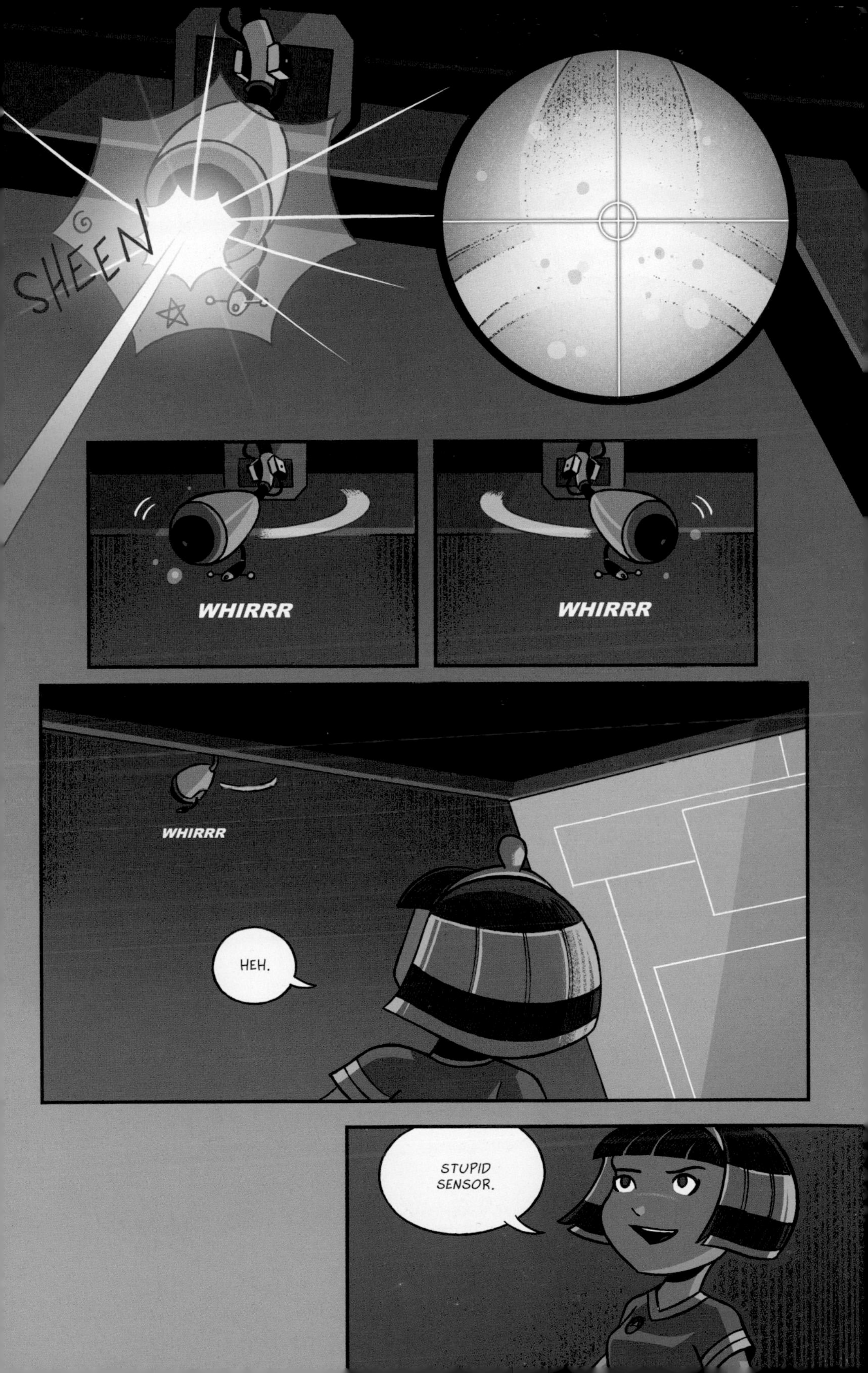
SHEEN
WHIRRR
WHIRRR
WHIRRR
HEH.
STUPID SENSOR.

WOW!

GO CLEO!

THIS IS GONNA BE A PIECE OF CAKE.

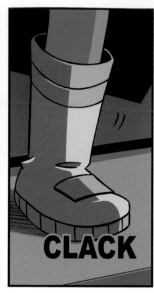

CLACK

BZZZZZZ

?

WEIGHT SENSOR. STRIKE **ONE**.

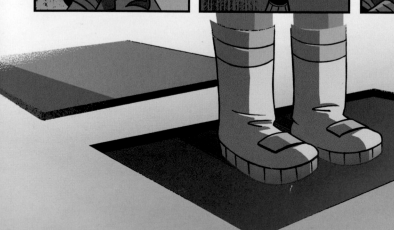

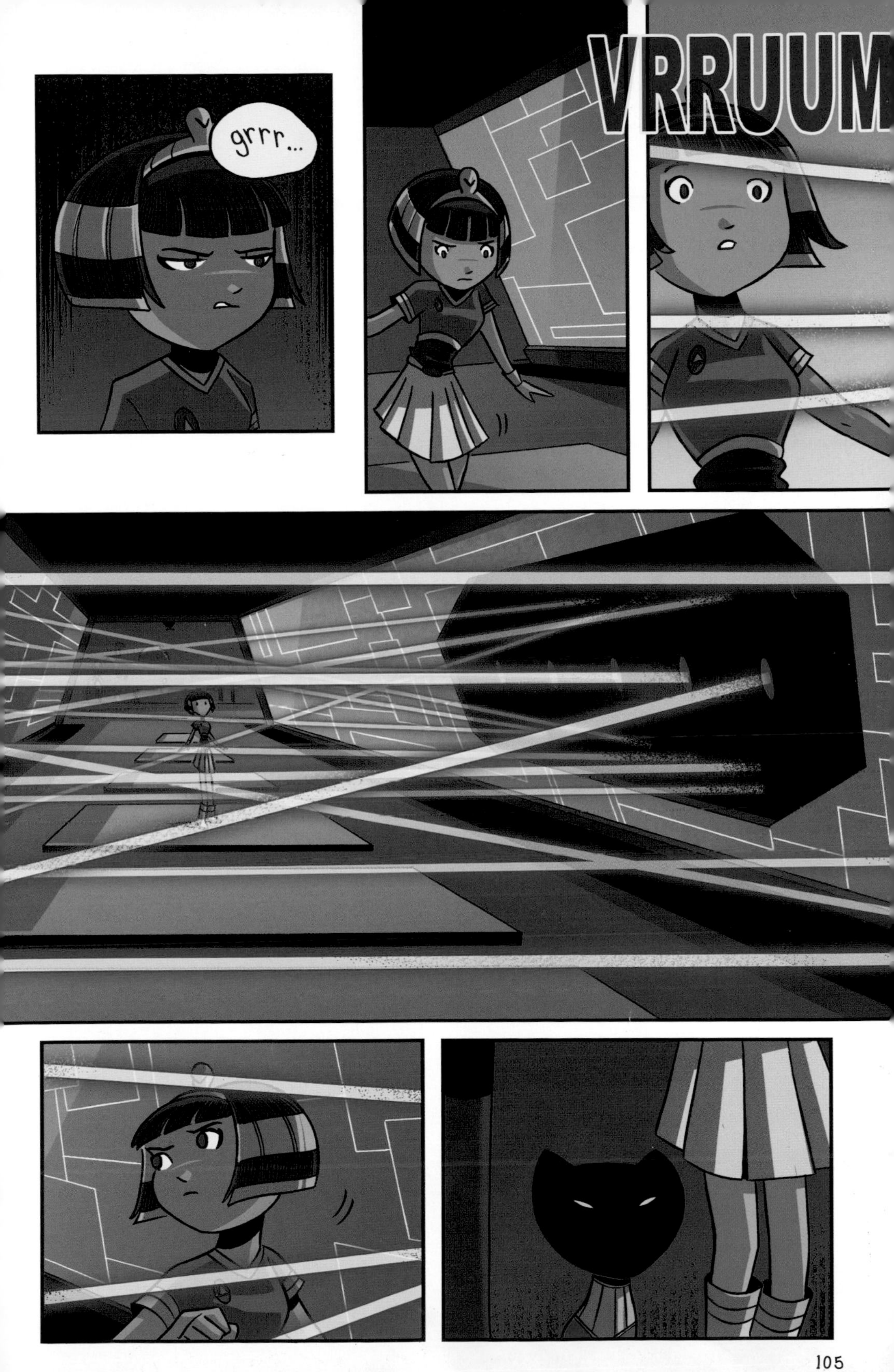
grrr...
VRRUUM

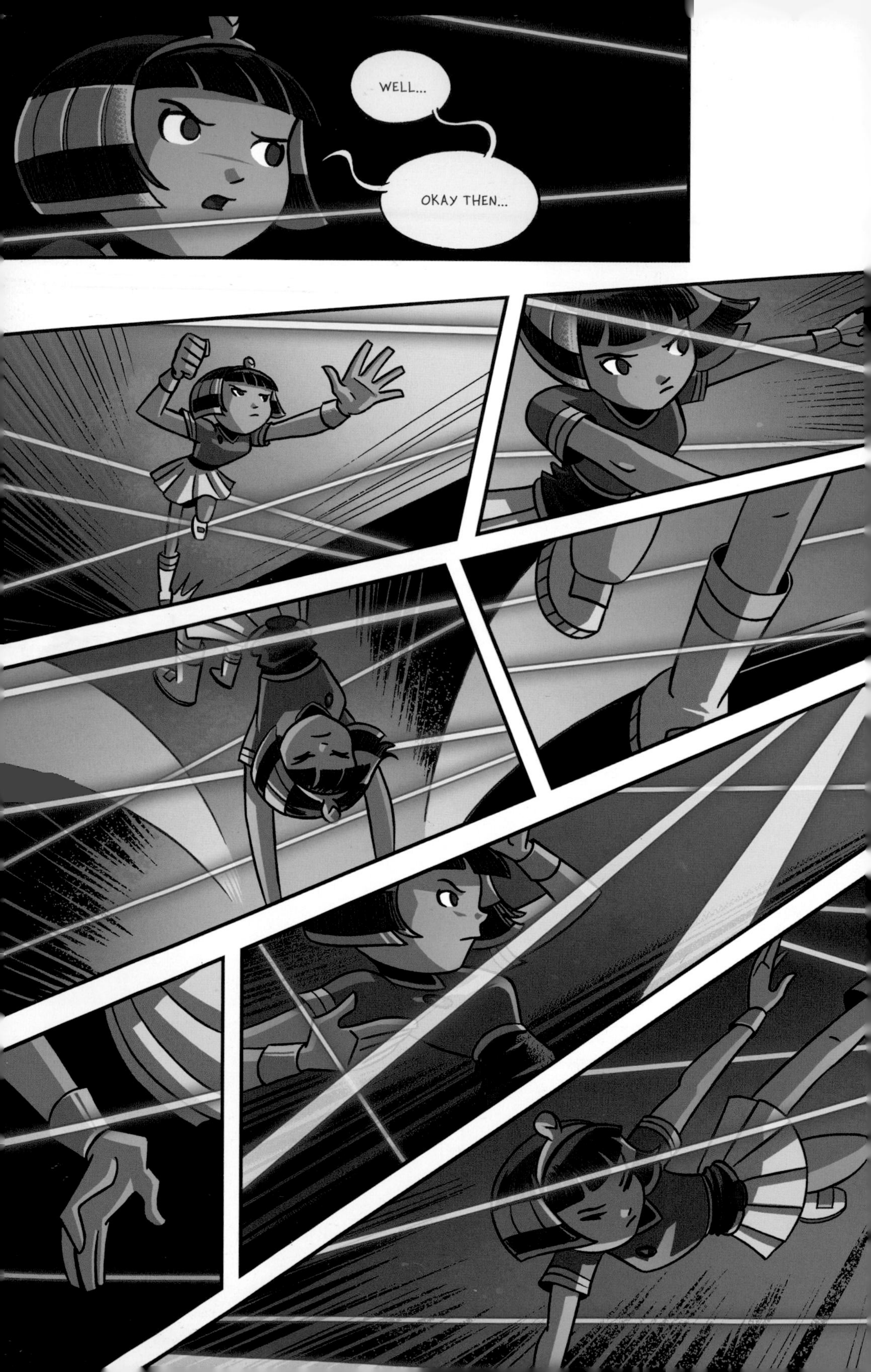
WELL...
OKAY THEN...

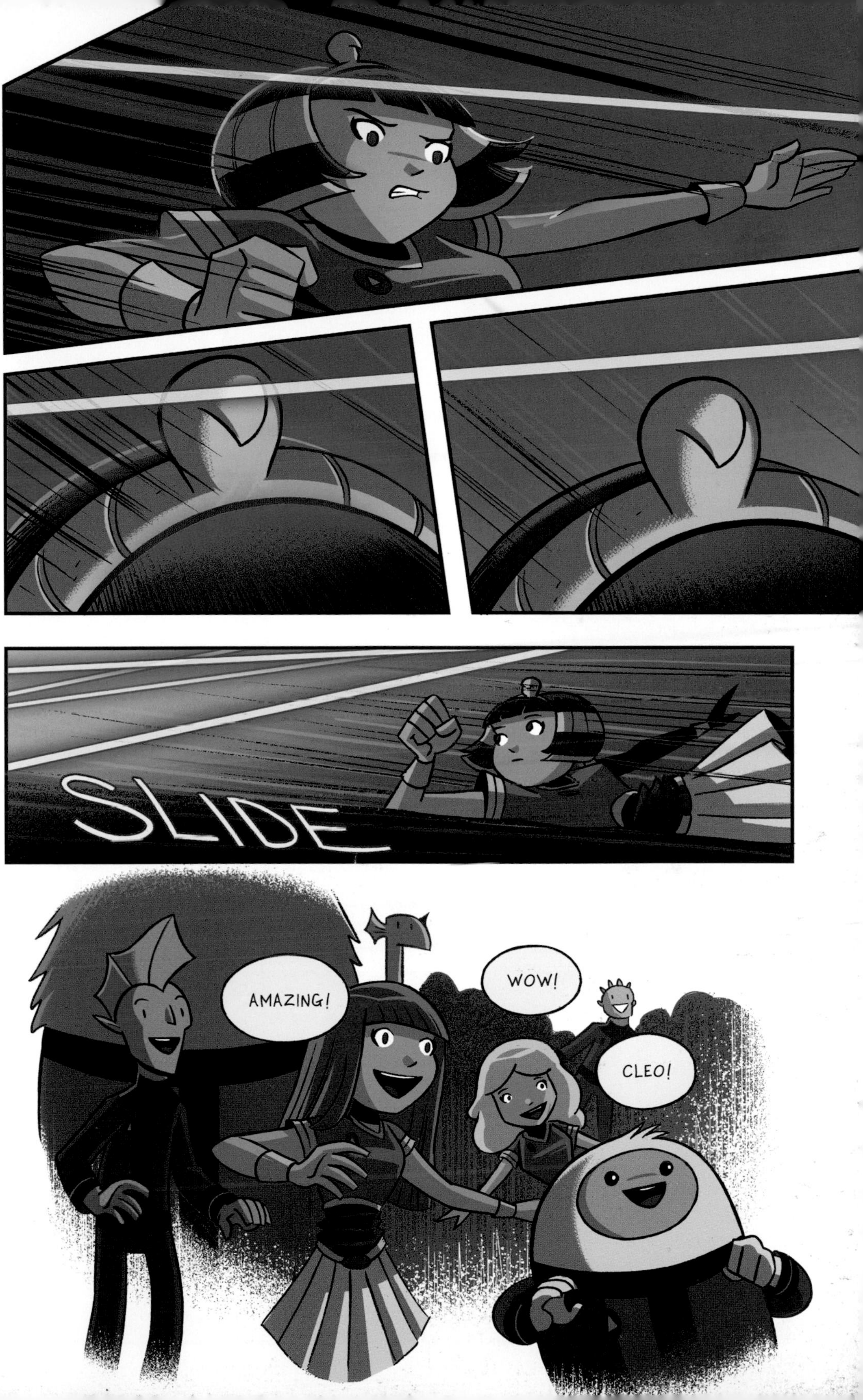
SLIDE
AMAZING!
WOW!
CLEO!

HUH.

CLACK **BZZZ**

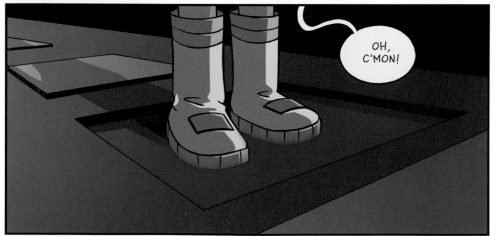

OH, C'MON!

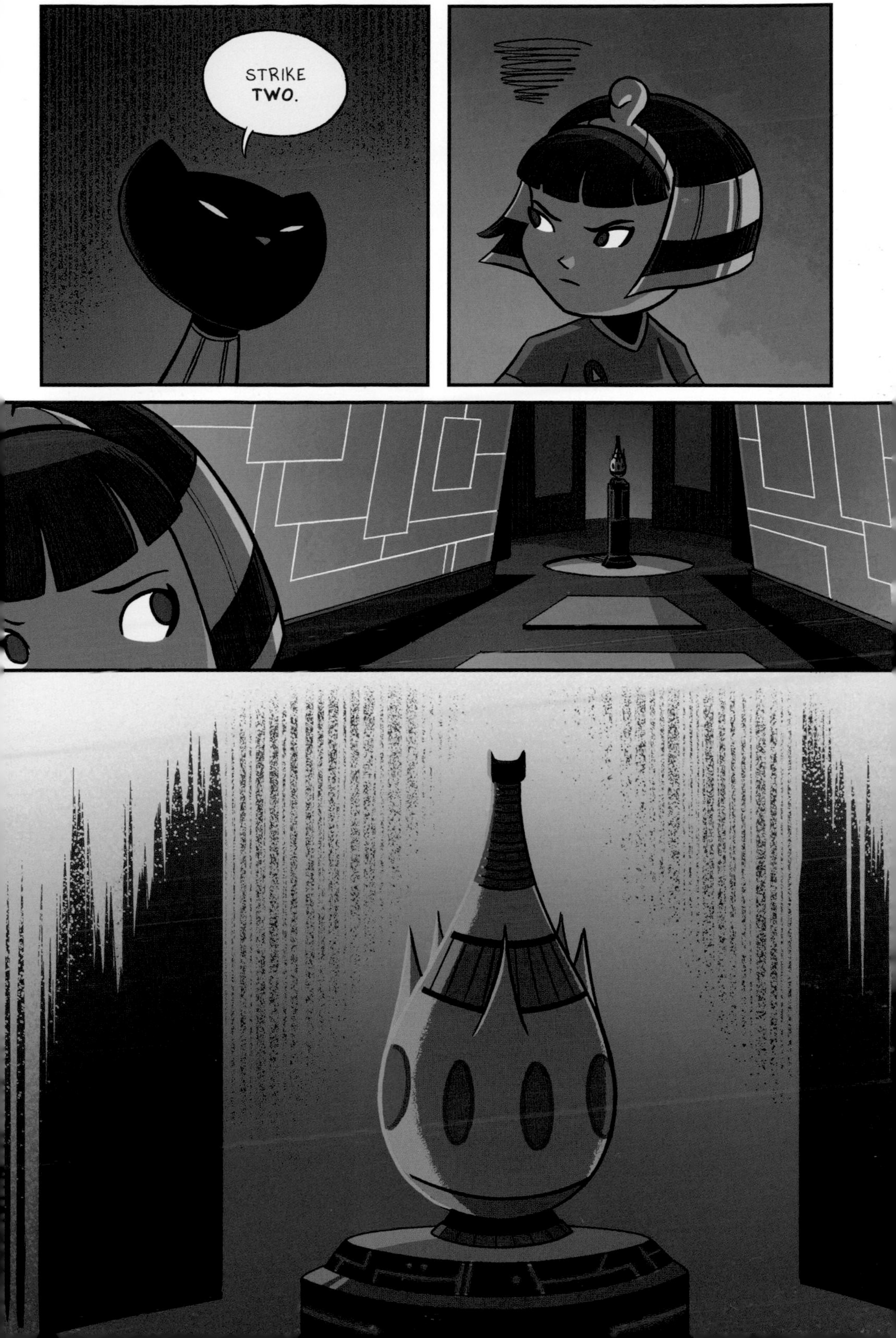
STRIKE TWO.

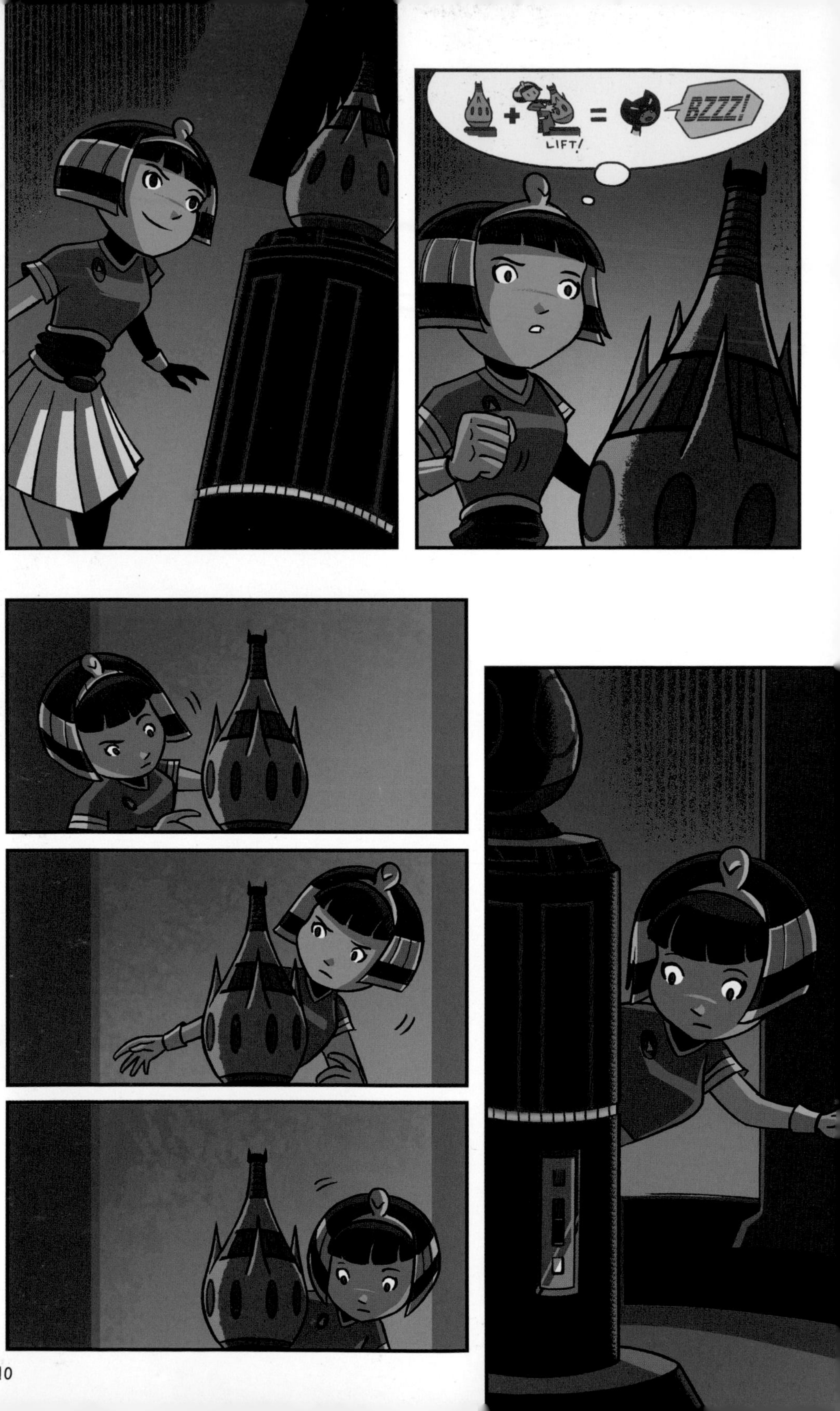
LIFT!
BZZZ!

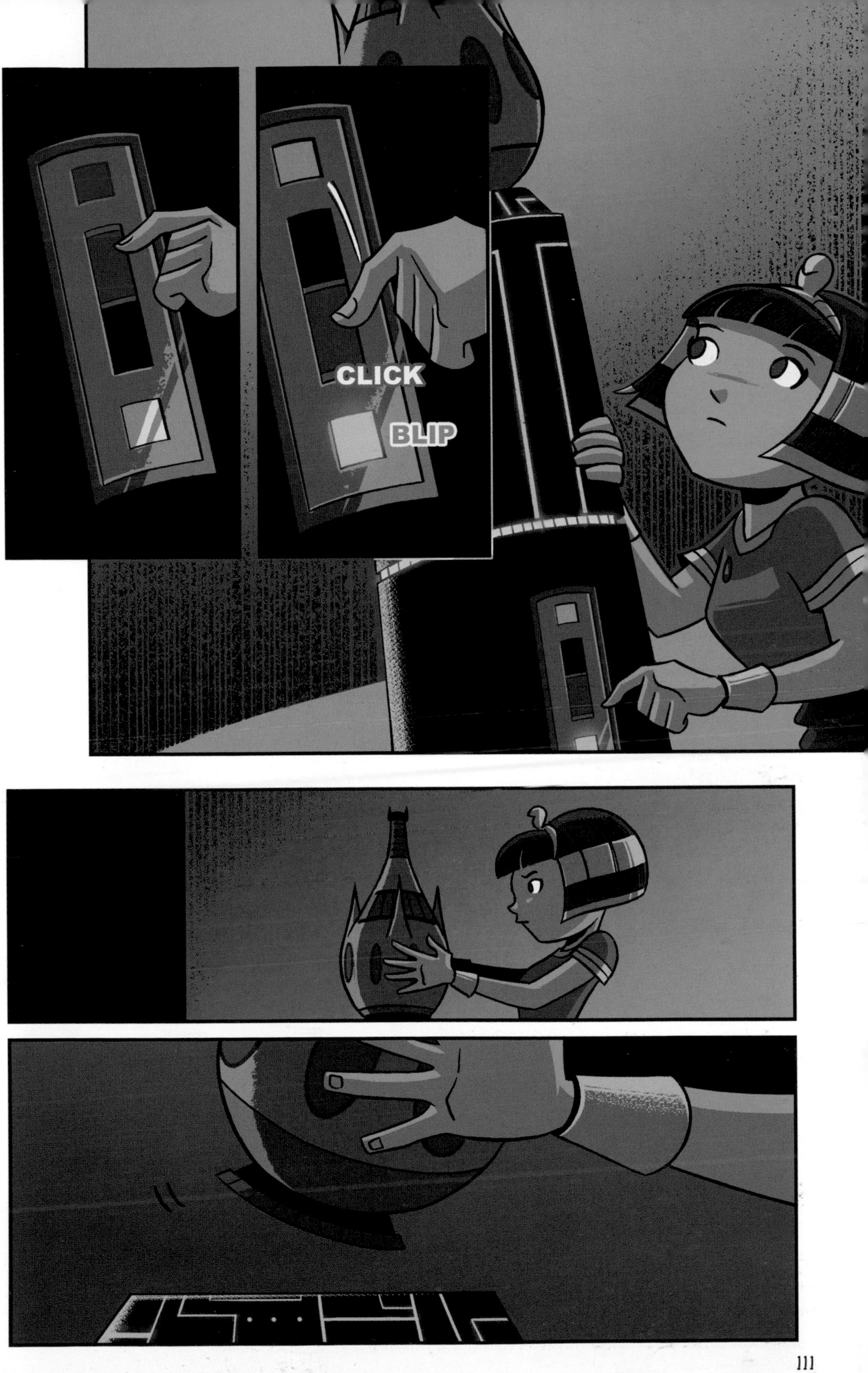
CLICK
BLIP

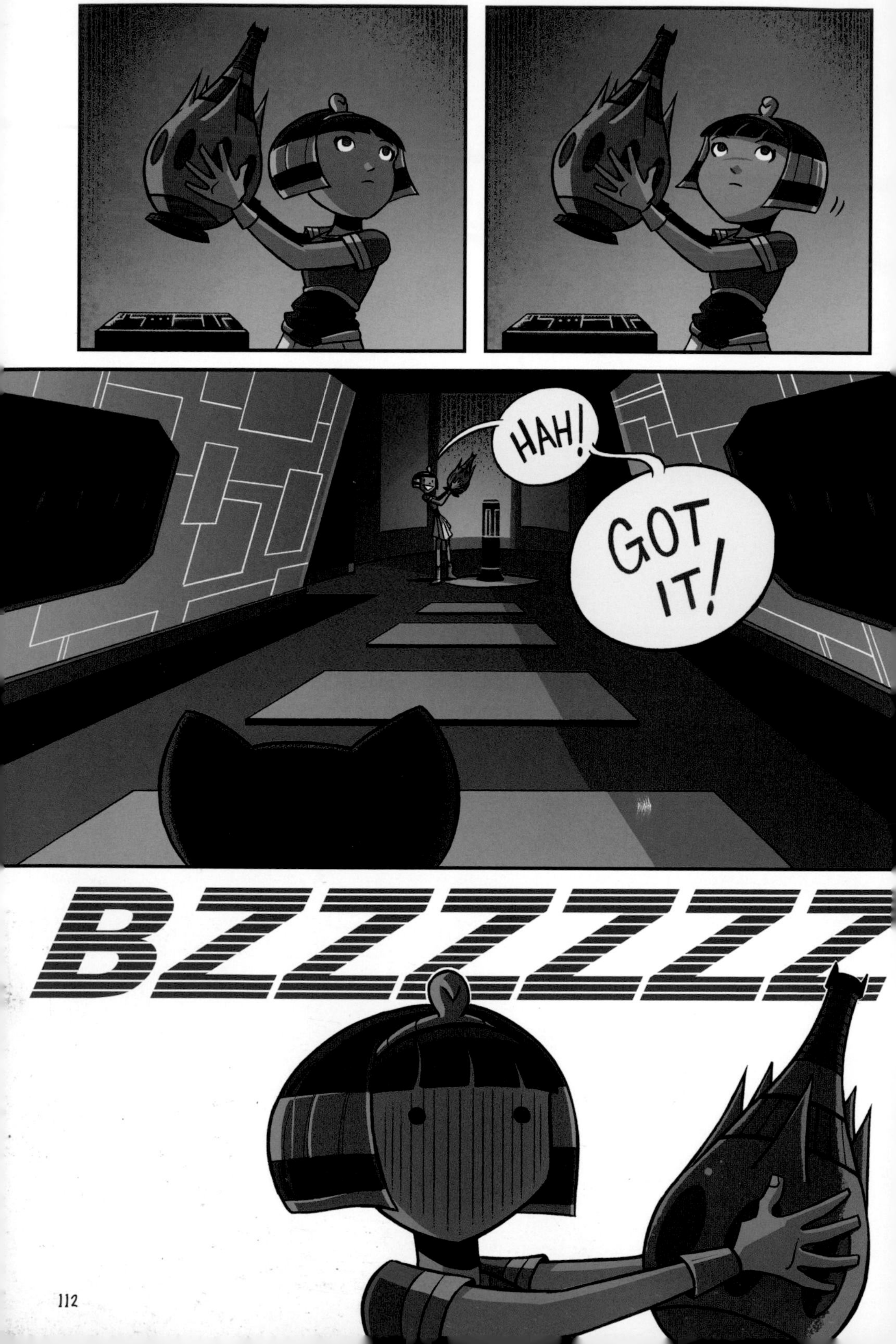
HAH!
GOT IT!
BZZZZZ

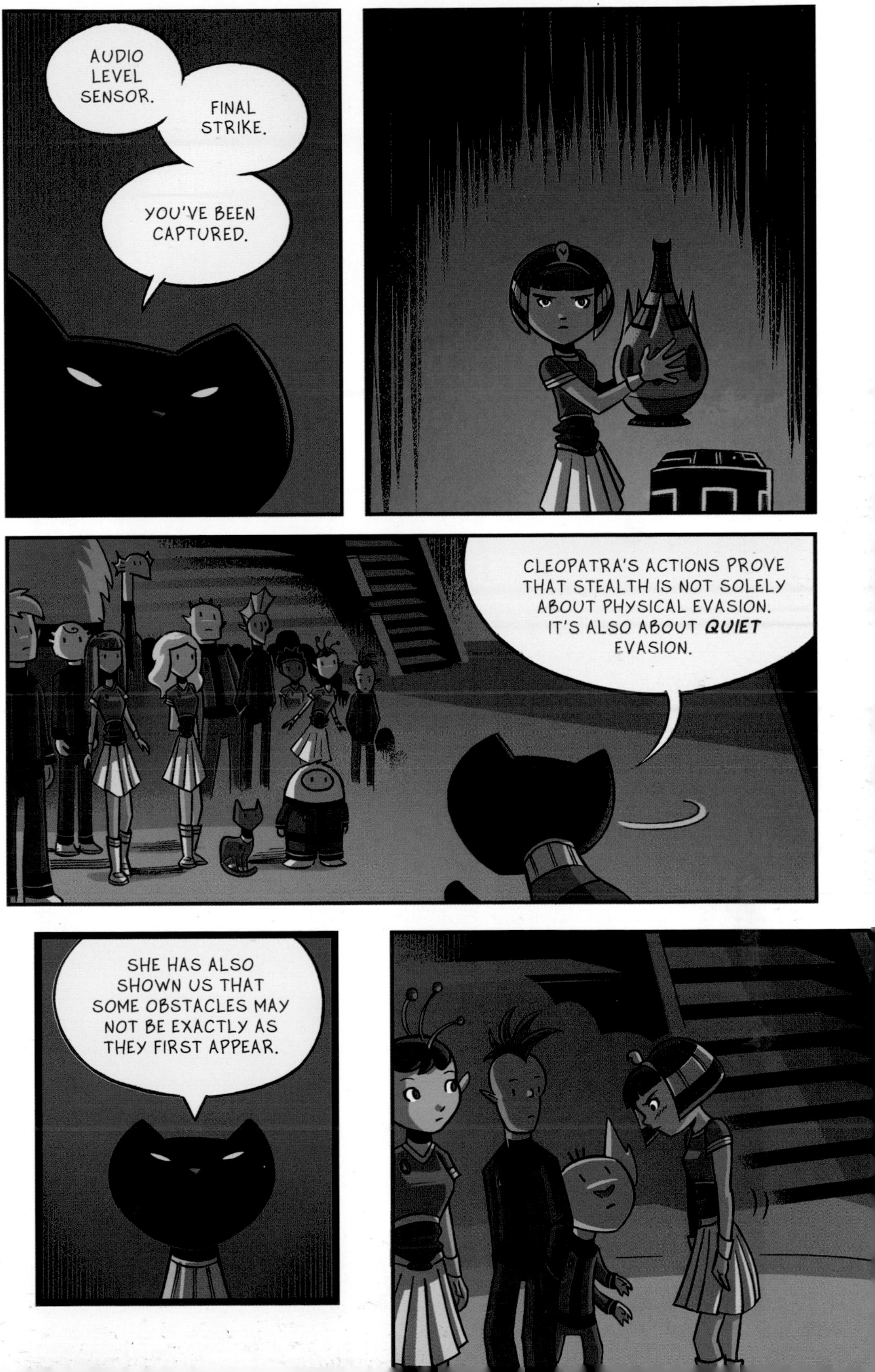
AUDIO LEVEL SENSOR.
FINAL STRIKE.
YOU'VE BEEN CAPTURED.
CLEOPATRA'S ACTIONS PROVE THAT STEALTH IS NOT SOLELY ABOUT PHYSICAL EVASION. IT'S ALSO ABOUT **QUIET** EVASION.
SHE HAS ALSO SHOWN US THAT SOME OBSTACLES MAY NOT BE EXACTLY AS THEY FIRST APPEAR.

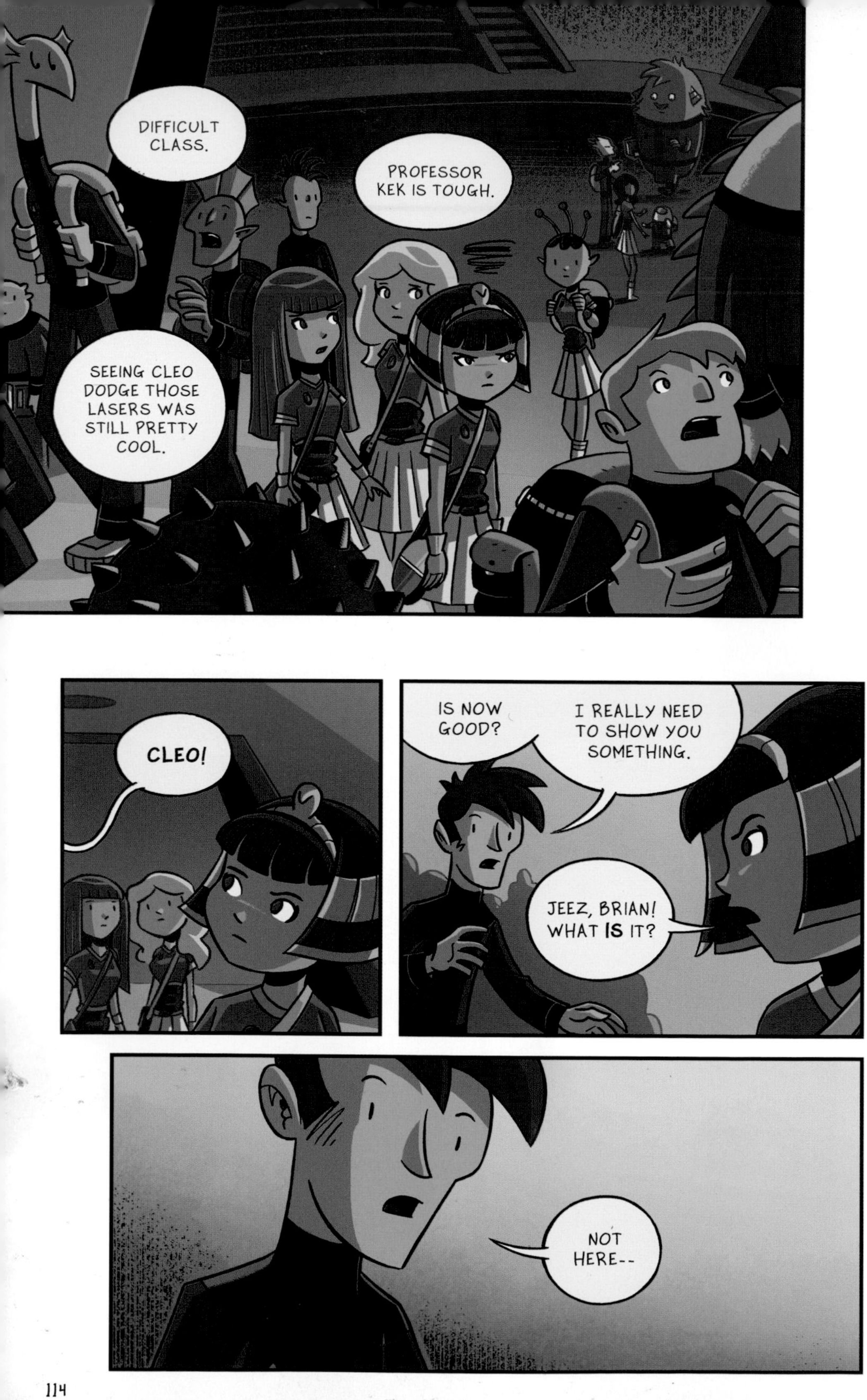
DIFFICULT CLASS.
PROFESSOR KEK IS TOUGH.
SEEING CLEO DODGE THOSE LASERS WAS STILL PRETTY COOL.
CLEO!
IS NOW GOOD?
I REALLY NEED TO SHOW YOU SOMETHING.
JEEZ, BRIAN! WHAT IS IT?
NOT HERE--

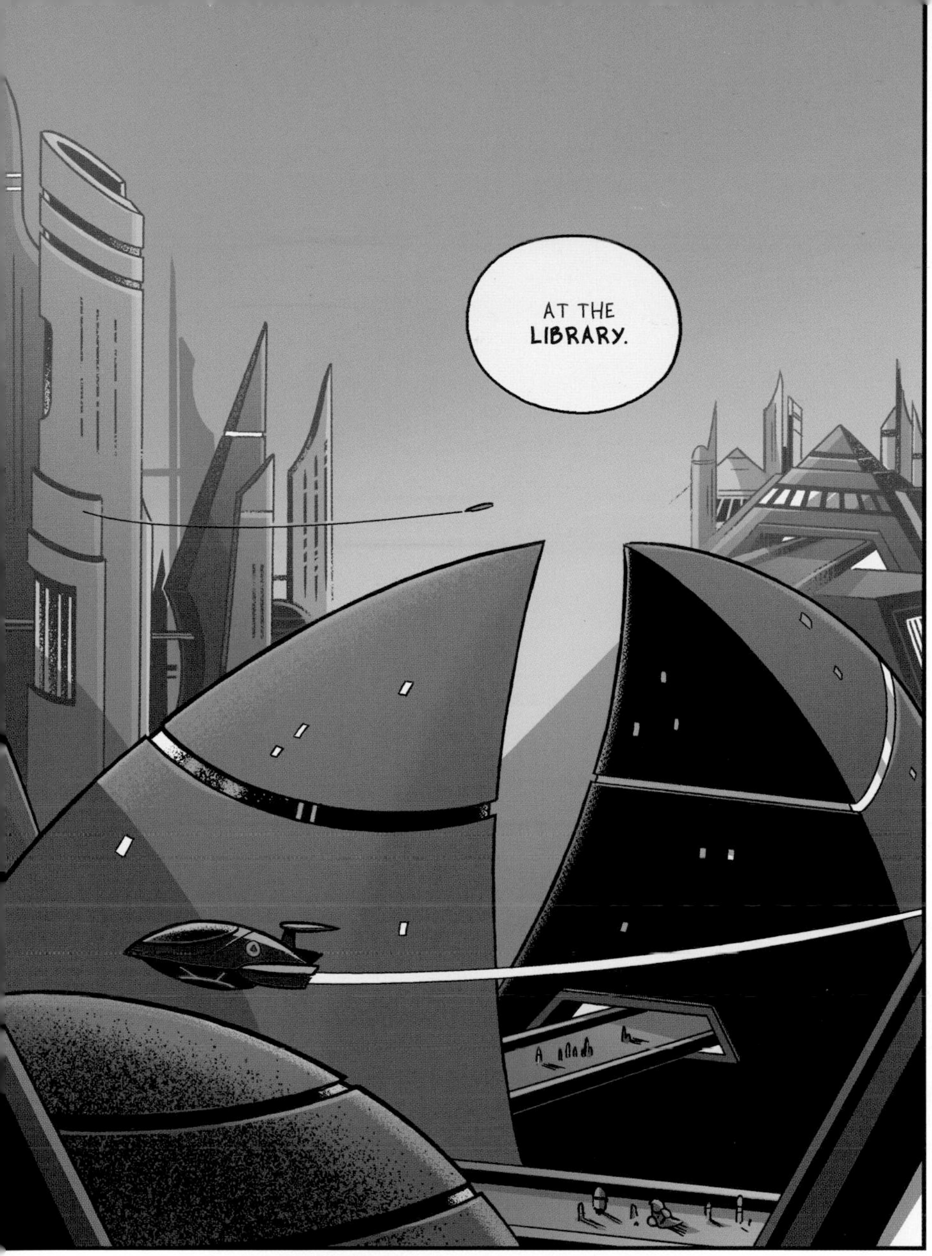
AT THE
LIBRARY.

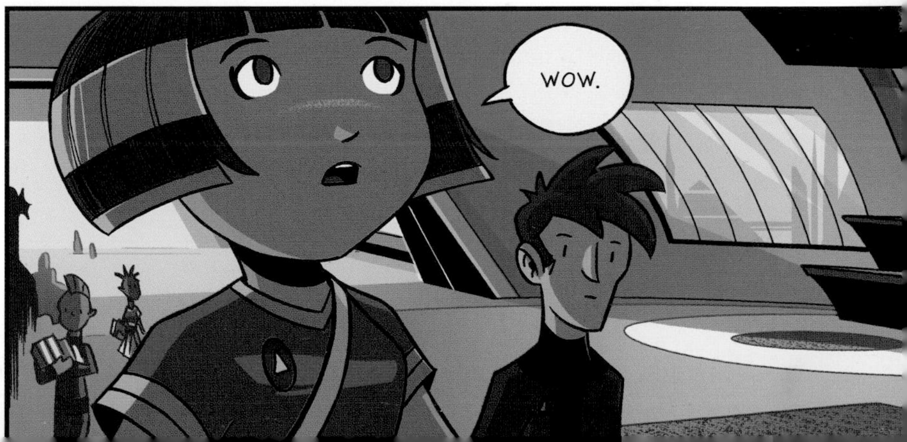
WOW.

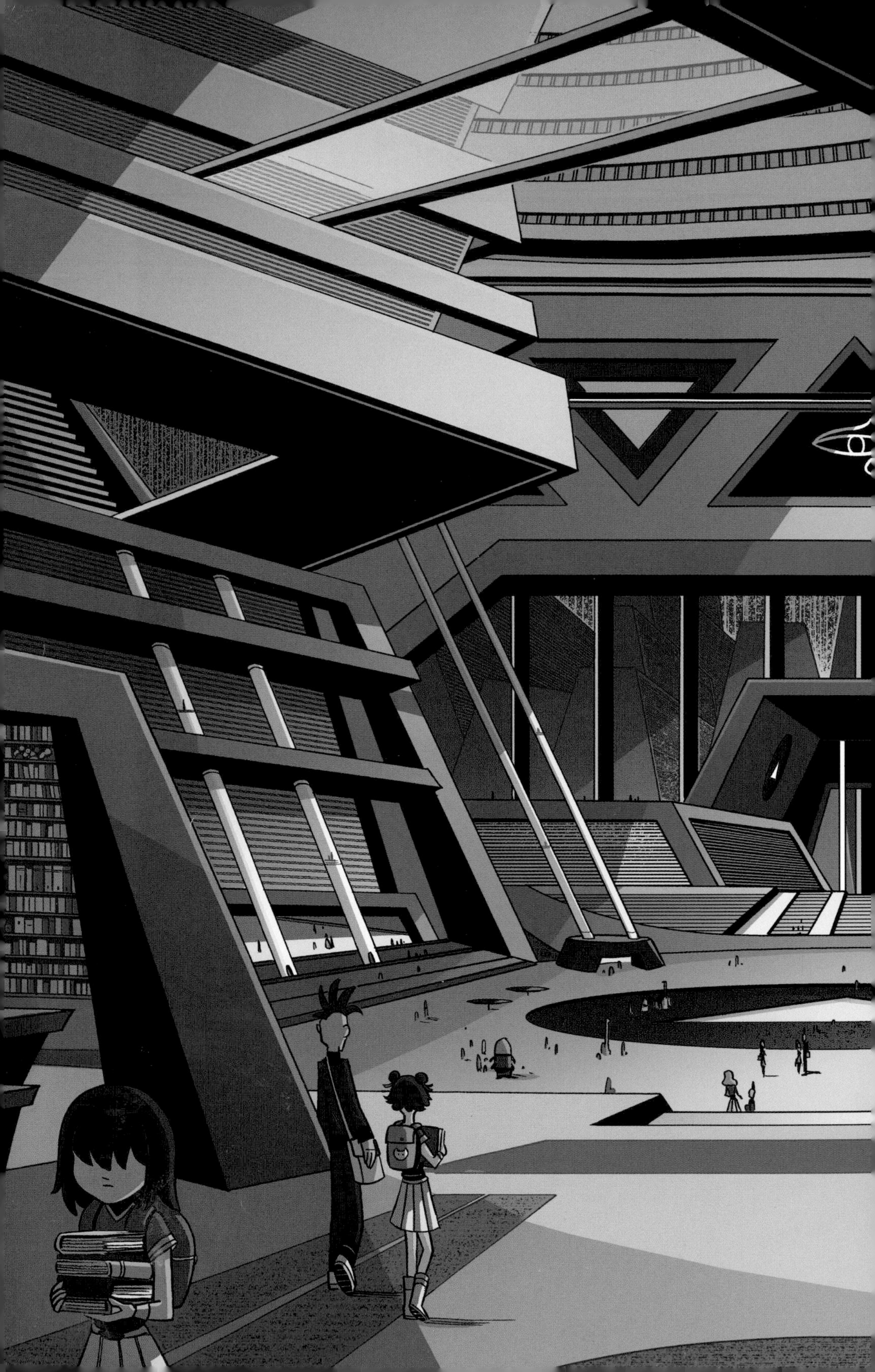

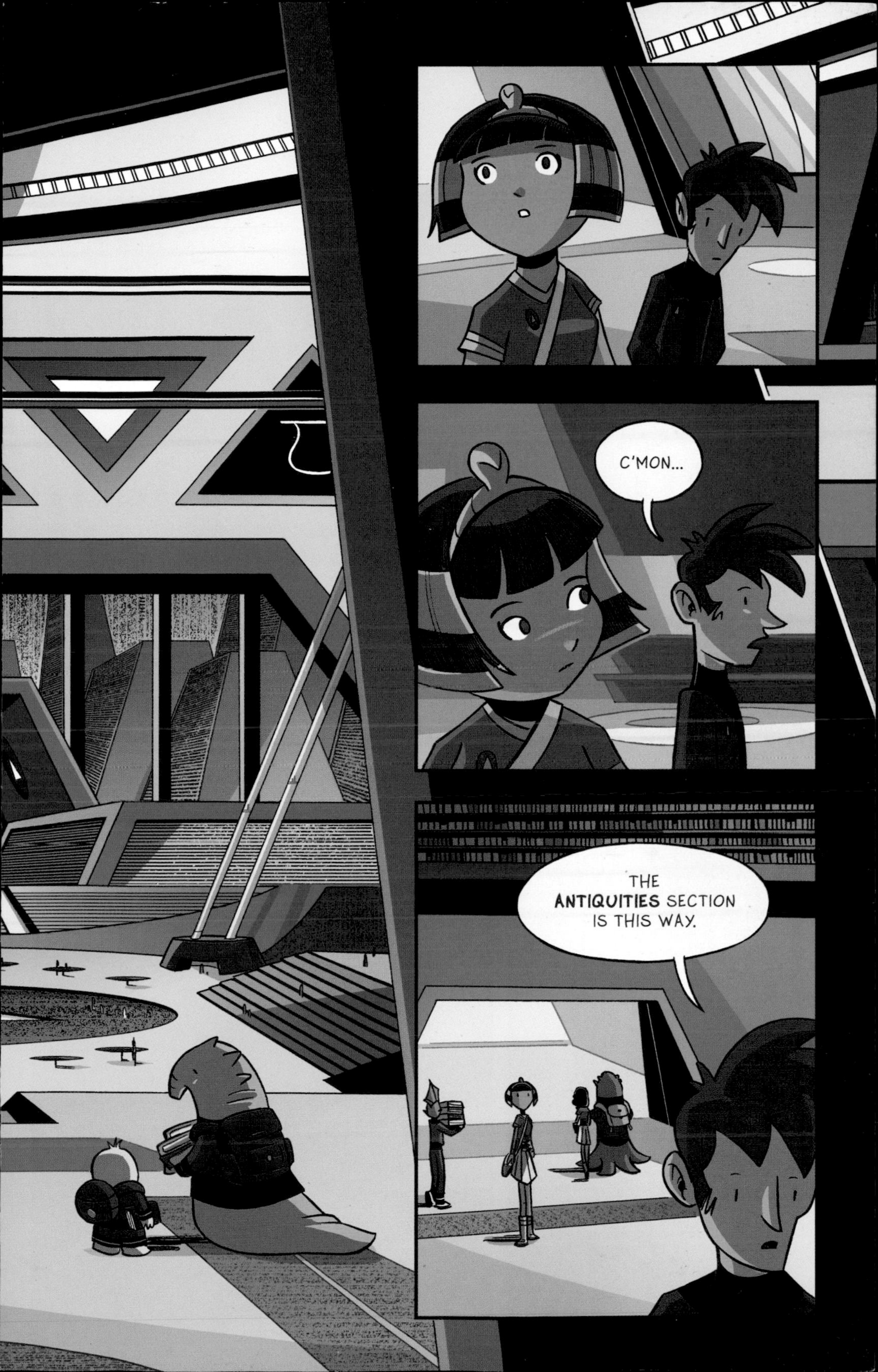
C'MON...
THE ANTIQUITIES SECTION IS THIS WAY.

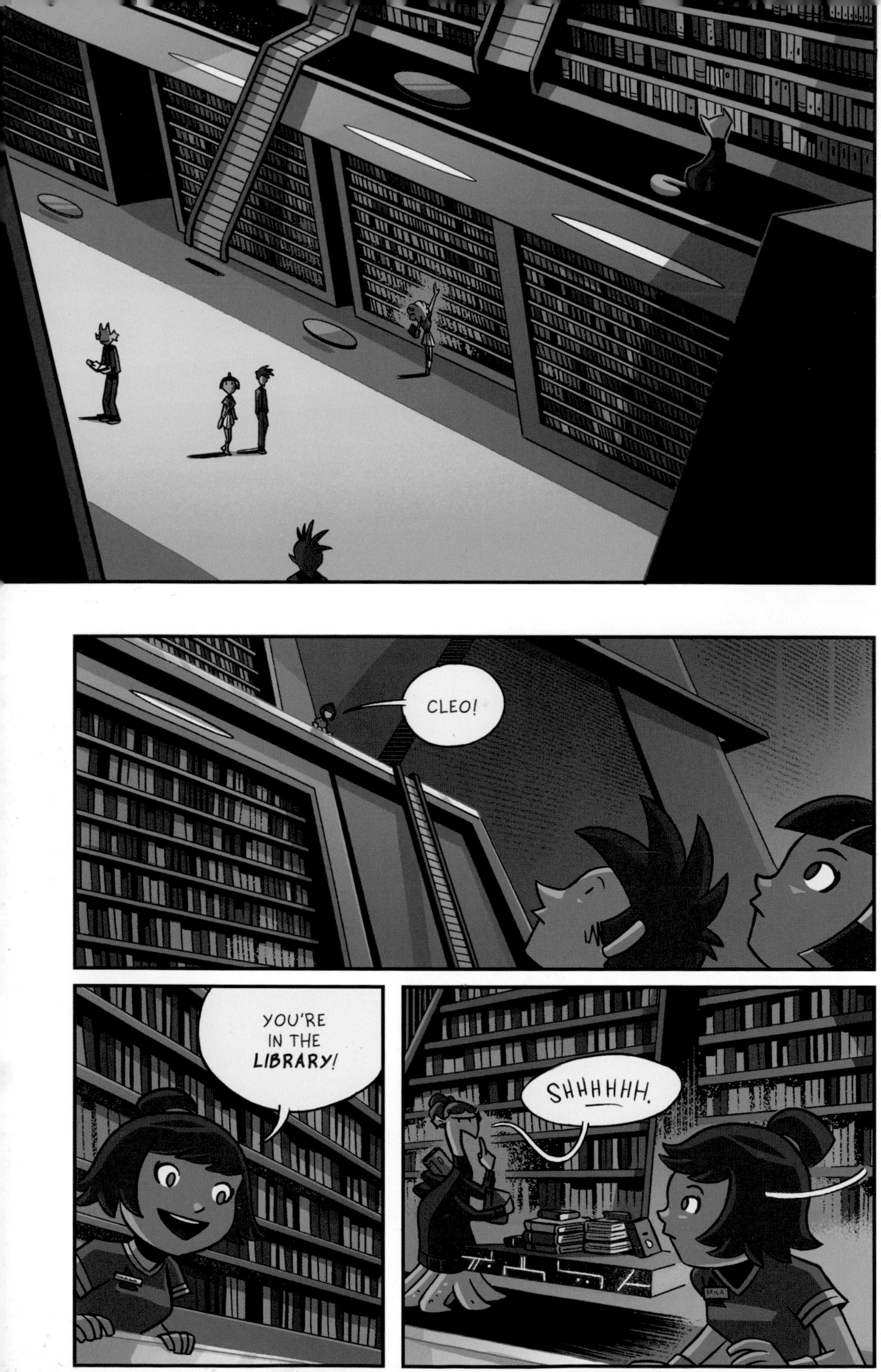
CLEO!
YOU'RE IN THE **LIBRARY**!
SHHHHHH.

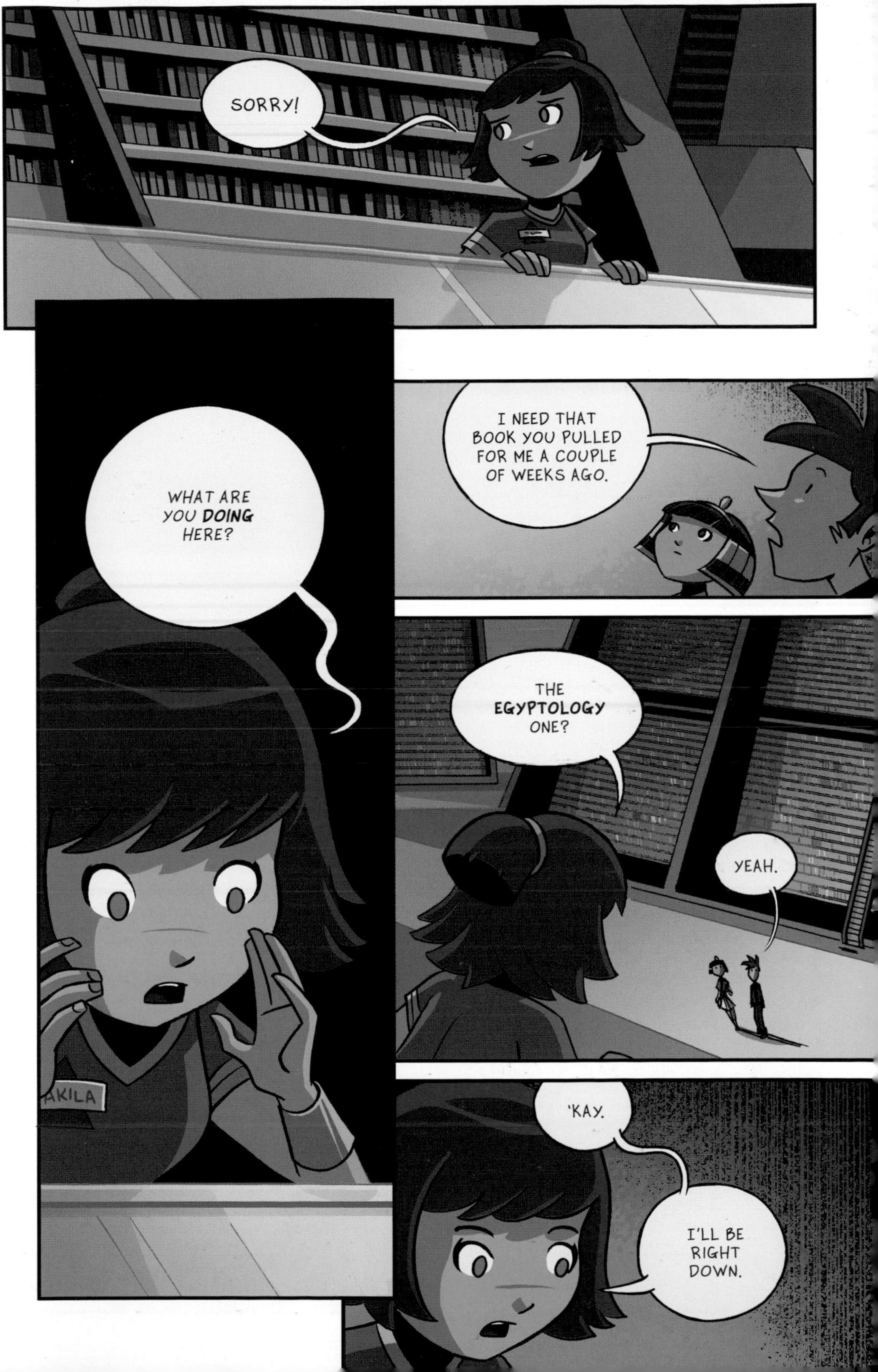
SORRY!
WHAT ARE YOU **DOING** HERE?
AKILA
I NEED THAT BOOK YOU PULLED FOR ME A COUPLE OF WEEKS AGO.
THE **EGYPTOLOGY** ONE?
YEAH.
'KAY.
I'LL BE RIGHT DOWN.

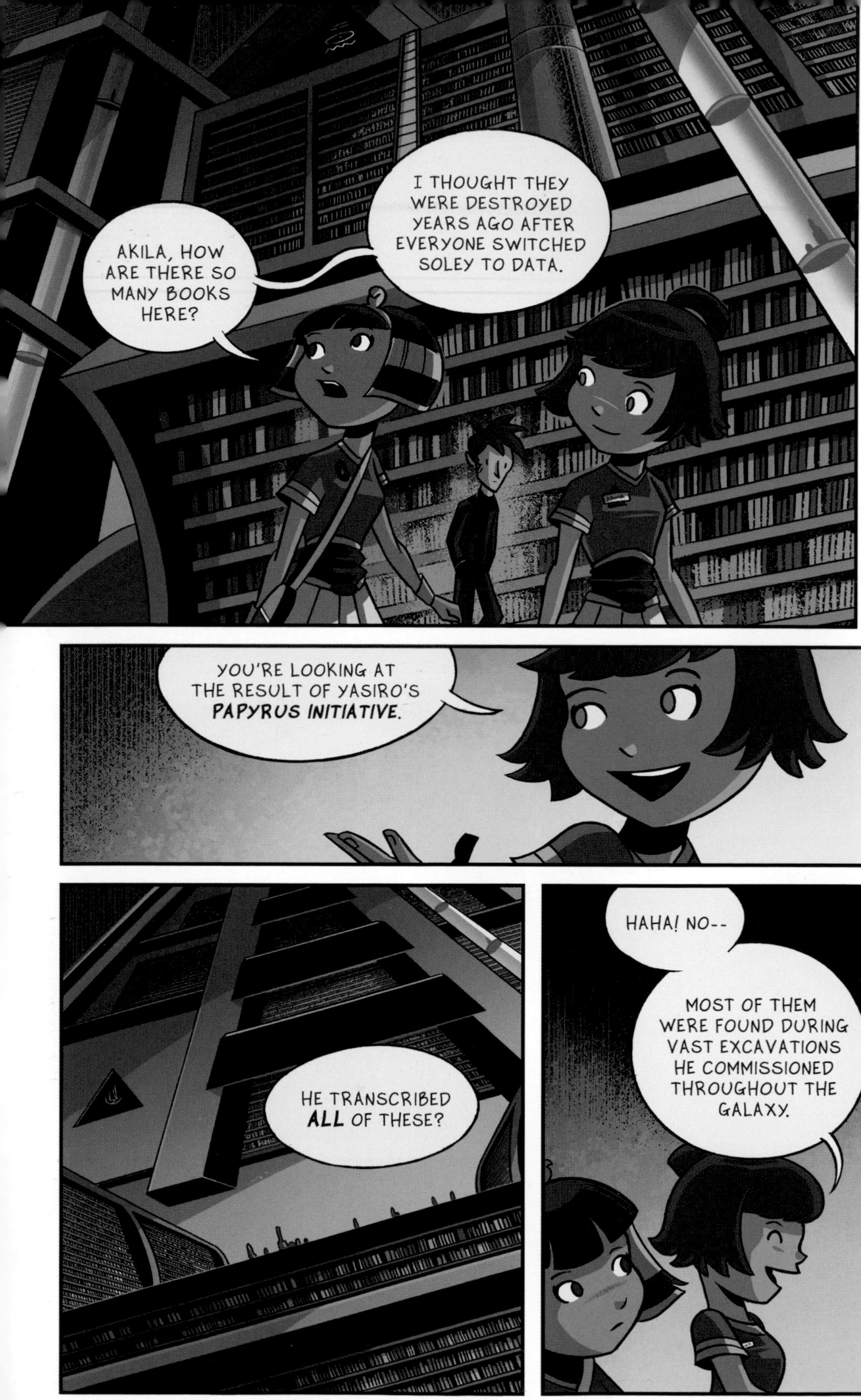
AKILA, HOW ARE THERE SO MANY BOOKS HERE?
I THOUGHT THEY WERE DESTROYED YEARS AGO AFTER EVERYONE SWITCHED SOLEY TO DATA.
YOU'RE LOOKING AT THE RESULT OF YASIRO'S **PAPYRUS INITIATIVE.**
HE TRANSCRIBED **ALL** OF THESE?
HAHA! NO--
MOST OF THEM WERE FOUND DURING VAST EXCAVATIONS HE COMMISSIONED THROUGHOUT THE GALAXY.

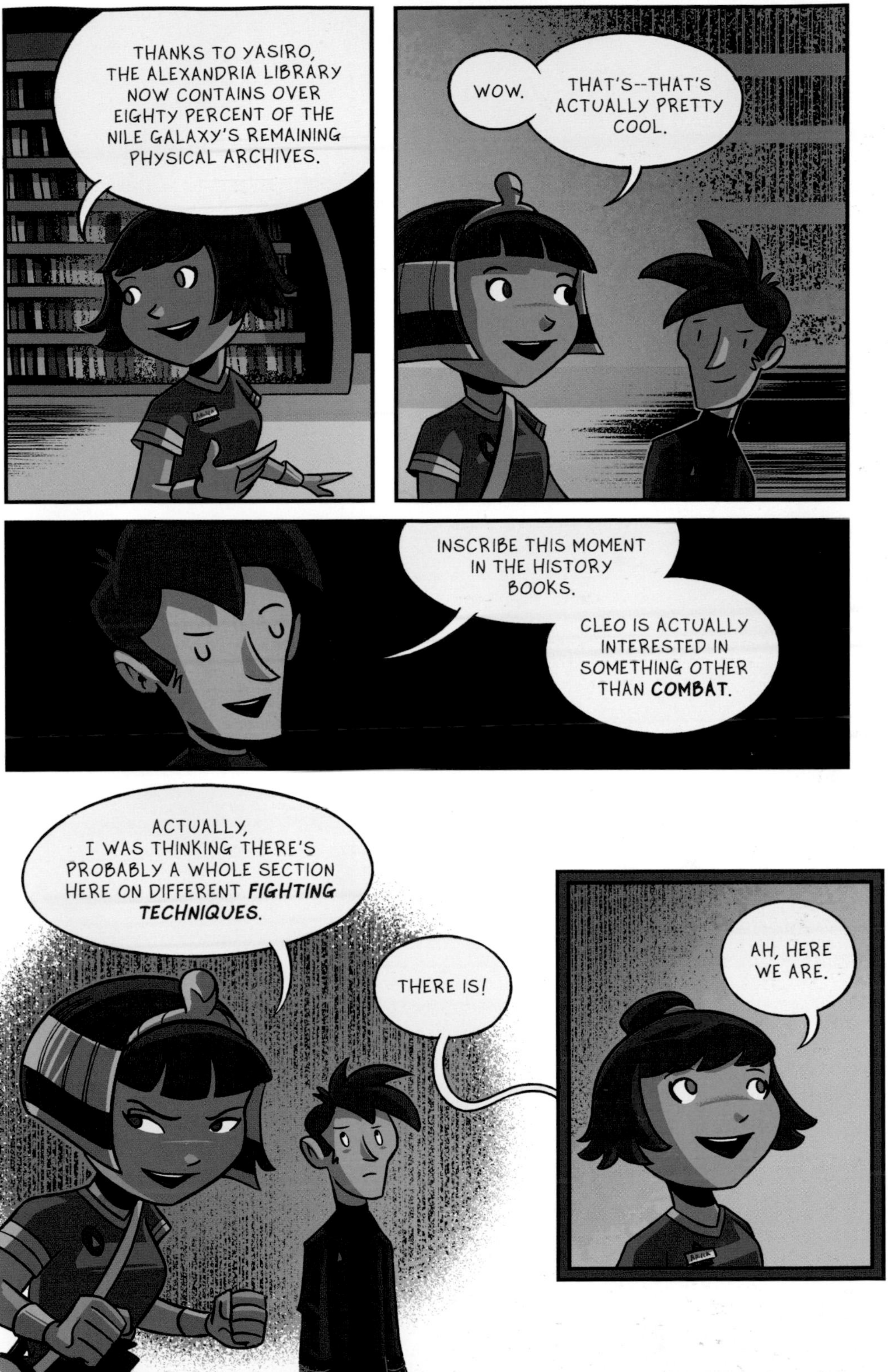
THANKS TO YASIRO, THE ALEXANDRIA LIBRARY NOW CONTAINS OVER EIGHTY PERCENT OF THE NILE GALAXY'S REMAINING PHYSICAL ARCHIVES.
WOW.
THAT'S--THAT'S ACTUALLY PRETTY COOL.
INSCRIBE THIS MOMENT IN THE HISTORY BOOKS.
CLEO IS ACTUALLY INTERESTED IN SOMETHING OTHER THAN **COMBAT**.
ACTUALLY, I WAS THINKING THERE'S PROBABLY A WHOLE SECTION HERE ON DIFFERENT **FIGHTING TECHNIQUES**.
THERE IS!
AH, HERE WE ARE.

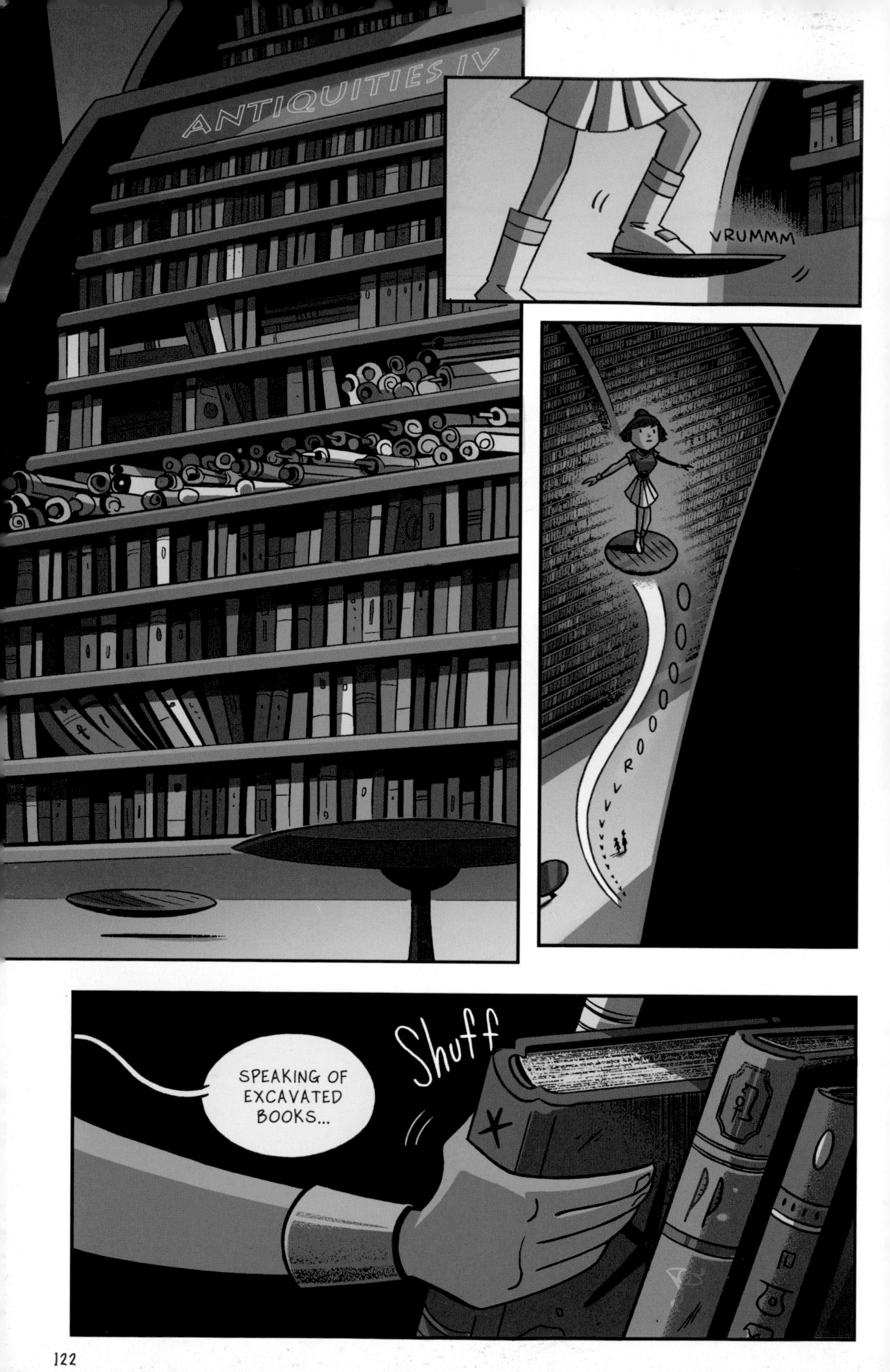
ANTIQUITIES IV
VRUMMM
VVROOOOOO
Shuff
SPEAKING OF EXCAVATED BOOKS...

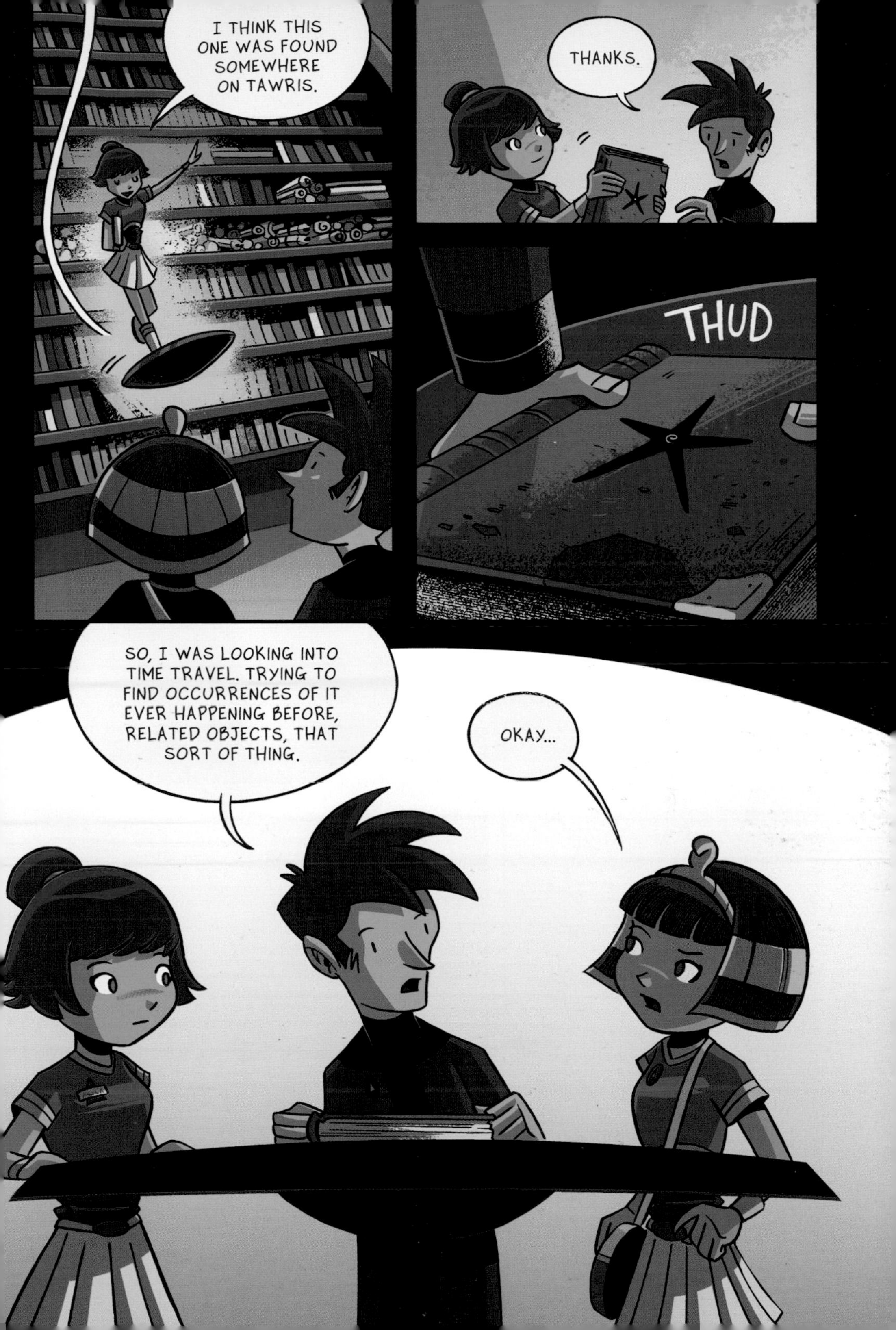
I THINK THIS ONE WAS FOUND SOMEWHERE ON TAWRIS.
THANKS.
THUD
SO, I WAS LOOKING INTO TIME TRAVEL. TRYING TO FIND OCCURRENCES OF IT EVER HAPPENING BEFORE, RELATED OBJECTS, THAT SORT OF THING.
OKAY...

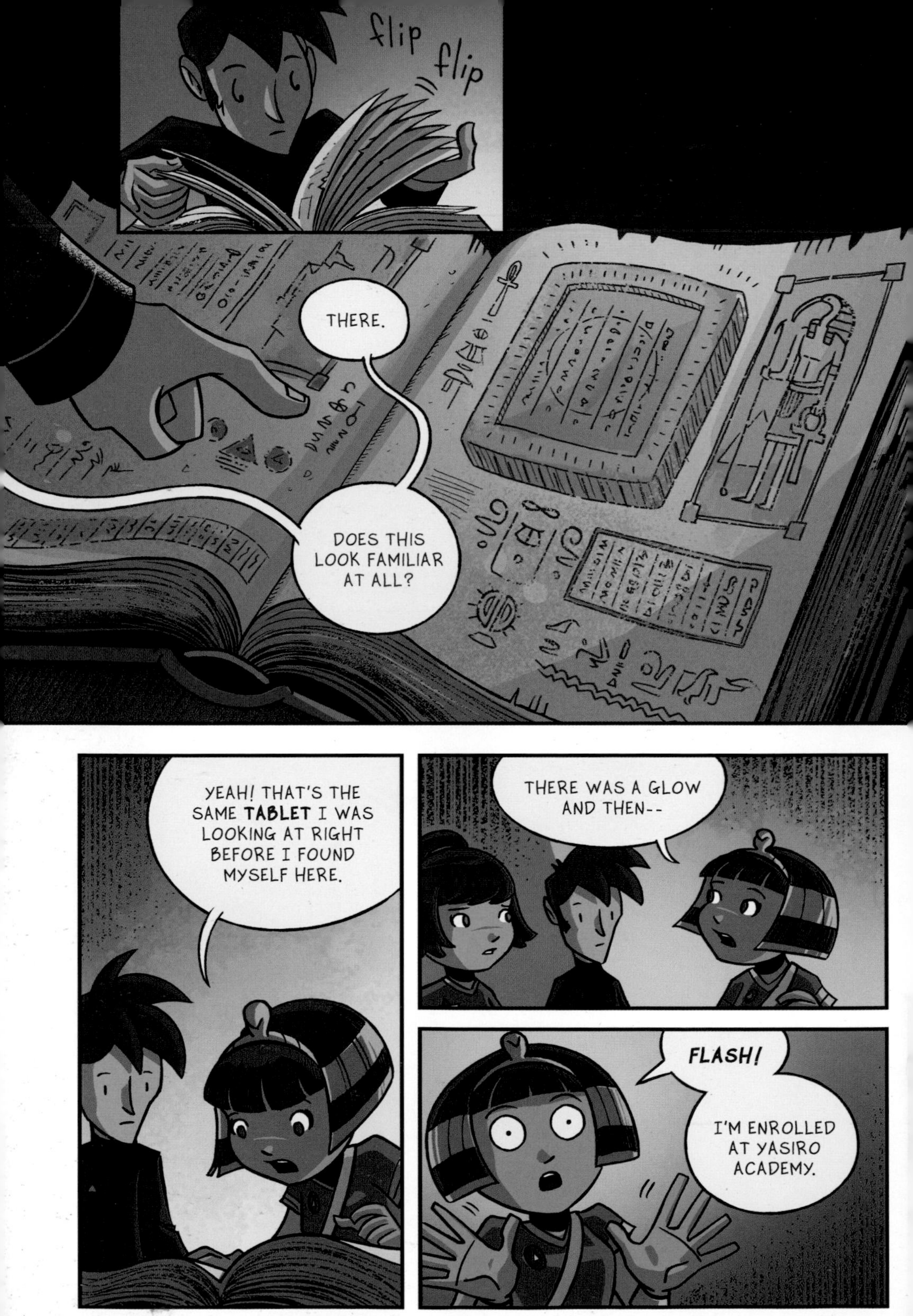
flip flip
THERE.
DOES THIS LOOK FAMILIAR AT ALL?
YEAH! THAT'S THE SAME **TABLET** I WAS LOOKING AT RIGHT BEFORE I FOUND MYSELF HERE.
THERE WAS A GLOW AND THEN--
FLASH!
I'M ENROLLED AT YASIRO ACADEMY.

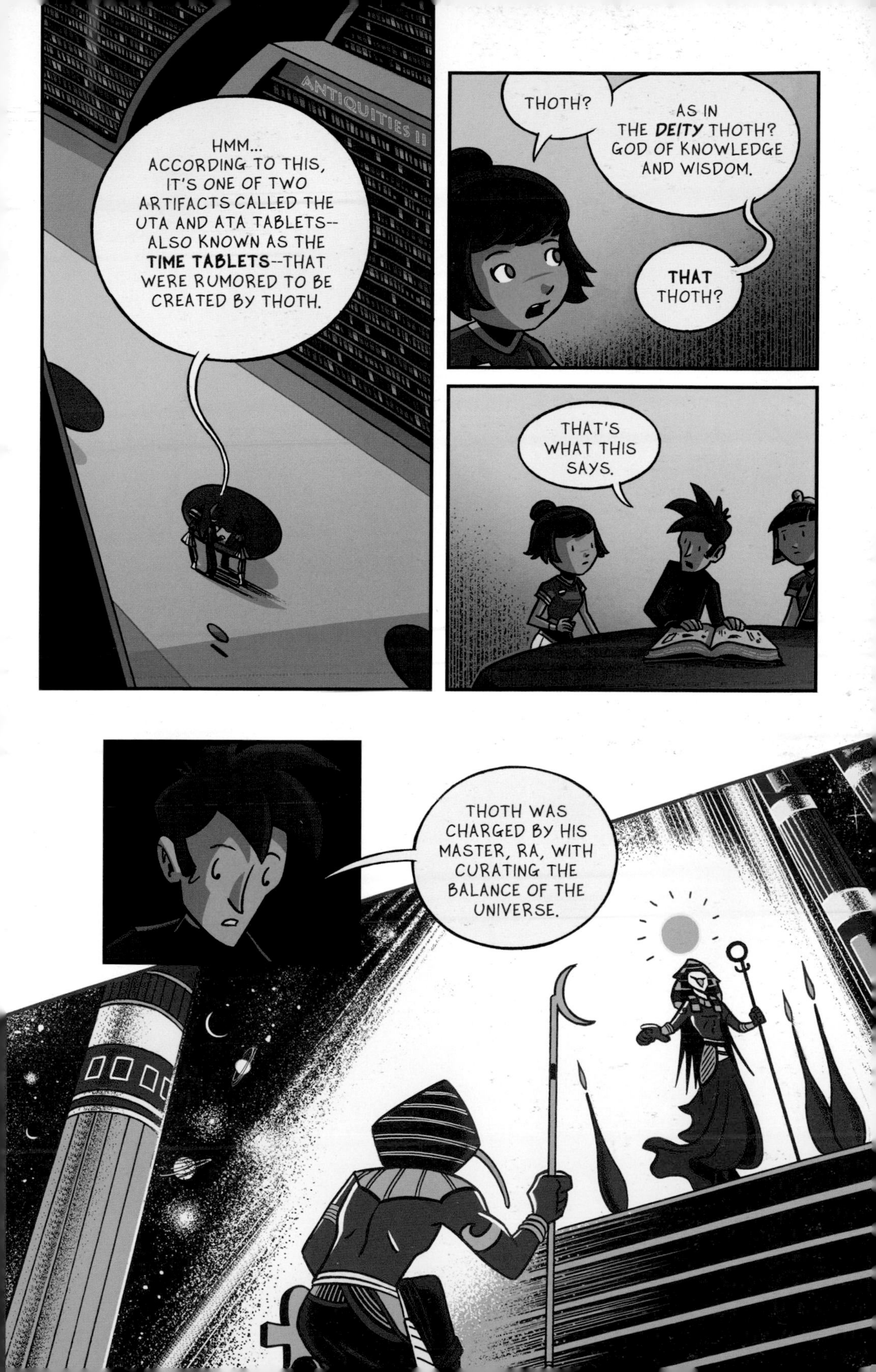
ANTIQUITIES II
HMM... ACCORDING TO THIS, IT'S ONE OF TWO ARTIFACTS CALLED THE UTA AND ATA TABLETS--ALSO KNOWN AS THE **TIME TABLETS**--THAT WERE RUMORED TO BE CREATED BY THOTH.
THOTH?
AS IN THE ***DEITY*** THOTH? GOD OF KNOWLEDGE AND WISDOM.
THAT THOTH?
THAT'S WHAT THIS SAYS.
THOTH WAS CHARGED BY HIS MASTER, RA, WITH CURATING THE BALANCE OF THE UNIVERSE.

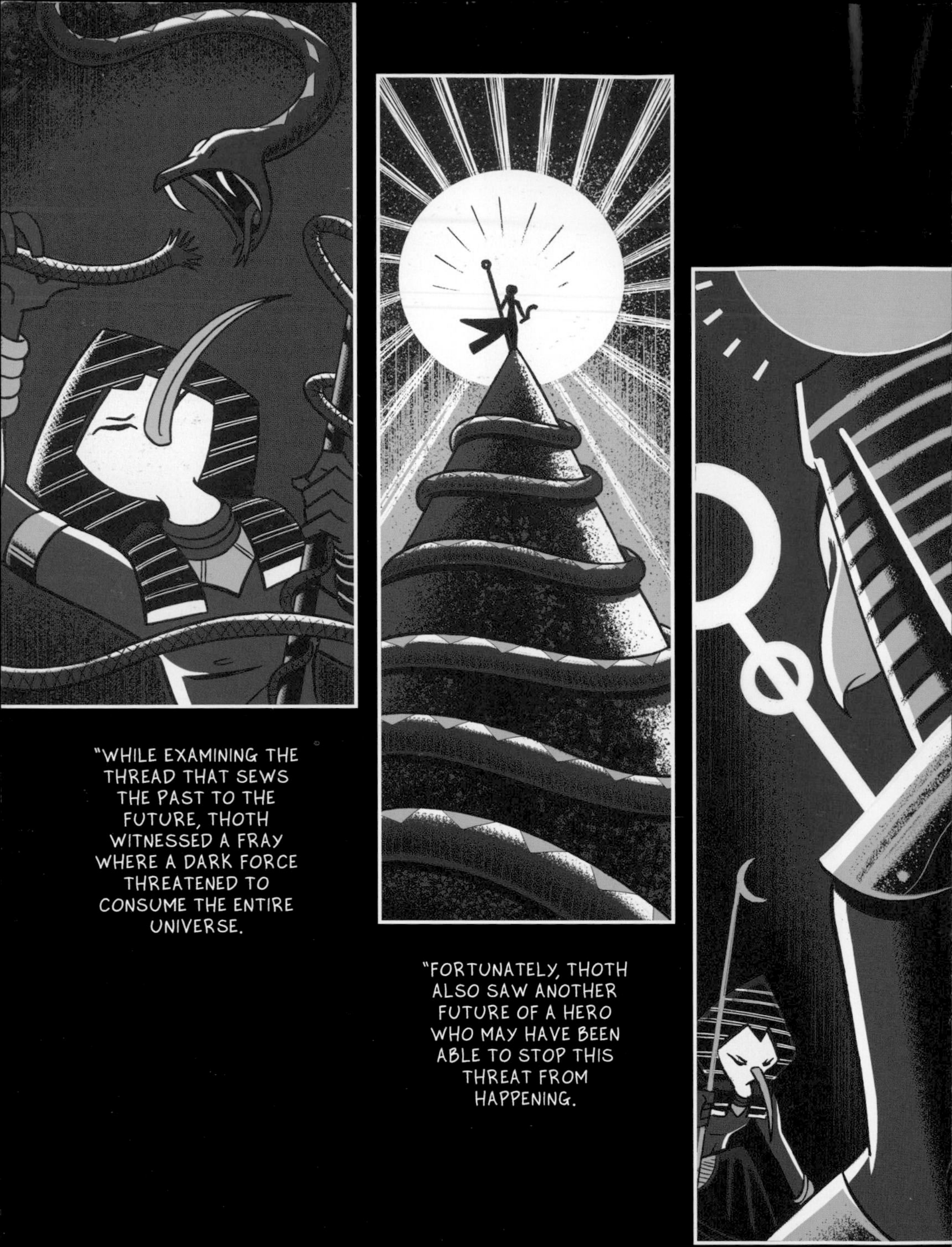
"WHILE EXAMINING THE THREAD THAT SEWS THE PAST TO THE FUTURE, THOTH WITNESSED A FRAY WHERE A DARK FORCE THREATENED TO CONSUME THE ENTIRE UNIVERSE.
"FORTUNATELY, THOTH ALSO SAW ANOTHER FUTURE OF A HERO WHO MAY HAVE BEEN ABLE TO STOP THIS THREAT FROM HAPPENING.

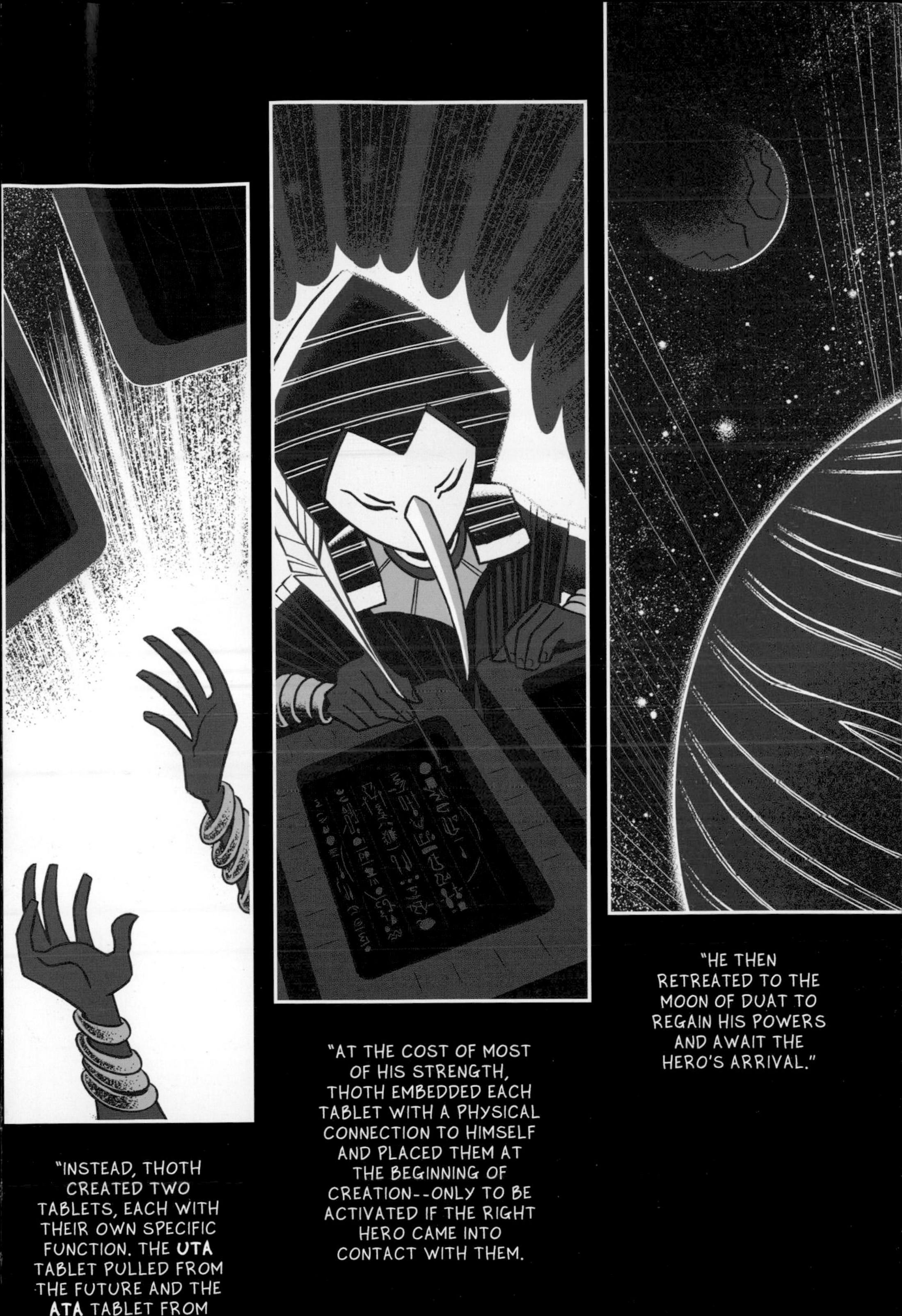
"INSTEAD, THOTH CREATED TWO TABLETS, EACH WITH THEIR OWN SPECIFIC FUNCTION. THE **UTA** TABLET PULLED FROM THE FUTURE AND THE **ATA** TABLET FROM
"AT THE COST OF MOST OF HIS STRENGTH, THOTH EMBEDDED EACH TABLET WITH A PHYSICAL CONNECTION TO HIMSELF AND PLACED THEM AT THE BEGINNING OF CREATION--ONLY TO BE ACTIVATED IF THE RIGHT HERO CAME INTO CONTACT WITH THEM.
"HE THEN RETREATED TO THE MOON OF DUAT TO REGAIN HIS POWERS AND AWAIT THE HERO'S ARRIVAL."

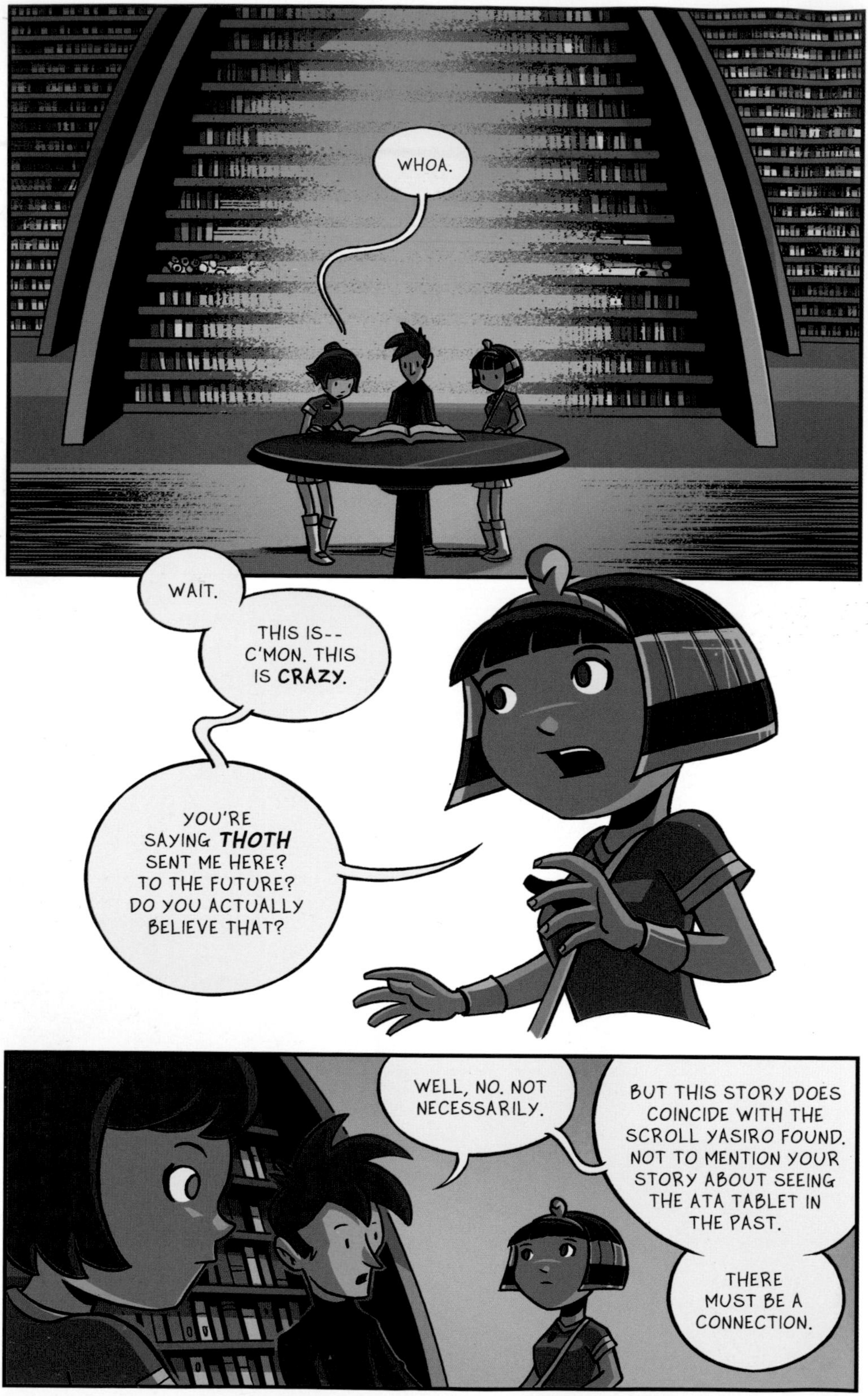
WHOA.
WAIT.
THIS IS-- C'MON. THIS IS **CRAZY.**
YOU'RE SAYING **THOTH** SENT ME HERE? TO THE FUTURE? DO YOU ACTUALLY BELIEVE THAT?
WELL, NO. NOT NECESSARILY.
BUT THIS STORY DOES COINCIDE WITH THE SCROLL YASIRO FOUND. NOT TO MENTION YOUR STORY ABOUT SEEING THE ATA TABLET IN THE PAST.
THERE MUST BE A CONNECTION.

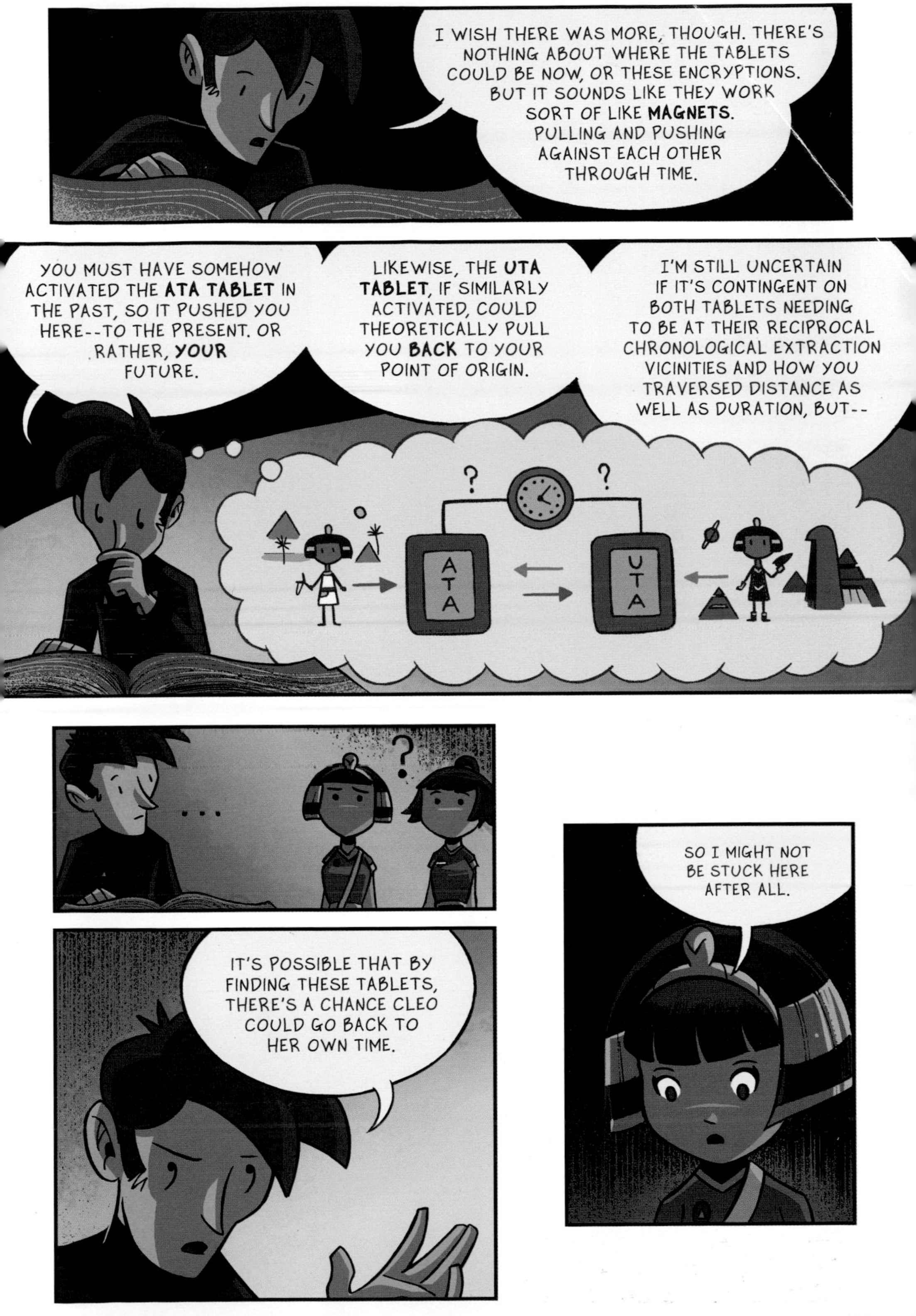
I WISH THERE WAS MORE, THOUGH. THERE'S NOTHING ABOUT WHERE THE TABLETS COULD BE NOW, OR THESE ENCRYPTIONS. BUT IT SOUNDS LIKE THEY WORK SORT OF LIKE **MAGNETS**. PULLING AND PUSHING AGAINST EACH OTHER THROUGH TIME.
YOU MUST HAVE SOMEHOW ACTIVATED THE **ATA TABLET** IN THE PAST, SO IT PUSHED YOU HERE--TO THE PRESENT. OR RATHER, **YOUR** FUTURE.
LIKEWISE, THE **UTA TABLET**, IF SIMILARLY ACTIVATED, COULD THEORETICALLY PULL YOU **BACK** TO YOUR POINT OF ORIGIN.
I'M STILL UNCERTAIN IF IT'S CONTINGENT ON BOTH TABLETS NEEDING TO BE AT THEIR RECIPROCAL CHRONOLOGICAL EXTRACTION VICINITIES AND HOW YOU TRAVERSED DISTANCE AS WELL AS DURATION, BUT--
?
?
ATA
UTA
...
?
IT'S POSSIBLE THAT BY FINDING THESE TABLETS, THERE'S A CHANCE CLEO COULD GO BACK TO HER OWN TIME.
SO I MIGHT NOT BE STUCK HERE AFTER ALL.

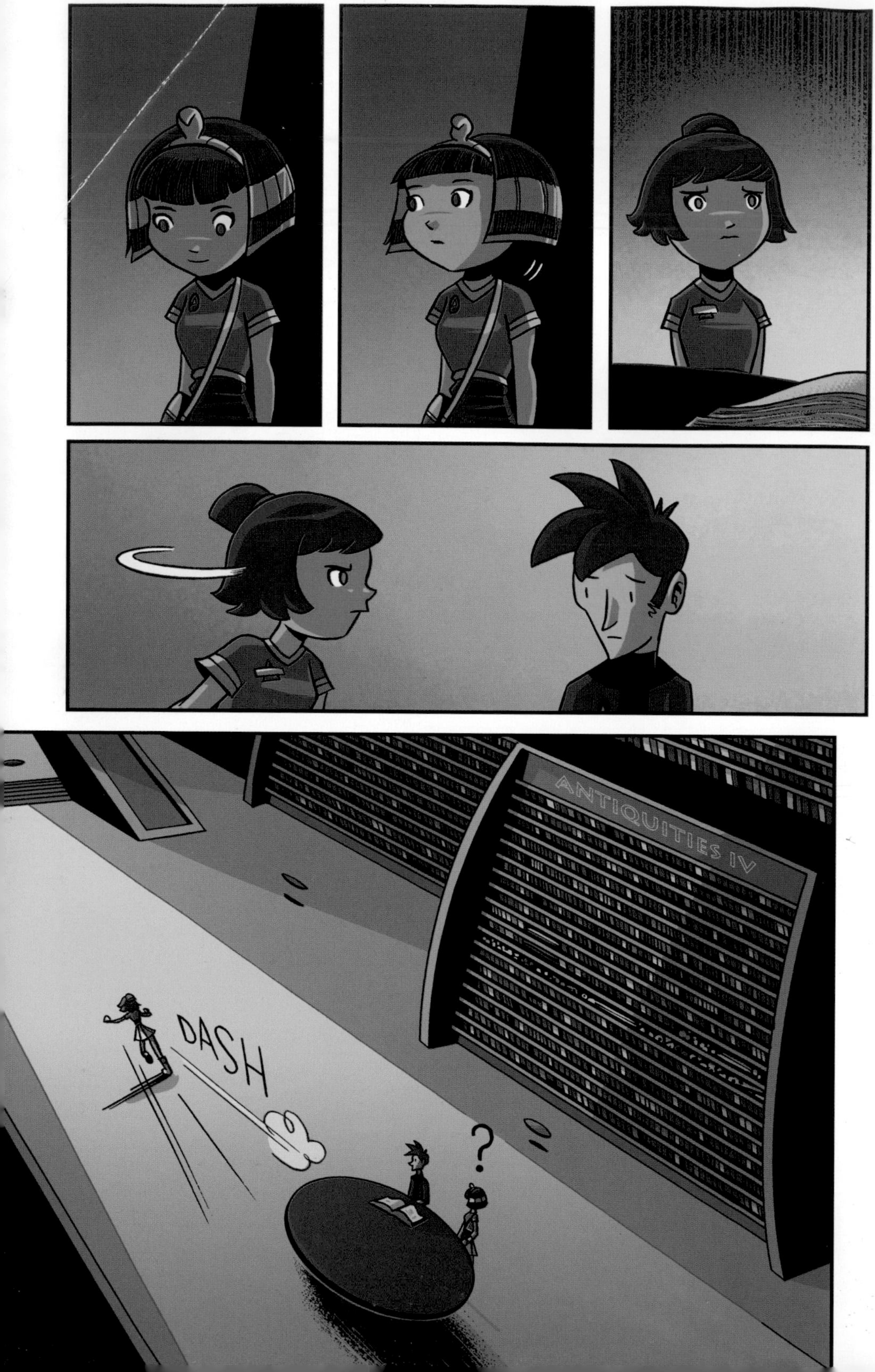
ANTIQUITIES IV
DASH
?

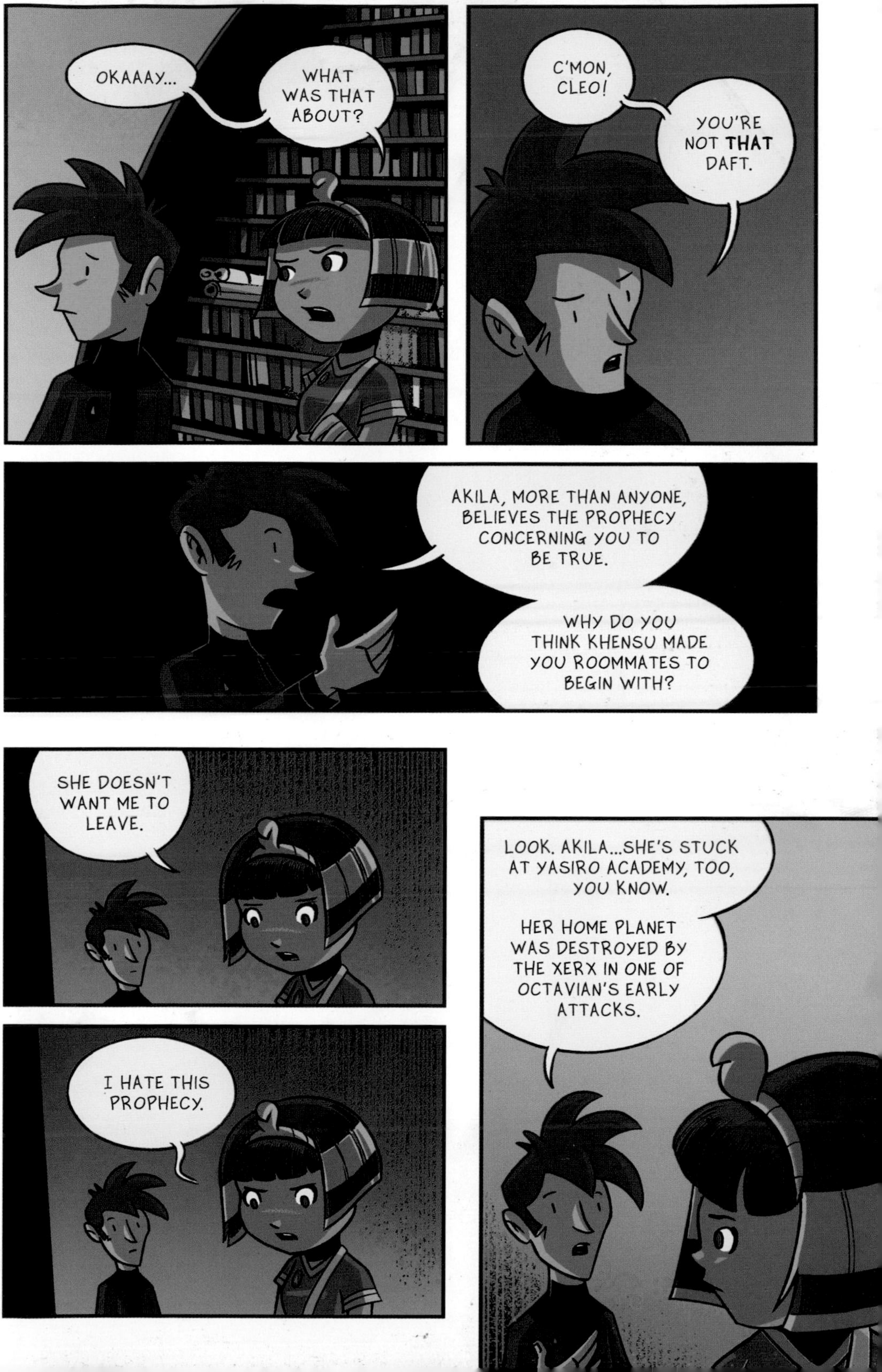
OKAAAY...
WHAT WAS THAT ABOUT?
C'MON, CLEO!
YOU'RE NOT **THAT** DAFT.
AKILA, MORE THAN ANYONE, BELIEVES THE PROPHECY CONCERNING YOU TO BE TRUE.
WHY DO YOU THINK KHENSU MADE YOU ROOMMATES TO BEGIN WITH?
SHE DOESN'T WANT ME TO LEAVE.
I HATE THIS PROPHECY.
LOOK. AKILA...SHE'S STUCK AT YASIRO ACADEMY, TOO, YOU KNOW.
HER HOME PLANET WAS DESTROYED BY THE XERX IN ONE OF OCTAVIAN'S EARLY ATTACKS.

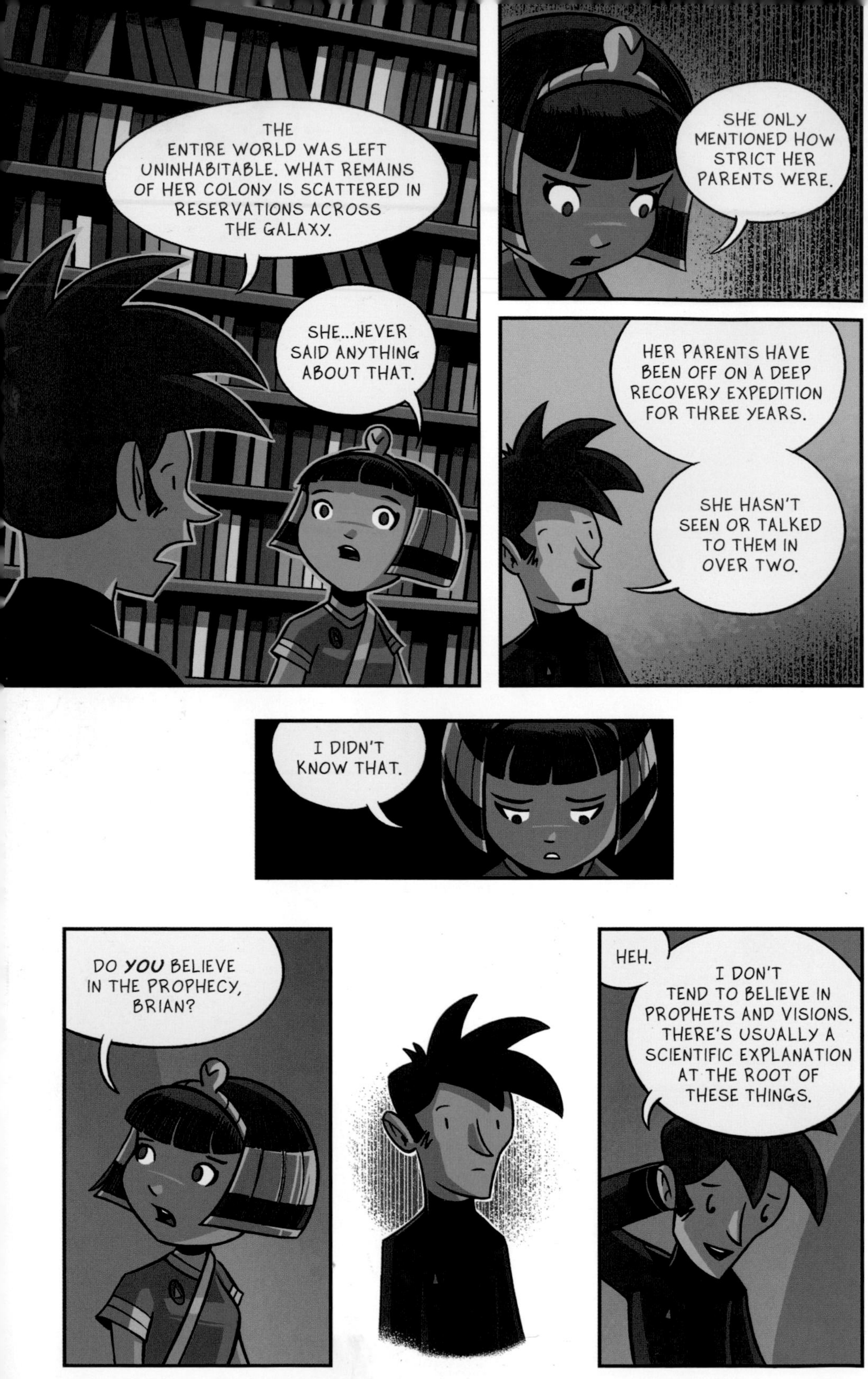
THE ENTIRE WORLD WAS LEFT UNINHABITABLE. WHAT REMAINS OF HER COLONY IS SCATTERED IN RESERVATIONS ACROSS THE GALAXY.
SHE...NEVER SAID ANYTHING ABOUT THAT.
SHE ONLY MENTIONED HOW STRICT HER PARENTS WERE.
HER PARENTS HAVE BEEN OFF ON A DEEP RECOVERY EXPEDITION FOR THREE YEARS.
SHE HASN'T SEEN OR TALKED TO THEM IN OVER TWO.
I DIDN'T KNOW THAT.
DO ***YOU*** BELIEVE IN THE PROPHECY, BRIAN?
HEH.
I DON'T TEND TO BELIEVE IN PROPHETS AND VISIONS. THERE'S USUALLY A SCIENTIFIC EXPLANATION AT THE ROOT OF THESE THINGS.

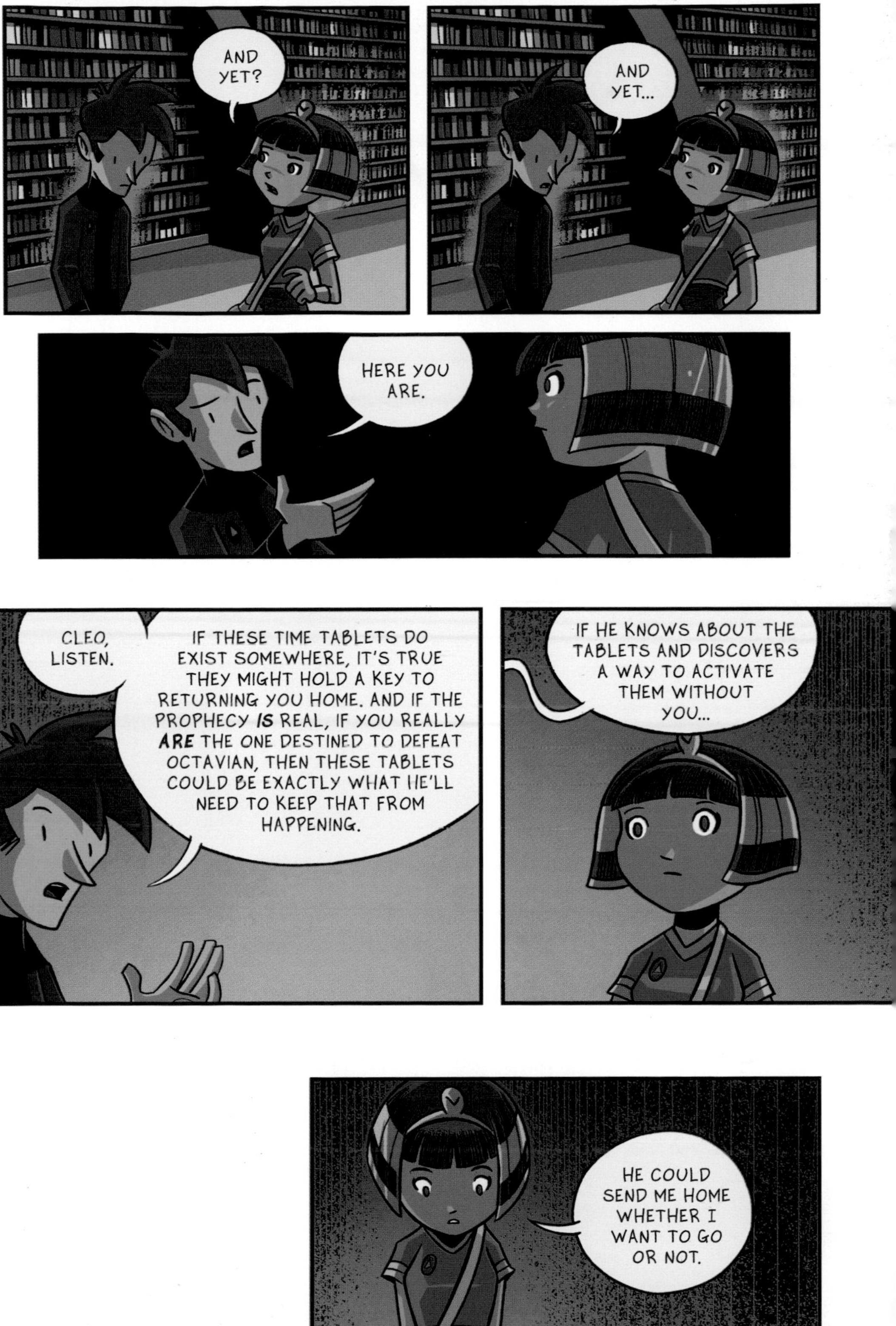
AND YET?
AND YET...
HERE YOU ARE.
CLEO, LISTEN.
IF THESE TIME TABLETS DO EXIST SOMEWHERE, IT'S TRUE THEY MIGHT HOLD A KEY TO RETURNING YOU HOME. AND IF THE PROPHECY **IS** REAL, IF YOU REALLY **ARE** THE ONE DESTINED TO DEFEAT OCTAVIAN, THEN THESE TABLETS COULD BE EXACTLY WHAT HE'LL NEED TO KEEP THAT FROM HAPPENING.
IF HE KNOWS ABOUT THE TABLETS AND DISCOVERS A WAY TO ACTIVATE THEM WITHOUT YOU...
HE COULD SEND ME HOME WHETHER I WANT TO GO OR NOT.

CHAPTER THREE

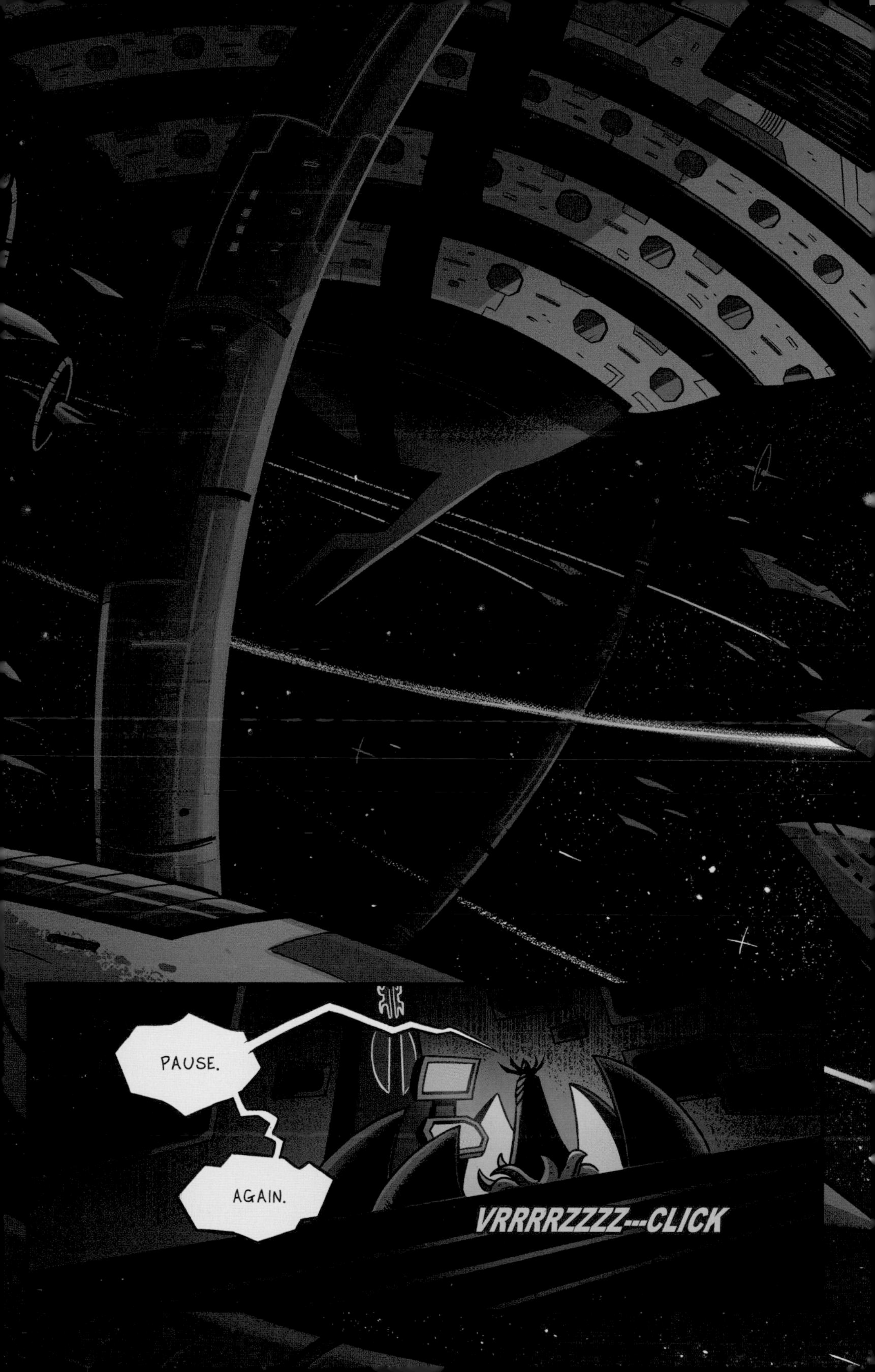
PAUSE.
AGAIN.
VRRRRZZZZ---CLICK

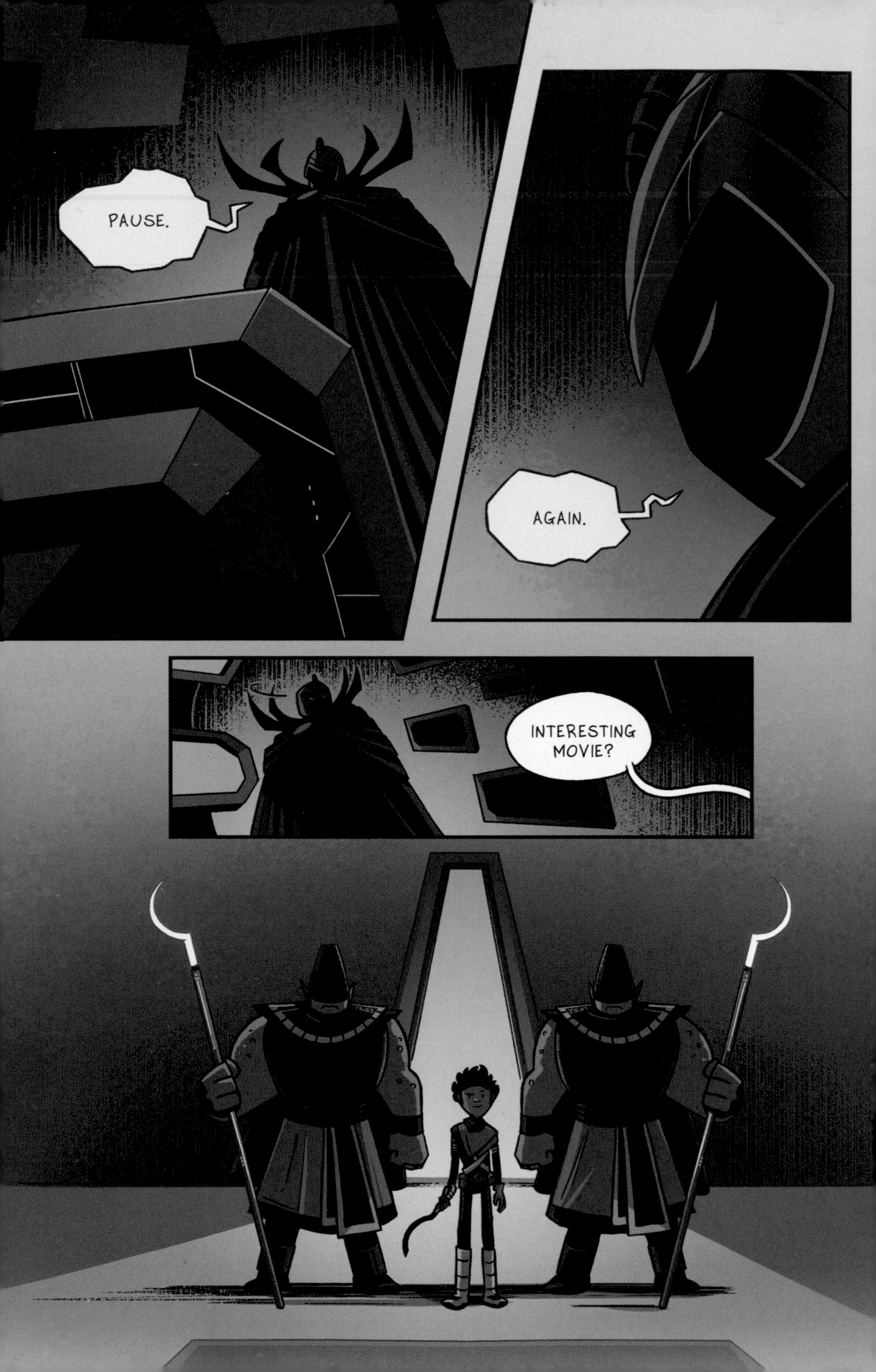
PAUSE.
AGAIN.
INTERESTING MOVIE?

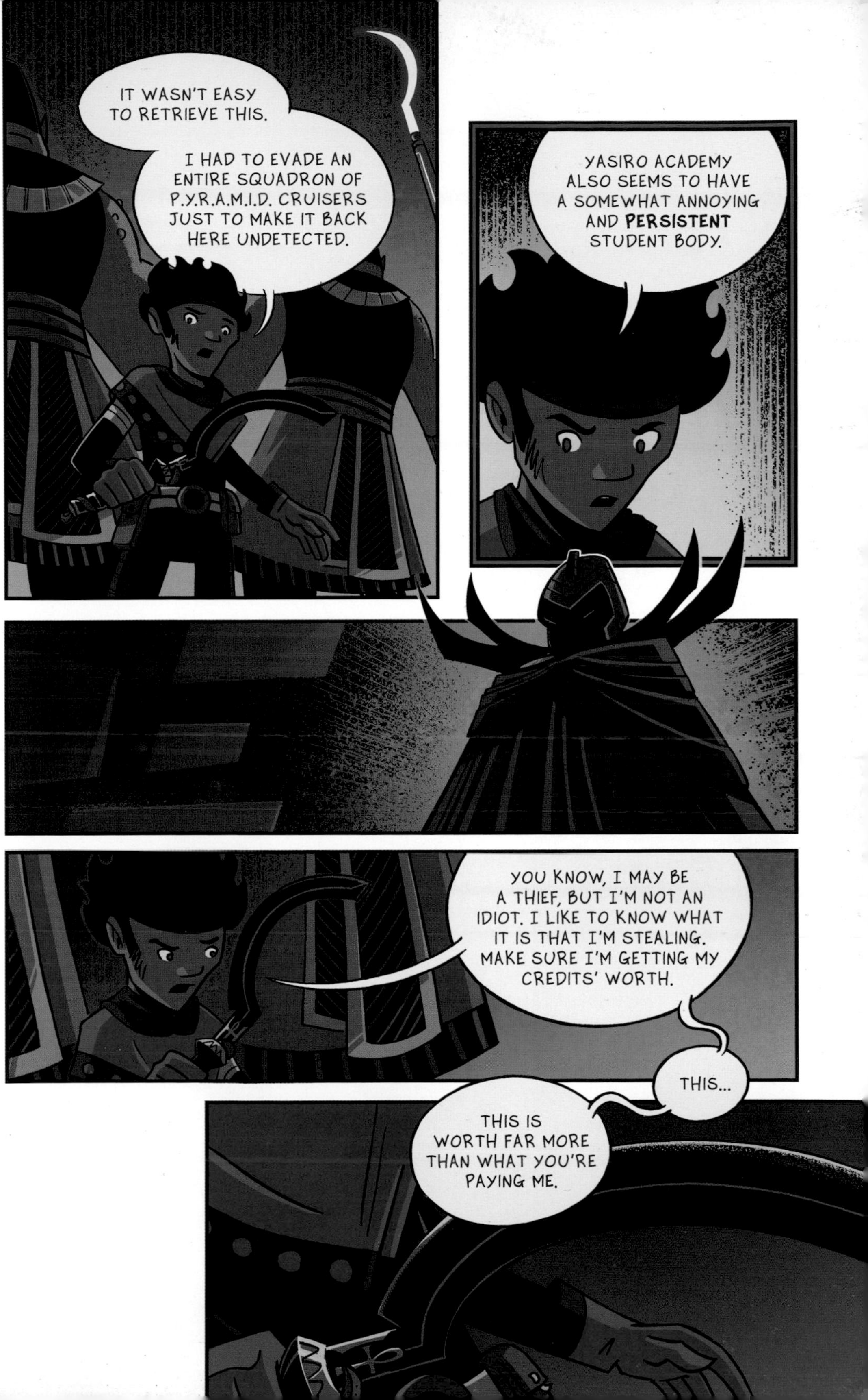
IT WASN'T EASY TO RETRIEVE THIS.
I HAD TO EVADE AN ENTIRE SQUADRON OF P.Y.R.A.M.I.D. CRUISERS JUST TO MAKE IT BACK HERE UNDETECTED.
YASIRO ACADEMY ALSO SEEMS TO HAVE A SOMEWHAT ANNOYING AND **PERSISTENT** STUDENT BODY.
YOU KNOW, I MAY BE A THIEF, BUT I'M NOT AN IDIOT. I LIKE TO KNOW WHAT IT IS THAT I'M STEALING. MAKE SURE I'M GETTING MY CREDITS' WORTH.
THIS...
THIS IS WORTH FAR MORE THAN WHAT YOU'RE PAYING ME.

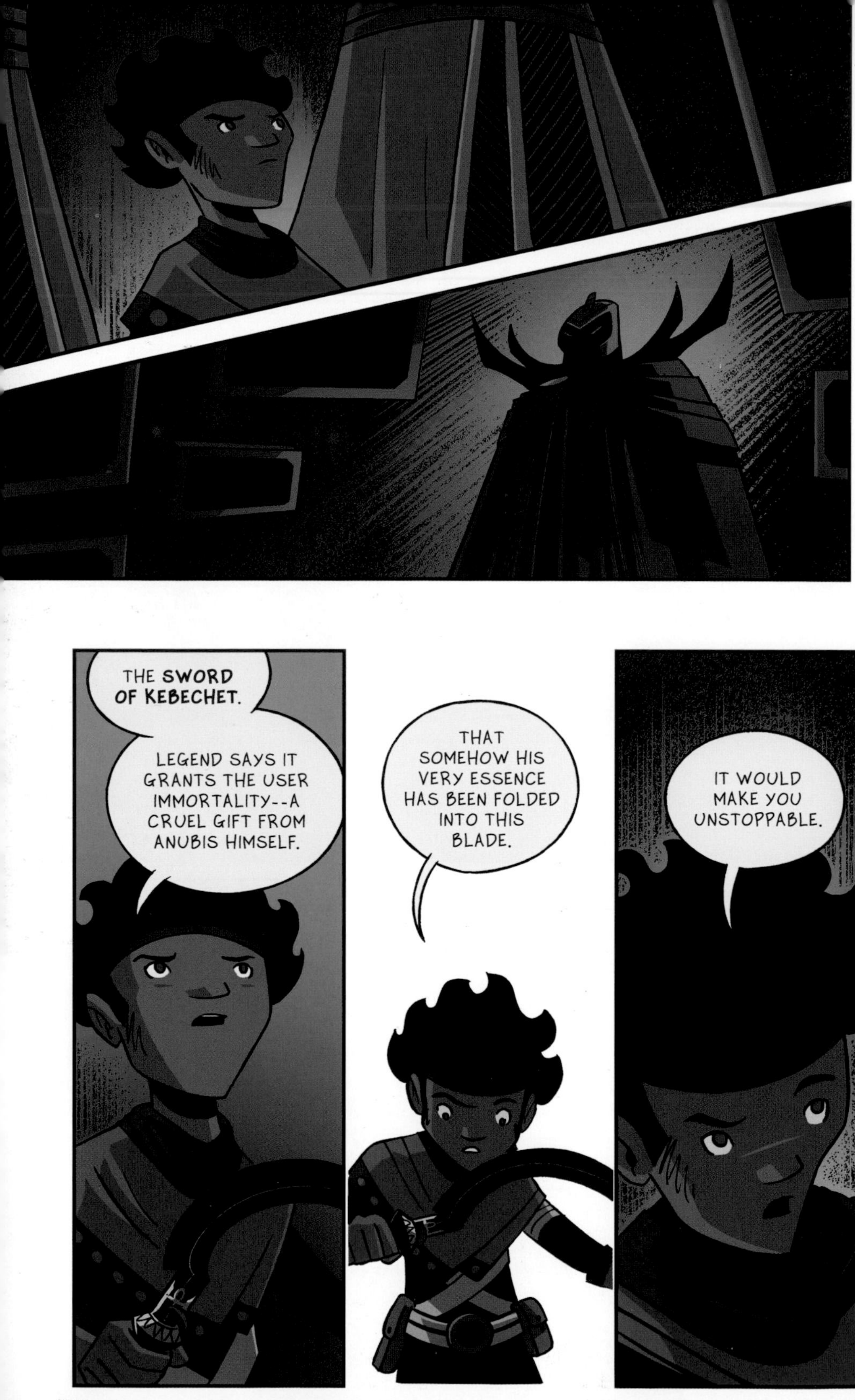
THE **SWORD OF KEBECHET**.
LEGEND SAYS IT GRANTS THE USER IMMORTALITY--A CRUEL GIFT FROM ANUBIS HIMSELF.
THAT SOMEHOW HIS VERY ESSENCE HAS BEEN FOLDED INTO THIS BLADE.
IT WOULD MAKE YOU UNSTOPPABLE.

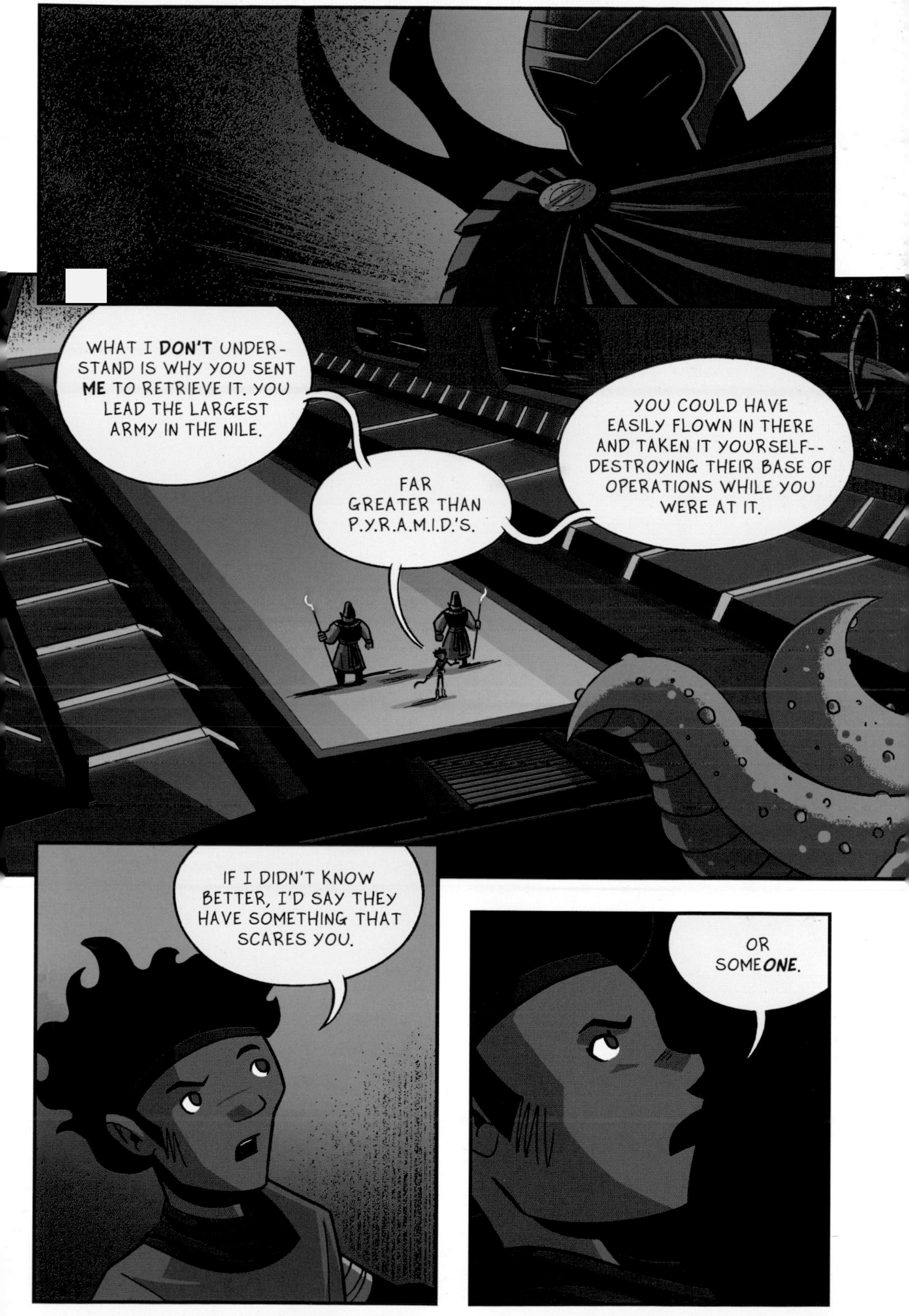

WHAT I DON'T UNDER-STAND IS WHY YOU SENT ME TO RETRIEVE IT. YOU LEAD THE LARGEST ARMY IN THE NILE.
FAR GREATER THAN P.Y.R.A.M.I.D.'S.
YOU COULD HAVE EASILY FLOWN IN THERE AND TAKEN IT YOURSELF-- DESTROYING THEIR BASE OF OPERATIONS WHILE YOU WERE AT IT.
IF I DIDN'T KNOW BETTER, I'D SAY THEY HAVE SOMETHING THAT SCARES YOU.
OR SOMEONE.

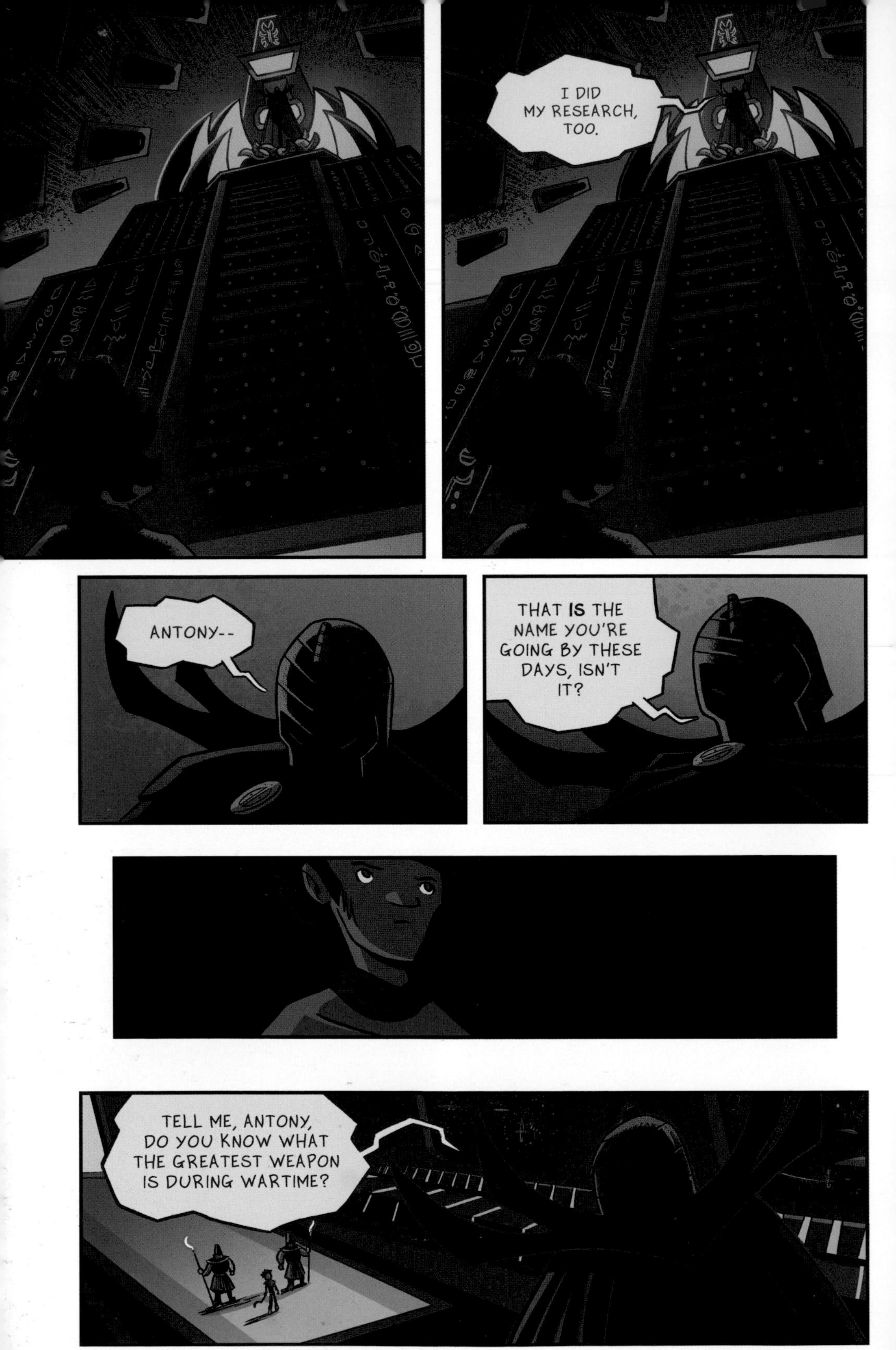
I DID MY RESEARCH, TOO.
ANTONY--
THAT IS THE NAME YOU'RE GOING BY THESE DAYS, ISN'T IT?
TELL ME, ANTONY, DO YOU KNOW WHAT THE GREATEST WEAPON IS DURING WARTIME?

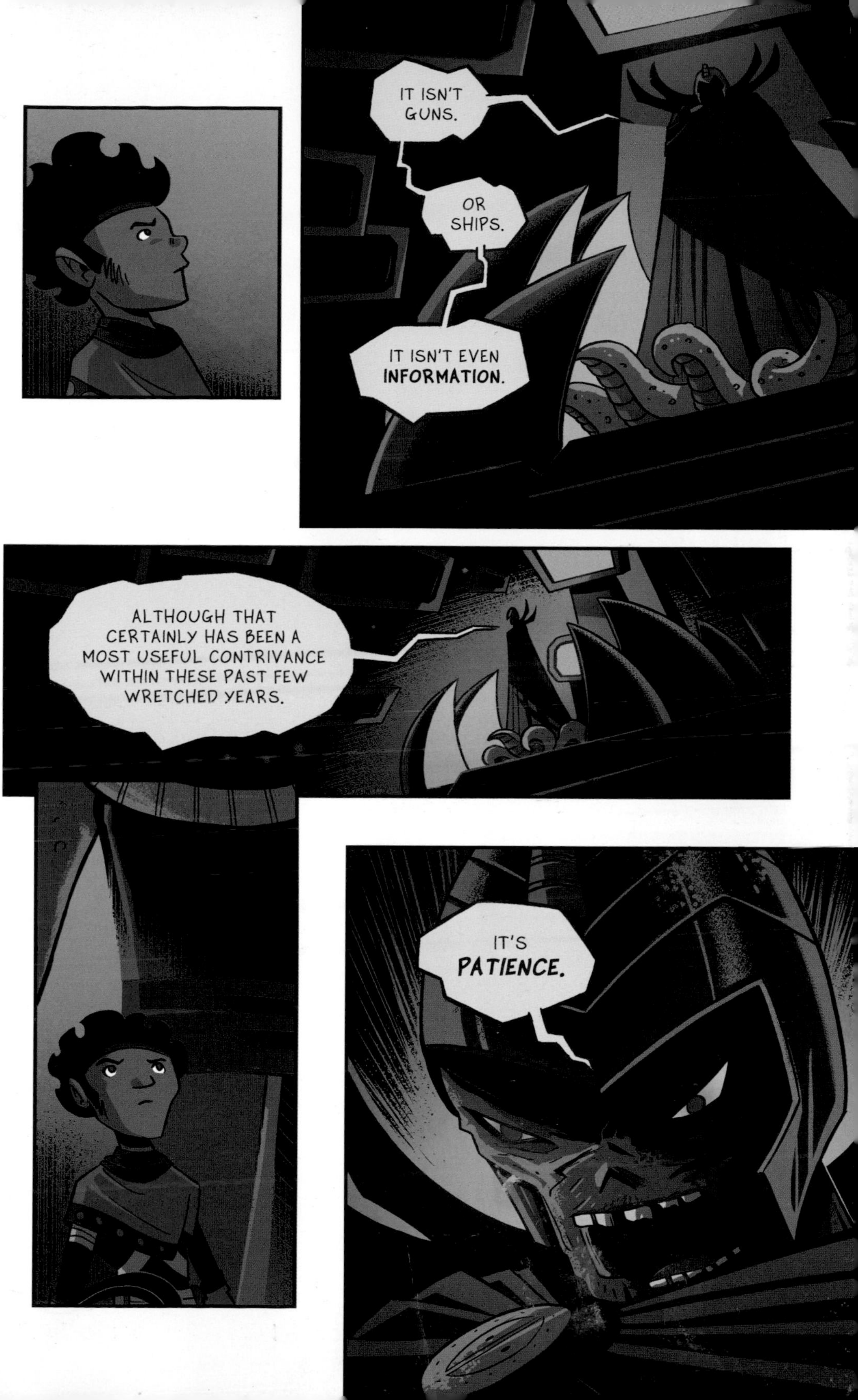
IT ISN'T GUNS.
OR SHIPS.
IT ISN'T EVEN **INFORMATION.**
ALTHOUGH THAT CERTAINLY HAS BEEN A MOST USEFUL CONTRIVANCE WITHIN THESE PAST FEW WRETCHED YEARS.
IT'S **PATIENCE.**

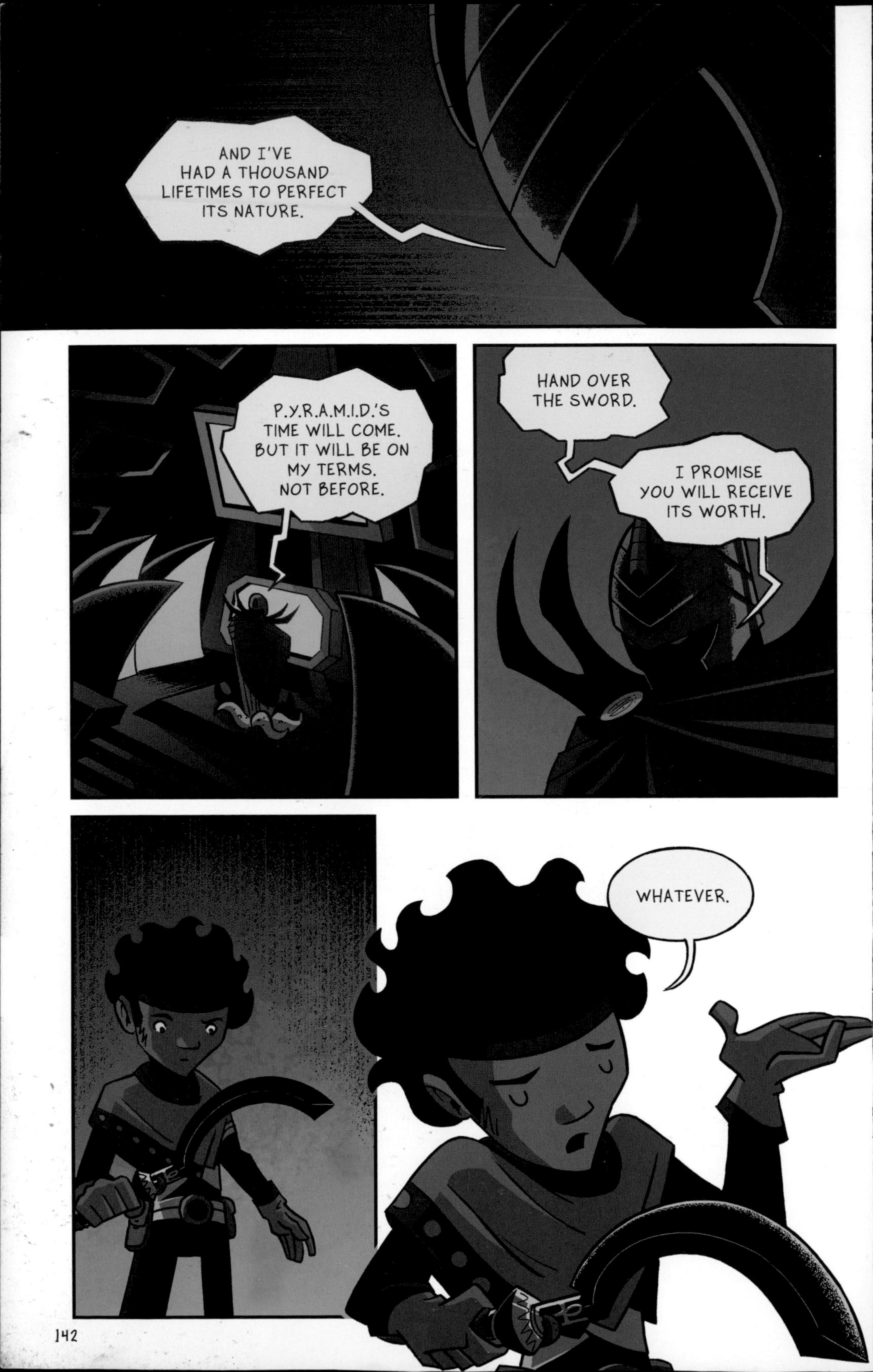
AND I'VE HAD A THOUSAND LIFETIMES TO PERFECT ITS NATURE.
P.Y.R.A.M.I.D.'S TIME WILL COME. BUT IT WILL BE ON MY TERMS. NOT BEFORE.
HAND OVER THE SWORD.
I PROMISE YOU WILL RECEIVE ITS WORTH.
WHATEVER.

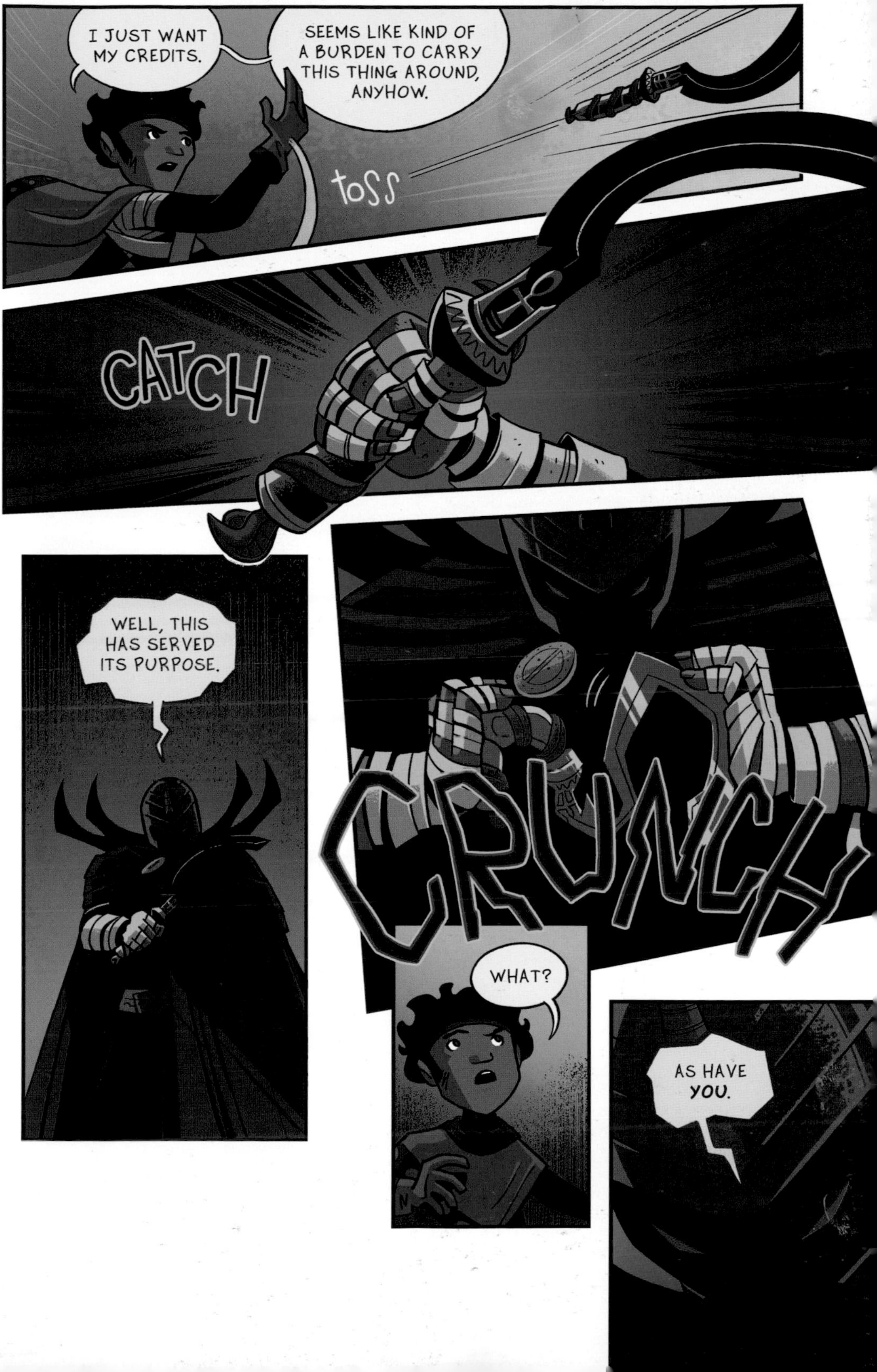
I JUST WANT MY CREDITS.
SEEMS LIKE KIND OF A BURDEN TO CARRY THIS THING AROUND, ANYHOW.
TOSS
CATCH
WELL, THIS HAS SERVED ITS PURPOSE.
CRUNCH
WHAT?
AS HAVE **YOU**.

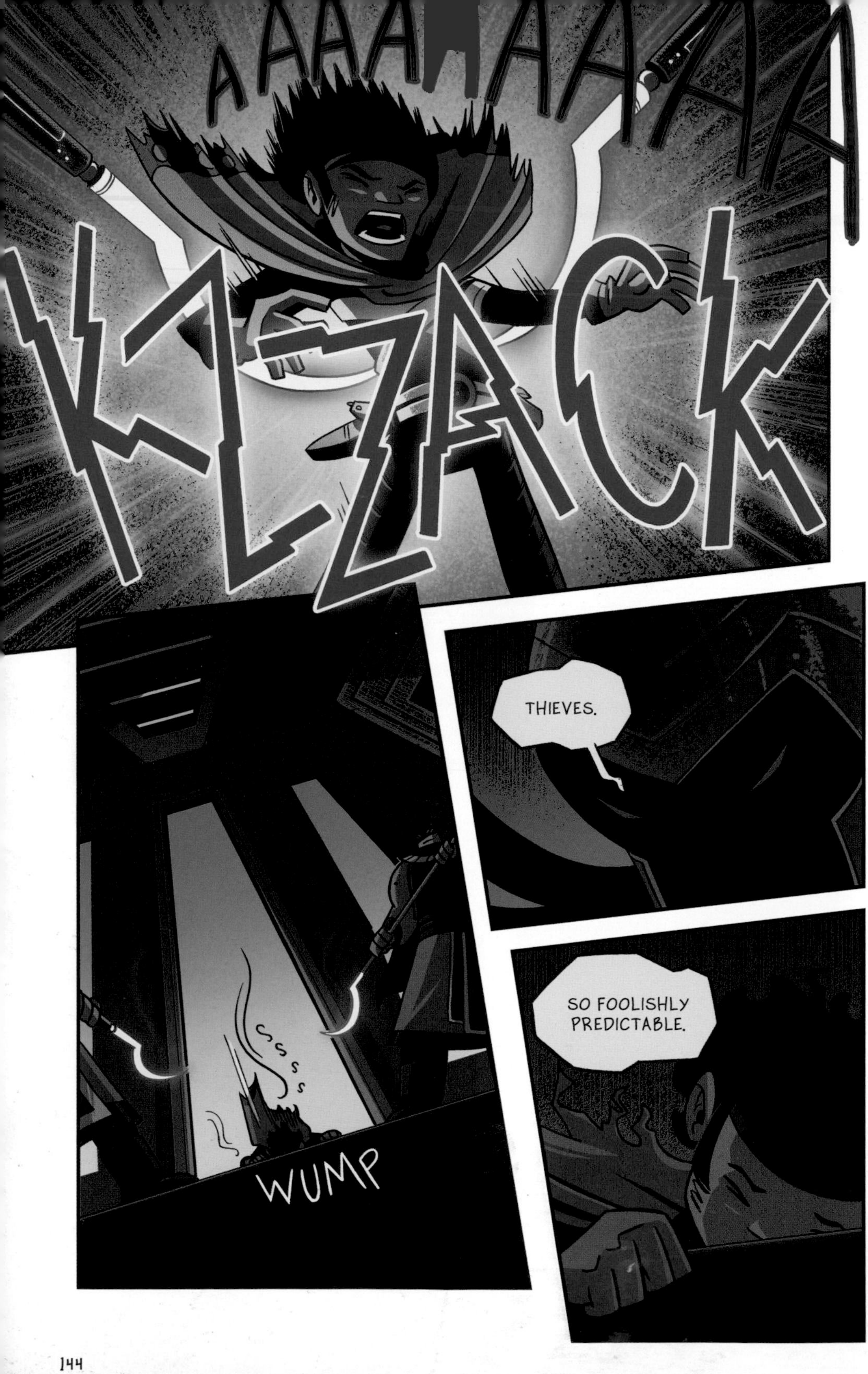
AAAAAAAAAAA
KZZACK
WUMP
Ssss
THIEVES.
SO FOOLISHLY PREDICTABLE.

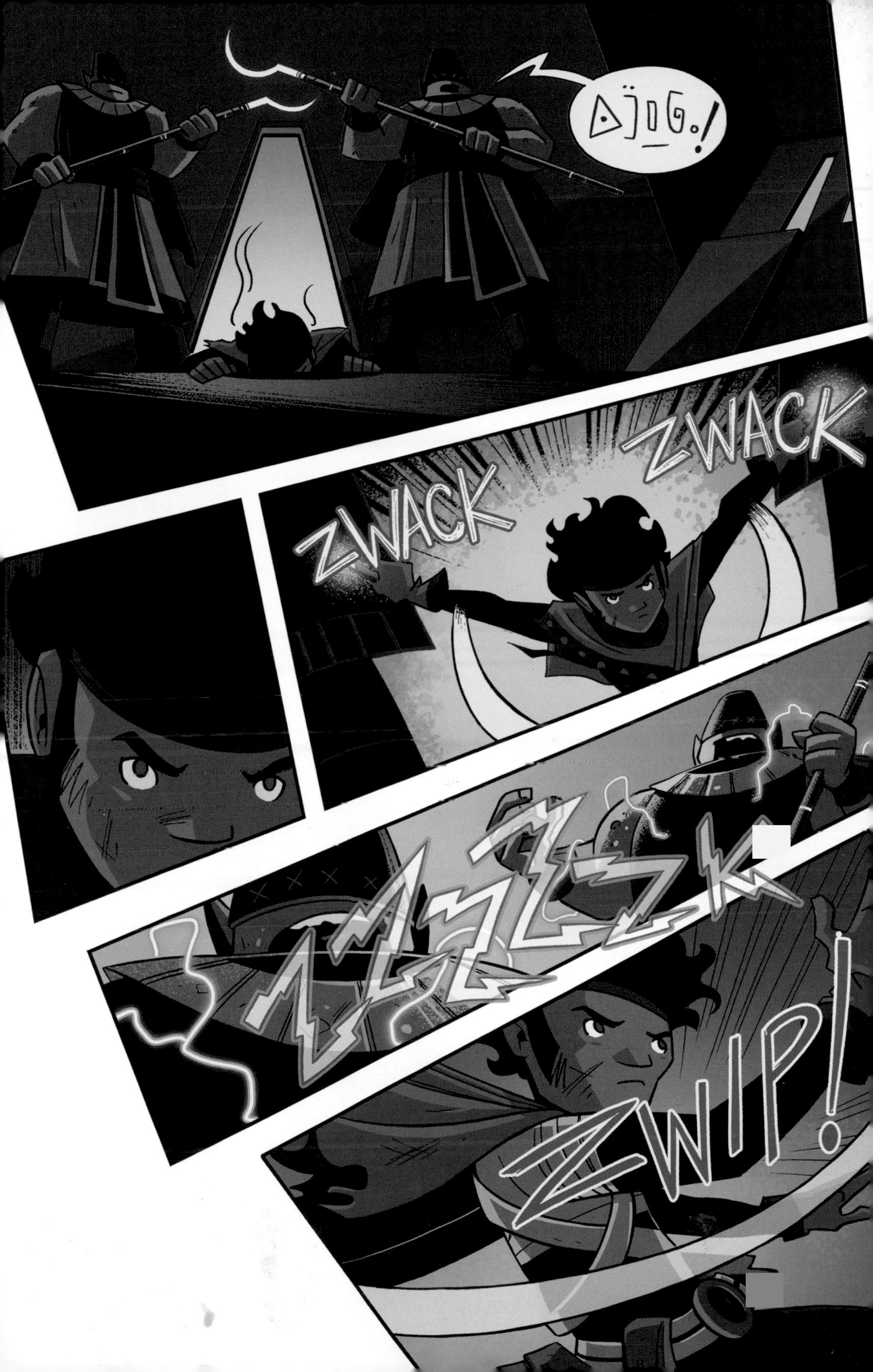
ZWACK
ZWACK
ZWIP!

ZZWIP

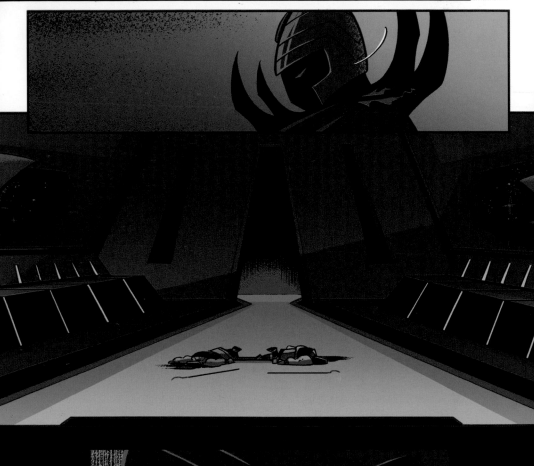

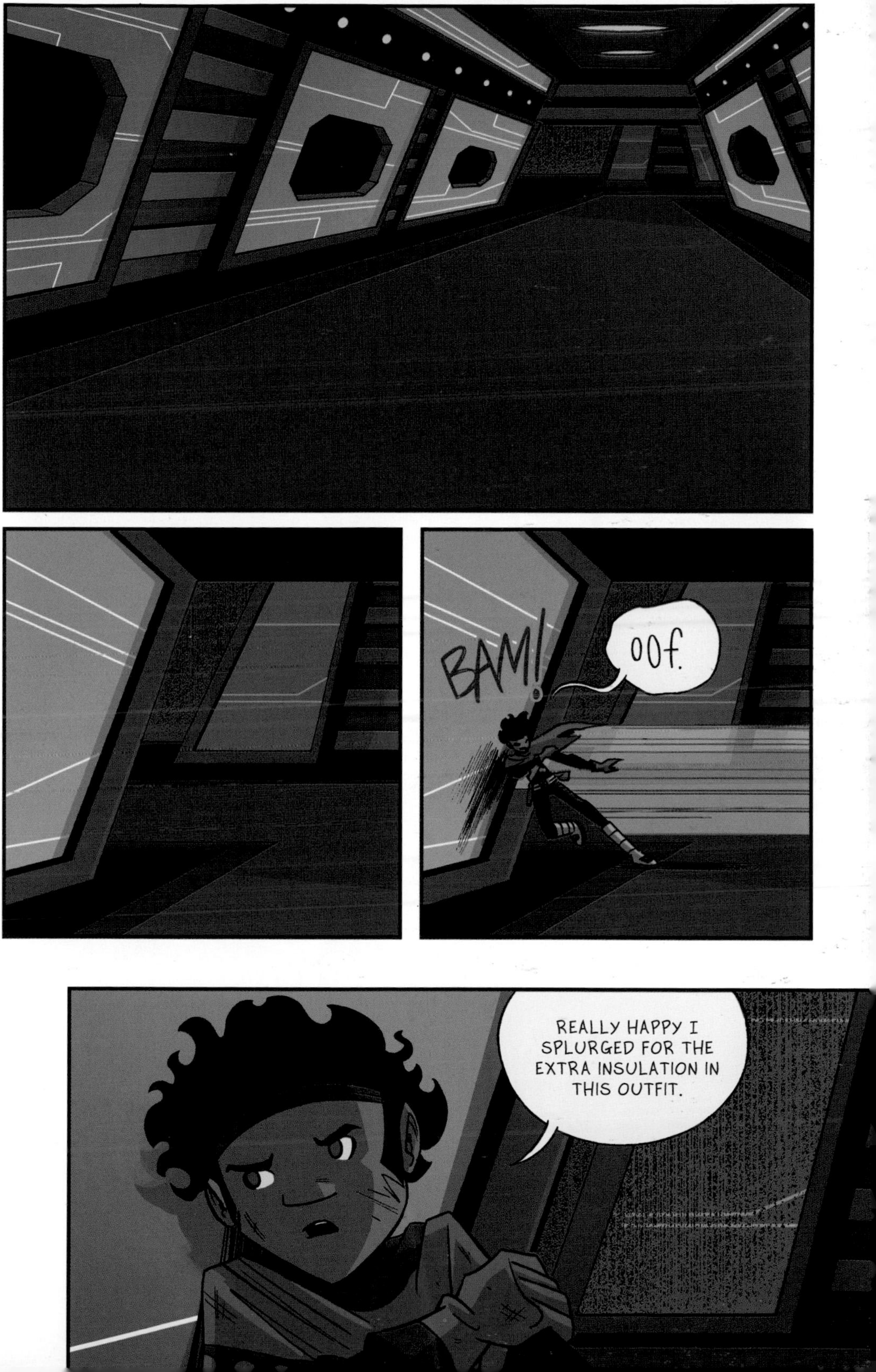
BAM!
OOF.
REALLY HAPPY I SPLURGED FOR THE EXTRA INSULATION IN THIS OUTFIT.

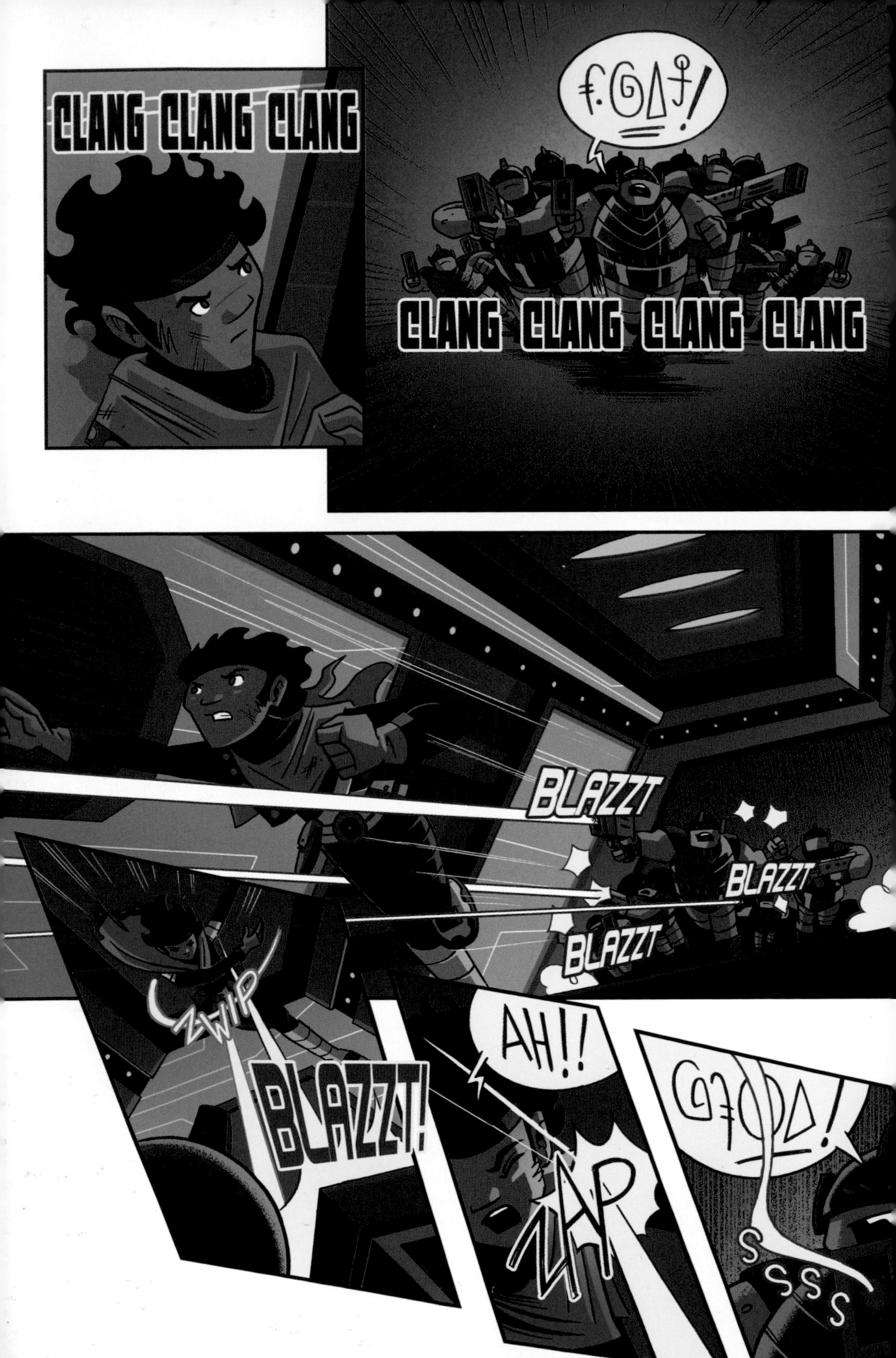
CLANG CLANG CLANG
CLANG CLANG CLANG CLANG
BLAZZT
BLAZZT
BLAZZT
ZWIP
BLAZZZT!
AH!!
ZAP
SSSSS

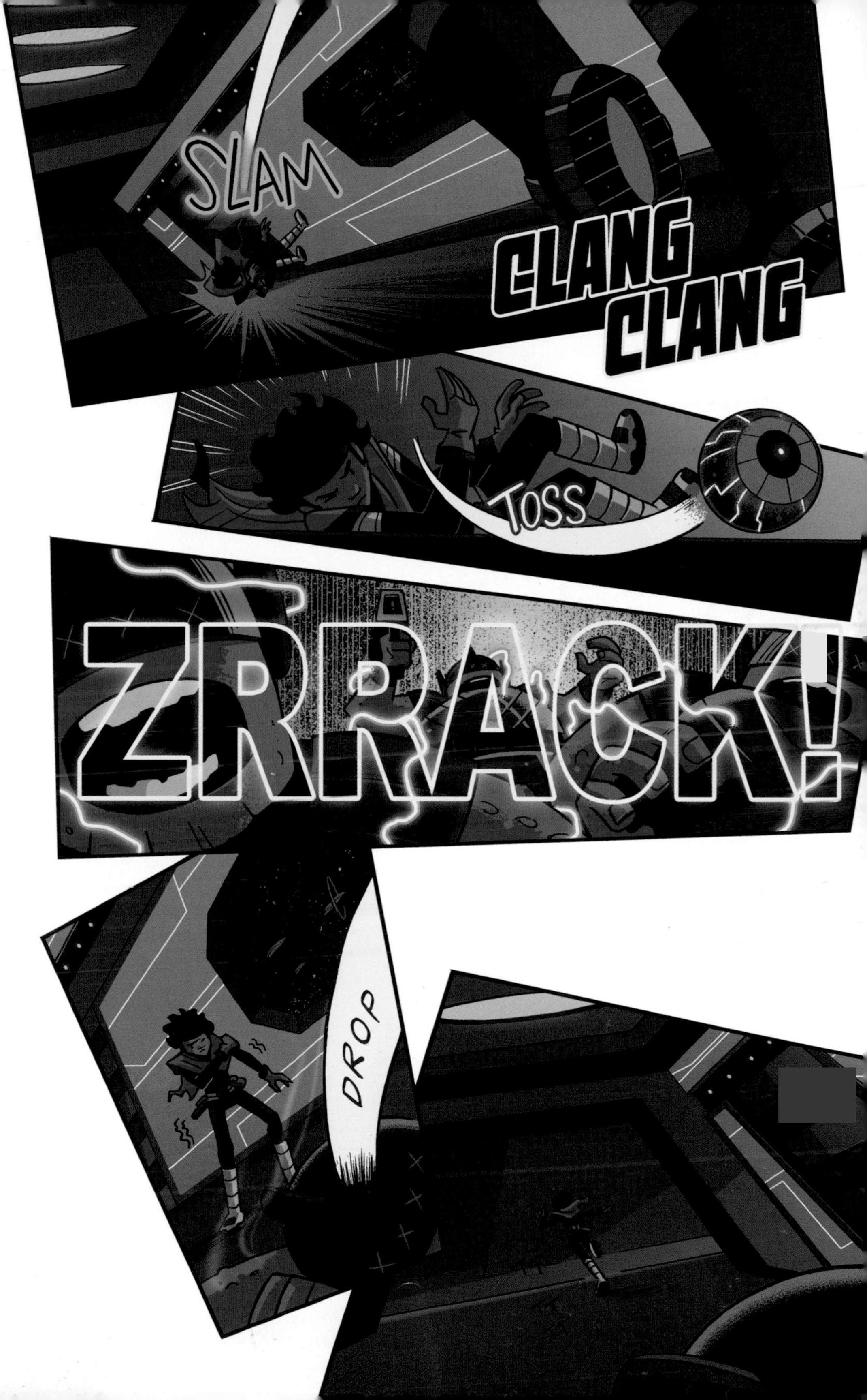
SLAM
CLANG
CLANG
TOSS
ZRRACK!
DROP

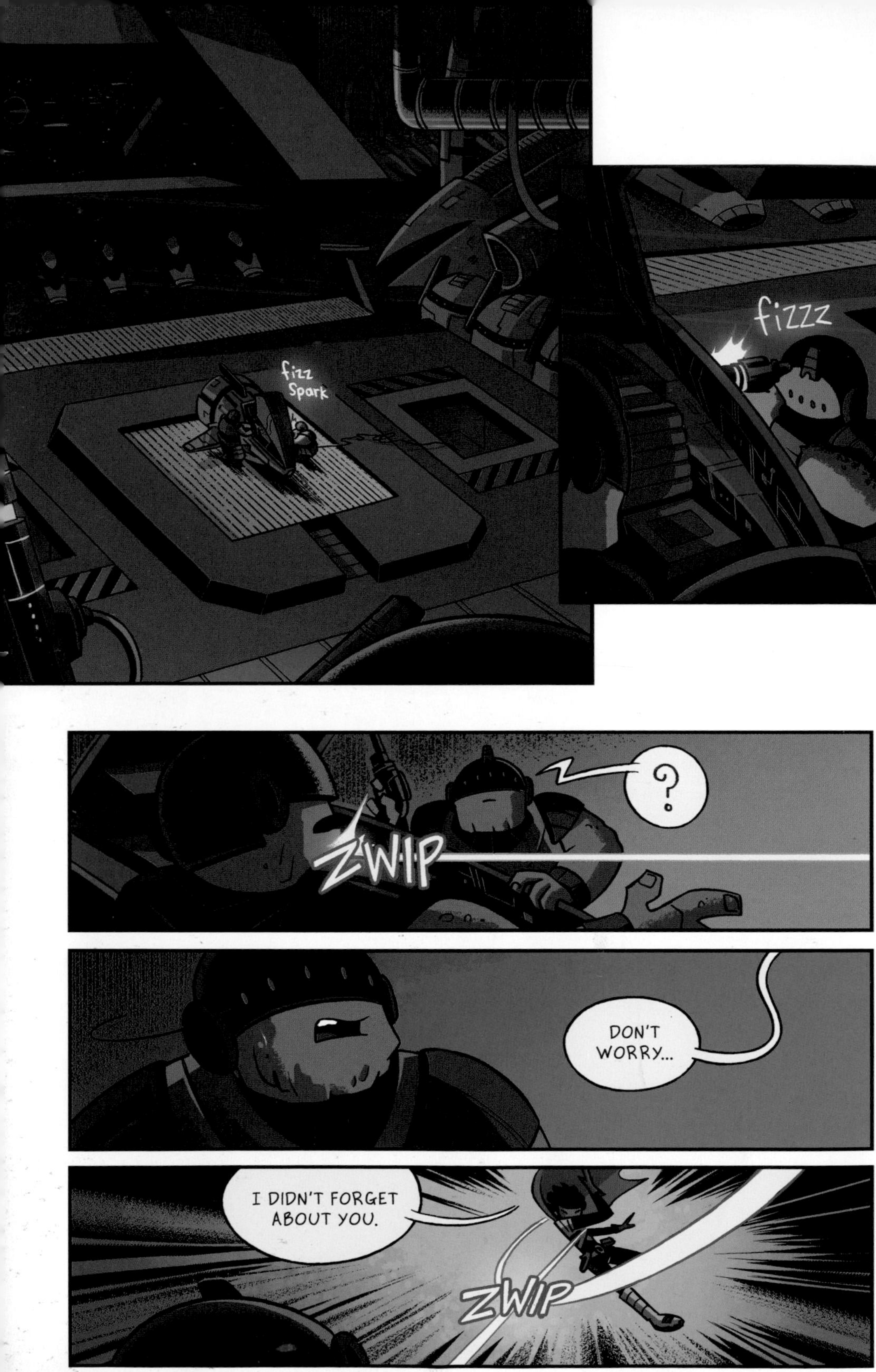
fizz
Spark
fizzz
?
ZWIP
DON'T WORRY...
I DIDN'T FORGET ABOUT YOU.
ZWIP

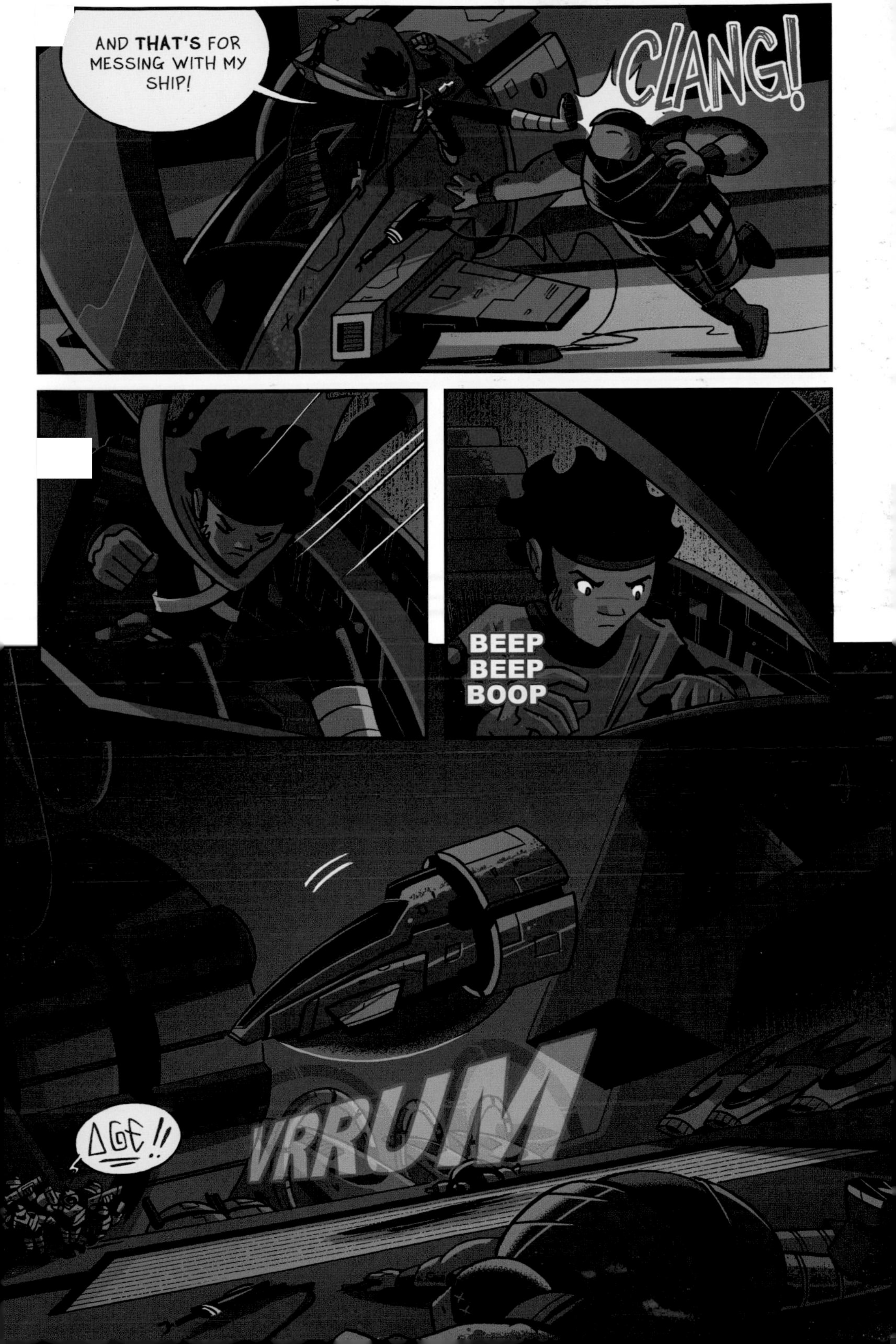
AND **THAT'S** FOR MESSING WITH MY SHIP!
CLANG!
BEEP
BEEP
BOOP
ΔGE!!
VRRUM

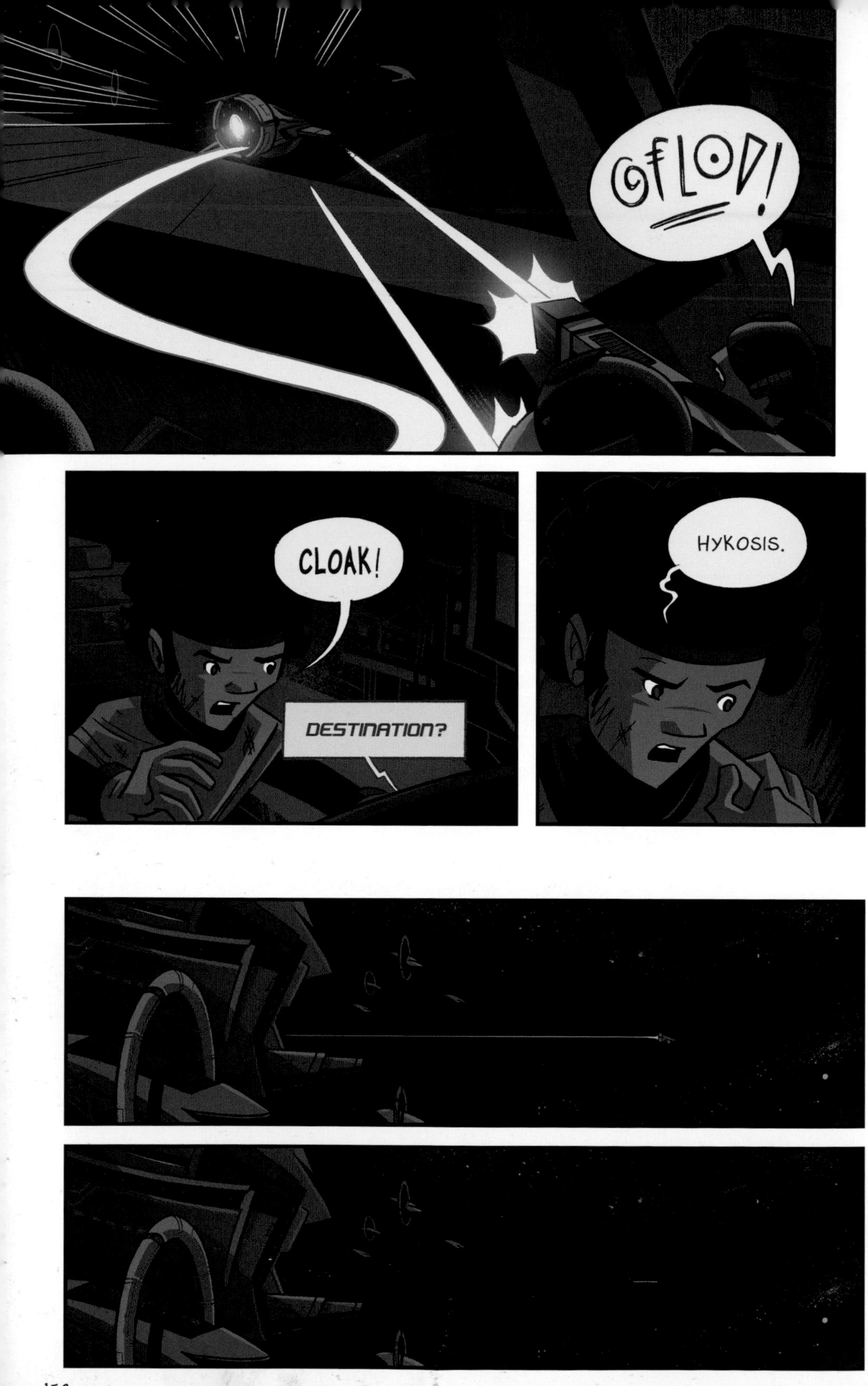
GFLOD!
CLOAK!
DESTINATION?
HYKOSIS.

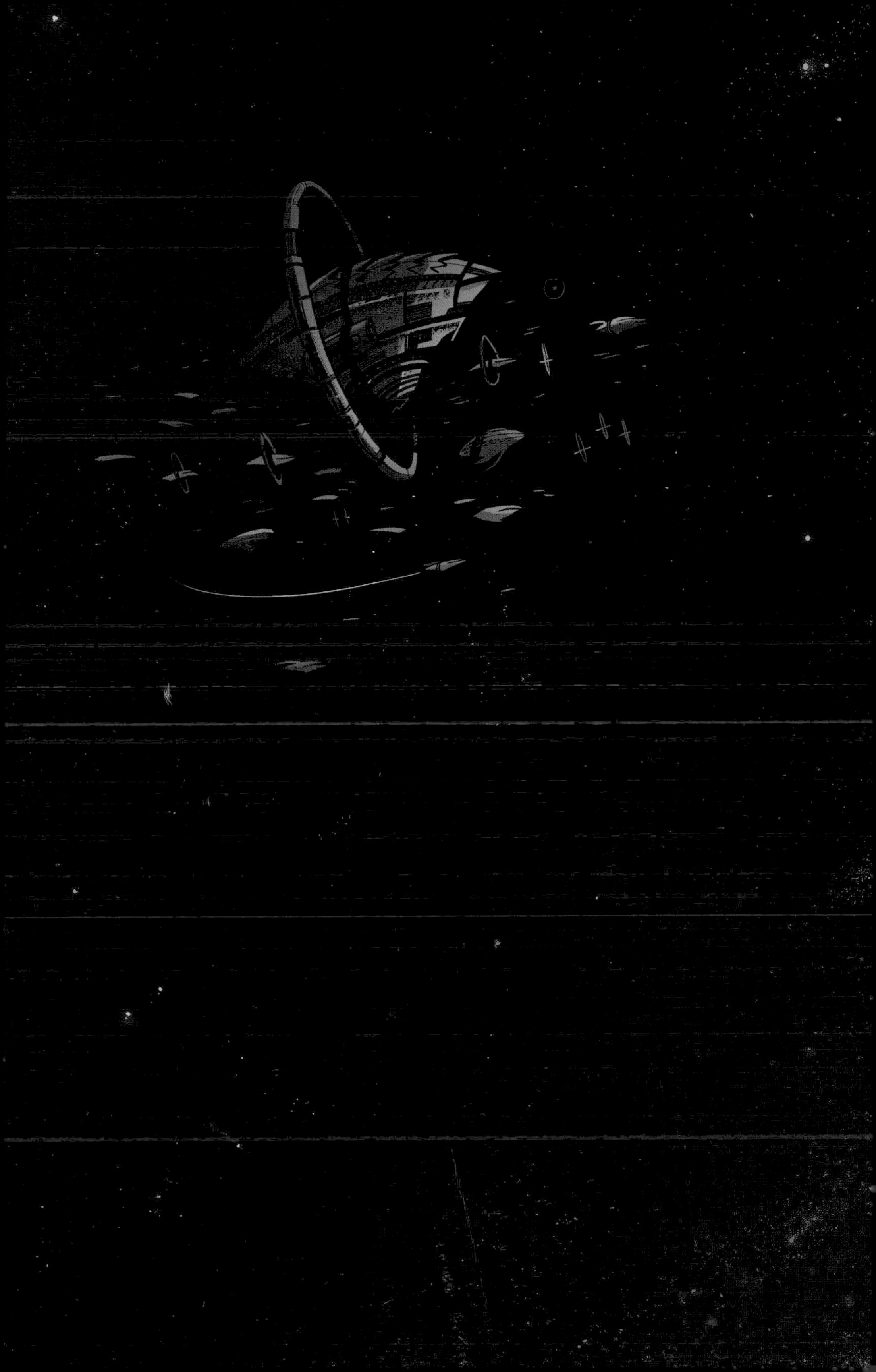

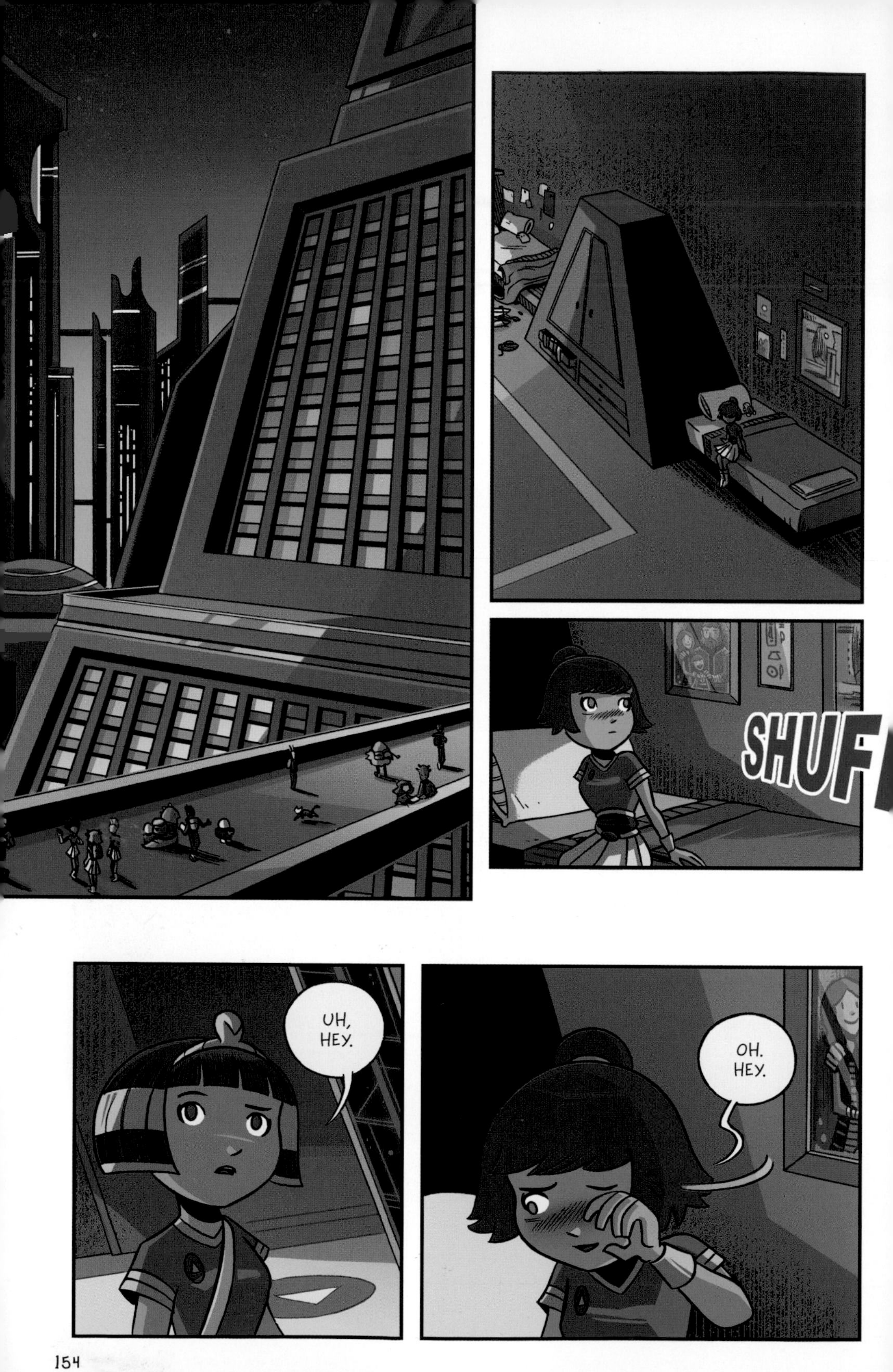
SHUF
UH, HEY.
OH. HEY.

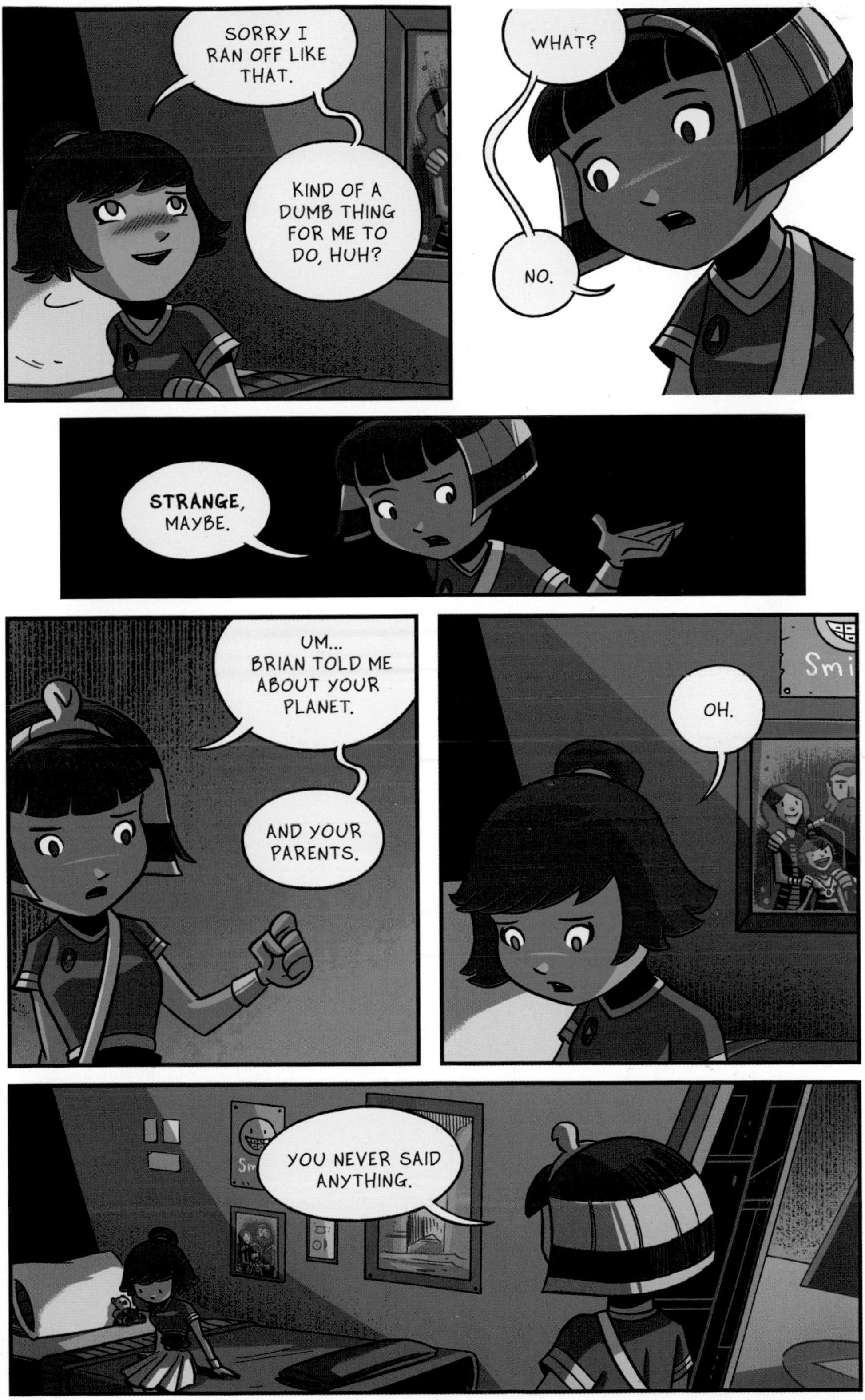
SORRY I RAN OFF LIKE THAT.
KIND OF A DUMB THING FOR ME TO DO, HUH?
WHAT?
NO.
STRANGE, MAYBE.
UM... BRIAN TOLD ME ABOUT YOUR PLANET.
AND YOUR PARENTS.
OH.
YOU NEVER SAID ANYTHING.

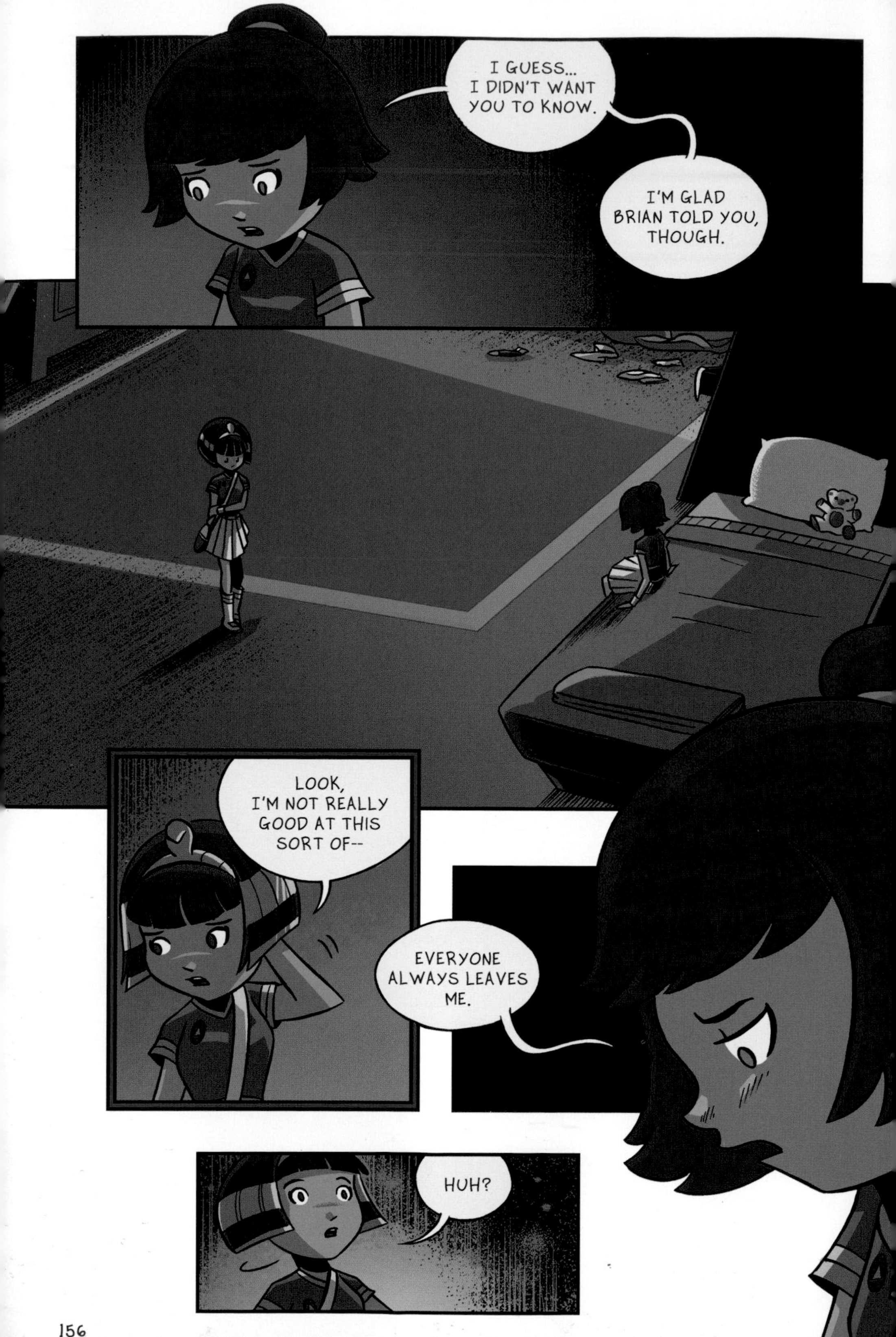
I GUESS... I DIDN'T WANT YOU TO KNOW.
I'M GLAD BRIAN TOLD YOU, THOUGH.
LOOK, I'M NOT REALLY GOOD AT THIS SORT OF--
EVERYONE ALWAYS LEAVES ME.
HUH?

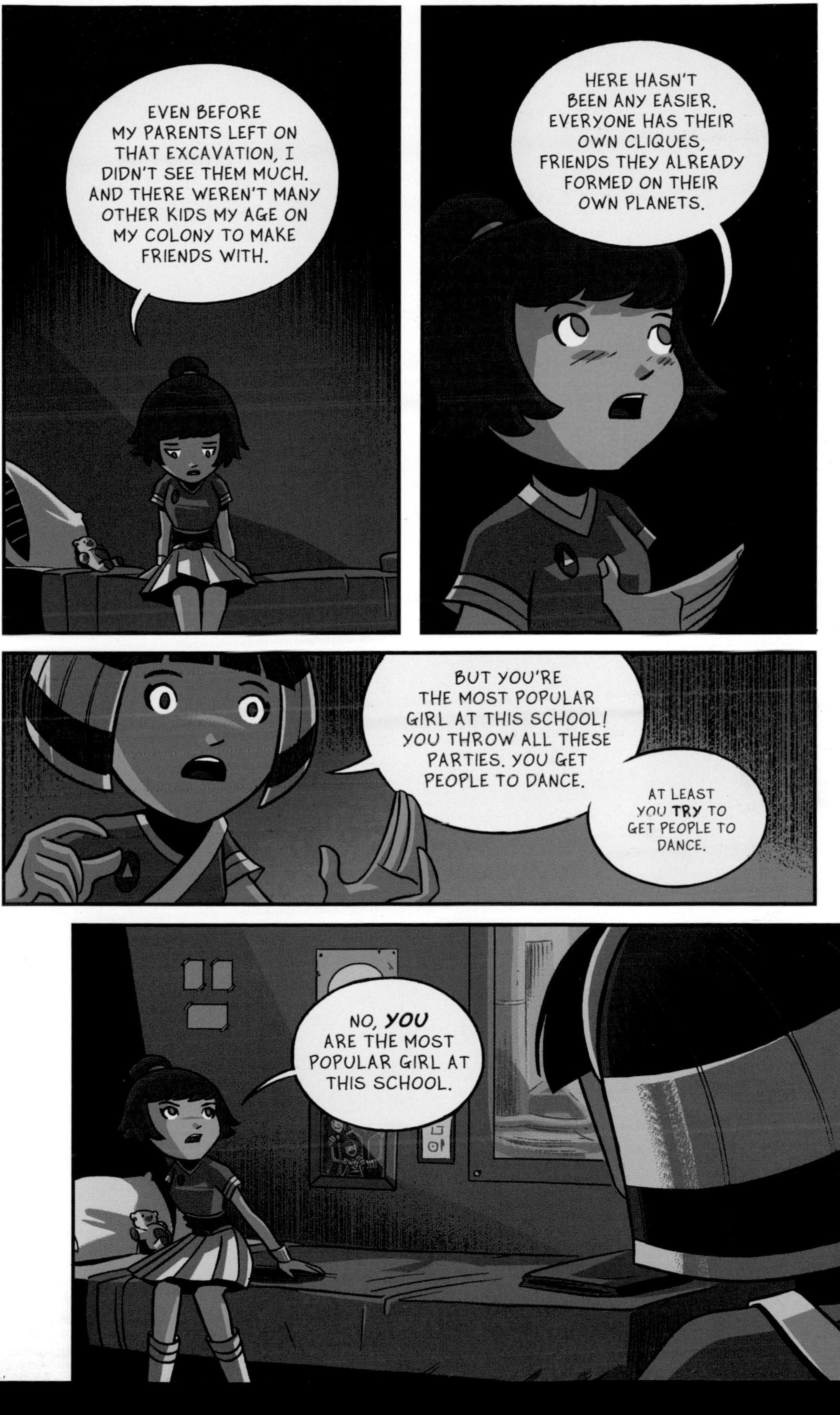
EVEN BEFORE MY PARENTS LEFT ON THAT EXCAVATION, I DIDN'T SEE THEM MUCH. AND THERE WEREN'T MANY OTHER KIDS MY AGE ON MY COLONY TO MAKE FRIENDS WITH.
HERE HASN'T BEEN ANY EASIER. EVERYONE HAS THEIR OWN CLIQUES, FRIENDS THEY ALREADY FORMED ON THEIR OWN PLANETS.
BUT YOU'RE THE MOST POPULAR GIRL AT THIS SCHOOL! YOU THROW ALL THESE PARTIES. YOU GET PEOPLE TO DANCE.
AT LEAST YOU **TRY** TO GET PEOPLE TO DANCE.
NO, ***YOU*** ARE THE MOST POPULAR GIRL AT THIS SCHOOL.

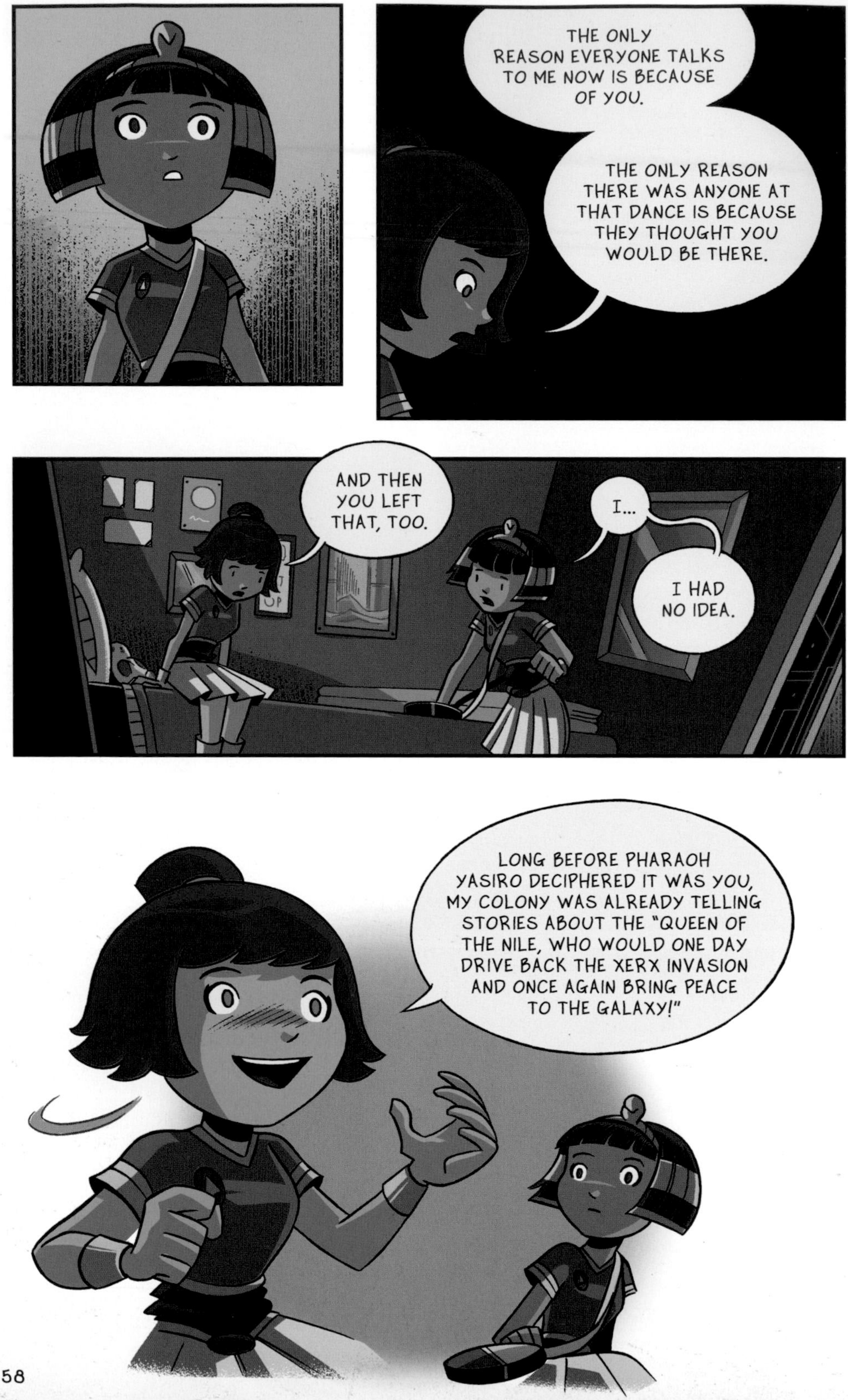
THE ONLY REASON EVERYONE TALKS TO ME NOW IS BECAUSE OF YOU.
THE ONLY REASON THERE WAS ANYONE AT THAT DANCE IS BECAUSE THEY THOUGHT YOU WOULD BE THERE.
AND THEN YOU LEFT THAT, TOO.
I...
I HAD NO IDEA.
LONG BEFORE PHARAOH YASIRO DECIPHERED IT WAS YOU, MY COLONY WAS ALREADY TELLING STORIES ABOUT THE "QUEEN OF THE NILE, WHO WOULD ONE DAY DRIVE BACK THE XERX INVASION AND ONCE AGAIN BRING PEACE TO THE GALAXY!"

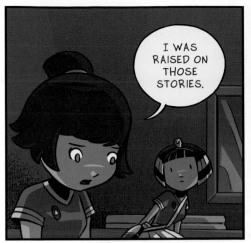

I WAS RAISED ON THOSE STORIES.

YOU'RE THE MAIN REASON MY PARENTS LEFT ON THEIR EXCAVATION TO BEGIN WITH.

IT'S ALL RIGHT. I MEAN... I GET IT. I KNOW WHY YOU'D WANT TO GO BACK TO YOUR OWN TIME.

YOUR FAMILY IS THERE. YOUR LIFE IS THERE. IT'S JUST...

IT WAS NICE TO HAVE A ROOMMATE WHO ACTUALLY HUNG OUT WITH ME.

OKAY, *NOW* YOU'RE ACTING DUMB.

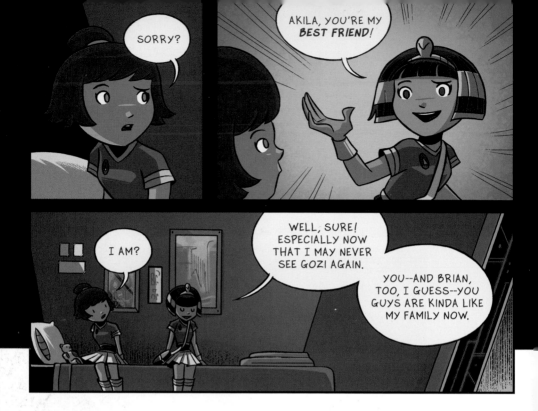

SORRY?

AKILA, YOU'RE MY **BEST FRIEND!**

I AM?

WELL, SURE! ESPECIALLY NOW THAT I MAY NEVER SEE GOZI AGAIN.

YOU--AND BRIAN, TOO, I GUESS--YOU GUYS ARE KINDA LIKE MY FAMILY NOW.

MY LIFE RIGHT NOW? IT'S *INSANE!* THERE'S A PROPHECY SURROUNDING ME, CATS TELL ME WHAT TO DO, A GIANT SQUID SITS NEXT TO ME IN GEOLOGY, NOT TO MENTION *ELECTRICITY...!*

YOU'RE ABOUT THE ONLY THING IN MY LIFE THAT'S EVEN REMOTELY NORMAL.

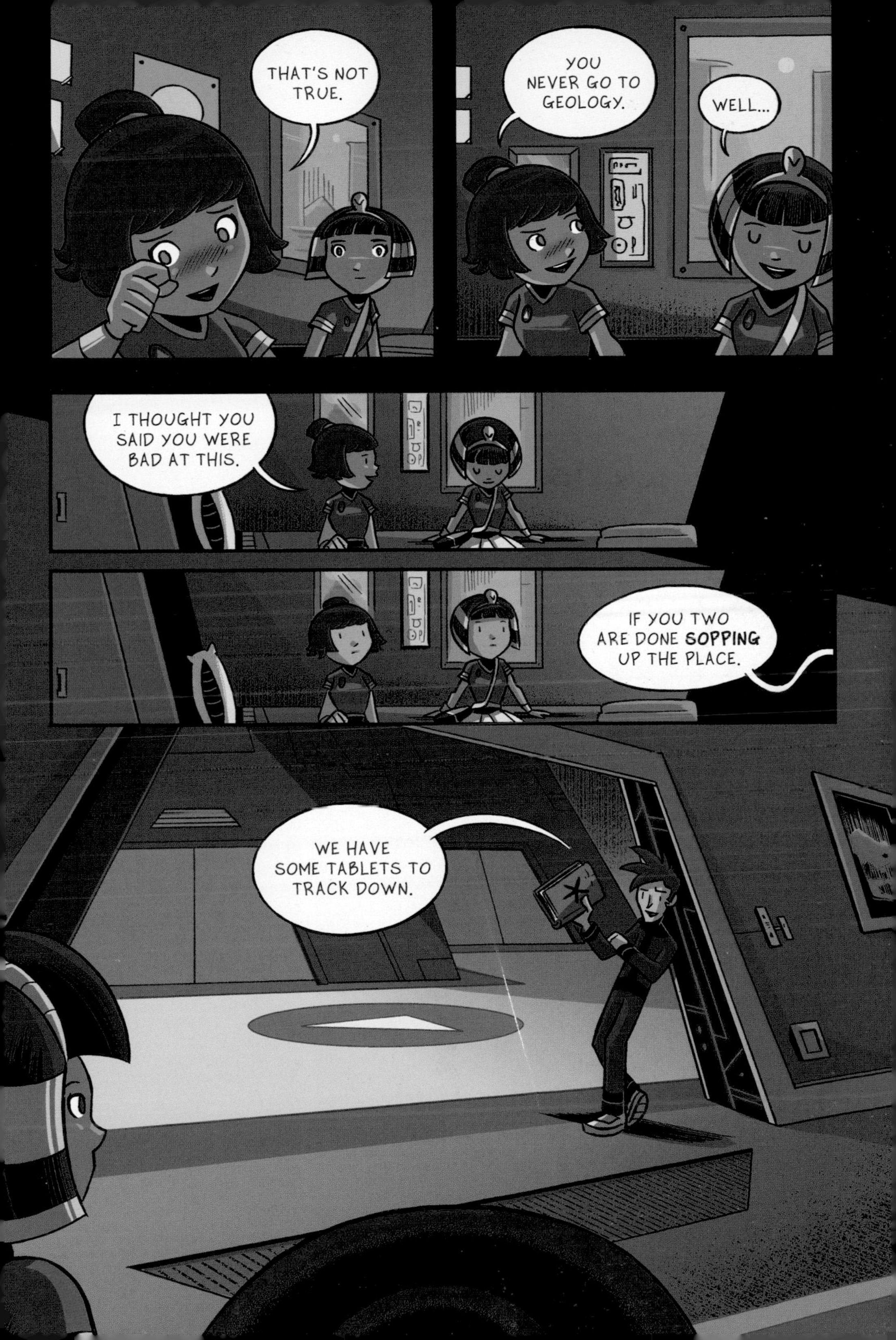
THAT'S NOT TRUE.
YOU NEVER GO TO GEOLOGY.
WELL...
I THOUGHT YOU SAID YOU WERE BAD AT THIS.
IF YOU TWO ARE DONE **SOPPING** UP THE PLACE.
WE HAVE SOME TABLETS TO TRACK DOWN.

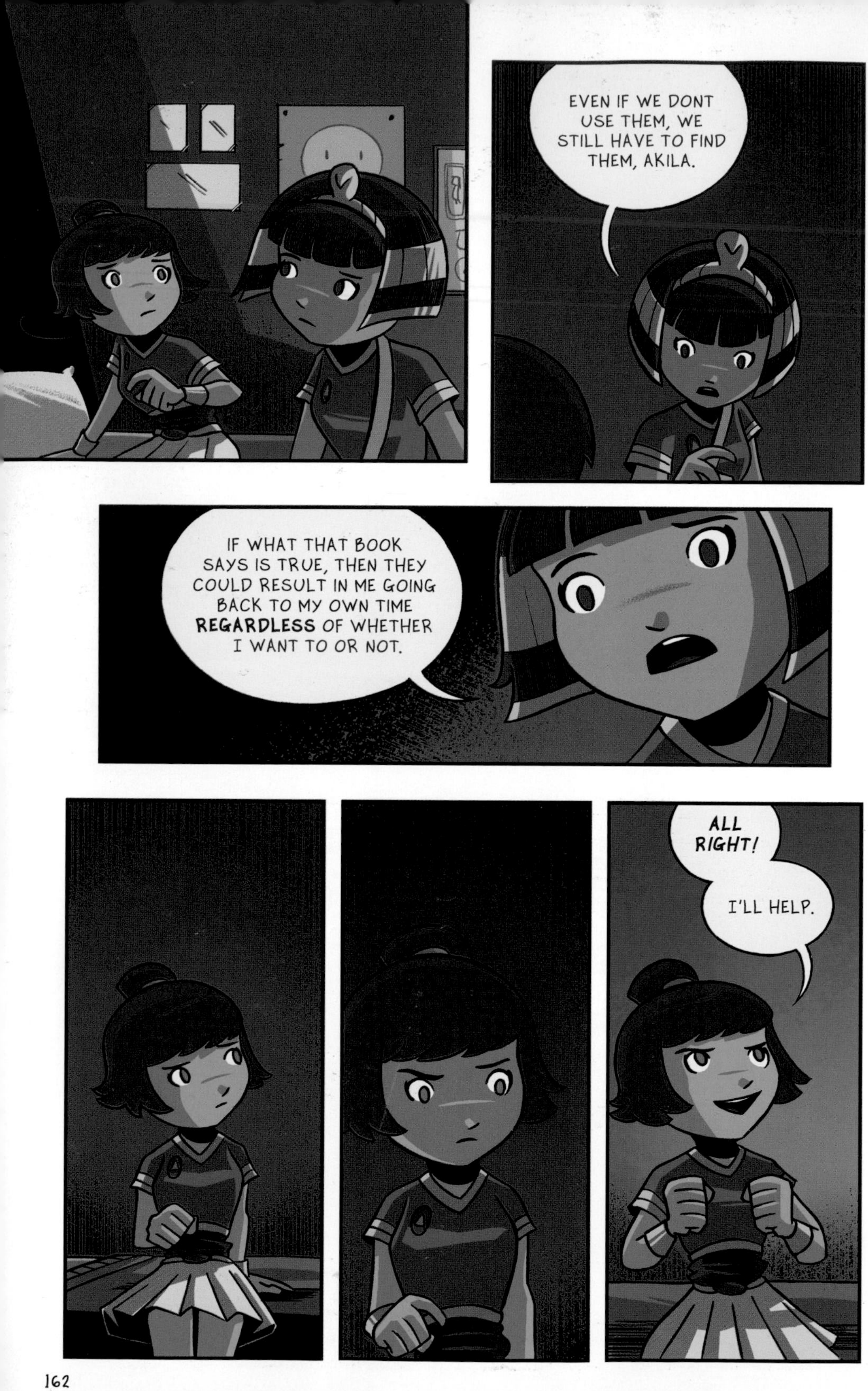
EVEN IF WE DONT USE THEM, WE STILL HAVE TO FIND THEM, AKILA.
IF WHAT THAT BOOK SAYS IS TRUE, THEN THEY COULD RESULT IN ME GOING BACK TO MY OWN TIME **REGARDLESS** OF WHETHER I WANT TO OR NOT.
ALL RIGHT!
I'LL HELP.

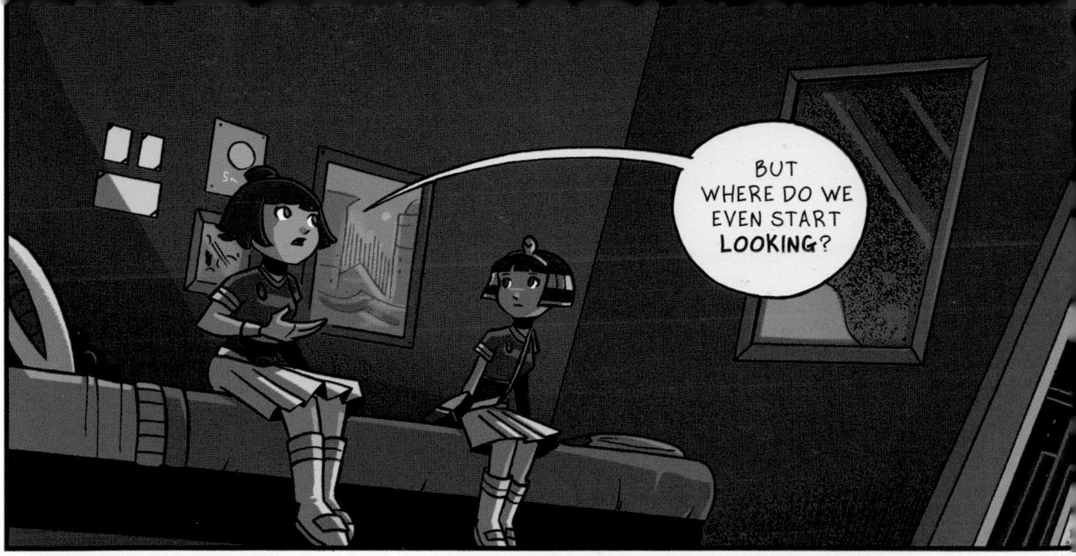
BUT WHERE DO WE EVEN START **LOOKING**?

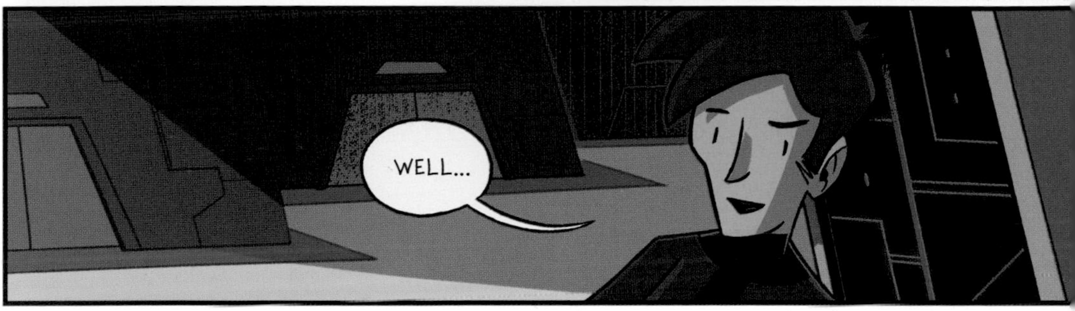
WELL...

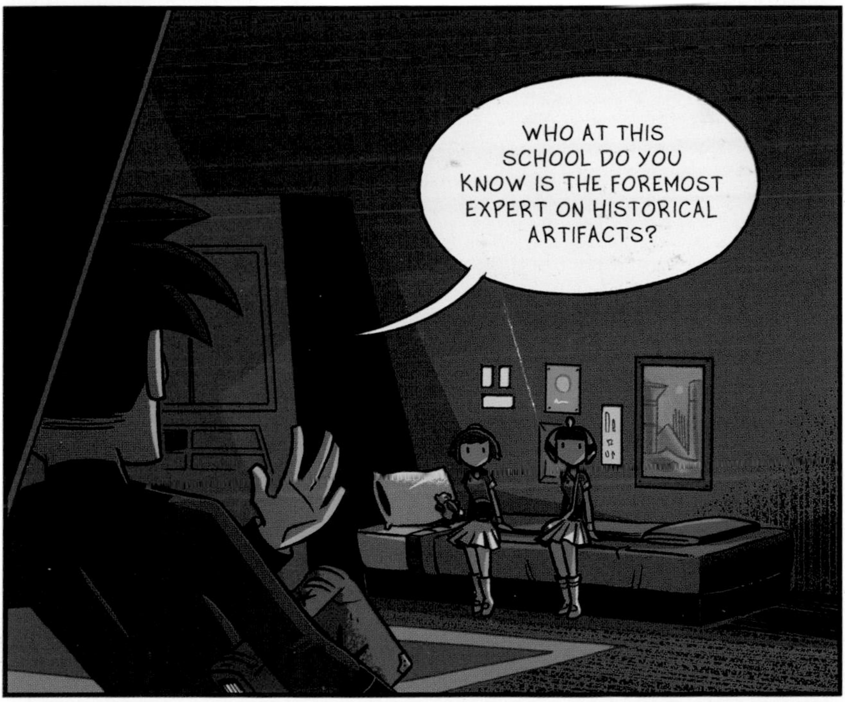
WHO AT THIS SCHOOL DO YOU KNOW IS THE FOREMOST EXPERT ON HISTORICAL ARTIFACTS?

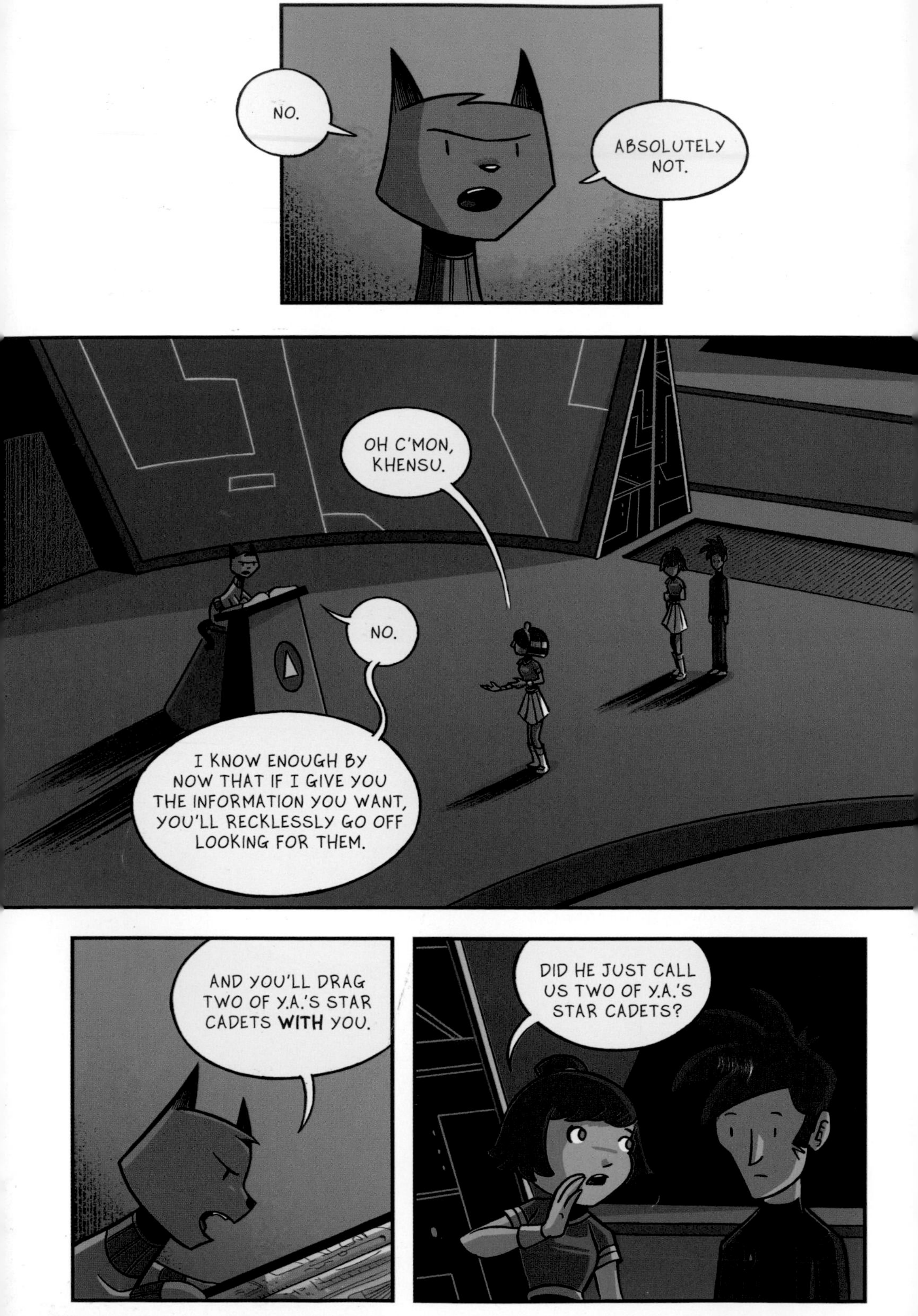
NO.
ABSOLUTELY NOT.
OH C'MON, KHENSU.
NO.
I KNOW ENOUGH BY NOW THAT IF I GIVE YOU THE INFORMATION YOU WANT, YOU'LL RECKLESSLY GO OFF LOOKING FOR THEM.
AND YOU'LL DRAG TWO OF Y.A.'S STAR CADETS **WITH** YOU.
DID HE JUST CALL US TWO OF Y.A.'S STAR CADETS?

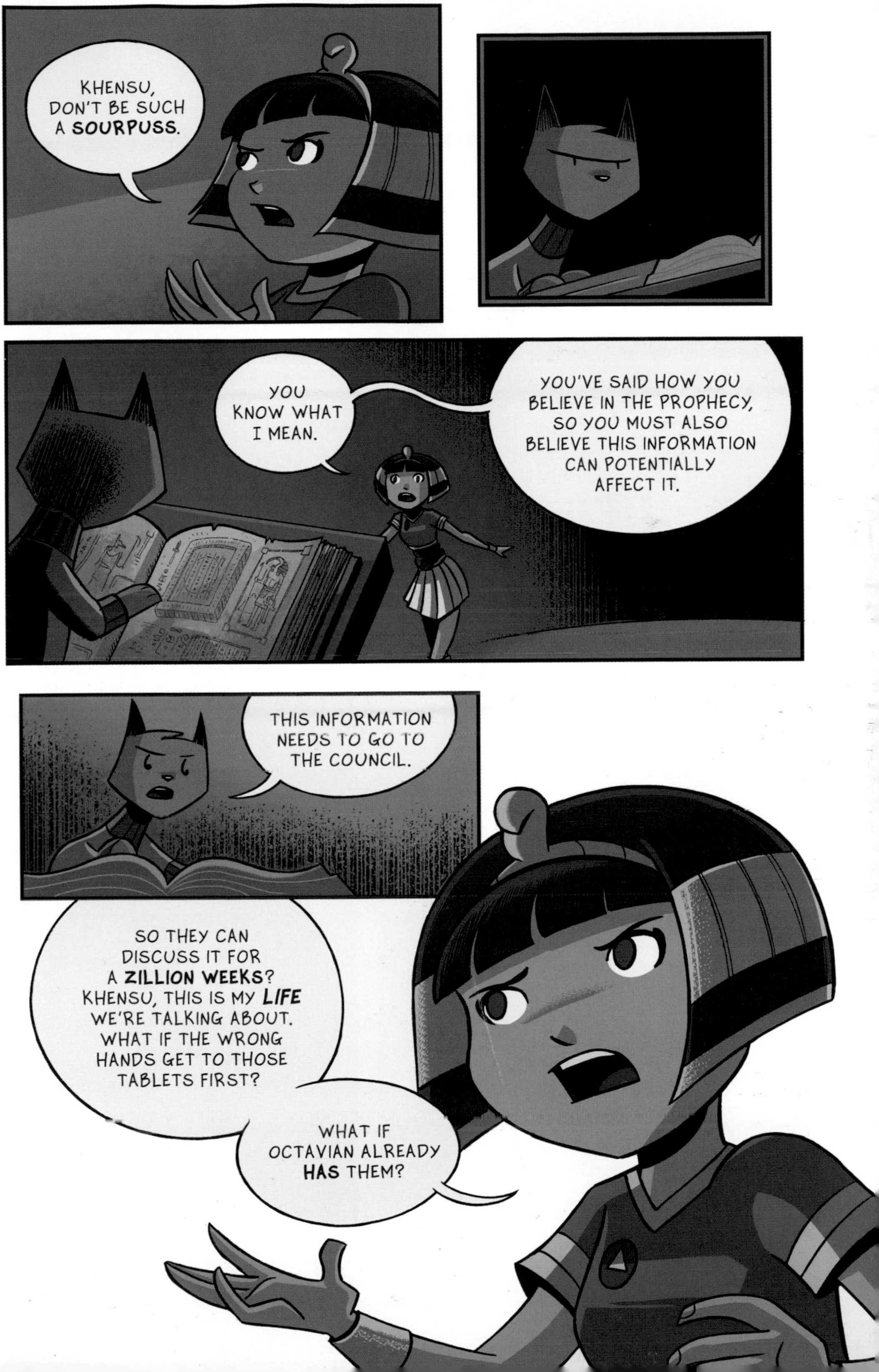
KHENSU, DON'T BE SUCH A **SOURPUSS.**
YOU KNOW WHAT I MEAN.
YOU'VE SAID HOW YOU BELIEVE IN THE PROPHECY, SO YOU MUST ALSO BELIEVE THIS INFORMATION CAN POTENTIALLY AFFECT IT.
THIS INFORMATION NEEDS TO GO TO THE COUNCIL.
SO THEY CAN DISCUSS IT FOR A **ZILLION WEEKS**? KHENSU, THIS IS MY ***LIFE*** WE'RE TALKING ABOUT. WHAT IF THE WRONG HANDS GET TO THOSE TABLETS FIRST?
WHAT IF OCTAVIAN ALREADY **HAS** THEM?

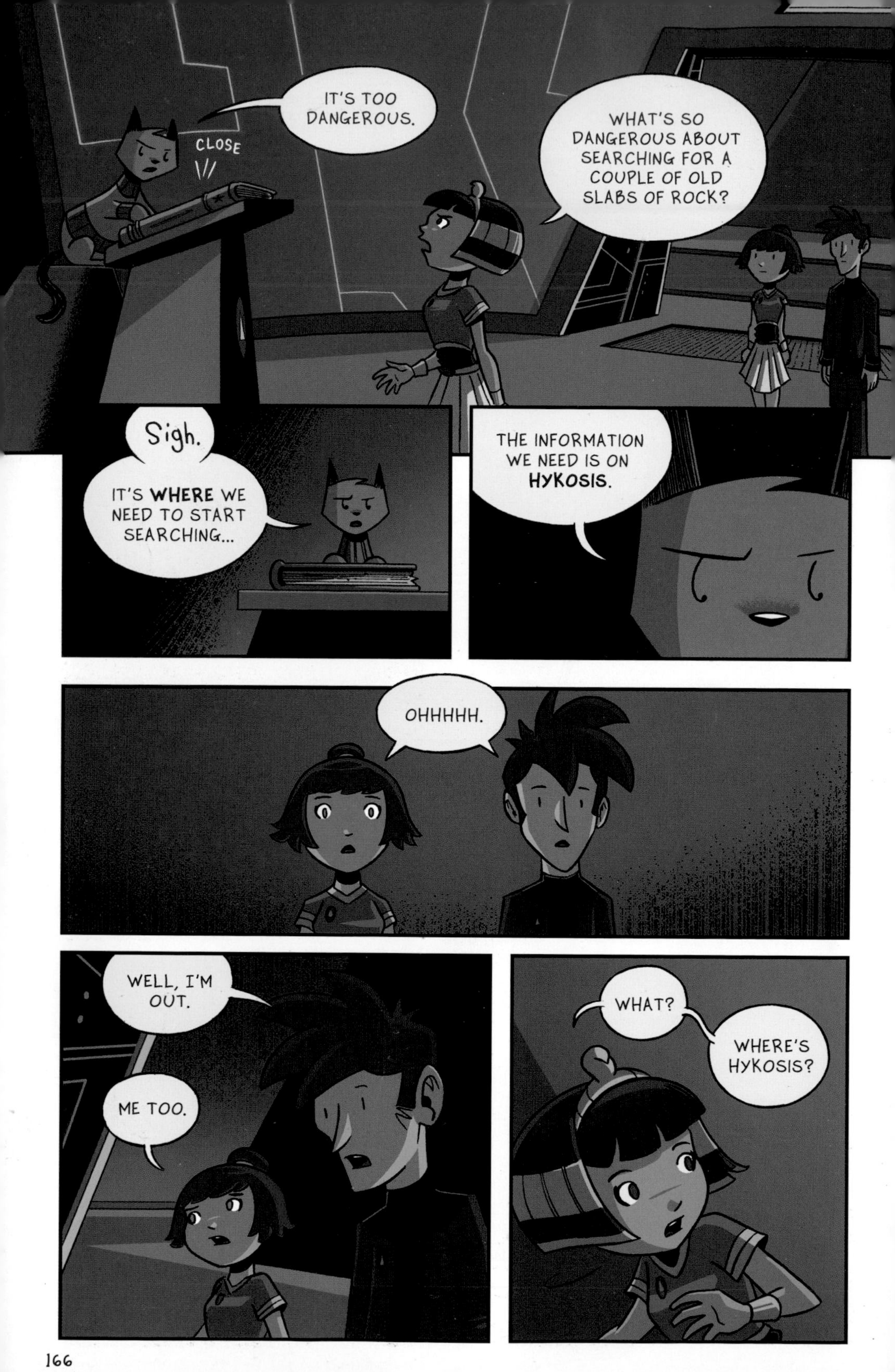
IT'S TOO DANGEROUS.
CLOSE
WHAT'S SO DANGEROUS ABOUT SEARCHING FOR A COUPLE OF OLD SLABS OF ROCK?
Sigh.
IT'S WHERE WE NEED TO START SEARCHING...
THE INFORMATION WE NEED IS ON HYKOSIS.
OHHHHH.
WELL, I'M OUT.
ME TOO.
WHAT?
WHERE'S HYKOSIS?

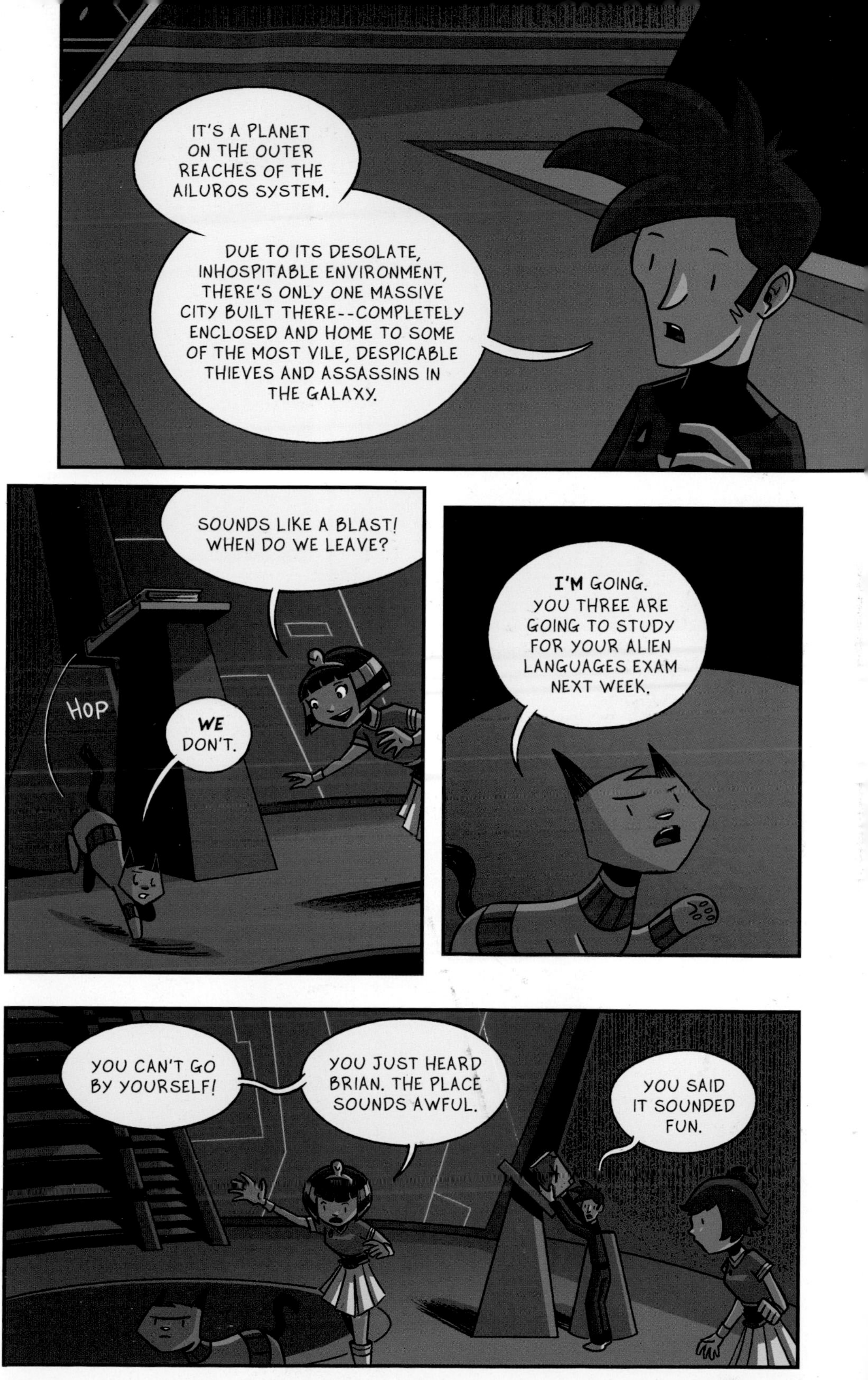
IT'S A PLANET ON THE OUTER REACHES OF THE AILUROS SYSTEM.
DUE TO ITS DESOLATE, INHOSPITABLE ENVIRONMENT, THERE'S ONLY ONE MASSIVE CITY BUILT THERE--COMPLETELY ENCLOSED AND HOME TO SOME OF THE MOST VILE, DESPICABLE THIEVES AND ASSASSINS IN THE GALAXY.
SOUNDS LIKE A BLAST! WHEN DO WE LEAVE?
HOP
WE DON'T.
I'M GOING. YOU THREE ARE GOING TO STUDY FOR YOUR ALIEN LANGUAGES EXAM NEXT WEEK.
YOU CAN'T GO BY YOURSELF!
YOU JUST HEARD BRIAN. THE PLACE SOUNDS AWFUL.
YOU SAID IT SOUNDED FUN.

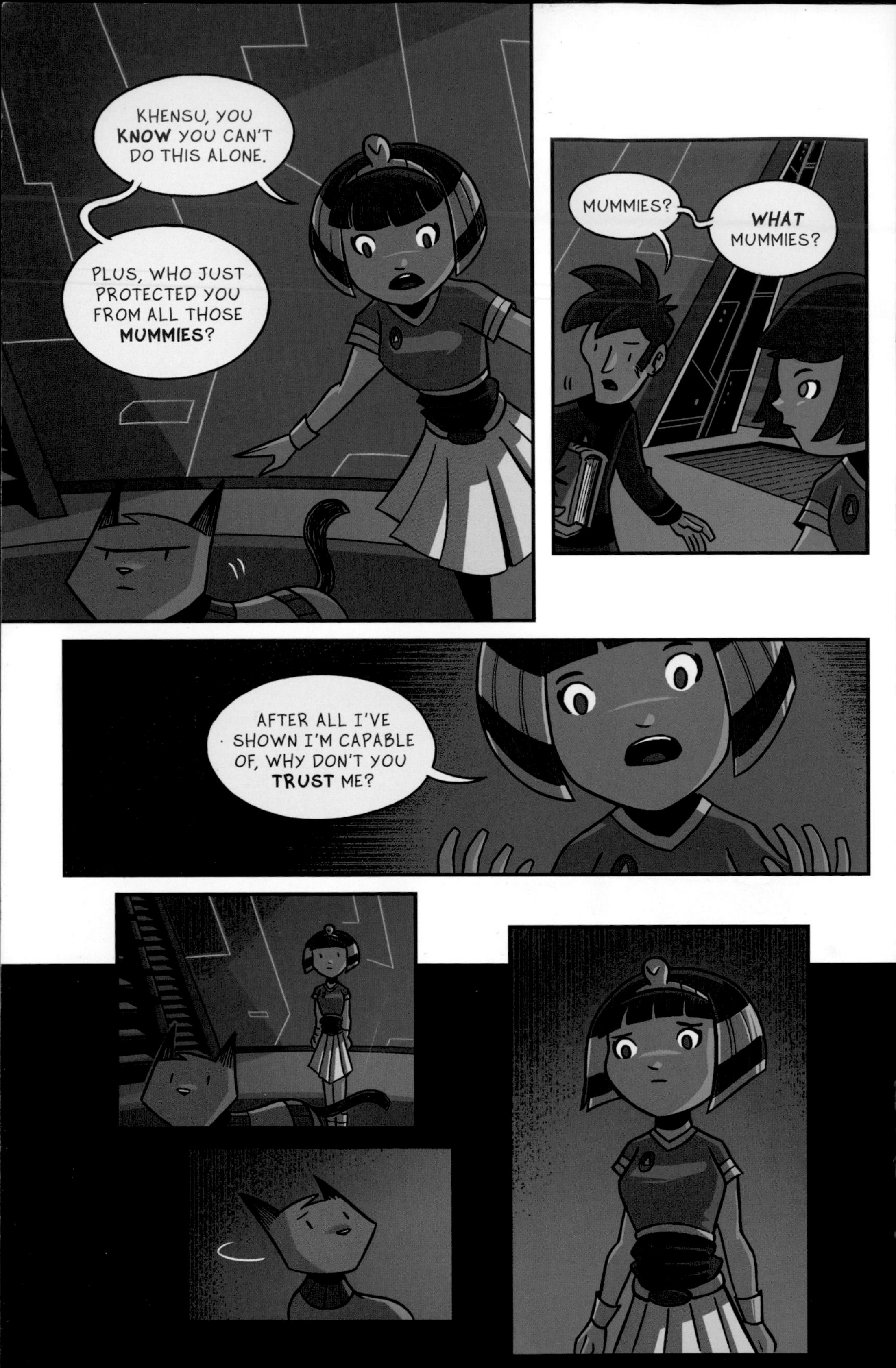
KHENSU, YOU **KNOW** YOU CAN'T DO THIS ALONE.
PLUS, WHO JUST PROTECTED YOU FROM ALL THOSE **MUMMIES**?
MUMMIES?
WHAT MUMMIES?
AFTER ALL I'VE SHOWN I'M CAPABLE OF, WHY DON'T YOU **TRUST** ME?

Sigh.

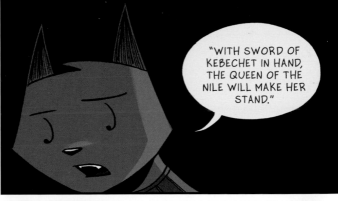

"WITH SWORD OF KEBECHET IN HAND, THE QUEEN OF THE NILE WILL MAKE HER STAND."

HUH?

IT'S...PART OF THE... A PROPHECY. IT SUGGESTS THAT BEFORE YOU CAN DEFEAT OCTAVIAN, IT'S NECESSARY FOR YOU TO HAVE THE SWORD YOU RECOVERED.

THAT'S WHY THE COUNCIL SENT YOU AFTER IT TO BEGIN WITH.

OKAY. WHY DIDN'T YOU JUST TELL ME THAT BEFORE?

DO YOU EVEN **BELIEVE** IN PROPHECIES?

WOULD IT HAVE MATTERED?

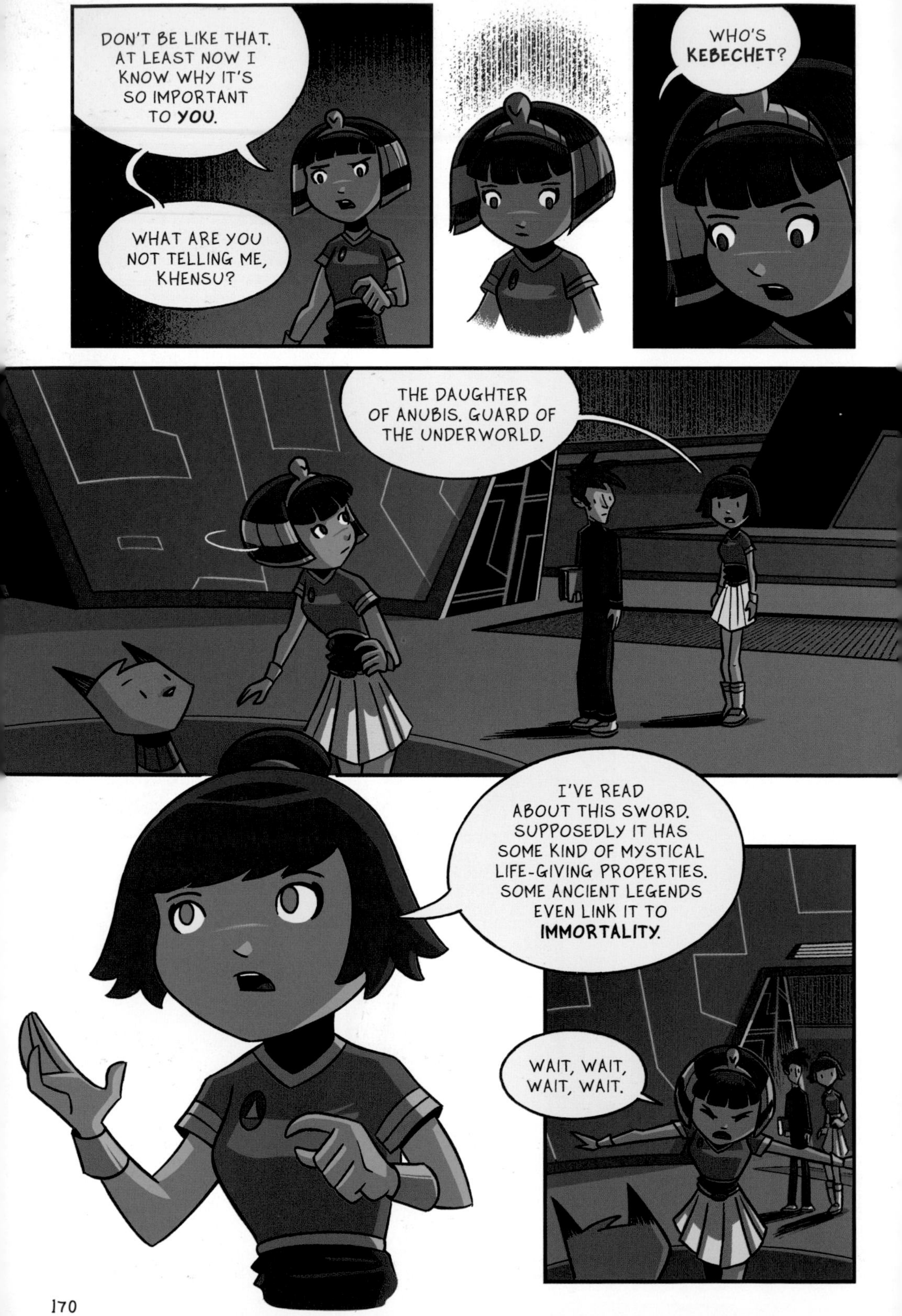
DON'T BE LIKE THAT. AT LEAST NOW I KNOW WHY IT'S SO IMPORTANT TO **YOU**.
WHAT ARE YOU NOT TELLING ME, KHENSU?
WHO'S **KEBECHET**?
THE DAUGHTER OF ANUBIS. GUARD OF THE UNDERWORLD.
I'VE READ ABOUT THIS SWORD. SUPPOSEDLY IT HAS SOME KIND OF MYSTICAL LIFE-GIVING PROPERTIES. SOME ANCIENT LEGENDS EVEN LINK IT TO **IMMORTALITY**.
WAIT, WAIT, WAIT, WAIT.

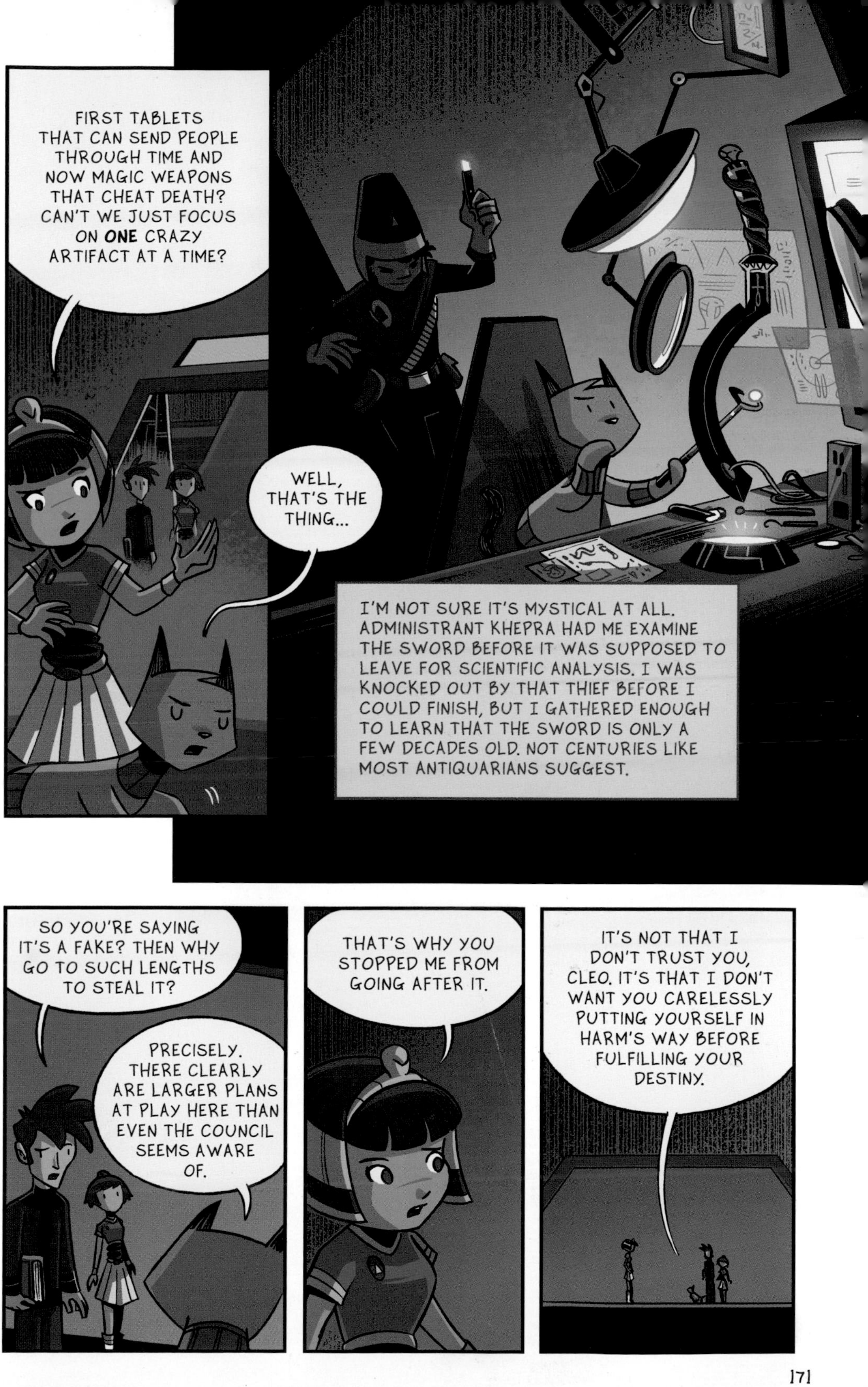
FIRST TABLETS THAT CAN SEND PEOPLE THROUGH TIME AND NOW MAGIC WEAPONS THAT CHEAT DEATH? CAN'T WE JUST FOCUS ON **ONE** CRAZY ARTIFACT AT A TIME?
WELL, THAT'S THE THING...
I'M NOT SURE IT'S MYSTICAL AT ALL. ADMINISTRANT KHEPRA HAD ME EXAMINE THE SWORD BEFORE IT WAS SUPPOSED TO LEAVE FOR SCIENTIFIC ANALYSIS. I WAS KNOCKED OUT BY THAT THIEF BEFORE I COULD FINISH, BUT I GATHERED ENOUGH TO LEARN THAT THE SWORD IS ONLY A FEW DECADES OLD. NOT CENTURIES LIKE MOST ANTIQUARIANS SUGGEST.
SO YOU'RE SAYING IT'S A FAKE? THEN WHY GO TO SUCH LENGTHS TO STEAL IT?
PRECISELY. THERE CLEARLY ARE LARGER PLANS AT PLAY HERE THAN EVEN THE COUNCIL SEEMS AWARE OF.
THAT'S WHY YOU STOPPED ME FROM GOING AFTER IT.
IT'S NOT THAT I DON'T TRUST YOU, CLEO. IT'S THAT I DON'T WANT YOU CARELESSLY PUTTING YOURSELF IN HARM'S WAY BEFORE FULFILLING YOUR DESTINY.

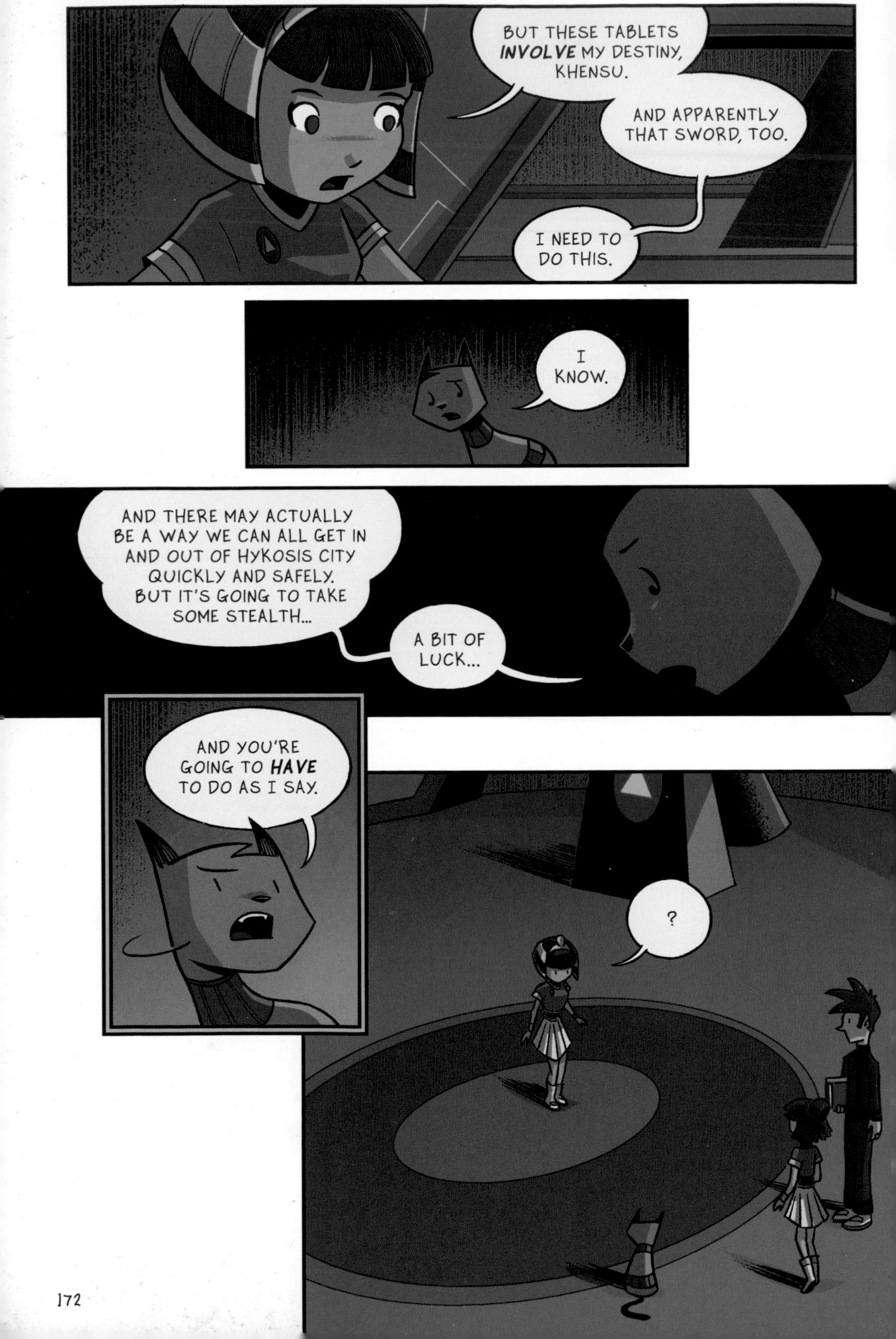
BUT THESE TABLETS **INVOLVE** MY DESTINY, KHENSU.
AND APPARENTLY THAT SWORD, TOO.
I NEED TO DO THIS.
I KNOW.
AND THERE MAY ACTUALLY BE A WAY WE CAN ALL GET IN AND OUT OF HYKOSIS CITY QUICKLY AND SAFELY. BUT IT'S GOING TO TAKE SOME STEALTH...
A BIT OF LUCK...
AND YOU'RE GOING TO **HAVE** TO DO AS I SAY.
?

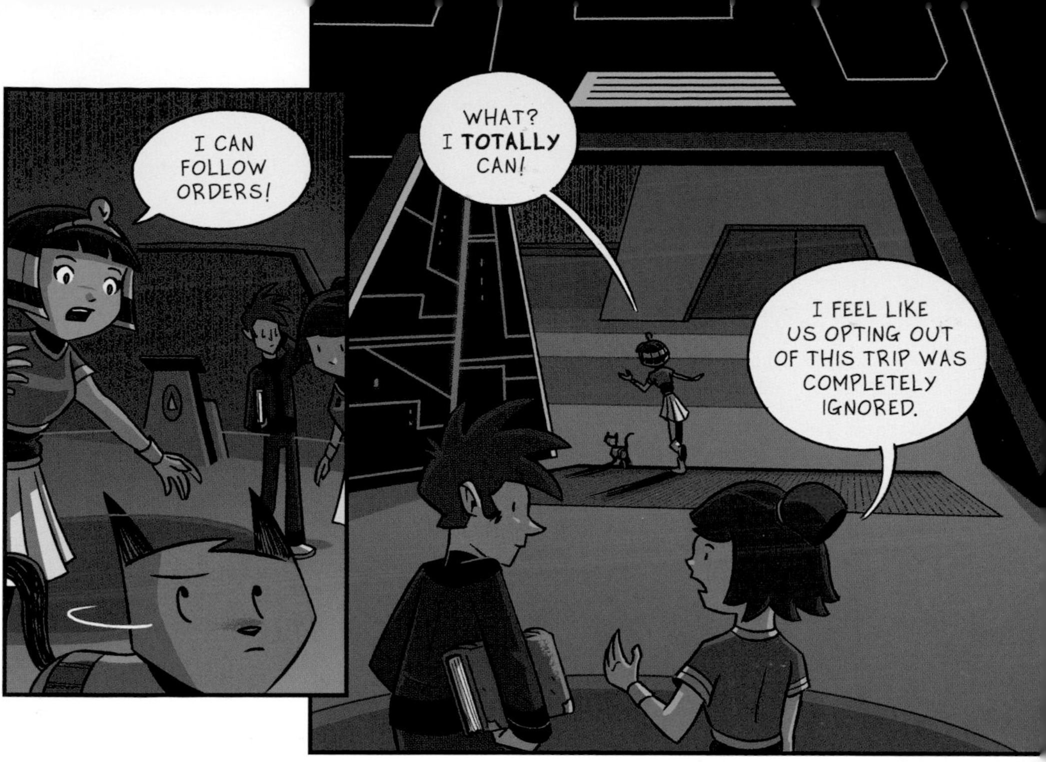
I CAN FOLLOW ORDERS!
WHAT? I **TOTALLY** CAN!
I FEEL LIKE US OPTING OUT OF THIS TRIP WAS COMPLETELY IGNORED.

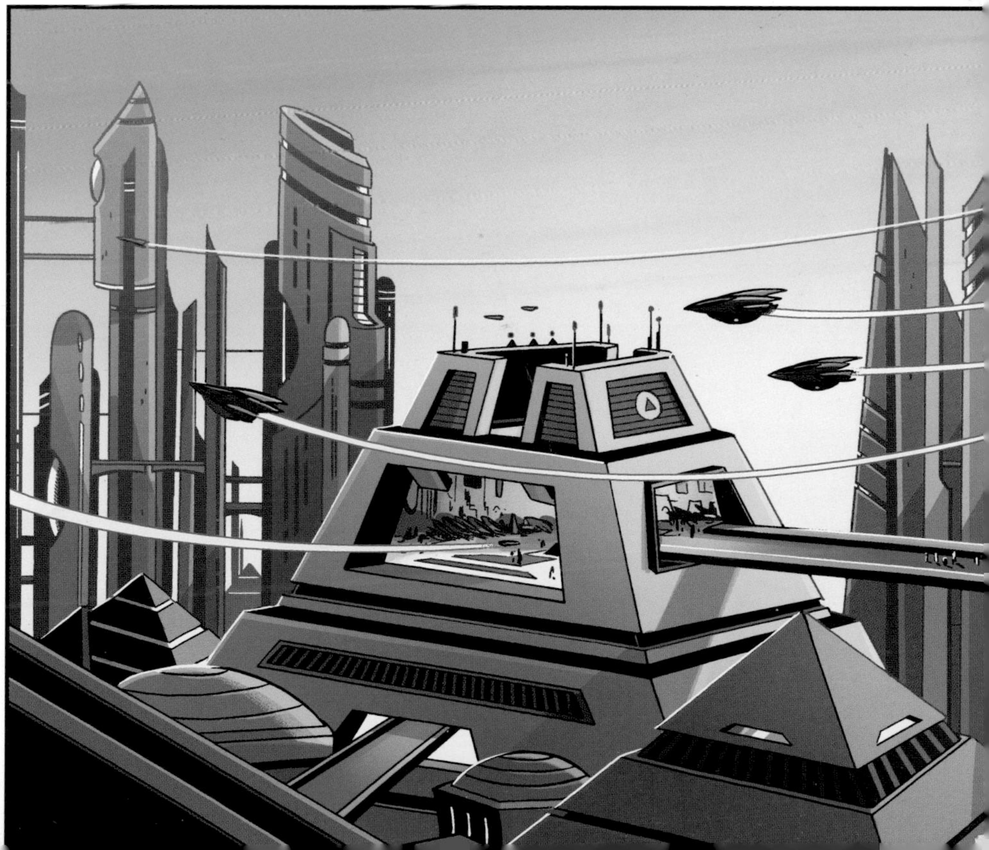

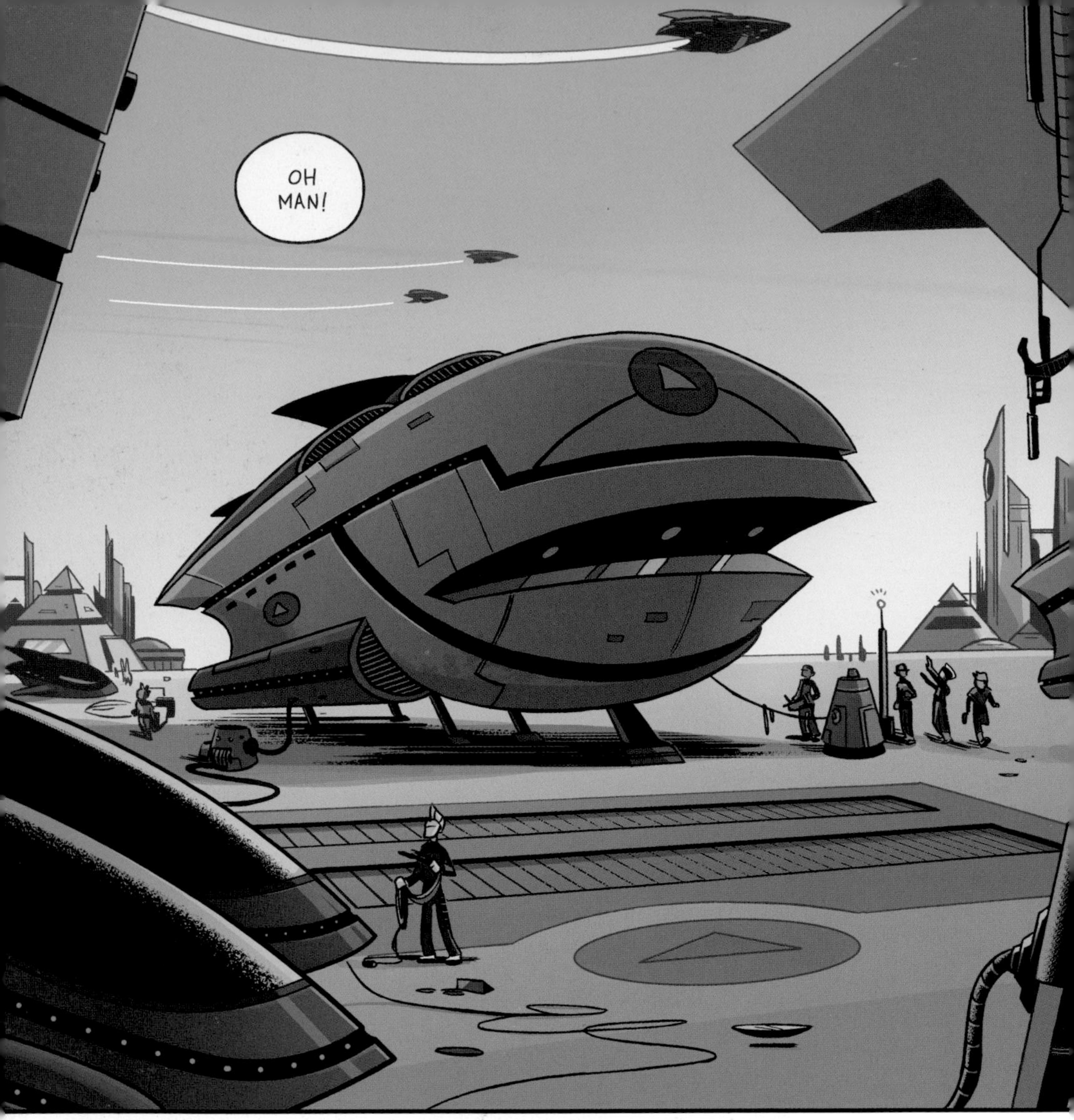
OH
MAN!

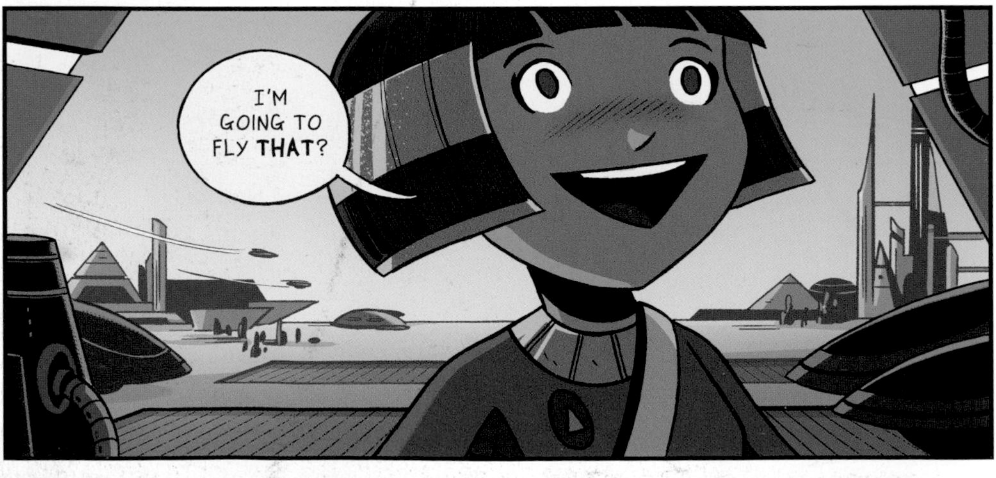
I'M
GOING TO
FLY **THAT**?

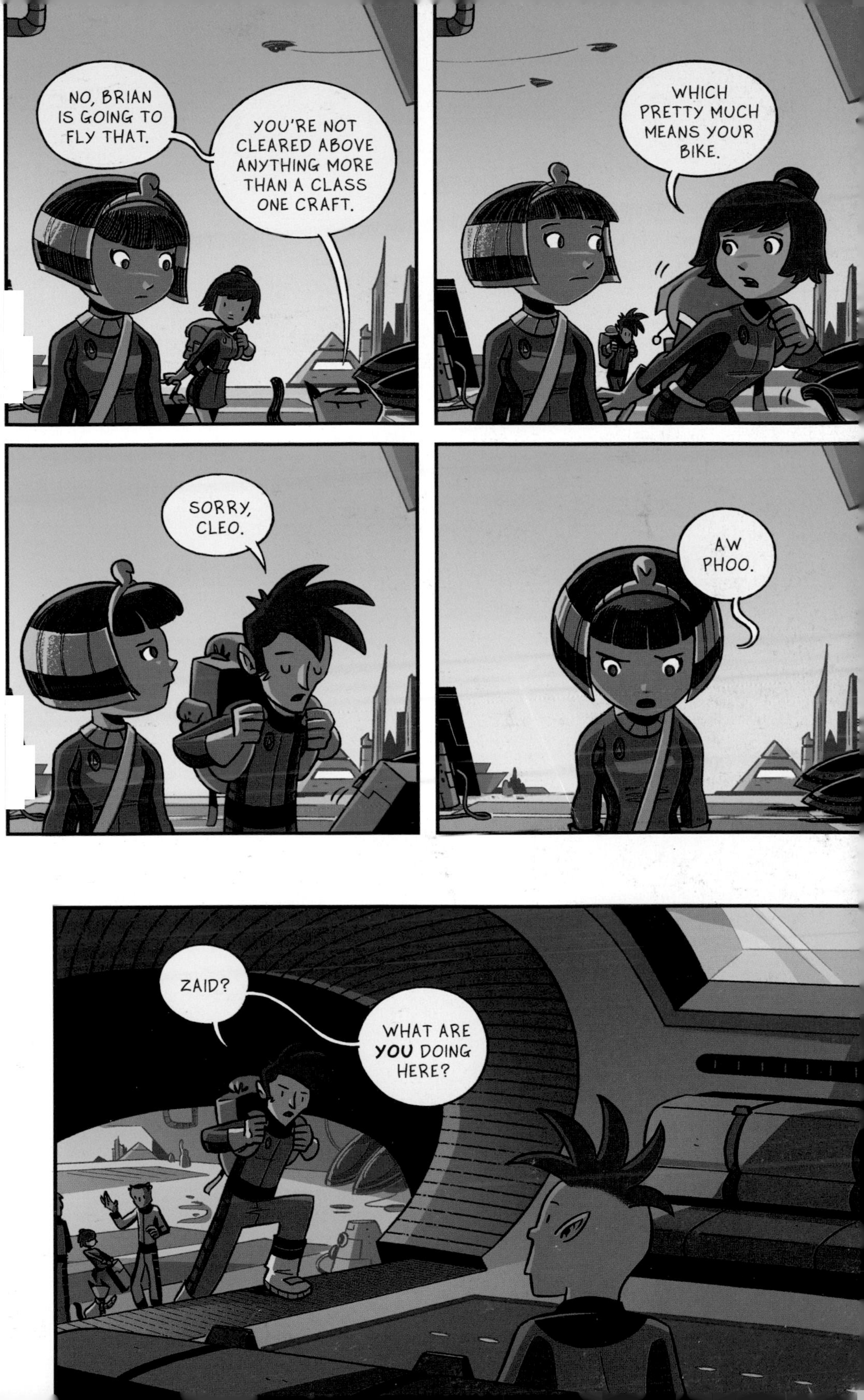
NO, BRIAN IS GOING TO FLY THAT.
YOU'RE NOT CLEARED ABOVE ANYTHING MORE THAN A CLASS ONE CRAFT.
WHICH PRETTY MUCH MEANS YOUR BIKE.
SORRY, CLEO.
AW PHOO.
ZAID?
WHAT ARE **YOU** DOING HERE?

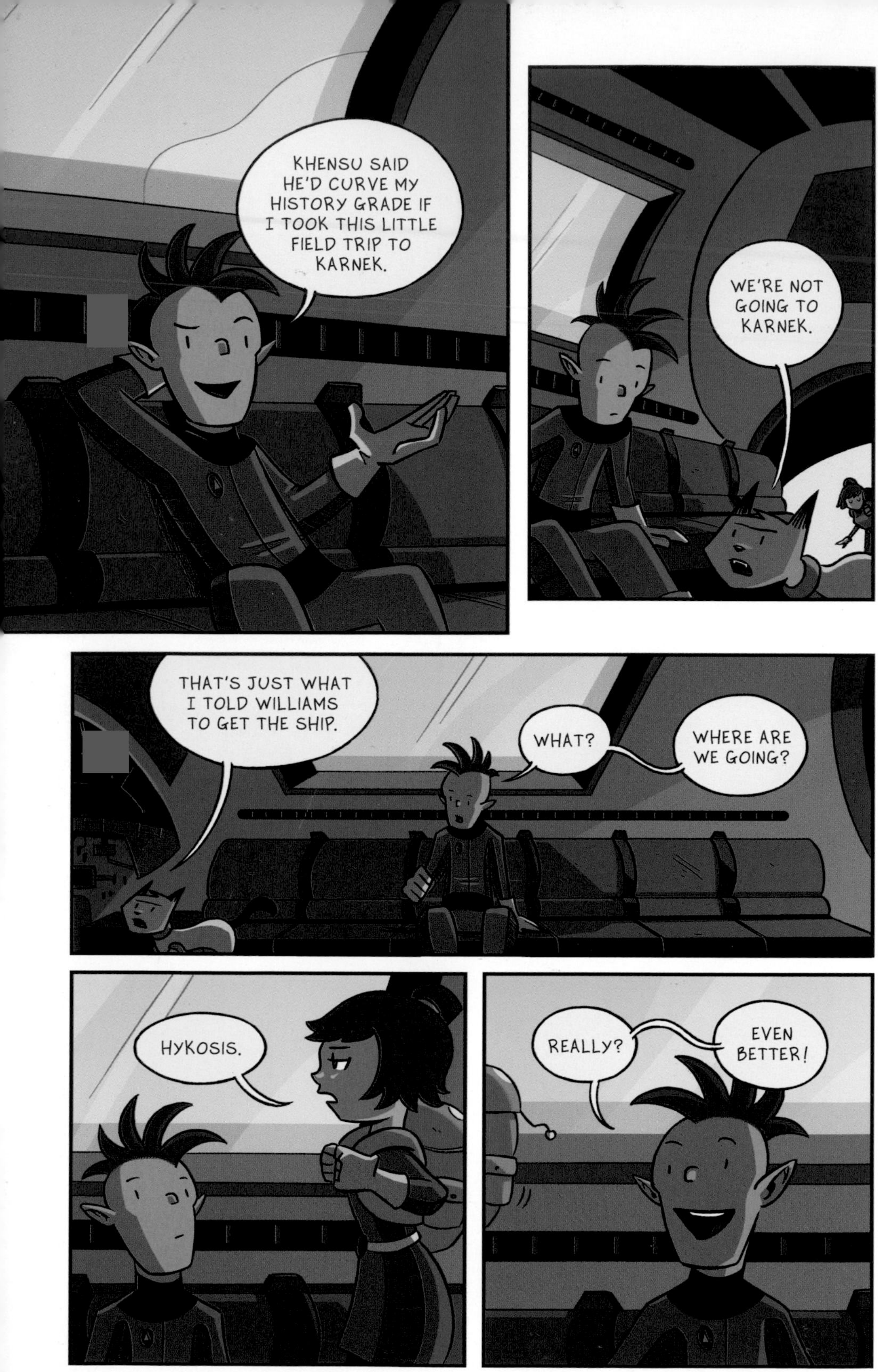
KHENSU SAID HE'D CURVE MY HISTORY GRADE IF I TOOK THIS LITTLE FIELD TRIP TO KARNEK.
WE'RE NOT GOING TO KARNEK.
THAT'S JUST WHAT I TOLD WILLIAMS TO GET THE SHIP.
WHAT?
WHERE ARE WE GOING?
HYKOSIS.
REALLY?
EVEN BETTER!

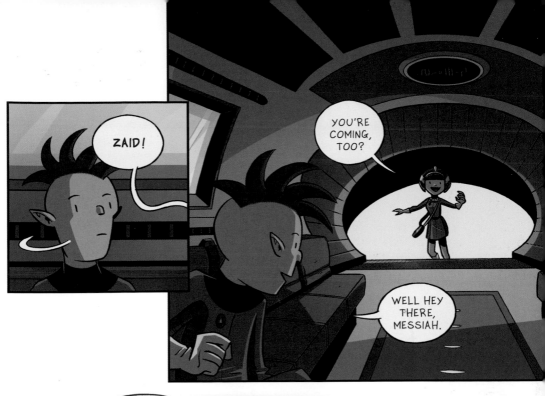

ZAID!

YOU'RE COMING, TOO?

WELL HEY THERE, MESSIAH.

SHOULD HAVE ASSUMED THIS LITTLE ESCAPADE HAD SOMETHING TO DO WITH YOU.

WELL, YOU KNOW. "SAVIOR OF THE GALAXY" BUSINESS.

WHY IS **HE** HERE?

WE NEED HIM.

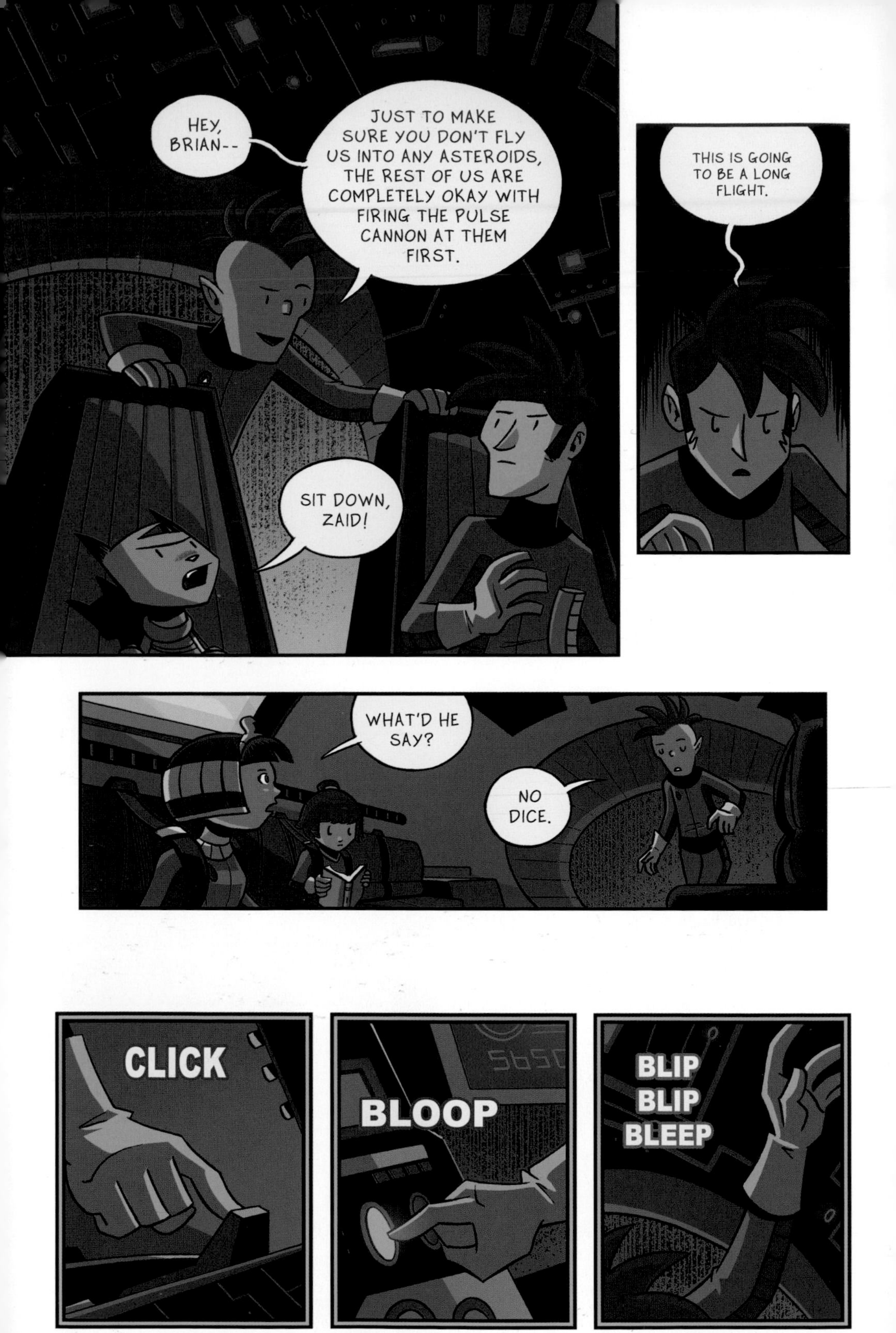
HEY, BRIAN--
JUST TO MAKE SURE YOU DON'T FLY US INTO ANY ASTEROIDS, THE REST OF US ARE COMPLETELY OKAY WITH FIRING THE PULSE CANNON AT THEM FIRST.
SIT DOWN, ZAID!
THIS IS GOING TO BE A LONG FLIGHT.
WHAT'D HE SAY?
NO DICE.
CLICK
BLOOP
BLIP
BLIP
BLEEP

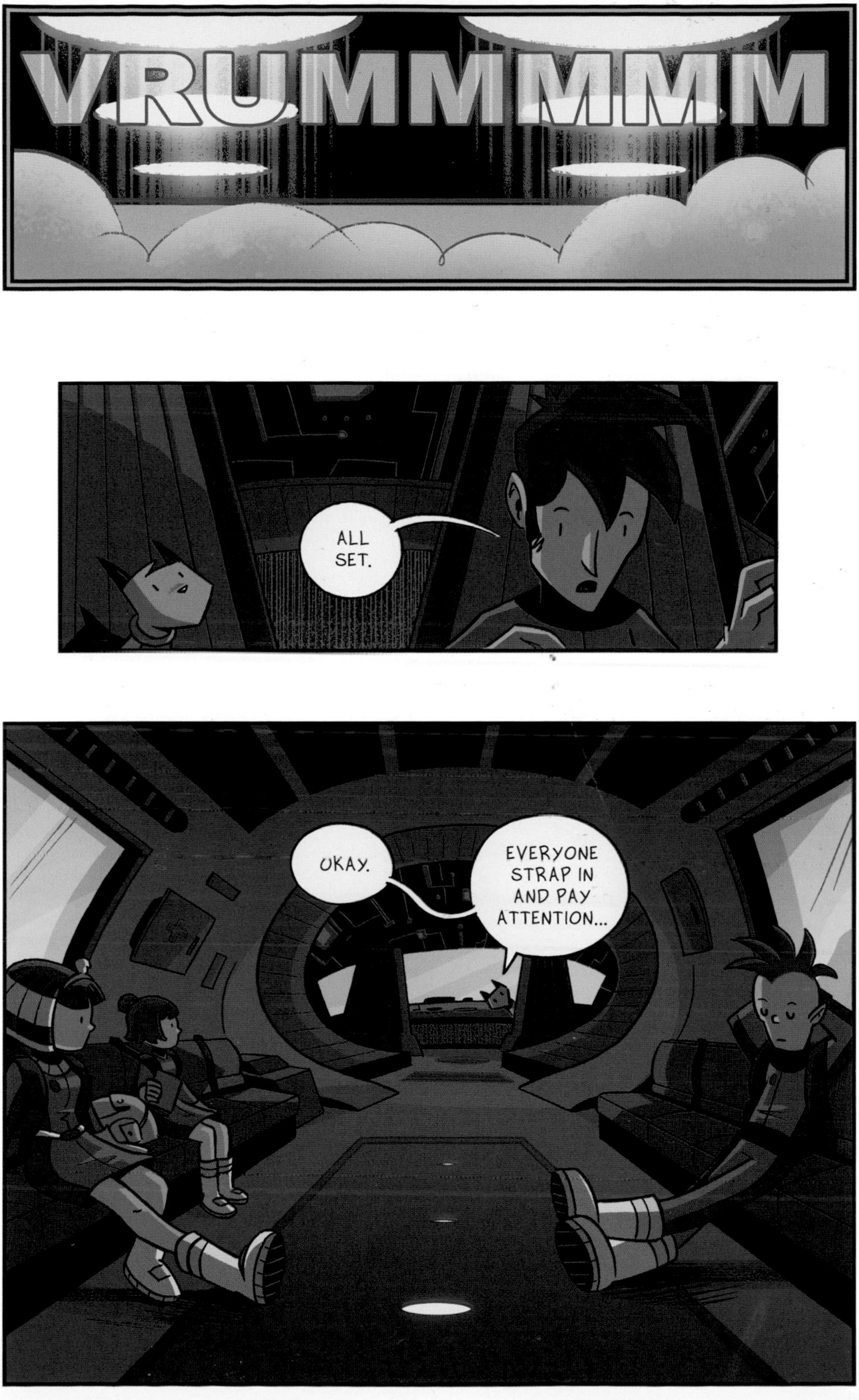
VRUMMMMMM
ALL SET.
OKAY.
EVERYONE STRAP IN AND PAY ATTENTION...

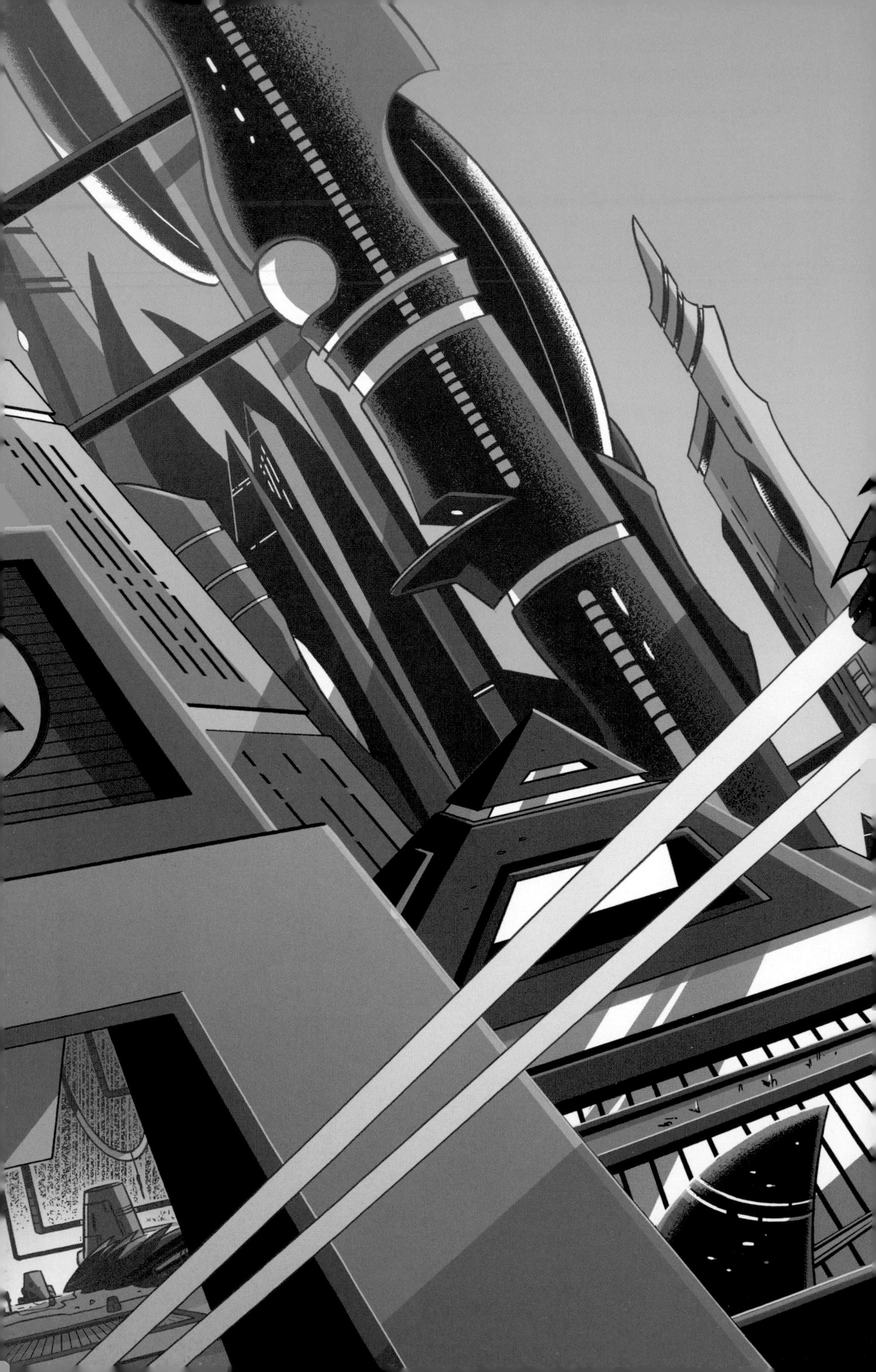

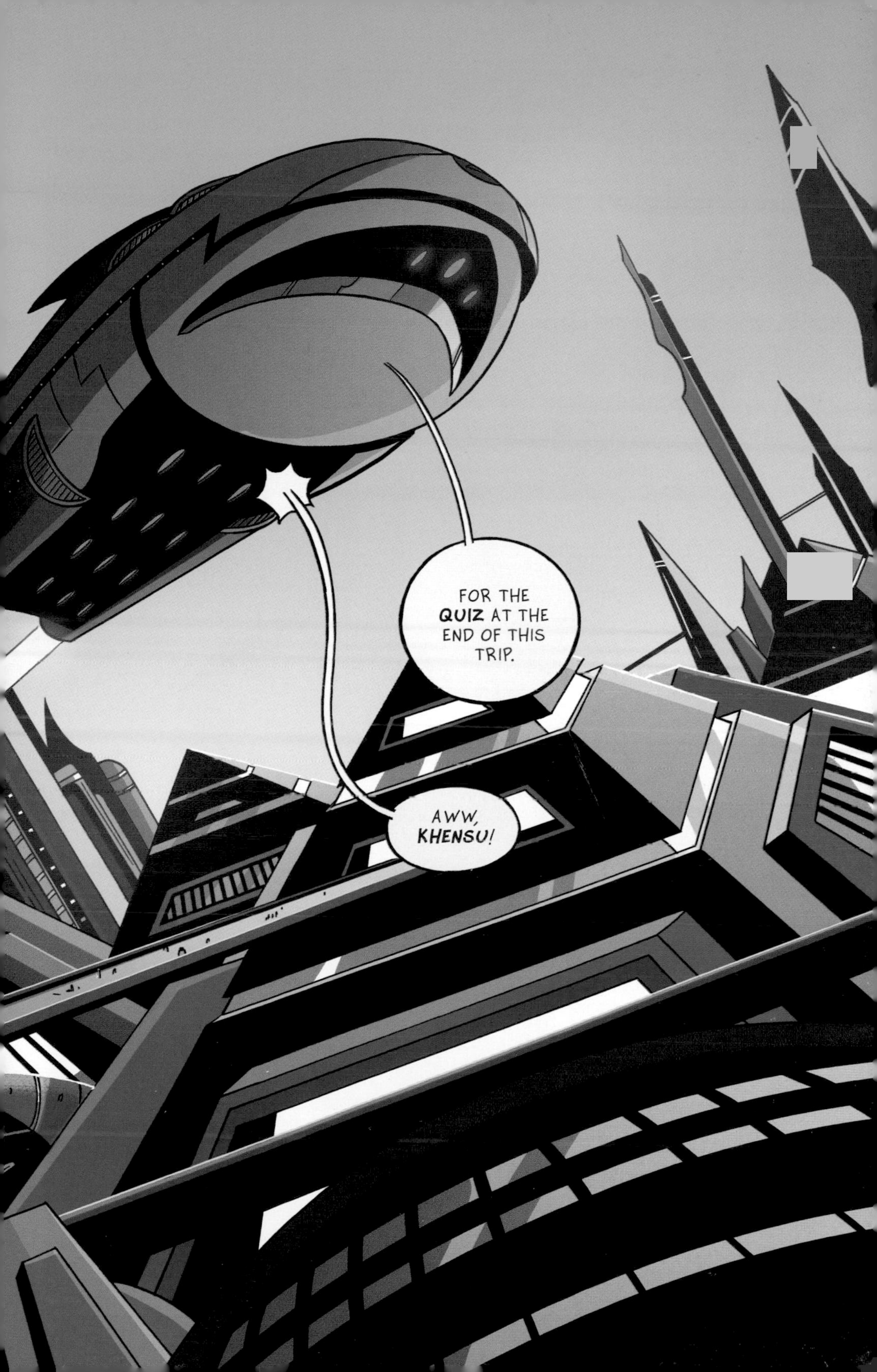
FOR THE **QUIZ** AT THE END OF THIS TRIP.
AWW, **KHENSU**!

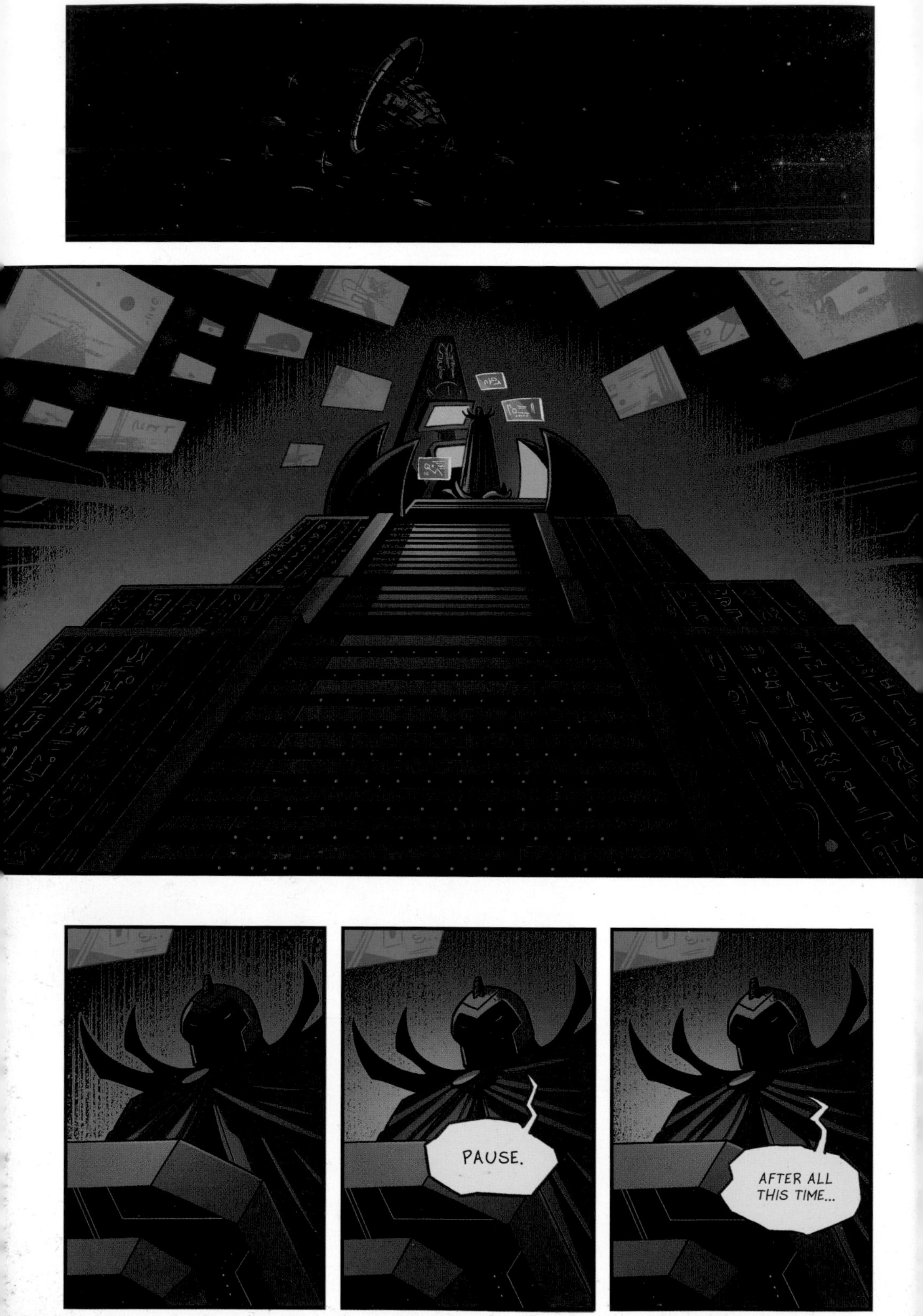
PAUSE.
AFTER ALL THIS TIME...

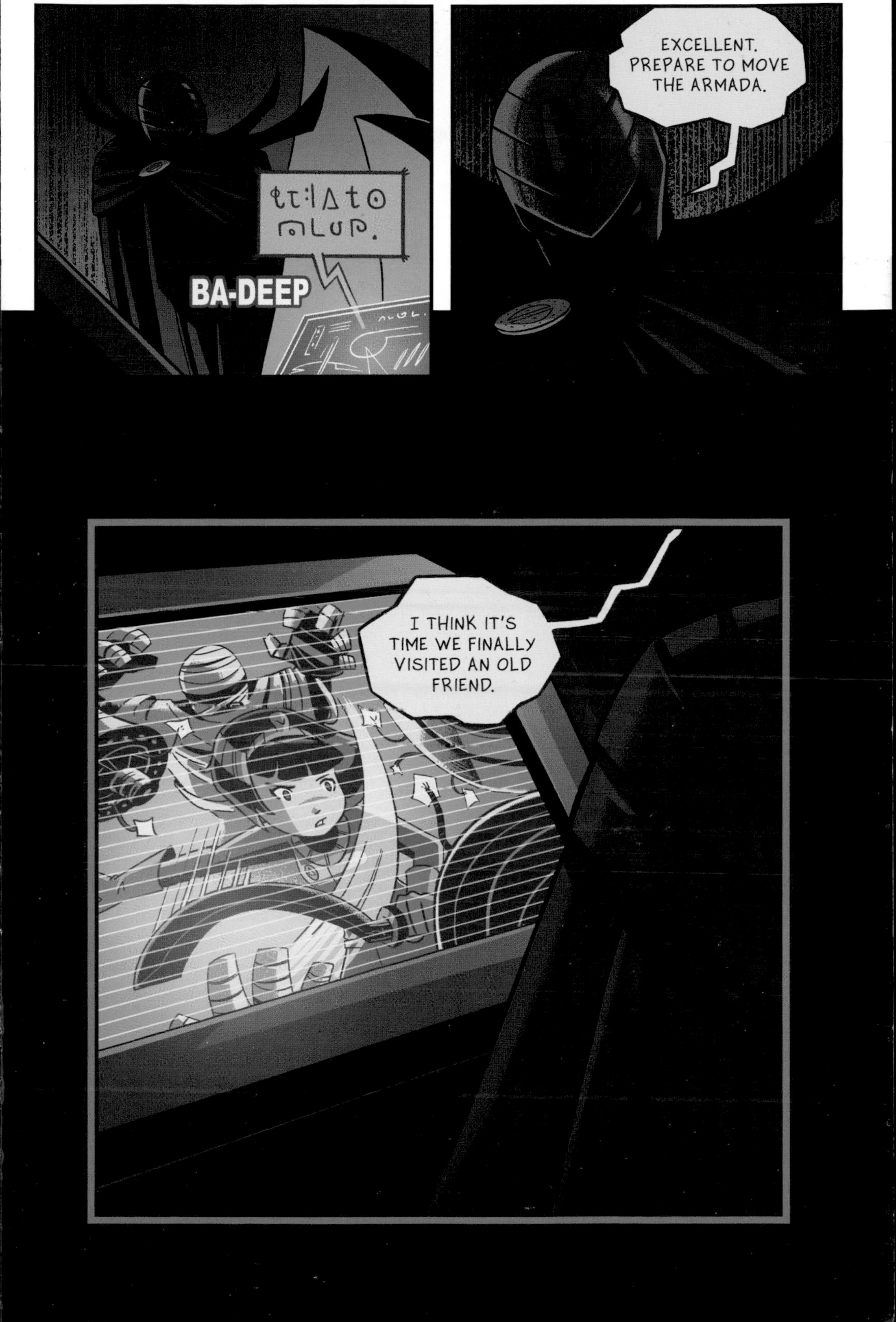
BA-DEEP
EXCELLENT. PREPARE TO MOVE THE ARMADA.
I THINK IT'S TIME WE FINALLY VISITED AN OLD FRIEND.

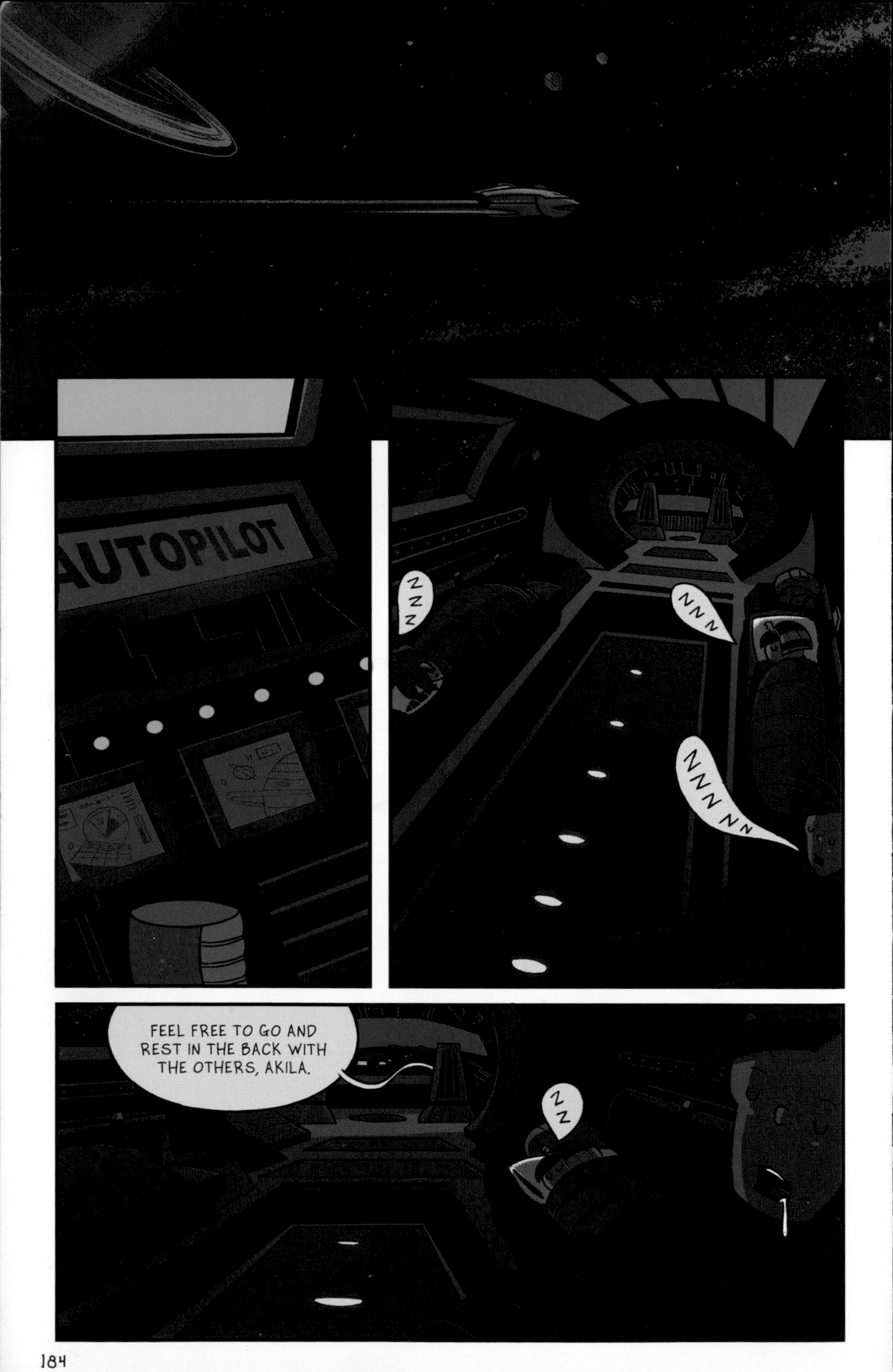
AUTOPILOT
ZZZ
ZZZ
ZZZZZ
FEEL FREE TO GO AND REST IN THE BACK WITH THE OTHERS, AKILA.
ZZ

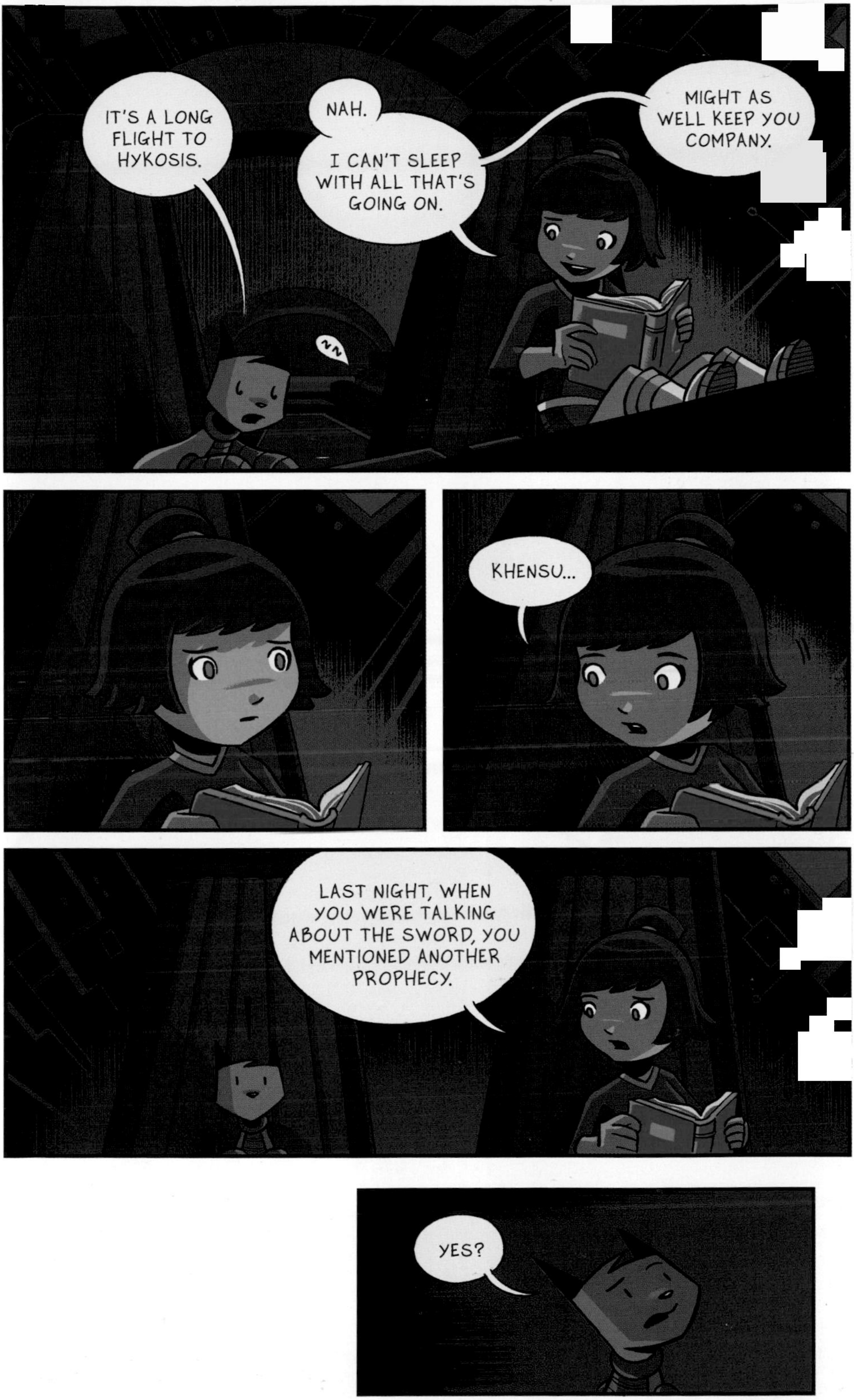

IT'S A LONG FLIGHT TO HYKOSIS.
NAH.
I CAN'T SLEEP WITH ALL THAT'S GOING ON.
MIGHT AS WELL KEEP YOU COMPANY.
KHENSU...
LAST NIGHT, WHEN YOU WERE TALKING ABOUT THE SWORD, YOU MENTIONED ANOTHER PROPHECY.
YES?

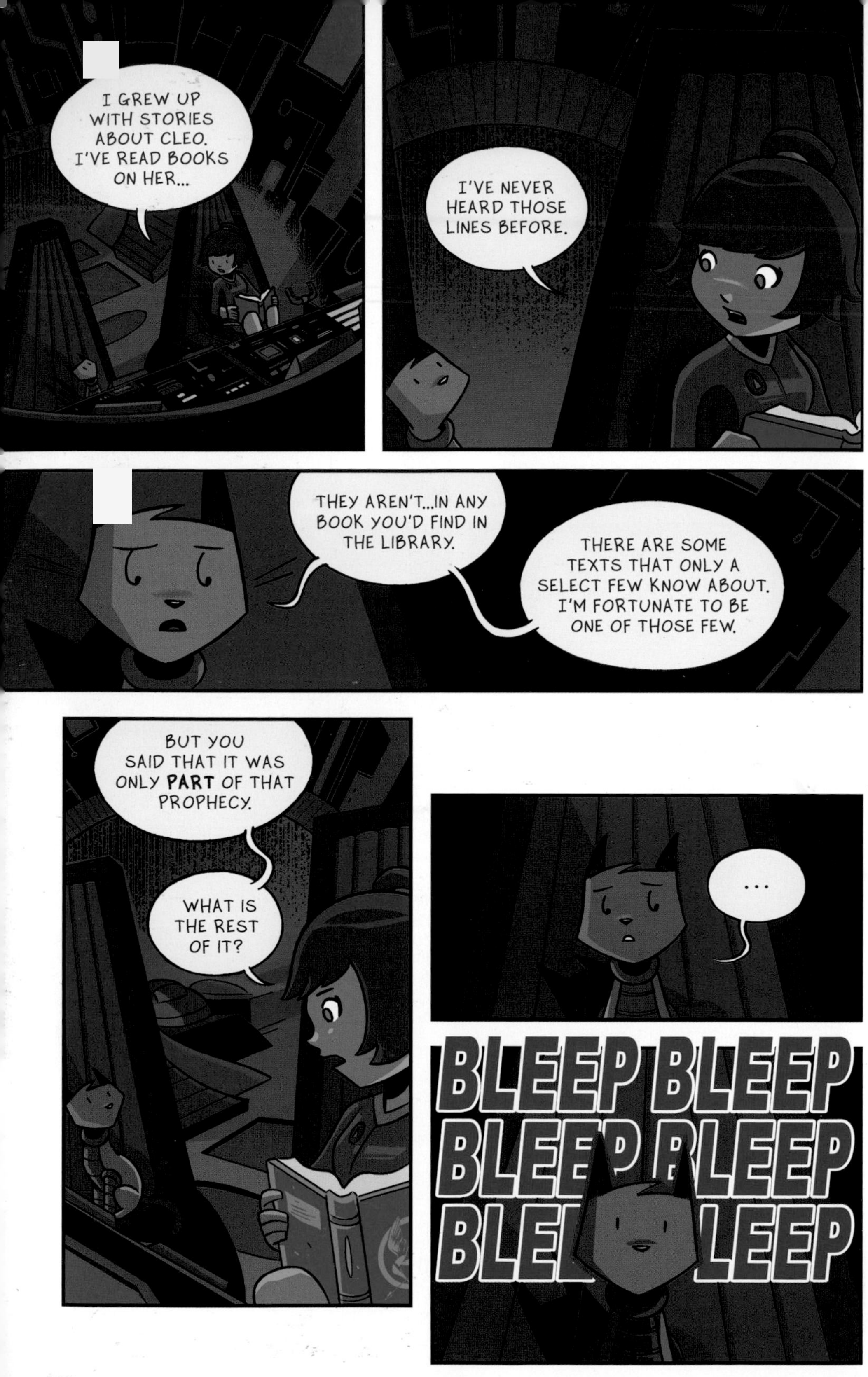
I GREW UP WITH STORIES ABOUT CLEO. I'VE READ BOOKS ON HER...
I'VE NEVER HEARD THOSE LINES BEFORE.
THEY AREN'T...IN ANY BOOK YOU'D FIND IN THE LIBRARY.
THERE ARE SOME TEXTS THAT ONLY A SELECT FEW KNOW ABOUT. I'M FORTUNATE TO BE ONE OF THOSE FEW.
BUT YOU SAID THAT IT WAS ONLY PART OF THAT PROPHECY.
WHAT IS THE REST OF IT?
...
BLEEP BLEEP
BLEEP BLEEP
BLEEP BLEEP

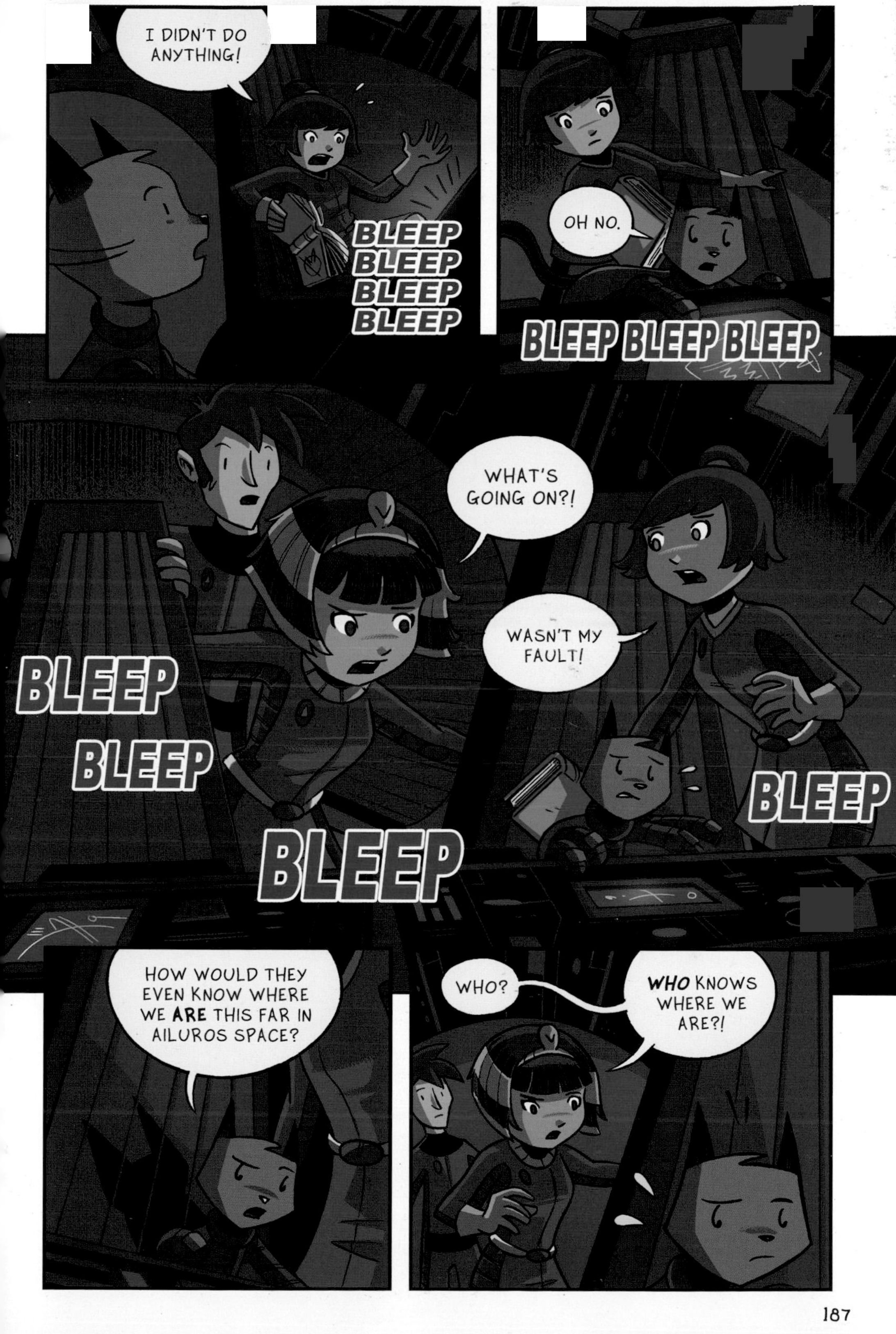
I DIDN'T DO ANYTHING!
BLEEP BLEEP BLEEP BLEEP
OH NO.
BLEEP BLEEP BLEEP
WHAT'S GOING ON?!
WASN'T MY FAULT!
BLEEP
BLEEP
BLEEP
BLEEP
HOW WOULD THEY EVEN KNOW WHERE WE **ARE** THIS FAR IN AILUROS SPACE?
WHO?
WHO KNOWS WHERE WE ARE?!

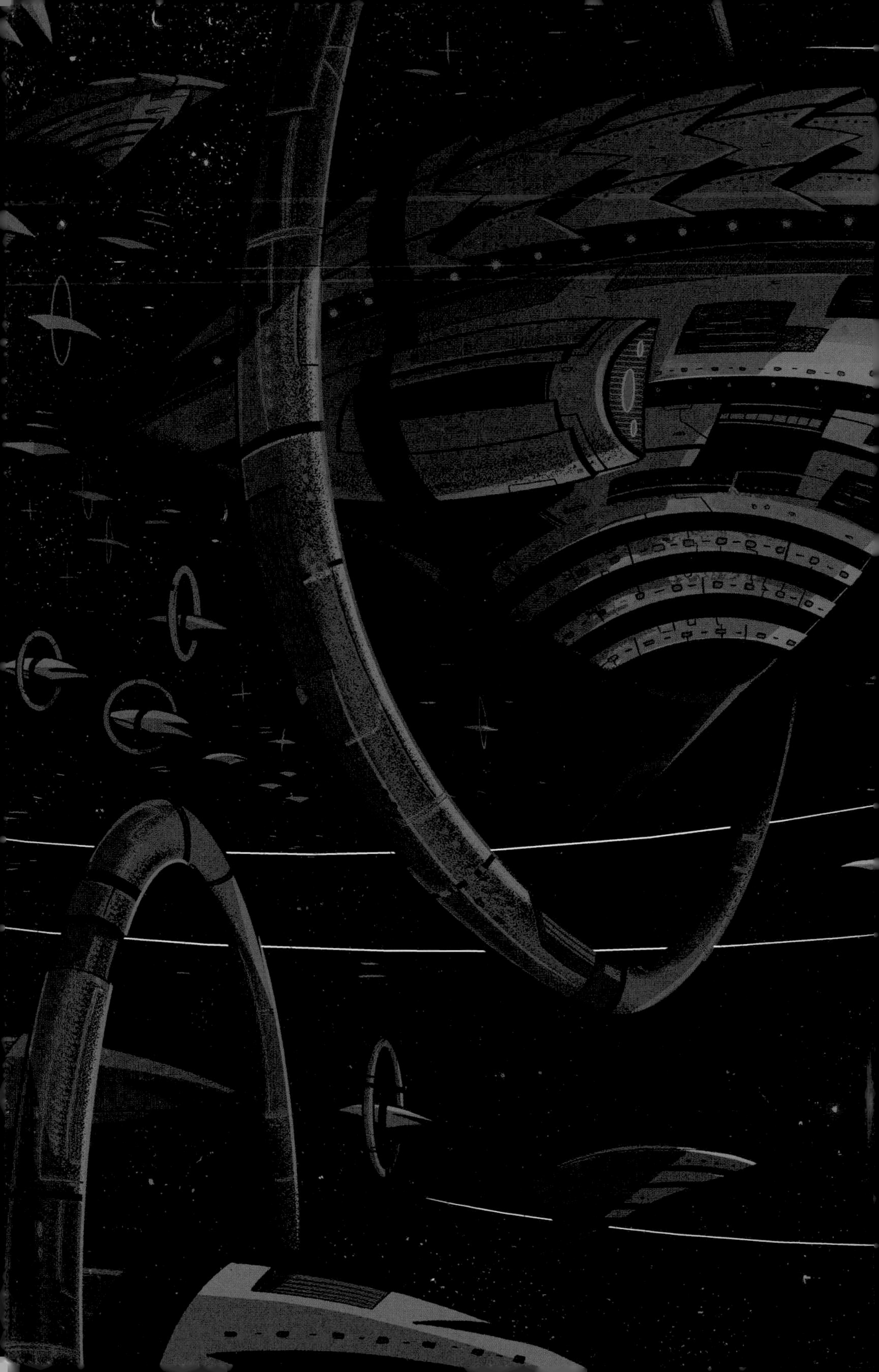

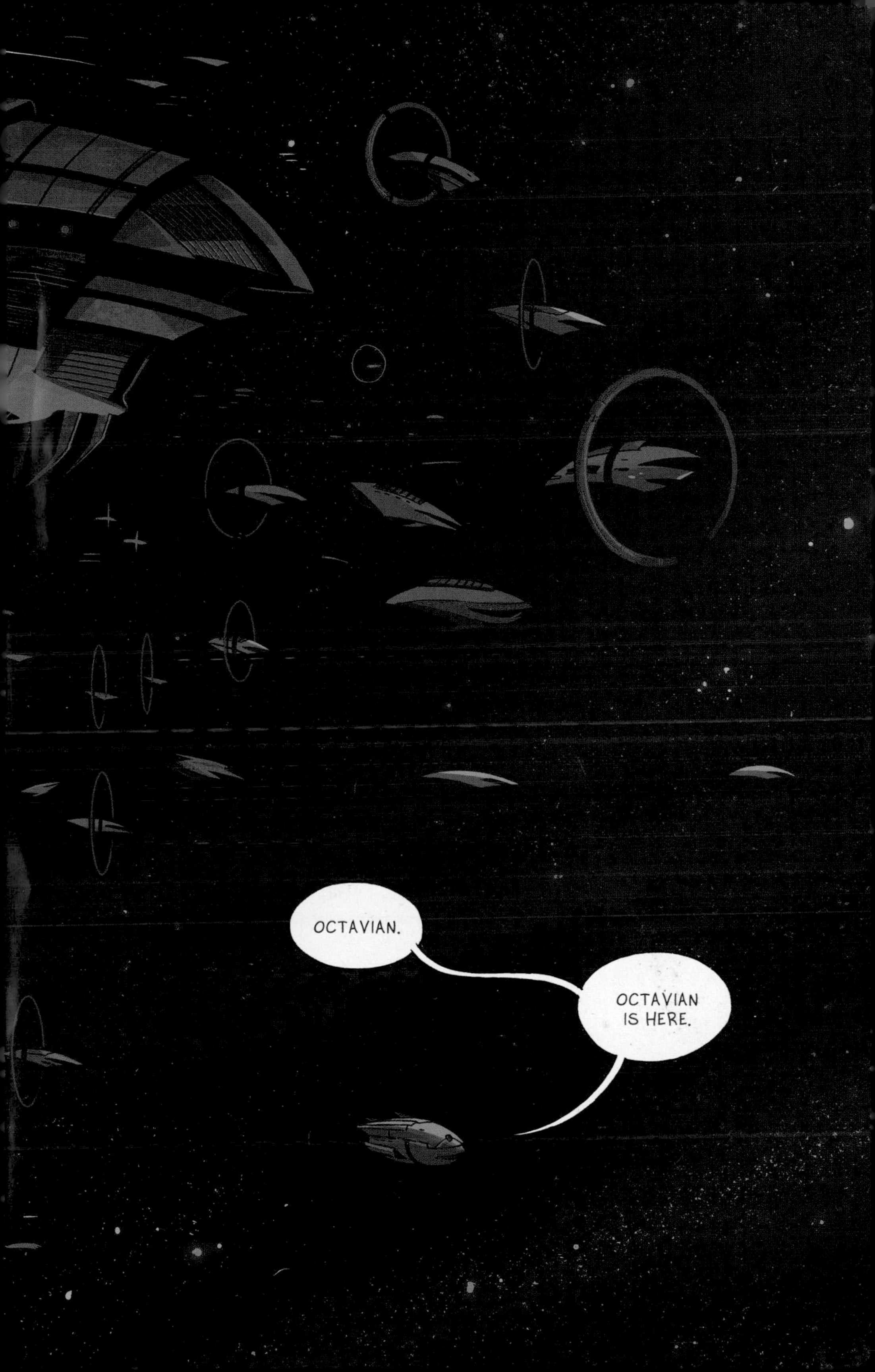
OCTAVIAN.
OCTAVIAN IS HERE.

ABOUT THE AUTHOR

A graduate of the Columbus College of Art & Design, Mike Maihack spends his time drawing pictures of cats, superheroes, space girls, and just about anything else he can think of that might involve a ray gun or two. He is the creator of *Cleopatra in Space, Book One: Target Practice* and the popular webcomic *Cow & Buffalo*; illustrator of the all-ages card game *Goblins Drool, Fairies Rule*; and has contributed art and stories to books like *Parable*; *Jim Henson's The Storyteller*; *Cow Boy*; *Geeks, Girls, and Secret Identities*; and the Eisner and Harvey award-winning *Comic Book Tattoo*. Mike currently lives in Tampa, Florida, with his wife, son, and two Siamese cats.

Visit Mike online at www.mikemaihack.com.

SPECIAL THANKS TO:

My amazingly supportive family: Jen Maihack, Sam and Barb Maihack, Brian and Jill Maeda, Patrick and Kim Tally, John and Darci Roberts, Chad and Jen Roberts, KeAli'i and Lindsey Rozet, Randy and Janice Meade, and — what the heck — my cats Ash and Misty (let's be more useful on the next book though, you two).

My wonderful Scholastic family (including but not limited to): Cassandra Pelham, David Saylor, Phil Falco, Lizette Serrano, Sheila Marie Everett, Tracy van Straaten, Bess Braswell, and Denise Anderson.

Judy Hansen, my literary guide through this tumultuous world of book publishing.

To all the teachers, librarians, booksellers, parents, and readers out there who have supported Cleopatra in Space thus far!

Last but not least, to Christ, my best friend and constant companion, who made certain I put as much love into every page of this book as He showed me every day I was making it.